C000139379

Taking Care of Business

J.D. de Roeck

Clink
Street

London | New York

Published by Clink Street Publishing 2018

Copyright © 2018

First edition.

ISBNs:
paperback 978-1-912562-17-6
ebook 978-1-912562-18-3

In memory of my Father
1935 – 2017
Greatly missed

Chapter 1

THREE YEARS AGO (JANUARY 2011)
ST PETERSBURG, RUSSIA

It was dark, the modest chamber lit only by the flicker of a roaring fire that did little to warm him. He knew it was time and dismissed them all. He would do this alone.

The study was sparsely furnished, a large desk at its heart, aged and scarred from years of wear. His old chair was set behind it, as it had been for so many years, now dusty from lack of use. There was a Chesterfield and a small table, both from a previous life yet still treasured for the history he shared with them. The heavy curtains were drawn against a Russian winter's night, but still the cold bit deeply into his failing frame.

It was a small room, lost among the vast halls and suites of the old palace that had been his home for so many years. It was his most private place, a refuge, pared back and simple.

The hour was late; the ornate clock on the mantelpiece recorded the passing of time relentlessly, its inevitability a stark echo of the life that was now ebbing from him.

He had achieved many things in his life, but, like so many great men in his country, he too knew regrets, the legacy of each tormenting him over the years, exacting a heavy toll.

There were many things he'd done in the early days that he knew would haunt him for the rest of his life. Now that the end was drawing near, he took some comfort in knowing that they did. At least he'd endeavoured to put things right, long ago accepting the full burden of his own guilt. He'd been complicit in all that took place, yet even now he only ever truly embraced the shame of it in private. He knew he could never be fully reconciled, and as the minutes ticked inexorably by, the torment that had plagued him for a lifetime troubled him more deeply than ever.

Over the years, Valentine had laboured to balance the scales, his philanthropy a price he was all too willing to pay. If there was a God, and, surely, he would have his answer soon, there would be a reckoning. He doubted that any God of worth would value such belated acts of kindness as fully paying down the debt. A debt stained with the blood of his enemies and those who stood in his way. That was how it was back then; surely any judgement would take such a context into account. But that was not his concern for now, at least not yet.

He'd done all he could to make his peace, and now one task remained. He clawed at the document on his lap, a pen painfully gripped between his trembling fingers. His eyes were failing; in the firelight no text was legible to him, but he knew where to sign. Now, with a shattering certainty, he accepted it was the right thing to do, the only responsible course of action and perhaps his last mortal act. He was resolved, and with the last vestige of his fading strength he would set this one remaining matter straight. It would define his legacy, and it would break the old man's weary heart.

The pen tumbled from his grasp, the ink spilling viscous from the nib and forming a black pool on the oak floor. It was an unsettling image for the old man. He made no attempt to recover the pen, but stared, transfixed. There had been so much blood in those early days, as dark and indelible as the ink that now spilled from the broken tip. The pen was a treasured gift from a wife taken from him so long ago, but now it was nothing more than a shattered instrument, a mere device, complicit in one last moment of defiance.

Valentine had done the right thing, and although he knew there could be no redemption in this life, he slowly closed his eyes one final time, to face his judgement in the next.

Chapter 2

The new mail notification appeared in the bottom left-hand corner of the screen. It displayed the opening lines of the message for a few seconds and then melted away before he could hit the reveal option. He had, however, seen enough to know that it was the email he'd been waiting for with a growing sense of dread.

He closed down the quote he was working on and clicked the email inbox. There was the usual flurry of spam and a few messages that would need dealing with, some urgent, others not so much. It never ceased to amaze Paul the sheer volume of rubbish people incessantly inflicted on each other through the medium of email; he deleted the spam as it appeared – delete, delete, delete...

The last email was from the US: Gideon@SecureCo.blablabla. He didn't know him; there was no reason he should. Secure Co. was a substantial concern, and he was new to the organisation, having only taken on the franchise three weeks earlier.

As he clicked on the email, he already knew it was going to be a distraction. It would entail at least five days out of the country, and, more importantly, five days out of the business. Then there were the travel costs and all the usual expenses that would inevitably accrue – accommodation, flights, taxis, perhaps some entertaining and his own "subsistence", the latter a nominal code imbued with an unwarranted sense of drama. Above all, the timing couldn't be worse.

For Paul, there was no choice. He glanced involuntarily at his in-tray, and in particular at the document on top of the growing mountain of filing he never seemed to get around to. His eye was drawn to a figure illuminated in yellow highlighter and annotated as "Paid in Full". The sum of a hundred thousand dollars loomed large on the page, a reminder of the commitment made, more an investment than a speculation, yet reason enough on its own to justify the trip.

There had been four franchises up for grabs in the UK, split broadly geographically: the north, south, Midlands, and basically everything inside the M25.

Paul pitched for the Midland region, or "Territory: Central" as it was described on the contract. Notwithstanding its name, his new patch stretched from the M25 to Carlisle and Newcastle. The southern region incorporated Wales, after his new colleague, Gary, argued to good effect that the south of England, excluding London entirely, wasn't a fair distribution of opportunity. Paul saw no issue relinquishing Wales. On balance, he had nothing personally against the Welsh but judged that the remaining extent of his territory contained prospects enough.

"Nice!"

He immediately focused on the one word in the email that really mattered. The location was Nice, Côte d'Azur, France. The Palais de la Méditerranée in Nice, to be more specific. His mood changed instantly. He might be the new kid on the block, but at least he knew his way around Nice.

He could readily recall a couple of excellent bars, some great restaurants, and was pretty familiar with the area in general, having holidayed there with Sophie annually for the last four years. Nice had become a habit. They would base themselves in the city and explore the coast down to Cannes and St Tropez in one direction and Monaco and Menton in the other.

On one occasion he'd surprised Sophie by arranging the trip to coincide with the Monaco Grand Prix, a once in a lifetime experience he had every intention of repeating. The whole Grand Prix trip had been exhilarating; even Sophie appeared to have been intoxicated by it. No matter how unlikely, he was certain they had both fallen under its spell.

Paul briefly considered calling Sophie with the good news and then quickly changed his mind. Things weren't great between them right now; an international sales conference was hardly conducive to fixing that. He quickly decided that taking Sophie wasn't a great option, leaving him with an even greater dilemma: how was he going to tell her she wasn't invited? One word about Nice and Sophie would instantly start planning the itinerary: lunch in Saint-Jean-Cap-Ferrat on Paloma Beach, mojitos in the beach bar of the Hôtel Martinez in Cannes, shoe shopping in St Tropez, Häagan-Dazs ice cream at the al fresco restaurant in Casino Square, Monaco. There just wouldn't be any time for any of that.

Paul opened and scrolled down the email attachment. The conference agenda was packed with motivational speakers, new product launches, workshops, Q&As and the ubiquitous keynote speech from Donald Ferranti himself, the self-styled founder and "beating heart" of Secure Co.

His sense of dread deepened. The schedule was a complete catalogue of everything he hated about corporate get-togethers, international or otherwise. In Paul's opinion, Secure Co. was a sales organisation first and last, each franchise working in its own target-driven silo. There was just no need for all the corporate self-indulgence that accompanied a set-piece get-together. All that mattered was the quality of the product and the commission rates. Everything else was just froth as far as Paul was concerned.

He'd seen it all before. No matter how glamorous the location, he could already visualise what lay in store. Endless stilted conversations with people he'd never met before and, in all probability, would never meet again. The seminar rooms and breakout areas were typically stalked by a mix of uber-competitive alpha males and over-compensating women, all genetically hardwired to exaggerate and embellish. He just wasn't cut out for all that corporate nonsense. Paul had long ago formed the opinion that whatever needed saying could be readily communicated in a well-worded email and save everyone the trouble.

He knew that not everyone felt the same – some revelled in such occasions. There would inevitably be the hard-core clique of long-serving international franchisees who would delight in ostracising the new guys or be fanatical in passing on the benefit of their self-serving experience. In among this lot there would, without doubt, be a few genuine people with the potential to make the event bearable. Finding them early in the piece would be the trick.

Doug had the potential to be a good guy. They'd met in London at The Westbury hotel in Mayfair, where the Secure Co. deal had finally been signed. Aged around forty-five, he was a Scottish gent of significant poise and character. Doug was a tall man, broad of shoulder with a full head of fair hair, softly spoken and possessed of a calming, measured manner. Doug held a great love of all things Scottish and a deeply held belief in the power of the Union, positions rationally reconciled during the course of dinner at the Brasserie Chavot after the meeting.

Having spent some time with Doug, Paul had quickly formed the view that he was a man of integrity, and he was much impressed with his knowledge of single malts.

Neither Gary nor Paul were experienced whisky drinkers, so, for educational purposes only, Doug treated them both to an impromptu tasting at no small personal expense. It had been late into the evening when they hit the Polo Bar at the Westbury. Each received a part measure of a selection of six whiskies, which Doug diligently lined up on the bar, Speyside to Island, with some iconic examples in between; light and heathery at one end, through to rich, dark and peaty at the other.

Doug's knowledge of the subject, at least to a novice such as Paul, seemed encyclopaedic as he jousted with the barman – a young "oik" who thought he knew it all and was singularly determined to rise to the challenge. Doug was effortlessly gracious in letting the lad have his moment in the sun, before gently including him in the tutorial. Classy!

Anyone would buy from Doug, a man of eloquent authority, a quick wit and a disarming charm. Where do I sign?

Doug took the north, Gary the south plus Wales, with Paul in the middle. Simon secured London for himself but, somewhat ironically, was unable to make the meeting in the heart of his own patch due to undisclosed transport problems.

Paul didn't have a lot of time for Gary. He was bright enough, but he lacked presence. Purely focused on the prize and devoid of tact, he possessed none of the poise of his colleague from the north. He was short, about five foot seven, slightly balding, and with an expanding waistline. His shirt was too tight and his jacket too large, with his fingers dangling from the sleeve giving the impression that he paddled as he walked. Gary wore cheap shoes, an expensive watch, maybe a fake, and endlessly fidgeted with his Ferrari key fob complete with a BMW ignition key attached.

Gary's ambition for the sale determined that all clients were mugs to be fully exploited and every sale was a victory. Gary was, as far as Paul could tell, completely without finesse. He was totally incapable of having a conversation without consulting his mobile phone, and he'd be inappropriately distracted by pretty much any female who entered his line of sight.

No, there was no point taking Sophie to Nice. There would be little pleasure in it for him, let alone for her, and anyway she had her own priorities right now, having just been made a partner at her firm. The truth was, Paul was inclined to concede, he was just as likely to be chastised for having the temerity to suggest a trip right now. His impudence would no doubt only serve to demonstrate how little he valued her career and further demonstrate the lack of sensitivity that apparently typified virtually every conversation they shared these days.

Paul would pick his moment to tell Sophie the news and then travel alone; it would be for the best.

He googled the hotel.

The Palais de la Méditerranée was a Hyatt Regency and, judging by its TripAdvisor reviews, it was a good solid base for the event. They'd never stayed at the hotel, despite their numerous trips to Nice, although Sophie often looked at it as a possibility. Whichever dates they chose to visit, there was precious little availability, if any, and never at a reasonable price. That didn't really surprise Paul that much, as the Palais de la Méditerranée enjoyed a fantastic location on the Promenade des Anglais. It was an iconic hotel dominating a much sought-after spot on the stunning seafront thoroughfare that had defined the city since the 1920s. Attracting business appeared to be the least of its problems.

Paul knew Nice well enough. It was a vibrant city with an historic old quarter, an impressive square, excellent shops, plenty of bars, a few museums, theatres, great restaurants, and, of course, casinos that were so synonymous with that part of the world.

Many an hour Sophie and Paul had walked… no… promenaded, as that is what one does in Nice, whiling away evenings trying to decide which of the many beachfront restaurants would send them scurrying to the cashpoint for a substantial top-up after dinner. A glass of rosé, a fish main course, a dessert to share and an espresso each, resulting in no change from a 150 euros no matter which one they chose. It never failed to amaze Paul just how expensive fish was on the beach in Nice despite the proximity of the resource.

Undaunted, Sophie had nominated the restaurant Castel Plage as their favourite, tucked away in the furthermost part of the beach, where the road narrowed to single lanes sweeping around the headland leading to the old harbour.

Paul completed the online registration form and hit *Send*. There was always next year for Sophie, and besides, Paul's attendance was as much an act of politics as anything else.

It was settled. He would drop the car off for its service over the weekend and then get a taxi to the airport in the early hours of Sunday morning. It was just easier that way.

The new mail message appeared in the bottom left-hand corner of the screen.

"Thank you for completing your online registra—" And then it melted away before Paul could fully appreciate the perfunctory gratitude he had no doubt the message would go on to convey, had he the enthusiasm to read it in full.

Chapter 3

THREE YEARS EARLIER (FEBRUARY 2011)
ST PETERSBURG, RUSSIA

"Sit down, Anatoly!" Nikoli demanded, slamming his fist on the table in his frustration with the younger man.

The room fell silent. It was not Nikoli's way; he was unfailingly calm in the boardroom, but not today.

Anatoly glared at the old man at the head of the table. His eyes were ablaze with anger, his mouth contoured with unrestrained hostility, his face flushed with an enmity long since held but suddenly reinforced and renewed. The documents in front of him lay scattered in disorder, discarded, rejected with a fury that had brought the meeting to an untimely halt. Anatoly had turned the pages in his impatience and immediately understood the devastating consequences of their contents.

"Please... sit," Nikoli urged him as he regained his composure. He indicated that Anatoly should retake his chair at the far end of the table; the gesture was well intentioned, calming and conciliatory, but futile all the same. He tried again as Anatoly fumed in silence, his features taking on a darker malevolence as the seconds slipped by.

There was nothing to be gained from antagonising Anatoly further. His temper was notoriously quick, frequently destructive, and the accompanying rages all too formidable. Nikoli had witnessed it all on so many previous occasions.

The younger man kicked his chair away, sending it spinning into the antique panelling that lined the sombre walls of the boardroom. He stormed the length of the room, wrenched the boardroom door open and slammed it shut behind him. All but Nikoli flinched as the huge mahogany door smashed into its ornate frame.

Thirteen men sat at the board table, and three more stood to one side, the attention of each fixed entirely on Anatoly as he took his leave. With the door closed, twelve men erupted simultaneously from their malaise; only Nikoli remained silent.

Beyond the boardroom, a young woman waited patiently for her father in the anteroom, Nikoli's secretary, Natalie, her only companion. Natalie was seated at her desk as always, ever-present, loyal, implacable, while Katia reclined rather less formally on a sumptuous sofa opposite. As faithful as she was long-suffering, Natalie's usual efficiency seemed to have deserted her briefly. Things were very different that morning. She was tense, tapping her fingers on the desktop, her breathing a little faster than the norm; she had known from the outset it would be a difficult meeting and was now only too aware of the escalating tensions from within.

"Perhaps you should wait for your father in his office..." she had quietly suggested earlier.

Katia had declined.

"We should catch up before I go. I might not see you again for ages," Katia said, pulling a long face to emphasise her point. "I'm going to miss you..." she added, and raised her glass in a gentle salute.

Natalie had poured Katia an ice-cold Diet Coke, which she sipped at sparingly, as was her way. Katia returned a smile imbued with a hint of gentle conspiracy. The choice of refreshment was more by way of tradition than personal preference these days. It had always been such a treat when she was younger – invariably frowned upon by her father, but otherwise an unchallenged indulgence permitted at Natalie's insistence. Katia rarely finished her Diet Coke these days, but she never refused it all the same.

Nikoli's voice was raised, his powerful baritone reverberating from the depths of the boardroom, the words lost but the tone unmistakable. Natalie engaged Katia in light conversation, as much to distract her from the sudden shattering of the harmony that so routinely typified company board meetings. As usual, she was quizzing her about her studies, her recent travels and, of course, she wanted to know everything about the latest boyfriend. Katia had been just five years old when she first met Natalie in her father's rather more modest offices in the outskirts of St Petersburg. But now she was eighteen, and while the questions were a little more in earnest, the answers remained just as coy.

But this wasn't like before. The heavy door leading to the boardroom was flung open and then slammed shut again with a venom that stunned both women into silence. They knew Anatoly well, his unpredictable ways, his terrible mood swings and unsettling reputation for casual violence; he wasn't a man to be trifled with.

Anatoly stormed through the anteroom with a look of pure malice on his face. He spotted Katia sitting on the sofa, her gaze determinedly averted. She became aware of his attentions as he approached and sipped nervously at her drink, her hands trembling uncontrollably, the fine crystal tumbler gripped ever more tightly. He was in front of her now and she could no longer ignore his presence.

"You bitch!" he cursed, pausing just long enough to clear his throat and spit his bile into her face. For a moment, it looked as though he would lash out – it was certainly in his nature – but he dismissed her with a wave of his hand and then walked on. Natalie rushed from the sanctuary of her desk to comfort the chairman's daughter.

"You bitch!" he repeated, and then he slammed his way out of the anteroom without a backwards glance.

There was uproar in the boardroom. Those inside were completely unaware of Anatoly's behaviour in the anteroom and solely preoccupied with all they had learned only a few short moments earlier. As the melee continued, Natalie held Katia reassuringly in her arms and wiped the spittle from her face. The girl shook uncontrollably, her pretty features blanched white with fear, her finely applied makeup streaked by tears that, even now, continued to flow.

In the boardroom Nikoli took control.

"Please, if you could leave us…" Nikoli addressed the three-man legal team that had delivered the documentation and provoked such controversy with Anatoly. Without a word, all three rose and left the room.

"Please, gentlemen, please." Calm and measured once again, Nikoli called the room to order.

"Gentlemen, gentlemen," Nikoli continued, "this is a good day. We have clarity, a new corporate constitution and a direction that we all feared would be lost to us."

The room was still buzzing with the news, so Nikoli gave them more time to come to terms with the scale of the revelations. A few minutes passed, the voices eventually falling silent one by one, and then, as was so often the case, all eyes turned to him for guidance.

"Thank you… thank you," he said calmly as peace descended without any further bidding from him.

"We have much to be grateful to Valentine for. Of all his great deeds this is surely among his bravest and, I'm sure you will agree, so typical of the man we all remember him to be." Nikoli always spoke with a deep affection for his recently departed friend.

The room buzzed with a quiet uneasiness.

"I have to tell you that what you have heard here today is true. Finally, it *is* settled. With his very last act in life, Valentine saved our company and all of us from the nightmare that would be Anatoly." Nikoli was studious and grave in his delivery.

"In removing his beloved son from this company, in casting his own son out of the very corporation he built from nothing to what we are today, he has done all of us a great service. I am sure you will agree with my assessment of Valentine's actions." He scanned the room for any sign of dissent that, in truth, he already knew he wouldn't find.

"There may have been a better way for Anatoly to hear the news – that, I accept. But who among us would take on that task alone? Better he hears of the changes enacted formally with us all present than for him to be given prior knowledge and the opportunity to react – as react we all know he surely will.

"I do understand that this is difficult, and I know some of you will not agree with what has happened – for my part I harboured reservations too. I have not been comfortable with the wealth that has fallen to me, and indeed to Katia, but Valentine would not be moved on the matter." Nikoli looked genuinely distressed, uncharacteristically awkward.

"I will address your concerns shortly. But firstly, we need to recognise that Valentine, as a devoted father, always intended to hand down the full extent of his own title in our company to his son. But despite his exhaustive endeavours to groom Anatoly to that task, he has, ultimately, and wisely in my view, chosen not to do so.

"We all know this was not Valentine's grand design. We all assumed that our counsel had fallen on deaf ears, but Valentine was courageous to the end and made a decision that would challenge, perhaps even haunt, any father. That decision, gentlemen, in my view, was inevitable. But it was Valentine's decision alone and could only be taken by him. Valentine has cut Anatoly out of the business completely and irrevocably, and in this single act he has spared the company from what would surely have been a damaging rule of tyranny and fear. We are all aware of what Anatoly is, and in the end, even his father had to recognise it too, and in doing so, face up to his responsibilities to us all.

"Gentlemen, Valentine *and you* – *all* of us together – have built a *great* company. With that greatness comes *great* influence and power, and with that comes *great* responsibility. In his final act, Valentine faced up to his responsibility and cut out the cancer that would surely have destroyed our business."

A mumbling consensus monetarily distracted Nikoli from his flow.

"Anatoly is nothing more than a psychopath!" a discordant voice boomed from the far end of the table. The consensus grew.

"I believe he might well be just that, but be aware, gentlemen, that he will not take this lightly. I urge you all to review your security. He is dangerous, and his father has not left him a poor man. He retains all of his father's business interests in Norilsk. These are considerable and very lucrative. He has resources, and we all know him to be vicious and unpredictable. He still has the wealth and power to respond to this slight. He will see it as nothing less than a betrayal."

A chorus of agreement filled the room. Nikoli pressed on, buoyed by the developing sense of unity.

"At the stroke of his father's pen," he continued, "Anatoly has lost all that he fully expected to have gained. No longer will he have the prospect of taking on Valentine's mantle, and he will never attain the power or authority of his father. All this and more has been denied him."

The room was in total accord now.

"Gentlemen, there is no doubt in my mind that Anatoly is little more than a corrupt, violent thug, and now, without his father to protect him, the world will finally see Anatoly for what he truly is. But be warned, he will not accept this readily."

The boardroom buzzed again with a mix of excitement and apprehension. Anatoly would certainly react, and they knew that none of them would be immune to his fury.

"One last thing…" he said, raising his hands in a bid to restore order.

"You will rightly be aware from the documents in front of you, that fifty per cent of Valentine's title passes to me and the remainder to a trust in which you are all trustees."

He scanned the desk briefly, selected a single document and held it up for all to see.

"This schedule explains in detail the circumstances in which the power of title contained within the trust can be exercised in our business. You will see, and I acknowledge to you today, that my holding is now substantially in excess of the fifty-one per cent required for absolute control of our company. I sense and understand why that might cause you disquiet. But be assured, in this agreement, all decisions, as set out in the schedule, will require a majority vote of the trustees in support of my own wishes for any matter to carry. This has been done to protect our company from the risk of too much power being centred in one man's hands. It was a burden to Valentine, and it would have been a travesty if such power had passed to Anatoly. This agreement is drawn up to Valentine and Yuri's approval based on decisions made together only days prior to his death."

Yuri Barkov, the company's lead counsel, sat at Nikoli's right hand nodding sagely. He acknowledged the questioning looks from his otherwise deferential colleagues, then spoke briefly.

"This agreement, and I commend it to you all, specifically reflects Valentine's dying wishes. He was determined that no one should face the torment he himself suffered in making such decisions in isolation. This is the way Valentine wanted it."

The consensus held and Nikoli continued once again.

"There is no doubt Valentine has handed me great wealth in my lifetime, and in turn to Katia and her family beyond that, and for that I will always love the man. But, more than that, he has handed all of us, equally, a shared authority so that we, all of us together, may live up to the full burden of our responsibilities and in doing so exercise those same responsibilities diligently, ethically and, most importantly of all, collectively."

All eyes were upon Nikoli. He intended to say so much more but the muffled sobs from beyond the boardroom door quite suddenly held his attention hostage. Much had been said already, and so much done, so with the board seemingly aligned, he called the meeting to a close.

"That is all I have to say for now. I suggest we adjourn, as these are unusual times and we all need to attend to our own personal matters. I suggest we reconvene next week and continue the great work that Valentine has so bravely passed into our care. Thank you and good day, gentlemen."

The meeting was over.

Nikoli rose swiftly from his chair and left the room. In the anteroom, he found his daughter being comforted by the irreplaceable Natalie, and both women were in great distress. He required no explanation. His familiarity with Anatoly's madness was all he needed to fill in the blanks. Valentine had only been dead for a matter of weeks and already Anatoly's actions were casting an ominous shadow. His contempt for his friend's only son redoubled in that instant, and for the first time since the early days he felt a fear that all too often in the past had chilled him to the bone.

Despite his antipathy towards Anatoly, Nikoli had loved his father like a brother. They had started the company together, working tirelessly over the years, and never once found cause for any form of dissent between them. It never troubled him that Valentine took the most part for himself, as there was so much else that was shared.

He had known Anatoly all his life and recalled his mother with an affection undiminished by the passing of time. He recalled Anatoly being a sweet child at first, full of fun and adventure. But following the sudden death of his mother to illness when he was just twelve years old, Anatoly changed.

Nikoli had witnessed it all. Anatoly became dark and withdrawn, his father too busy or too distracted by the business to notice the demons that troubled his beloved boy. Valentine would see no wrong in his child and would accept no counsel, not even from Nikoli. The boy became damaged and dangerous.

Nikoli stood quietly aside as Valentine dealt with the terrible things his son did, the people he hurt and even the girl he, and his equally twisted cousin, callously left to die on a Mediterranean hillside. Valentine dealt with it all as best he could, but still Anatoly descended further into a world of corruption and violence. The depth of the darkness that consumed his friend's son made even the great man recoil. Nikoli bore witness to Valentine's despair as he dispatched his fixers to clean up the mess his son's growing depravity created.

Valentine often spoke of the redemption he saw for his son in the business; surely such a great endeavour would give him direction and exorcise the bile that drove him?

In the end it was Anatoly himself that brought his father to the only conclusion he could. Anatoly never sort redemption, never felt the guilt; he was never haunted by his actions. Valentine was only too aware of his own failings and could barely allow himself to judge his son, but instead he blamed his own frailties for passing on the weaknesses that gave Anatoly the stomach to carry out his own misdeeds.

Finally, Valentine recognised that Anatoly did not perceive the pain of others; he felt no empathy, no contrition. In all the years since his own guilty actions, Nikoli was at Valentine's side as he took each and every opportunity to make good, seek amends and put things right. Valentine always acknowledged it was never enough, but he could only live with himself knowing he had accepted his full part in it. It was Anatoly's absolute rejection of blame, his failure to recognise the evil that had become his world, that drew Valentine's hand across that page and, ultimately, ensured the fate of the company without Anatoly at its helm.

His son was beyond Valentine's help now, but before his death he'd grieved for his lost son and even prayed for his soul as his own mortality lent focus to his legacy. He'd never been a religious man, but in the end, and for the first time in his life, Valentine had called on a greater power, not for himself, but in the hope that with God's grace and his own prayers a "greater power" might succeed where he had known only failure and despair.

SUNDAY

SEPTEMBER 2014

Chapter 4

SUNDAY

A rush of cold air hit Paul as he stepped out of the taxi and onto a crowded pavement outside the entrance to the departure hall at East Midlands airport.

It was 5.30 am, his flight scheduled for departure one hour and forty minutes later at ten past seven. If the trip was the precursor to a holiday, no doubt somewhere sunny but not too hot, he would happily spend a full two hours with Sophie, enjoying a coffee and pastry together, or Paul would just sit and read while Sophie did her "thing" in duty-free. But travelling on business and unaccompanied, the whole airport experience just grated that little bit more, each irritation testing what small measure of patience he could still draw on at such an early hour.

With a packed five days of meetings and a black-tie formal dinner to attend, he wheeled a full twenty-two kilos of luggage to the check-in desk with a briefcase balanced on top as carry-on. If it hadn't been for the black-tie dinner, Paul had already convinced himself, with a concerted effort and a little self-discipline, he could have avoided the hold altogether, cramming everything into an overhead-locker-sized suitcase, but that just wasn't to be.

That niggled away at him perhaps more than it should, but Paul took no pleasure in the formality of such events. He couldn't comprehend how anyone could derive any joy from such an outdated formula as the set-piece gala dinner. The whole thing seemed incongruous to him. Firstly, he wasn't aware of anyone from the UK attending the event accompanied by their spouse, so, at best, the dancing would be an interesting exercise in international diplomacy, and secondly, Secure Co. was a modern, West Coast, commercial enterprise. Surely relaxed informality was the order of the day? He'd readily accepted the premise that, in business, the Americans had all but done away with even the most modest convention of ties, favouring casual over formal as the norm. A black-tie dinner appeared, at least to him, to be the antithesis of their modern day work style, with their beanbag seminars and blue-sky thinking zones. He assumed the whole thing was merely a cultural misunderstanding, his American hosts, through lack of international sophistication, believing British businessmen still wore bowler hats, the Austrians waltz the night away, while the French conspiratorially smoked stinking cigarettes in darkened corners.

In Paul's experience of doing business in America, they dined at 6 pm and were in bed by ten. He doubted that any of the American contingent, which would be considerable, would endure much beyond the dinner itself, leaving the Europeans free to party the night away.

Whatever the reason for the arcane formality, it was the dinner jacket alone that required him to take his place at the back of a long queue in order to check-in a suitcase at five forty-five on a Sunday morning in September. The queue was longer than he expected but the staff efficient.

It wasn't long before he was sipping an extra-shot café au lait and working his way through an almond croissant. As he immersed himself in what could reasonably pass for a French-style continental breakfast, albeit at East Midlands Airport, it struck him as akin to a method actor preparing for a role. The charade was due to begin in earnest the following morning, with the obligatory conference registration meet and greet followed by a "get to know you" light lunch reception from 1 pm.

His mood darkened. The first day would almost certainly be the worst. Paul was in no doubt that practically everyone he met on Monday morning would be truly "delighted to make his acquaintance", albeit through a thinly applied veneer of sincerity. Typically, he found such acquaintances ingratiatingly fascinated to discover whatever it was that actually "made him tick", while awaiting even the most tenuous opportunity to eulogise about themselves. In Paul's experience of such events, on the first day he would generally meet a sanitised and polished version of a fellow delegate, with a more authentic iteration emerging as the days passed. The true depth of any deception would inevitably reveal itself in the death throes of the black-tie gala dinner, when alcohol and familiarity would contrive to lift what remained of the veil and the curtain finally fell on the entire event.

The truth about any sales-based business, or at least the truth as far as Paul was concerned, was that the commercial discipline itself was little more than a performance, and Nice would, without doubt, provide all concerned with a truly international stage. Lights, camera, action…

There was little he was looking forward to in the next few days, and he self-consciously contemplated which version of himself he could deploy to get through the worst of it. Without Sophie or even a book for distraction, there were another forty-five minutes before boarding, plenty of time to decide…

His mind slipped back to the previous morning. He'd called Sophie and invited her to stay over. Unsurprisingly, she saw through his plan in an instant.

"I'm not getting up at stupid o'clock and taking you to the airport. You can be so selfish, Paul!"

Paul didn't doubt it from her tone.

"What about just coming over then? I'll cook."

They both knew he wouldn't. Paul never cooked, but it was worth a shot. He shuddered a little inside. Was he really that shallow? The plan had been crystal clear in his own mind all along. Sophie staying the night before he travelled to Nice raised the very real prospect of a decent home cooked meal and maybe a little fun at bedtime – it had been a while – and then an early morning lift to the airport, which was fully factored in as a bonus. Maybe Sophie did have a point; perhaps he was being a little selfish after all.

"Christ Paul!" he recalled her saying. *"When are you going to understand that this is just not working for me?"*

Paul had treated the question as rhetorical. If pressed for an answer it would have been inconclusive at best.

Probably never, he considered to himself, but he remained silent on the subject at the time.

There was no doubt he still loved her, and he was sure she still loved him too, but it was getting tougher to tell. Although they still did things together, they never seemed to do anything meaningful as a couple any more. They chose Sophie's new settee together the previous month, but that was really the point; it was her settee, for her flat, and was nothing at all to do with *them*.

"I'll get a taxi," Paul had said mournfully.

She chose to misunderstand, permitting herself to assume, with some justification, that he still fully expected her to stay the night, cook the dinner and just skip the early morning drive.

"You could always let yourself out once I've left for the airport."

After all, Sophie did still have a key to his place, although he was only too aware that he could no longer say the same about hers. And that was another significant development that he chose to dismiss when it happened, but which frustrated him now as he filled the time in contemplation of such matters. Apparently, he remembered with an increasing degree of irritation, Sophie needed her front-door key back for a while, something she raised in a conversation initiated almost immediately after a heated discussion on the merits of her "having her own space". The reason given at the time? Her sister, Donna, who always regarded Paul with the look of someone experiencing a life-changing disappointment, was planning to visit and would need the key for the duration of her stay. As it turned out, and for reasons that were never explained, Donna never actually did.

"I'm not coming over! This is not working for me, Paul!" She sounded serious; the emphasis was on "not".

"I understand. Don't worry, I'll get a takeaway."

"Christ, Paul, it's not about the bloody cooking!"

"Look, you're angry and upset," he'd interjected, desperate to take the heat out of the conversation. *"Don't worry about it. I'm probably being a bit unsensitive,"* he admitted in an attempt to steal her thunder.

"Insensitive, you moron. You're being insensitive!" She became exasperated with him, but she was never happier than when correcting him in some way or another. He might have loaded the dishwasher the wrong way, or washed up in the wrong order. "Don't leave your shoes here… don't leave your toothbrush there… in fact, why don't you just leave…?"

Paul was forced to consider that things weren't looking good between them. He was prepared to concede that much of it was almost certainly his own fault.

"We need to talk…" he recalled her saying before she hung up. *"When you get back, Paul, we need to talk…"*

It wasn't the first time. Paul experienced a familiar sinking feeling as the phone went dead before he could even say goodbye. Sophie clearly meant "the talk", and it wouldn't even be the second time either. Having reconciled twice in the last twelve months alone, he'd been subjected to "the talk" several times before. But this time it felt a little bit different. This time it just felt… final.

A PA announcement broke his train of thought and the family at the next table rose to leave. A well-thumbed newspaper remained in their wake. Paul watched silently as the beleaguered mother and her three manically overexcited children made their way to the departure gates. Dad seemed oblivious to it all. Paul liberated the newspaper, tidied the sheets into a foldable format and ironed it flat with his hand. At least he would have something to read on the flight.

Paul stirred the remnants of his cappuccino and checked his iPhone. It was more by way of habit than for any particular reason. There were no messages, why would there be? After all, it was still early, the flight information screen nearby confirmed it, the time: 6.45 am.

Gate 14 was displayed on the monitor. He scooped up his coat, newspaper and briefcase and joined the herd making its way to the departure gates. Paul still had Sophie on his mind. After a few moments of consideration, he decided he'd give her a ring once he landed in Nice and tell her just how much he was missing her. Before turning the iPhone to flight mode, he took the precaution of setting a reminder, just in case he forgot.

Chapter 5

Anatoly paced from one side of the room to the other.

Yuri Barkov, who for so many years had been Anatoly's father's most trusted legal advisor, sat silently awaiting a reaction. He didn't have to wait long.

Anatoly drew himself to his full height, towering over the lawyer as he stood on the opposite side of his desk. His eyes pored over the documents as if seeking an alternative conclusion. He was in denial, unconvinced, his head shaking, his mood as volatile as Semtex. Any other version of the facts seemed preferable to him. Anything other than the conclusion Yuri had given him in such considered and compelling detail.

Yuri had explained it all, but despite the logic of his arguments, Anatoly refused to accept it. Yuri was tired, exhausted by his work and now seemed determined that his silence would be an end to it.

"And you're quite sure there is nothing you have missed?" The benign tone in Anatoly's voice belied the menace it carried. It was the calm before the storm.

"Quite sure," the old man said dismissively. For almost three years he had worked on the documentation.

There were no more questions.

Anatoly's patience broke.

He grabbed the desk phone, complete with handset, and smashed it across the ageing lawyer's face. Yuri's head shot backwards as if hit by a high velocity round and blood sprayed from his nose and mouth. Anatoly threw the phone back on the desk contemptuously. The handset fell from its cradle seemingly in an act of disrespect that angered him still further. Anatoly snatched up the instrument again, only the handset this time, as if intent on teaching the errant object a lesson. He brought it down hard onto the old man's face with venomous power. Once, twice, three times he smashed it viciously into his face, tearing into his thin skin and crashing into his frail bones.

As quickly as it had started, it was over. The handset was discarded dismissively onto the desk once more.

"You dare to tell me nothing can be done!" It was more of an accusation than a question. Anatoly wiped his blood-spattered hand on the old man's shirt. Spittle foamed at his mouth.

"You do it, or I will kill you and every piece of shit you have ever known. Do you understand me?"

He didn't understand. There was no way he could. Yuri lay slumped in his chair, limp and bleeding, rendered unconscious from the blows. He was in his seventieth year and didn't have the strength to withstand such an assault.

"You…" Anatoly turned his attention to the others. "Check the old fool is all right." He pointed indifferently in the direction of the two junior lawyers in the room.

"If he's dead, I will kill both of you. Wake him up."

Neither man moved. The first to do so would put himself in the direct line of fire. But Yuri needed help and there was no one else. The younger of the two lawyers blinked first. He could claim no medial experience but could tell Yuri wasn't dead… not yet. Relief washed over him. It was selfish and weak but he feared Anatoly wouldn't hesitate to honour his threat if the old man died. At least it was good news for now. He wouldn't have to tell Anatoly he'd just killed a man.

Three years earlier, Yuri had served Anatoly's father as his most trusted legal advisor and the company's lead counsel. He was now slumped beaten and unconscious at his own desk. The young lawyer hesitated and his colleague recoiled; both were traumatised by the treatment meted out to such a man. He was a mentor to the two younger lawyers, and a man who on so many previous occasions had proved to be the legal powerhouse that saved Anatoly from facing the justice his countless acts of brutality rightly deserved.

"He's not dead, sir," the young lawyer ventured with all the conviction he could manage. "But he is unconscious, sir. He needs help. He needs a doctor."

"I hardly touched him. Wake him up!" Anatoly commanded. He might have gone too far, perhaps struck him more times than he initially intended, but that prospect didn't concern him. If Yuri died, he died. It was of no great consequence to Anatoly.

The young lawyer stared back blankly at Anatoly, his heart racing. There was nothing he could do. Yuri's condition was deteriorating at an alarming rate. There was a chilling rattle in his breathing, and what little colour there had been in his features had drained from him completely.

Anatoly relented.

"Get him a doctor and then tell him to fix it. This isn't the end for him. I will tell him when it's finished. Make sure he understands." He wiped his mouth on his sleeve. "I'll say when it's over. Do you understand?"

The two young lawyers nodded nervously with no obvious sign of comprehension. There was nothing to understand; Anatoly's behaviour was beyond reason and his actions were those of a madman.

Anatoly left the room cursing the old man's incompetence.

*****

It was three years since Anatoly's father died. Three years less two weeks since Anatoly had learned the full depth of his father's betrayal. In the intervening time he'd tasked Yuri to break the new constitution, invalidate the contracts and undermine the new trust arrangements that had ripped his legacy from him.

Anatoly understood violence and pain, but he couldn't comprehend that mere words on a page could stand between him and everything his father had built in his name. This wouldn't be the end of the matter and, with Yuri's blood still fresh on his hands, Anatoly finally accepted that if it was going to get done at all, it would have to be done another way. His way…

*****

As Yuri fought for his life, the memory of Valentine's last request haunted him.

"Yuri, my old friend…" Valentine had said three long years earlier, "it is my dying wish that you take on the most precious of all responsibilities for me. I have asked so much of you over the years, but nothing is more important to me than this. You have been my friend and my counsel for as long as I can remember. I have no right to ask this of you, but I beg you…"

Yuri acquiesced immediately, such was his affection for the old man. The undisguised regret on Yuri's face was acknowledged by Valentine, who was fully aware of the sacrifice he was asking him to undertake. It was the most poisoned of chalices, eternally linking Yuri's fate with the machinations of the old man's beloved son, forsaking all else to protect and keep the very worst of men safe in his lifetime.

Yuri had been there from the start. He had picked up the pieces for Anatoly time and time again over the years. He knew nothing would change. Anatoly learned nothing of his father's ways during his lifetime, and he would certainly suffer no censure from Yuri now he was gone. It was folly to think otherwise.

But Anatoly had been obsessive, single-minded in his madness. He'd kept a low profile over the previous three years since his father's death, since his father's "betrayal". There was nothing to distract Yuri from the work Anatoly had instructed him to undertake. But Yuri saw no reason to believe that Anatoly had changed at all. There was no evidence that he could. There were still the rages, the violent explosions of temper, but only those in his inner circle had been exposed to them in recent times. That alone proved to be enough to keep Yuri's desk free of other distractions. Nothing was to detract from the ageing lawyer's work. If that meant a degree of moderation on Anatoly's part, then that price had been paid in full. But it wouldn't last.

He'd given Yuri just one task. His sole purpose was to dismantle the very framework his father had worked so tirelessly to create in his final weeks. Yuri had known he was never going to do it. It was a source of comfort to him that he, of all men, knew there was nothing he could do. Yuri had drawn up the paperwork himself explicitly to Valentine's instructions, and he'd executed his work well. He'd left no omissions; there were no arguments unreasoned; there was quite simply no room for debate. His work was irrevocable in law when it had first been drafted, and nothing had changed to weaken the finality of it since.

*****

The old lawyer would practice no more. He never recovered from his injuries and he never spoke again. He died in pain and in isolation just two desperate weeks later. His family mourned his passing, but the fear of further reprisals kept them away from his bedside and ultimately his funeral. It was a pitiful affair. Anatoly attended to pay his last respects. It was just one more calculated act of contempt. He spoke a few miserly words in tribute but made no attempt to conceal his obvious pleasure at the meagre attendance at the old man's graveside.

Chapter 6

The plane wasn't full but boarding seemed laboured. A few frequent flyer types had managed to smuggle what, to Paul, appeared to be oversized suitcases on board and were now engaged in the task of stowing them in the overhead lockers. It took an eternity as they determinedly forced them into the available space, which was barely adequate to accept their bulk. It wasn't entirely lost on him that he was no more than a dress code away from being one of them himself.

Paul stashed his briefcase under the seat in front of him, sat down and buckled up.

A familiar and manically exuberant family pushed their way down the plane in his direction. Dad brought up the rear, deaf to the shrieks of his offspring and indifferent to his wife's futile efforts to bring them to heel. Paul assumed, somewhat judgementally, that they might be more familiar with travelling on one of the tacky budget airlines, where fighting for seats so they could all sit together or paying a king's ransom for the privilege were the only options. As they scrambled into the seats immediately behind him, he was forced to consider just how much of a premium he might be prepared to pay to avoid sitting anywhere near them at all.

He placed his briefcase on his lap and worked the combination lock to 5555. Once open, he slipped his iPhone inside next to a fully charged iPad. He spun the dials before re-stowing it, somewhat awkwardly, under the seat in front of him once again. At least he'd be able to get on with some work during the flight, and after all, since landing in his inbox, there were a few emails that, although not pressing, he could at least occupy himself with.

The captain announced "final checks for take-off" at a volume that set a number of babies bawling and wailing in unison. The toddler behind him increased pitch, drawing the attention of a member of the overworked cabin crew, she smiled professionally at the howling baby's mum before tripping over his poorly stowed briefcase. She whisked it away before he was even aware there was an issue. With her smile still intact, but clearly strained, she and the briefcase disappeared down the plane as if by way of a personal favour. Paul could only imagine that even if he could summon the will to query her actions, its removal would almost certainly be justified under the pretext of health and safety. He quietly despaired as the volume and intensity of the baby's crying continued unabated.

"I'll get it back to you as soon as possible, sir," the flight attendant said on her return, her words barely audible above the din and her smile a preview of the sort of sincerity he hadn't expected to encounter until conference registration at the earliest.

"Thank you," he said in compliant resignation.

As the plane began to taxi, he scanned the headlines of his second-hand newspaper, ever more grateful for the distraction.

Russian Mafia Compete For Slice Of Illegal Weapons Trade In North Africa.

Paul read on.

Evidence has emerged that Russian organised crime bosses are looking to spread their sphere of influence into North Africa and the lucrative trade in illegal arms. An escalation in activity is at the centre of a potentially deadly conflict with the Papé crime syndicate based in Marseilles. The Russians, who are well organised and well financed, have opened up new lines of supply using their established connections through smuggling, trafficking and racketeering operations in the area.

The business of smuggling arms into North Africa was, at one time, the sole preserve of French organised crime, but as more routes across the Mediterranean have been opened up, due mainly to failing North African regimes, the proliferation in opportunities is now being exploited by Russian criminal elements.

The increasing volatility and politic unrest in the area has seen demand for illegal weapons soar. An increasing number of potential new customers are now in the market and there appears to be no shortage of suppliers coming forward to fulfil the demand.

Russian attempts to steal market share are being blamed for starting what appears to be a turf war being played out in the darkest recess of Marseille itself and as far afield as Norilsk in Siberia…

The article ran to two full columns, but succumbing to the weariness of the early start, Paul placed the newspaper back on the empty seat next to him in favour of closing his eyes. He blocked out the noise, settled back and, remarkably, he slept.

*****

The plane landed at ten twenty-five local time, a mere five minutes late.

Paul's briefcase was returned in good order and the passage through Nice Airport was straightforward and uneventful. He met Doug at the adjacent luggage carousel and they exchanged pleasantries and agreed to share a taxi.

"Palais de la Méditerranée," Doug informed the driver as they entered the white Mercedes. It was a short taxi ride from the airport to the hotel, not more than ten minutes depending on traffic conditions.

Bathed in sunshine and bustling with morning traffic even on a Sunday, it was pleasant to be back in Nice. Paul's mood lifted further as they passed by familiar landmark hotels and beachfront restaurants, and he allowed himself to enjoy the journey in quiet reflection.

Doug was in a free-flowing conversation with the taxi driver. His comments elicited a laugh and a comprehensive response. Doug cracked a broad smile in return. "*Oui! Oui!*" he responded at intervals, and then he settled back still grinning at the driver's musings. Paul smiled warmly at his fellow traveller; he understood nothing of what was said, despite Doug's apparently impeccable French, but saw no reason to admit it.

Paul took a few euros from his wallet as they approached the hotel. He was determined to settle the taxi fare himself, after enjoying Doug's generosity at the whisky-tasting in the Polo Bar. He was out of the cab first and well before an attentive concierge had time to get to the door. He tendered the fare and received change from the driver without a word passing between them. Paul used the universal language when paying for taxis in foreign climes; gestures and grunts were all he required, and he was fluent enough in both.

"Thanks, I owe you," Doug said casually.

"You're welcome," Paul said, and then he trailed behind his colleague, dragging his own suitcase as the concierge was already preoccupied with Doug's.

"Monsieur, please, please."

The second concierge spoke a passable version of Franglais, having already calculated, quite rightly as it happened, that Paul couldn't possibly understand French. He gestured for him to leave his luggage where it was.

"I'm okay. I'm okay. It's not a problem. Thank you."

The concierge looked completely relaxed either way and pointed out the location of the reception desk, while Doug's bags were whisked away in the opposite direction.

The reception lobby was a large, spacious hall entered from the porte-cochère via an automatic revolving door. A smell of lavender and mint filled the air; the temperature was cool and the atmosphere restful. Hyatt Regency, Paul suspected, had developed a "brand essence" that was being systematically pumped into the lobby – a cynical corporate trick, and it was, quite frankly, fantastic.

The interior of the hotel was art deco, highly polished mid-tone woods, marble floors and ornate lighting. To either side of the entrance doors were oversized sofas, armchairs and coffee tables, variously occupied by an Asian family and a group of businessmen who could quite possibly be attending the Secure Co. event itself. Paul didn't recognise any of them, and he confidently suspected that neither did Doug.

Beyond the seating areas, and set off to the right, was the concierge desk, and an American couple attempting to communicate via an improvised version of semaphore. To the left there were two large reception desks set at ninety degrees to each other, complete with immaculately attired staff at both. Straight ahead, the large spacious lobby ran further back to a bank of three lifts, and opposite those were two desks, complete with computers and comfortable chairs, provided for the use of hotel guests.

It was typical in terms of its scale and facilities, but given the styling and the disarming fragrance copiously wafted into the space through the highly efficient air-conditioning, Paul declared himself content as he waited for his turn to check in.

Doug was up first.

"There you are, Mr Sterling. You are on the fifth floor. The lifts are to your right and your luggage will be up shortly. If there is anything you need during your stay, my name is Andrea, please do not hesitate to ask. Enjoy your stay, sir."

Doug turned to head for the lifts and then paused.

"Do you fancy a coffee maybe, or perhaps we could take a stroll... or do you have other things you need to take care of?"

"A bit of fresh air would do us good. Meet you down here in about thirty minutes?" Paul suggested.

"Make it forty-five," Doug replied.

"Great!"

As Doug headed for the lifts, Paul was handed a small branded cardboard pouch with two plastic key cards tucked snugly inside.

"Seventh floor, Mr..." Andrea looked down at her paperwork. This was the same girl who gushed so easily with "Mr Sterling" but now tripped over "Smith"!

"Monsieur Smith," she finished. "Your bags will be up as soon as possible, but we are rather busy right now. Do let me know if you need anything in the meantime."

What? No name? No "enjoy your stay"? Paul was forced to confront the possibility that he was unduly weary from the flight and the early start. Even minor irritations were beginning to grate unreasonably on his nerves. Doug was right to give it forty-five minutes. He needed a break.

Chapter 7

PRESENT DAY, SUNDAY (SEPTEMBER 2014)

The lift doors opened.

"Doors opening, seventh floor," the lift chimed in French, but that much Paul could work out for himself. Eat your heart out, Doug.

He was greeted with the beaming smile of a man whose enthusiasm for life knew no bounds.

"Hey, hey, mate. How are ya?" Gary was in the lift lobby on the seventh floor and could hardly control his delight at their chance meeting. Three hundred attendees and, other than Doug, Gary was the first one Paul met.

"I got in last night – got on the piss. I'm just going down for some breakfast. Are you gonna join me?"

Gary reminded Paul of an overexcited puppy compulsively waiting for someone to throw the proverbial ball. Paul consulted his iPhone, which had conveniently updated itself to local time. It was 12.20 pm; he was way beyond breakfast.

"I've just arrived, Gary. I've got a bit of work to do…"

Paul was desperately trying to think of something that would sound credible if Gary pressed him on it. He did. Paul imagined, quite wrongly as it turned out, that even Gary wouldn't think it entirely unreasonable not to want breakfast at twelve-twenty in the afternoon, not least considering that breakfast service, in all likelihood, had stopped several hours earlier.

"Come on. There's plenty of time for all that. Come and have some breakfast," Gary persisted. He was bouncing with enthusiasm. "Come on, what's the matter with ya? A bit of breakfast won't hurt ya."

Paul was beaten.

"I'm meeting Doug in the lobby at one o'clock. Why don't you just join us? I'm sure we can get something to eat then. Why don't you just skip breakfast, Gary? We can get some lunch in town."

What was he saying? Paul was looking forward to spending the afternoon with Doug but entertained no desire to renew his acquaintance with Gary at all.

Gary could hardly contain himself.

"It's a date," he declared, virtually dancing with enthusiasm.

Paul was horrified. He thought Gary was about to start throwing fake punches in a matey sort of way.

"It's a date..." Gary repeated.

It's not a date, it's nothing like a bloody date, a silent voice boomed inside Paul's head. "See you in the lobby then," Paul said with a smile bordering on sincere.

"See you, mate. Hair of the dog," Gary said for no obvious reason.

The image of a neurotic terrier with a serious obsessive-compulsive disorder flashed through Paul's mind.

Gary spun on his heels and headed back to his room, fortunately down a corridor in the opposite direction to one signposted to room 733.

Small mercies! Paul thought.

Straight ahead and then a right, left and right again. Room 733 was at the back of the hotel.

For Paul, when staying in a hotel for the first time, there was invariably a moment of mild suspense as he swiped the seemingly mandatory magnetic key card in the obligatory electronic lock. The act of opening the door would reveal the true nature of his lodgings, a moment invariably followed by either mild elation or abject disappointment, with very little in between.

Paul pushed open the heavy door. Result!

The room was spacious and flooded with light from a huge window forming the entire width of the far wall. A sliding patio door opened onto a balcony overlooking the rear of the hotel – not too picturesque, but pleasant enough. A measure of privacy was provided by tall frosted-glass screens that separated the balconies from adjacent rooms. A pair of comfortable patio chairs and a table provided a mild incentive to relax and absorb a view that consisted almost entirely of balconies of similar design surrounding a small private square.

Paul slipped one of the plastic keys into a slot on the wall. The lobby light illuminated on cue, while a gurgling sound overhead implied the air-conditioning unit had got the message too.

The bedroom itself benefited from a large lobby and a set of huge wardrobes secured by three full-height wardrobe doors. Secreted within was a typical hotel safe and an amply stocked minibar with an eye-watering tariff stuck forebodingly to the door. The lobby had four doors leading off it: one to the bedroom and two more giving access to the bathroom and a separate WC on the left.

The bathroom was good too. The floor and walls were fully tiled in a light honey-coloured marble. On the right, a large bath took up the entire length of the wall. Straight ahead, a huge mirror occupied the space over a vanity unit with two basins complete with designer taps. To the left and behind the door was a separate glass shower cubicle fitted with an impressive douche and a further hand-held shower attachment, which, it occurred to Paul, would meet most aspirations. Stylish and practical, he fully approved. It was a delightful bathroom and to his eye immaculately clean. Whether it would pass the "Sophie Test" was a different matter.

Less satisfying was the separate toilet facility, essentially a small room, or more accurately a cell, to the left of the bathroom. It was fine in itself, but he couldn't understand why any hotel designers would separate the WC from the bathroom without providing a small washing facility within it. It just didn't make sense to him. Notwithstanding this design flaw, it too was cleaned to a sparkle and smelt pleasantly enough of fresh mint.

However, his heart sank a little as he tried the door directly opposite the bathroom. It was locked. He turned the simple thumb turn lock provided and pulled the door open only to reveal another door immediately beyond. There was no means of opening the second door from his side and his worst fears were confirmed. He'd been allocated an adjoining room, separated by two, almost certainly inadequate, independently locking doors.

Paul hated adjoining rooms in hotels. Having no children or similarly needy dependents, he had no appreciation of their value and plenty of experience of their inadequacies. No matter how good the joiner, no matter how competent the design, he would invariably be able to hear everything that was going on in the room next door. That was fair enough on the balcony but utterly unacceptable in the bedroom.

Paul doubted Doug would have been allocated an adjoining room – that's just not how the world works. He resigned himself to the prospect that the occupants of room 732 would be largely nocturnal, extremely noisy and totally inconsiderate. The family on the plane came to mind, or worse, an amorous couple with the stamina of Olympic gold medallists, completely oblivious to the frailty of their own privacy.

The saving grace was the final door that, when closed, separated the lobby from the bedroom itself and afforded some small measure of soundproofing if the worst came to the worst.

Paul considered changing rooms. Then there was a knock at the door that made the option more complicated; his suitcase had arrived rather sooner than he expected. Paul opened the door to a porter who placed the suitcase on the luggage rack and unzipped it, which Paul felt was a little invasive for his tastes.

The porter drew the sheers, presumably to give Paul a little more privacy since he'd already experienced the view, and then proceeded to remove and re-insert the plastic room key in the energy-saving device as if performing magic. Paul had already worked it out for himself, but he allowed the porter to finish his routine. Lights went off and back on again, which required no verbal explanation, and the gentle hum from the air-conditioner resumed, much to the porter's approval. He pointed at the location of the heating controls, smiled and then stood stock still, expectantly awaiting his reward. The porter left the room, pausing somewhat indelicately to check the magnitude of his guest's appreciation.

Paul waited for the bedroom door to close before doing anything at all.

An enormous bed dominated the bedroom, with a crisp white duvet, masses of pillows and a couple of soft, brightly coloured cushions for decoration. Bedside tables with attractive lamps, two easy chairs and a coffee table were all tastefully arranged. Opposite the bed, a huge TV dominated an equally huge desk complete with a bowl of fruit, a sharp looking fruit knife and an attendant welcome letter. To the side, a luggage rack, replete with his suitcase now open, revealed the devastatingly creased dinner jacket Paul had so painstakingly folded to avoid that precise outcome.

Forty-five minutes is not going to be nearly enough time to sort that lot out, he mused. Paul was resigned to the possibility that just about everything would need ironing before wearing, and he wondered why he'd bothered with the laborious task of folding it all in the first place. It was invariably the same outcome no matter how careful he was during the packing process. On holiday, who cares? On business, it was a different matter completely.

Needless to say, the one thing he didn't have in his room was an iron and ironing board, which to his mind was probably the one thing that everybody was likely to actually *need* at some stage during their stay. Paul was staying in a five-star hotel, according to the website, and five-star hotels don't expect their clientele to be bothered with such menial chores as ironing. Why would they, when they can charge a small fortune for doing it for you on the pretext of service.

On the upside, the Nespresso machine was going to get a good workout, starting now. Located to the left of the massive TV, eight of the delightfully coloured capsules were arranged in pairs in a small wooden display box, with the machine jauntily placed at an angle behind.

Having made a lungo and ordered the essential iron and ironing board from reception, he settled down on a chair with the welcome letter for light reading. It was accompanied by a single bloom as a final flourish. A gerbera, Paul decided, and he felt pretty confident he was right. Tragic!

The welcome letter contained the usual platitudes, well intended but vacuous all the same: an invitation to join Donald Ferranti for drinks at 6 pm that evening, for all the early birds, and a reminder that registration started at 11 am the following day, with a welcome lunch to follow at one o'clock. He tossed the letter aside.

The joy of it all, he thought. *And so it begins…* Having decided not to bother with the unpacking, other than to hang up the dinner jacket and two similarly creased lounge suits, he kicked back on the bed and did nothing much for half an hour.

A message to "Call Sophie" was displayed on the iPhone. Paul decided to call her later. He reset the reminder and then hit the *Home* button to clear the screen.

Chapter 8

THREE MONTHS EARLIER (JUNE 2014)
NICE, COTE D'AZURE

Oleg thumbed the photograph nervously and shuffled uneasily in his chair.

"Just a little information and a mobile telephone number, Oleg, that's all... and when we have everything we need, we will arrange for you to go home. It's all quite simple. There's no need to make this into something unpleasant."

Alex oozed confidence and smiled casually as he leaned forward to emphasise his point. His immaculate white shirt stretched taut across his chest as he moved, his crisply ironed sleeves, rolled twice, revealing powerful forearms and an even tan.

The Russian spoke quietly over the clatter of the early morning diners.

The café was busy, but Alex had steered Oleg away from the crowd. He sat opposite him, at a table in a corner, the one furthest away from the windows and away from prying eyes. Alex made it all sound so casual, but Oleg already knew he was in serious danger. They all were.

"And you won't hurt her?" he asked nervously, his voice faltering.

"Why would we hurt her?" Alex sounded incredulous at the prospect. "It's such a simple thing, Oleg. There's no need for anyone to get hurt."

He didn't believe him. That's what they did! Whenever they did anything at all, someone always got hurt.

"How can I know for certain? If I do this for you, how can I be certain she will be safe?"

"You have my word, Oleg."

Oleg noticed the twitch of impatience in his face, the hardening of his tone. His reassurance lacked any conviction and Oleg knew he couldn't trust this man. He was already certain his own life was at risk, but could the others be saved if he did exactly what he was told?

He looked up nervously and swallowed hard. His hands began to shake involuntarily. He tried to steady them, placing one across the other on the table as he gripped the image ever more tightly.

"What about Katia…" Oleg could barely finish his sentence. "What about Katia? If I tell you what you want to know, what about her?"

The tall Russian interrupted him angrily.

"The Shapiro girl is none of your concern. Have a care, Oleg, this is not a negotiation! Just some information, a telephone number and a little cooperation is all we need right now, but don't push me."

Alex mellowed; a pretence of concern furrowed his brow.

"Where she goes, who she sees… that's it. That's all we need. No one needs to get hurt…"

Oleg couldn't speak. He just stared at the photograph in silence. Alex switched moods in an instant.

"Oleg," he snarled, "you need to understand that what is done with her is none of your business. It will be so much better for you if you don't ask stupid questions."

He snatched the photograph from Oleg's trembling hand and slammed it down hard on the table in front of him. He jabbed his fingernail into the image of the child, cutting through the paper and disfiguring the young girl's features.

"You need to focus!" Alex barked.

Oleg struggled for breath. He couldn't bear to look. Alex reached over the table with a giant paw, grabbed Oleg by the chin and snapped his head around to face him. He snatched up the damaged image and held it inches from his nose. Oleg felt his bowels work involuntarily and fought to control them. Tears began to fall. He raised a hand to wipe them away but Alex grabbed his arm with a grip that burned into his skin.

"There is no way out of this. I am trying to help you here." Alex scanned the room self-consciously as he spoke. He was attracting unwanted attention. He seemed to relent a little.

Alex released his arm and placed the photograph back down on the table. He lowered his voice and closed in. Oleg could smell his breath, feel the heat from it as he whispered the words.

"He will kill them all, Oleg. You know he will." His head shook despondently to emphasise the point. "He will send the Roman and kill them all. He will take his time. He will start with the girl and he will make your sister watch. Anatoly will insist on it. He will force your sister to watch that twisted bastard, Roman, kill her own daughter." He paused for effect. "It's his way. You know what Anatoly is capable of!"

Oleg felt lightheaded, his heart racing, the sound of it hammering in his ears.

"Do you want to put your sister through all that? Do you?" Alex added.

Oleg sobbed silently, desperate to avoid drawing attention that would antagonise Alex further.

Alex moved his lips to Oleg's ear and continued.

"Yes, Oleg, he will take his time, my friend... Then he will start on the father, and when he has finished with him, he will take your sister..."

Oleg was falling apart.

"She is a fine looking woman, your sister... perhaps he will let the Roman have some sport with her first, and then..."

Alex paused for effect and then smiled.

"But none of this is necessary, Oleg, none of it. Why are you making me say these things?" Alex spoke as if all Oleg's troubles had just found a happy resolution.

"I'm sorry..." Oleg said.

"You have to do this. It's all very straightforward..." Alex finished his espresso in a single sip and placed the cup back down noisily on its saucer. "If you don't do as I ask..." He shrugged his shoulders indifferently. "Well, my friend, that is all very straightforward too... you should know what will happen to you if this is not done. When they are gone, Oleg, all of them... when it is done and they are all dead... I will kill you too. He will make me do that part myself. It's just the way it is... It is inevitable. This is not hard to understand. It's such a simple thing for me because, like you, I will have no choice. It's not personal, Oleg, it's just business."

Oleg sobbed.

"You know him, Oleg. He always takes care of business."

"I know." Oleg's sobbing continued.

"Good!" he said breezily. "You need to understand what I'm saying to you, but the truth is neither of us has a choice here. Look, it's just a little information, nothing more. That's all I need from you. It's so simple. No one will even know you were involved and you will already be back home safely with your family in St Petersburg. There is no decision for you to make here, Oleg. You are going to have to do this for me and, if not for me, then do it for your sister and for the girl!"

Alex eased back in his chair and scanned the room again.

Oleg picked up the photo. A salty tear fell upon it and ran slowly down the image of his sister's child. A second tear landed on the image of Elena, his youngest sister, just three years his junior. She stood contentedly behind little Eva, pushing her on the swing in the park. He knew it well. He and Elena had played on that very same swing many times, but that was all so many years ago. Nothing had changed... everything in the photo was just as he remembered it. The park had been a happy place for them, an escape for a few hours at a time whenever they could steal the opportunity together. When they were there, they could be anywhere, anywhere but home, temporarily transported far away, playing games and living out modest yet magical fantasies far from their dismal existence in a loveless and squalid tenement. And now there was this...

Little Eva was so innocent. A pretty girl with a pretty smile, she reminded him of Elena when she was the same age. Her innocence tore at his heart and his breath failed him. He gasped for air and gripped the photograph rigidly in one hand as the other clawed at his chest.

"Pull yourself together, Oleg!" Alex snapped. All pretence of a smile was banished by the authenticity of the scowl that replaced it.

"You're being ridiculous! Little Eva will grow up to have daughters of her own one day and she will live to take good care of your sister in her old age. What I ask of you is nothing, and you have no choice anyway. So, keep that photograph and remind yourself what is at stake here. I have plenty more photographs and I can always find her if I should need more... Think about what I've said today... I'll be in touch."

Oleg's breath caught in his throat.

The tall Russian rose to leave.

"Sort yourself out, Oleg, and don't screw this up. It would be such a tragedy if anything happened to that girl."

Finally, the oxygen starved to him in his panic returned to his aching lungs. Oleg said nothing. He wasn't capable of speech even if he could find the words.

"And Oleg, get me that *special* telephone number. I want that straight away. Let's just call it an act of good faith."

They both knew he would do exactly as he was asked. There had never been any doubt.

Chapter 9

Paul deposited his English money, 400 euros, a couple of credit cards and his travel documents into the safe. He tapped his default passcode into the number pad on the door and hit the *Lock* button. The sequence 5555 was now the code for the mini-safe in room 733. He self-consciously determined he would change that habit now he was in the security business; common sense told him he should know better anyway.

Deciding to perform a little magic of his own, he left the plastic key card undisturbed in the energy saving device by the bedroom door and picked up the spare instead. Paul discarded the branded cover and slipped the second of the two room keys into his pocket. The gentle hum of the air-conditioner continued uninterrupted as the bedroom door closed behind him with a reassuringly secure click.

Back in the corridor, Paul noticed, quite incidentally, that all the bedroom doors were along one side of what was, in fact, a gloomy soulless passageway. A series of five covered windows, one opposite each bedroom door, was on the other. It was a casual observation, nothing more, but he was mildly intrigued that the glorious afternoon sunshine that would otherwise brighten a dark and miserable corridor was almost totally excluded by heavy Roman blinds. He raised one corner of the blind at the last of the windows with no great expectation of the view. Suddenly he felt something hit him, followed by a searing pain in his left shoulder, and he toppled forward, almost pulling the blind from its mountings.

A huge man had rounded the corner and, without breaking step, barged into him with considerable force. Six feet five at least, nineteen stone minimum, and barely an ounce of fat to soften the impact of a clumsy, jarring collision. Paul didn't see his face, just the back of his ample head as he strode purposefully down the corridor. His light blue jeans, lumberjack shirt and close-cropped light brown hair were all of another era, but the phone he pressed to his hideously bulbous cauliflower ear was every bit today's technology.

Paul was tempted to remonstrate with him for his clumsiness and lack of courtesy, but there was something about him being six feet five, nineteen stone and, not least, the potentially countless rounds spent in a boxing ring that persuaded Paul to hold his counsel. He decided to let the man's indiscretions go this once and consoled himself with a brief rub of his shoulder and a mild expletive he sincerely hoped the huge man didn't hear.

He didn't, for which Paul was mightily relieved. The relief was short-lived, however, as the man paused outside room 732, produced a small plastic key card of his own, and let himself in.

"*Da… Da!*" he spat into the phone that remained pressed firmly to his appallingly disfigured ear. The enormous man effortlessly pushed open the heavy bedroom door and disappeared inside.

Shit! Paul thought, *Russians. There goes the neighbourhood!*

*****

"Doors closing," Paul translated as the lift doors duly closed. The lift was empty but the button for the ground floor was already illuminated.

Paul was surprised and a little irritated to see that neither Gary nor Doug were in the hotel reception. He plopped himself down in one of the oversized chairs and tried to get comfortable. Sitting back was hopeless, resulting in his legs sticking out in mid-air like a small child. Sitting forward just felt awkward, and the very least he wanted to achieve was to appear at home and composed. He struggled with both.

He consulted his iPhone. No messages and only spam on the email, but it was Sunday after all. It was more by way of a habit than in expectation of any great revelation, something to do as he waited. He recalled how the same habit had been a source of irritation when Gary had done it so persistently in London and, having already determined to mend his ways on passcode security, he now resolved to address this newly acknowledged tic as well.

The lobby was quiet. Most people were probably either in their rooms or making their way to restaurants for a bite of Sunday lunch. Paul slipped his phone into his back pocket, removing the temptation to meddle with it, and picked up one of the magazines that were neatly displayed in the middle of a coffee table.

As he thumbed through the glossy publication, cursorily scanning the pictures, he became aware that sections of the text were in English. The editor had produced his work in both French and English and, in doing so, had substantially broadened the publication's appeal. *Clever,* Paul thought as he scanned an article discussing the merits of ownership of some the Côte d'Azur's most expensive properties.

Apparently, Paul learned with a genuine degree of interest, forty of the region's sixty most valuable properties were now in Russian hands, the Russians being the latest crop of nouveau riche to take up residence on this most sought-after piece of French coastline – the Cap Ferrat and Cap d'Antibes being the most sought-after of all.

There was a brief article about a well-known oligarch buying the former, post-abdication, home of Edward and Mrs Simpson. A snip at 30 million euros with a further reputed hundred million spent on renovations.

A celebrity feature was accompanied by a beautifully posed series of photographs of a young woman, Katia Shapiro, who had recently turned twenty-one. According to the article, she was the only daughter of yet another oligarch, and as a result she was rich beyond reason. Her interests were fine art, socialising and travel. Her "most favourite thing", according to the article, was enjoying ice cream in the Häagan Dazs restaurant in Casino Square with her girlfriends.

Paul had to smile. It was a treat he'd enjoyed with Sophie on a number of occasions, but there was one very significant difference. He and Sophie managed to refrain from the afternoon shopping spree and the cocktails at the Hotel Hermitage that completed the oligarch's daughter's Friday afternoon ritual. Katia's weekly pilgrimage clearly carried a heavy price tag too, as was readily evident from the dozen or so designer shopping bags by her feet in a full-length photograph on page 21.

The girl was stunning, with soft Russian features, immaculate grooming and a figure to match. Her long straight brunette hair framed a beautiful smile, and her eyes, ice blue, were clear and confident.

Katia Shapiro, Paul mused.

He shook his head slowly and let out a breath. He allowed himself to speculate for a while. At what cost to ordinary Russians citizens had so much wealth been accrued by one family in the few short years since the fall of communism? How could such extraordinary, extreme wealth, enough to comfortably fund such privilege, possibly have been made?

Spotting Doug's approach, he closed the magazine and placed it back roughly where he'd found it. Doug had dressed for the occasion, and the jeans and pullover had been replaced with chinos, a light blue oxford shirt and a blue sports jacket. Sunglasses had been strategically placed on his head ready to be dropped into position at the appropriate moment.

Gary was following in his wake, his fingers dangling from a dark brown jacket. He was paddling away and making ground, he caught up with Doug before either of them reached Paul, but Gary was unable to find the right moment to spring his surprise.

"Look behind you," Paul suggested, levering himself out of the chair.

"Gary!" Doug boomed – his emotions were clearly mixed.

"Ay, mate. How are ya? How long ya been here?" Gary was vigorously shaking Doug's hand almost before it was offered. He pointed roughly in Paul's direction, his excitement all too evident. "I met this old bugger at the lift. We're on the same floor!" In Gary's world, being on the same floor was a measure of worth in some way. "Seventh!" he declared, as if it signified something worth sharing.

"Fifth," said Doug, playing along.

"Fifth, ay? I thought that was the staff floor!" Gary was on the verge of hysteria, euphoric at the outcome. "Just the fifth! What have ya done wrong? Who have you pissed off then?" Doug glanced at Paul with a look of utter dismay.

He felt compelled to explain himself.

"I thought it would be good for Gary to join us. Are you up for that?" Paul already knew the answer.

"Of course, the more the merrier," Doug declared. He glared in Paul's direction a second time.

"What's on the agenda then?" Gary demanded, bouncing from one foot to the other.

"We're in Nice. That's the Promenade des Anglais…" Paul suggested, sweeping his arm in an exaggerated arc.

"So, what have ya got in mind then?" Gary looked vacant.

"We're going for a walk, Gary," Doug clarified with a sigh of resignation.

"Can we get a beer and something to eat?" It was fair enough. Gary had skipped breakfast and Paul hadn't seen Doug eat a morsel all day.

The hotel forecourt was busy. There were a number of luxury cars parked up under the vast canopy and a taxi was dropping off new arrivals. The entrance to the casino was to the right and beyond that were a cluster of restaurant tables which appeared sparsely populated given the time of day.

Negotiating the road by the nearest crossing, they made their way to the promenade itself. It was teaming with life. Pedestrians, cyclists, bladers and skateboarders of all ages, variously competent on their chosen mode of transport, jockeyed for position. The marked cycle path was a hazard to be negotiated with care, well utilised by those it was intended for, yet largely unnoticed by pedestrians at no small risk to themselves.

At intervals, large white timber pavilions afforded shade to the benches beneath. And every so often, individually styled entrances gave access to steps that invitingly announced the presence of restaurants and bars that spilled out each season onto the stony beach below.

More benches placed closer to the edge of the promenade were in constant use, the view uninhibited by railings or safety paraphernalia of any kind. The unprotected, precipitous drop to the beach, and the sea beyond, gave rise to much comment and a conclusion that being treated like adults was refreshing and uplifting in equal measure. They applauded the French for standing up for common sense and for preserving a spectacular panoramic sea view.

The afternoon drifted pleasantly by in conversation and at times in quiet contemplation. Walking far beyond the famous old Hotel Negresco, they then retraced their steps returning by the same route. The views in each direction were equally satisfying. Rounding the headland under the castle, they passed the war memorial and continued on to the old harbour. The port was under considerable renovation, but still pleasant enough.

A large ferry proudly declared its dual destinations of Corsica and Sardinia in huge letters along its side. Past the ferry terminal, dozens of luxurious yachts, sailing boats and a couple of racing catamarans were moored in the old port. Paul and his colleagues, like so many before them, contemplated at length the merits of each, as if choice was the only obstacle to ownership.

After taking in the harbour from the comfort of a small bar, they finally decided it was time to eat. Paul was stunned when he consulted his iPhone, having already made an impressive, if unconscious effort, with regard to his earlier resolution. It was way past six o'clock and they had, quiet inadvertently, missed the opportunity to get better acquainted with Donald Ferranti back at the hotel. They barely discussed it as an option – no one had shown any enthusiasm for the idea when they did – and it was certainly never Paul's intention to attend. Sunday was a day to enjoy the city and, as it turned out, to get to know his UK partners that little bit better.

Nothing had occurred during the afternoon to dim his opinion of Doug, and even Gary had grown on him a little. Yes, he was crass, excitable and irritating, but he was also bright, full of fun and great company.

"Fuck it, let's get a pizza!" Gary said, exploding into life.

The glasses on the table betrayed them, a pretty French maiden having cynically seduced them into drinking far more than they intended. It was only the cooling of the evening, the fading light and a stiffening sea breeze that broke the spell.

"*Le billet s'il vous plaît, mademoiselle.*" Doug was at his fluent best.

"No, you don't," Paul objected. "I'm getting this!"

"No, you bloody well both don't!" slurred Gary, slamming a 100 euro note on the table in triumph. "I've had a bloody marvellous time and I'm damn well paying."

Gary spotted the French maiden.

"The billet thingy, please, luv. Whatever he said, give it to me."

Paul had some sense of what was coming next.

"I bloody wish she would give it to me!" Gary managed to laugh and leer simultaneously.

"Come on, let's go. You can get the pizzas if you like," Paul said, getting to his feet.

He stuffed a 50 euro note into the small ceramic pot already well lined with tickets and handed Gary his 100 euros back. They left with Gary declaring his undying affection for all things French, but, in particular, a pretty young waitress at the D'Harbour Bar in Nice.

Chapter 10

SUNDAY

"This is it!" Gary declared enthusiastically.

He seemed elated and relieved at his find. The restaurant was located at the entrance to the historic flower market. The tables were set in lines on the broad patio and largely covered with umbrellas and canopies in combination. The perimeter of the restaurant was framed by large white planters with maturing olive trees, each specimen underplanted with what Paul confidently suggested was erigeron. Double tragic!

Soft lighting and Café del Mar-style music added to the ambience as the evening light faded and the sky was blushed red with the setting of the sun. Period buildings to the rear and side of the restaurant protected patrons from the full glare of the road yet afforded views across the promenade and out to sea. As they approached, the gentle hum of contended diners spilled invitingly out on to the street.

Indeed, Gary had found *it*, and *it* was, without doubt, an excellent choice.

A young hostess guided them to a table set for four, just one row back from the pavement. There were still plenty of tables but the restaurant was filling fast.

"*Trois bieres, s'il vous plaît.*" Gary looked chuffed with himself.

Doug burst his bubble.

"I'm going to have wine actually."

Doug was a born leader of men.

"I'll join you," Paul said, happy to follow.

He'd already consumed more than enough beer, and there was no way he was going to go drink for drink with Gary – he was clearly on a mission.

"*Une biere et une bouteille du vin rosé, s'il vous plaît,*" Gary said as the girl hesitated at his side.

She'd instinctively worked out the pecking order and waited on Doug for confirmation.

"How's that, Dougie boy? How's that for a bit of the old lingo?"

"Fine with me," he said. "Very impressive."

Doug nodded his approval and Gary beamed wildly. Paul had no idea if his manic expression was induced solely by the beer or merely as a product of his natural disposition.

"*Merci, Mademoiselle,*" confirmed Doug, and the girl was gone.

"This is a wonderful town…" Gary started, but then he stopped dead, mid-sentence. He lowered his voice and leaned forward in his chair. "They've got a game going. Shall we join 'em?" The expression of utter excitement on his face was as exaggerated as Paul had ever seen it.

Paul was sitting with his back turned slightly towards the table Gary was referring to. It was on the front row and nearest to the pavement.

Three men occupied it, with playing cards distributed as if for a hand of poker. Piles of loose change lay uncounted in front of each man. Paul hadn't noticed them when they first sat down, which was something of a wonder; they were all huge men, and loud too.

"Best not," Paul suggested.

"Mug's game. I've never been a gambler." Doug backed Paul up. His contribution was conclusive.

The poker players were already boisterous. Clearly fuelled by alcohol and adrenaline, each man appeared even more slovenly than the next. They lounged at the table, enveloped by a thick noxious fog, the inconsiderate and foul smelling by-product of their strong continental tobacco. The table groaned under the weight of empty beer glasses, and the contents of the ashtray spilled out onto the marble tabletop. Voices were raised and things look set to deteriorate as the evening drew on. They had been drinking heavily, each beer seemingly accompanied by a vodka chaser, a dozen shot glasses littering the table, stacked in pairs or lying on their side. The game gave every impression of going deep into the evening, and there was a palpable sense of growing unease from their fellow diners.

The waitress returned with their drinks order. She distributed them from memory, a bottle of Heineken and a chilled beer glass for Gary, a huge wine glass each for Doug and Paul. She presented the wine for Doug's approval, then poured a little of the very pale rosé wine into each glass and invited them to order their food.

As the waitress left, Paul adjusted his position slightly so he could see the comings and goings on the promenade. He took a sip of the perfectly chilled Domaines Ott and settled into his chair. His revised orientation also afforded him a better view of the card game as its intensity continued to grow.

The first man was sitting with his back to Paul and the other two were facing him, but one was almost totally obscured from view behind the first.

The man with his back to Paul appeared to be marginally shorter than the others from what he could tell, with a slighter frame but still powerful and perhaps more athletic than his colleagues. He had a full head of dark hair, his close-fitting crisp white shirt, with sleeves neatly rolled, revealing muscular arms tanned from sustained exposure to the Mediterranean sun. This man was doing most of the talking and he was doing it all in Russian.

"The town is just full of Russians," Paul said under his breath.

Gary heard him, and Paul was immediately alarmed at what he might say next. Subtlety wasn't one of Gary's strengths based on Paul's limited experience of his company, and he had certainly drunk more than enough to dull even his most rudimentary levels of tact and discretion. He didn't need to worry on this one occasion, however. Even Gary had scoped the situation for himself.

It was clear that his colleague had a better view of the other two men than he did, and he could sense that even in his somewhat relaxed state his new friend was uneasy about something. Paul shifted in his seat again to get a better view of the second of the three men at the table. He understood Gary's disquiet immediately. He was a huge, powerful, brutal looking man, his presence unsettling and intimidating. Even the man in the white shirt seemed to be cautious of this comrade, and it was of no surprise to Paul that, of the three, this man had started to accumulate the largest pile of coins in front of him. He slammed another winning hand down on the table and the man in the white shirt folded without revealing his cards while enthusiastically congratulating him on his continuing good fortune.

This man wore a faded denim shirt, jeans, white trainers, sports socks, and there was a cheap looking leather jacket draped across the chair next to him. His head was closely shaved – maybe a number two – which did nothing to soften his appearance.

He turned in Paul's direction as if suddenly aware of his attentions. Paul averted his gaze instantly. When he looked back, the Russian was once again focused on his cards, and the prospect of another "pot" which was taking on significant proportions in the middle of the table.

He was a bear of a man and significantly over six feet tall. His face seemed unnaturally clammy, his skin pale and greasy, strangely pockmarked, perhaps from some distant childhood disease. He appeared humourless and on edge.

The beer glasses on the table were empty and the pockmarked man stuck his hand in the air like a child in a classroom. He turned to see a waitress at the table next to theirs pouring wine for a young couple.

"You, beer here, I want," he bellowed in a hideous staccato English.

The girl did her best to ignore him, but it was impossible.

"*Oui!*" she said, and muttered something less compliant under her breath. She finished pouring the wine and hurried off towards the bar.

The pockmarked man stood, stretched to his full height with no regard for etiquette, and set off in the direction of the toilets. It was then that Paul saw the last of the three men properly for the first time.

He remained seated at the table in conversation with the first. There was no mistaking him. He was the same build. It was the same seventies' lumber-jack shirt, the same close-cropped light brown hair and the same deformed bulbous ears. It was the Russian Paul had encountered at close quarters in the corridor outside room 733.

He looked even meaner from the front than he did from the back. A scar ran from his right eye in a red crescent to the bottom of his right ear. This was the man who had barged into him in the corridor, and this was the man who occupied the room next to his at the Palais de la Méditerranée. The Russian hadn't recognised Paul as far as he could tell, but Paul wasn't surprised. He'd been so engrossed in his telephone call at the time he probably hadn't registered the incident in the corridor at all.

All three of the men were unsettling in their own ways, but he was the meanest looking of them all. Paul was glad when the pockmarked Russian returned and took his seat. The last of the Russians was once again largely obscured by his colleague's huge frame, reducing the chances of Paul coming to his attention. He determined there and then that he preferred to remain anonymous when it came to his new next-door neighbour.

"They're staying at the hotel… or at least the one with the scar is. I bumped into him earlier," Paul offered by way of an explanation for his distraction.

"I doubt they're attending the conference…" Gary quipped.

"You never know… Have Secure Co. expanded as far as the motherland yet?" Doug asked with no expectation of an answer.

The food duly arrived.

Despite the card game going on next to them, the meal and the conversation was most enjoyable. Paul restricted himself to two glasses of wine and Doug comfortably polished off the rest. Gary just kept on going – one more beer for the road and he'd call it a day, but he never actually did. The conference was starting in the morning, and Paul was determined not to be nursing a hangover. Gary seemed singularly untroubled by the prospect.

Paul finished off the very last of his quatre fromages as the Russian in the white shirt got to his feet and left the table. The two thugs were left unat-tended for a while. They immediately became more subdued in his absence, noticeably lowering their voices and becoming more conspiratorial. On a positive note, at least the card game was concluded and the Russians had placed an order for food. The ambience in the restaurant improved markedly.

In the absence of their colleague, the pockmarked Russian reached out a huge paw and grabbed an unoccupied table next to his, pulling it towards him. A waitress went over to remonstrate with him but it was pretty futile. He just waved her away dismissively. As she retreated, he stood up to retrieve the chairs that were originally at the table but were now marooned in no man's land and proceeded to rearrange the restaurant to his satisfaction.

The waitress came back with the manager, who again remonstrated with the Russian, and Paul had to admire his commitment to the cause. It was to no avail though, and the Russian just waved him away too. Ignoring all the protests, both Russians took up new positions at their extended table with their backs to Paul, facing the road and looking out to sea.

"Pudding anybody?" Gary enquired.

"Really?" Paul replied.

"It's not a night out without pudding," Gary said, in a tone that implied Paul needed to get with the programme.

Doug was relaxed about it either way, so they waited for the waitress to return with the menu.

As they chatted, the missing Russian returned to the restaurant and the reason for the rearranging of the furniture was immediately clear. He was accompanied by two more dinner guests. There was a buzz around the restaurant as the two girls made their way through the diners to where the hastily rearranged table now awaited them. They were introduced to the two thugs, whose mood lightened immediately on making their acquaintance.

They were stunning. The girls wore high heels, shimmering sheer stockings and identical electric blue, body hugging dresses to just above the knee. Both had long blonde hair, one light and straight, the other luxuriously thick, set in a series of sweeping curls that framed her face, spilling onto her shoulders. The girls had incredible figures, doll-like faces and they were breathtakingly beautiful. It was all change at their table now. The girls sat opposite the three men and suddenly it was all smiles and silly giggles.

Paul couldn't take his eyes off the girls and noticed that Gary was equally captivated.

"They're working girls, you know. It's such a shame," Doug said, and they both knew he was right.

Paul had known it from the moment they entered the restaurant.

"But they are such beautiful girls," Paul said almost unconsciously. He was immediately aware that his comment might have implied that it would be that bit more palatable if they weren't so lovely. His colleagues graciously let the remark go by without comment.

The girl with the mass of curly blonde hair diligently engaged Paul's nemesis in conversation. Paul was instantly appalled on some level he couldn't explain. The girls were Russian too, he supposed, as the conversation seemed to flow easily between them. Both girls set to work as he imagined they had done on countless occasions before; they were naturals: confident, charming, convincingly flirtatious and devastatingly beautiful.

"They'd cost a bloody fortune if you ask me," Gary said. "They aren't earning tonight though," he stated, as if his conclusion was unquestionably obvious.

"What do you mean?" Doug was intrigued.

"I've been watching them," Gary said with a shrug of his shoulders. "It's obvious."

"They've only just arrived. How can you possibly know something like that?" Paul was almost annoyed by Gary's total conviction, but unsure why it should be so affecting. Perhaps it was just the thought of the two young girls with the Russians that inflamed his mood. Gary had done nothing to annoy him for hours, which, as it happened, took Paul by surprise in its own right.

"Look," he said, "it's not about the girls, it's about the blokes." Gary wasn't so casual now. He waited for Paul and Doug to get a little closer before he continued. As distasteful as the whole scene was, Paul was keen to hear what the oracle had to say.

"Right... if you ask me... and you have" – Gary was enjoying his moment – "the tall one is the local contact and the two thugs are here on business... bad business no doubt, but business all the same. The tall one..." Gary pointed at him and Paul immediately grabbed his hand, pushing it back down onto the table "Yeah, right, sorry," Gary spluttered. "The tall one... well, I think they're his girls. After all, he's the one that went off to fetch them."

"So?" Paul interrupted.

"So..." said Gary, "booking girls like that for dinner – and then you know what – is going to cost loads, a thousand pounds a night at least, assuming they're going to take them back to their hotel... and let's face it, they are." Gary paused. "Do those thugs look like 'thousand pound a night' call-girl types to you?"

Paul had no idea what a thousand pound a night call-girl type would look like, but Gary must be right. They couldn't possibly look like these two animals.

"So, if they can't afford them, it's obvious, the other guy's paying... or they're his girls and no one's earning tonight." Gary was warming to his task. Doug and Paul were incredulous at the amount of thought Gary had invested in the matter.

"Look, that guy has the tan, he's the local, and the other goons are fresh in town from Siberia or some other Soviet shithole. I bet they're not even here legally. Smuggled in to carry out some bastard's dirty work. They look like they'd kill you just as soon as look at you, if you ask me."

Gary had gone too far.

"Bloody hell, Gary, that's a bit strong." Paul had heard enough.

Doug joined in. "The secret to being a successful international assassin is surely not to look like one, Gary. They're probably here on their holidays and the girls are part of the tour for guys like that," he said.

Gary would have none of it.

"Trust me, mate. Fifty quid a tug crack whores maybe, but these girls are something else." Gary had a point.

"Really, guys!" Paul wasn't happy with the way the conversation was going at all.

"Look, it's obvious! That guy is clearly nervous of the other two. Not really surprising is it! They look evil to me. He's been trying to please them all night. He should have just rolled out the dancing girls earlier and taken the rest of the night off. Those two would have been just as happy... Who wouldn't?" Gary seemed pleased with his deductions.

"Gary, they are human beings, you know, not just—" Paul was interrupted.

"I know, I know. I'm not saying it's all right or anything. I'm just saying there's more to it than just a couple of hookers on a job..." Gary looked a little sheepish.

"I don't know, Gary. It all seems such a shame if you ask me." Paul was already resolved to leave. His appetite for "pudding" had waned, and there was still no sign of the waitress with the dessert menus.

The episode had put a dampener on the night as far as Paul was concerned, and Doug looked ready to leave too. Paul suddenly felt very uncomfortable. He'd made his decision.

"I think I'll skip dessert if that's okay. Early start and all that..."

Paul took one more look at the table of Russians before he left. He felt an unexpected sense of sadness, which was completely at odds with the newly discovered sense of revelry on their table. It just seemed tragic and inappropriate. Paul dropped 50 euros on the table. He knew it was easily his fair share.

"Fair enough, Paul," Doug said. "See you in the morning."

"Cheers, mate. See you tomorrow!" Gary called after him as he left.

Paul walked the short distance back to the hotel in silence and alone.

MONDAY

SEPTEMBER 2014

Chapter 11

MONDAY

Paul awoke suddenly. He wasn't sure at first what caused him to stir, but something was wrong. There was a loud bang from the bedroom lobby and he heard a female voice. He was disorientated, and he couldn't be sure if what he was hearing was real or imagined.

There were a few seconds of silence followed by the same sound again. There was no mistaking it this time. The bang wasn't so loud on this occasion; it seemed further away perhaps, and then he heard the female voice again. No words were spoken, just a muffled cry followed by a groan. No discernible words, just sounds.

Paul couldn't be sure. Was someone in trouble or was it something else? Whatever was happening, it was playing out in the lobby of room 733, in his bedroom or perhaps in the corridor just outside. Paul was momentarily torn. Did he switch the lights on or just shout out? *What the hell is going on?*

More cries – more of a whimper this time – and then silence once again.

Paul tried to shake the sleep from his mind and assimilate what was happening. There was limited evidence of anything sinister taking place but, for reasons he couldn't yet fathom, he felt a deepening sense of foreboding. He heard the sound again and felt the hairs on the back of his neck rise.

Something was very wrong, and he couldn't just hope it went away or convince himself it was nothing to do with him. It was happening and he couldn't just ignore it. More cries. This time they were more urgent. He was certain it was panic he could hear; there could be no doubt about it.

A man's voice broke his malaise. It was suppressed, as if trying not to be heard, but there was no disguising the ferocity of the outburst.

The light was still on outside on the balcony and the bedroom curtains were thin, certainly thinner than one would expect from a hotel of five-star quality. Paul's eyes were slowly becoming accustomed to the half-light, and he could see the door between the bedroom and the lobby was slightly ajar.

He pulled the duvet away and instantly became aware of his nakedness. He searched briefly for something, anything at all, to wear.

There was the male voice again. It took on a primeval quality now, dangerous and unsettling. Paul was across the bedroom and at the door to the lobby in a couple of seconds. Silence again; just his own exaggerated heartbeat and the racing, rushing sound of his blood flowing, supercharged with adrenaline, through his veins. His breath caught in his throat, his mouth dry. He swallowed hard and eased the door open.

He stood to one side, allowing what little illumination there was from the balcony light to penetrate as far as possible into the bedroom's lobby. Paul braced himself and entered.

A further cry, loud and unrestrained; it was unmistakably female this time and then it changed again. Simpering, pleading; it was the sound of someone he was finally convinced was in great distress. It was obvious now that the sound wasn't coming from his bedroom lobby at all but from the room next door. He could see the soft glow of light seeping under the twin doors that separated room 732 from his own.

Suddenly the realisation hit him. A wave of relief washed over him and his raging pulse began to slow. The couple in the room next door were having sex! That's all it was after all. It might be nasty, aggressive sex, but it was just that all the same. Noisy, possibly dangerous, sex. Each to their own, but for all that, it was just sex and none of his business. The curse of the adjoining room had struck once again.

For Christ's sake. I should have moved rooms when I had the chance! He berated himself silently for his lack of conviction earlier in the day. Now he was stuck in that room for a full week and, as a consequence, condemned to put up with whatever sexual proclivities the lovers next door subjected each other to. It could be days before they checked out. It could be the full week.

Despite the mounting frustration that immediately accompanied his revised conclusion, he suddenly felt that he was the one intruding on their private moment. Perhaps it was the lateness of the hour, or the fact that he was standing conspicuously naked and overtly eavesdropping on his neighbours. He felt ridiculous, somehow inappropriate, and momentarily rather alone. Then he remembered, and the image of the scar-faced thug and the girl in the restaurant flashed through his mind. He was briefly distracted by it as a surge of contempt and anger preoccupied him.

He consoled himself with the conclusion that, despite his contempt, there was nothing sinister to confront, and that conclusion in itself was accompanied by no small measure of relief. It was the way of the world and nothing at all to do with him. If he shut the lobby door and pulled the duvet over his ears, he knew eventually he would get back to sleep. He was angry with himself for not closing the lobby door in the first place.

The male voice boomed out again, deep and intimidating. He sounded furious this time. Paul heard the sound of a slap, not playful but vicious and brutal. The girl's cries were desperate, and he knew then it was something more. Again he was torn. He could either go for the telephone and call for help or bang on the door and make his presence known. Before he could decide, there was the muffled yet unmistakable sound of a scuffle. A suppressed howl forced him to think again. This time it was the man that was in pain. Then a scream... a female voice, chilling and intense. The girl was in serious trouble...

What the hell is going on? There was no time to get help. It had to be him; he couldn't let it go on. Finally, Paul was thinking straight. Room 732 was the Russian thug's bedroom, the bruiser from the corridor, the man with the ugly scar at the pizza restaurant and the guy with the blonde escort. Whatever he was doing to her now, it had to be stopped.

More cries, and then the unmistakable sounds of a struggle as he imagined the girl helplessly trying to escape the huge man.

He's attacking her! There was no other explanation now. It was the only thing that made sense. The girl didn't stand a chance. He was a massively powerful man and looked every bit the primal animal. Paul knew he didn't stand a chance either, but he was compelled to intervene.

He grabbed a towel from the bathroom and wrapped it around his waist to cover himself up and then pressed the bedroom door handle down hard to enter the corridor, but before he could open the door more than an inch, he froze.

In the split second he slammed his door handle down, he heard the door to room 732 being flung open. He caught his breath, his heart racing. He was fighting his own personal battle with fear, but he needed to go out there. He couldn't live with himself if he just stood by. He pulled slowly, silently inching the heavy door open, but he couldn't see anything, just the corridor and nothing out of place. He opened the door further.

There was a sickening thud, and the body of a girl landed heavily on the far side of the corridor opposite his bedroom door. There was a bestial roar of pure malice from the man who was now only inches away from him yet completely oblivious to his presence. He cursed at the girl, his English rudimentary but intimidating all the same. He threw something at her from the room. It was an electric-blue dress.

He heard the man retreating back into his bedroom as the girl spotted him crouching in the doorway of room 733. He raised his finger to his lips, Paul's eyes imploring her, *Keep quiet for all our sakes!*

The girl was naked, blood trickling from her nose and smeared across her face. Tears rolled down her cheeks and across her lips, where they mixed with spittle from a mouth contorted in pain. Her eyes were wide and pleading in her desperation.

"Stay quiet!" Paul said in a barely audible whisper. She didn't move. There was no acknowledgement, no sense of comprehension. Paul needed to wait for the door to room 732 to click shut, and it took an age. Every second seemed brutal. How could he wait and just leave her lying there? But he knew there was no choice. The click was his cue, and he was at her side in an instant.

"It's okay. It's okay," he whispered.

It was ridiculous. She was far from okay and far from safe. They both knew it. If the door to room 732 opened again they were both in trouble. Paul had surrendered any advantage he perceived he might have the second he broke cover. The Russian would take Paul down in a heartbeat and there would be nothing he could do about it. She would be at his mercy once again.

"Can you stand? Do you speak English?" *Calm down, Paul, one question at a time,* he urged himself. But he needed to gain her trust and get her out of the corridor as quickly as possible. Paul didn't know why the man had thrown her out of his room, and he didn't know the extent of her injuries, but his instincts told him he could come back at any moment. That couldn't possibly be good for the girl. Perhaps he would to try to make it right in some way, or more likely he'd try to finish the job. Either way, Paul was certain she wouldn't be safe with him. He was out of control, evidently capable of extreme violence, and the girl was utterly terrified.

Damn it! The door to room 733 was all but closed. Paul lunged for it. He didn't have a key, and if the door shut they would be locked out, both of them stuck in the corridor together. Worse, the Russian would almost certainly hear the door click shut as his own had done only a few moments earlier. The door closed heavily onto Paul's fingers as he scrambled to prevent it from locking.

"Stay there," he mouthed, and he signalled for her to stay put and stay quiet.

She didn't move, didn't answer or even meet his gaze. She just sobbed. She made no effort to cover herself. She just lay there naked in the corridor, utterly broken.

Paul dashed back into the room, ripping off his towel and wedging it in the doorway to hold it open. In an instant he'd grabbed two more towels from the bathroom and was back in the corridor at her side. She hadn't even noticed his momentary exposure, her eyes still full of tears as she tried to

wipe blood from her hands. She looked horrified at the sight of it
them together to little effect.

It was only as Paul tried to wrap the towel around her shoul
finally seemed to comprehend what he was trying to do. At first, she flinched,
pulling away. She drew a deep breath, as if in pain, and wiped away the tears
that rolled down her face. But still the tears kept falling.

"It's okay. You need to get out of the corridor. He might come back…"

She regarded him intently. He felt her eyes burning into his. She was looking straight into his soul, and perhaps something there told her it was safe.
She eased herself forward so he could pass the towel over her back, and she
pulled it close around her.

"Can you stand?" he whispered.

"Yes, I think so," she whispered back in perfect English with just a hint of
Russian in her accent. She understood.

"You speak English?"

Paul could hear noises from 732 again. There was a strong possibility the
Russian was coming back.

She nodded urgently. "Yes, English…" She too could hear the noises emanating from room 732. They needed to move.

Paul helped her to her feet. The towel fell away slightly and he could see
yet more blood on her stomach – just a smear but more than he would have
expected from what he'd seen of her injuries.

"Where are you hurt?"

"I'm okay," she said, and with that he helped her into room 733.

He removed the towel he'd previously used to hold the door open and then
closed the bedroom door quietly behind them. The relief was immediate.
With the door locked and the lights still off, he guided her through to the
bedroom and sat her down in the easy chair nearest the desk.

He returned to the bedroom lobby. A thread of light was still seeping under
the twin doors that separated him from the man in room 732. Paul grabbed the
redundant towel, previously used as a doorstop, and silently pushed it into the
crack at the bottom of the connecting doors. Only then did he switch on a light.

He double-locked the bedroom entrance door and put the security chain
on for good measure. He was tempted to check the thumb turn lock on the
connecting door but decided against it. The slightest noise would alert the
man to his neighbour being awake and potentially a witness to his brutality.
That was a risk he didn't need to take.

Paul could still hear him moving around in the room next door. There was
the occasional outburst in a cruel and primitive dialect. It was as if he was
still arguing with someone.

A wave of dread crashed over him. *Shit! Does he have someone else in there?* Paul needed to know.

Closing the door between the lobby and the bedroom again, he went back to the girl. She sat staring at the floor, with the light from the single lamp on the desk illuminating the room. He felt he needed to ask her about the other girl from earlier in the evening, and then he stopped himself. She would wonder how he knew there was another. It had been all but impossible for him not to spot her and her friend at the restaurant, but he doubted he would have warranted a second glance from either of them. There was the real possibility that the question would unsettle her, frighten her in some way, and that was the last thing he wanted.

Walking past her, again with his finger pressed to his lips, he quietly closed the balcony door, locked it, and rearranged the curtains for optimum privacy.

"Were you alone with him in that room, or is there someone else in there?"

"Alone, no one else," she answered.

"Okay, okay, that's good."

He sat on the bed opposite her and then sprang to his feet and went to the bathroom. He returned with a box of tissues, which he set down on the coffee table at her side. She seemed to appreciate the gesture. She pulled a couple of sheets from the box and then scrunched them into a ball in her hand without pausing to use them.

Paul left her there for a moment. The jeans he'd worn to the restaurant earlier that evening were lying casually discarded over the back of the desk chair. He grabbed them and slipped them on. He found a clean polo shirt in his suitcase and offered her a t-shirt. She took it without a word but just placed it over her knees. He had a better idea. He ventured back into the lobby and recovered one of the huge towelling "one size fits nobody" dressing gowns from the wardrobe.

He took a moment to listen for any activity next door. The Russian's voice was louder than before. It sounded like he was on the phone, perhaps to one of the men from the restaurant earlier in the evening.

Paul picked out a bottle of fiendishly expensive mineral water from the minibar and went back into the bedroom.

"Here, put this on," he said gently.

She took the dressing gown and started to wrestle with it.

"Thank you," she managed.

But she was struggling to manage the dressing gown. Paul held out his hand to take it back. The belt was wound tightly around the huge garment in a way that it would deter all but the most determined user. After separating the belt from the gown, he handed the two parts back to her, one element at a time.

"Thank you," she said again.

She rose slowly to her feet, letting the bath sheet and t-shirt fall to the ground, naked again for a moment, before being completely swamped by the huge dressing gown that only served to make her look smaller and more vulnerable than ever.

She sat down and began to sob.

"I'm so sorry," she said. "I'm so sorry." The floodgates opened and she was inconsolable.

"It's okay. It's okay." Paul tried to comfort her, but he sensed she was sorry in a more fundamental way – sorry for what was happening to her. And he sensed there was anger with it too. None of what she was feeling appeared to relate to him. He determined to stay silent and give her some time. It was all he could do; he already knew he didn't have the words to make things better.

He wanted to console her, and the urge to hold her was natural but it would have been the wrong thing to do. She'd already suffered at the hands of one man in the confines of his hotel bedroom. There was no way he was going to give her any cause for concern in his. He would keep his distance and just be there for her.

His silence didn't last long.

"Would you like some water?"

He broke the seal on the bottle of mineral water and passed it to her. She took it and held it for a moment while she wiped away more tears. He sat on the bed opposite her, unsure of what to do next. There was nothing much he could do for now; he would have to wait for her to get a little composure back.

There were so many questions. What was her name? What happened? Who was the Russian? What did he do to her? Above all, he needed to know how badly hurt she was and if she needed proper medical assistance.

After a few minutes, he ventured a question.

"Where are you hurt?" he asked.

She drew herself up in the chair and there was a little more steel in her eyes. She took a sip of water, which clearly hurt. She winced and put her hand to her mouth.

"Did he hit you?"

Just give the girl a chance! Paul berated himself again. She was a mess, but she was getting herself together. He needed to give her just a little longer.

More for something to do than for any other reason, he picked up the iPhone from the bedside table where it was charging. There were no messages, and just a few spam emails dropped into the inbox.

It was 3.20 am. He closed down the phone and placed it back on the bedside table. The girl was looking a little more settled now, and, taking a deep breath, she pushed her long golden hair away from her face, tucking it behind her ears.

Just below her left temple a large lump was forming, an abrasion that Paul hadn't noticed before. He winced for her – it looked angry and raw.

"I'm so sorry. That looks so painful," he said quietly, breaking the silence once again.

She let her hair fall forward, covering the damage as if embarrassed by its presence. As she put her hand up to feel it, she was visibly shocked to discover the extent of the weal on the side of her face.

"It's okay. It'll soon go down. It probably feels worse than it looks," he said, trying to reassure her. "Are you hurt anywhere else?"

The tears had stopped, but she looked utterly lost. She was distraught, afraid, and she looked so vulnerable as she rocked backwards and forwards in the chair. She was naked but for an ill-fitting bathrobe, her face and hands bloodied, her body bruised and in pain. She looked every bit the victim of a desperate trade. She was an eternity away from somewhere she might call home. Nowhere would feel safe to her right now, and he couldn't begin to imagine how isolated she must feel.

She reached out and grabbed Paul's hand. It took him by surprise.

"Thank you," she said. "Can I stay here for a while? I don't know where else to go right now. I don't know what to do…" Her voice trailed away. He felt shattered for her.

"Of course, of course. You can stay as long as you need to," he reassured her, without giving a second thought to what he might be getting himself involved in. "But we need to call the police—"

"No. Please no. No police." Her eyes fixed him again, but they were full of panic now.

"But he's really hurt you. We have to report it," Paul said, but he realised he was probably being naïve.

His mind flashed back to her flying through the air and slamming into the wall. It was pure chance that she wasn't more seriously injured. She'd been attacked, and no matter what the circumstances, in his view her abuser should face the consequences of his actions. Paul's instinct was to call the police but that failed to take into account the consequences of such an action for the girl herself. Her protests were immediate, heartfelt and desperate. Right now, she had to be the priority.

He was suddenly acutely aware of her plight. A young girl trying to survive, eking out an existence in a foreign country, he could have no idea what kind of treatment she might get at the hands of the French police. It occurred to him then that she would know that with far greater certainty than he could. She might, in all likelihood, be just as desperate to avoid the gendarmerie as she was to get away from her attacker in the first place. Perhaps she wasn't even legal and had no right to be in the country. Maybe she had been trafficked by some Mafia-style gang. Paul considered that his imagination might be running away with him, but what was he supposed to think? He recalled a disturbingly graphic TV documentary on the subject, and he'd read the odd incendiary article in the *Mail on Sunday*. It was Sophie's paper of choice, sensational and judgemental, but right now Paul was convinced of the potential validity of every word. He had no idea what type of people this girl was involved with, but perhaps the consequences of reporting the incident to the police would be far worse for her than the predicament she currently found herself in.

"No police! Please! No police," she repeated.

"If you're sure that's what you want?"

"It is. Thank you." The girl seemed to calm down appreciably as the prospect of police involvement diminished.

"Is there someone you can call? A friend maybe? Or someone who can help you?" He held out his iPhone for her to take.

"No, no one can help me. There's no one I can call."

"But won't someone be worried about you?" Paul couldn't believe that anyone, not even a scumbag of a pimp, would let a young girl go off with those men without at least being on call for just such an emergency. Even for the sort of men that he assumed must run this trade, she must be valuable to them. Someone must be looking out for her.

And she was beautiful. Despite the cuts and the bruises, the tears and the tangled hair, despite the ill-fitting dressing gown, the smudged makeup and the desolate look in her eyes, she was still breathtakingly beautiful.

"I just need a little more time, please."

There was no need for him to answer her. She already knew he wasn't going to kick her out. He just smiled weakly and nodded.

"Of course," he said. "Take as much time as you need."

He tried again. "Can you tell me where you're hurt?"

If he wasn't going to call the police, Paul was determined to make sure she wasn't seriously injured. That at least he could do.

She shook her head.

"It's not bad, just my face." She touched her nose and then the side of her head where the lump was forming. She scraped her hair back again to show him, and Paul felt he'd just been let in on a secret.

"But the blood here?" Paul pointed to his own stomach to indicate where he'd seen it earlier on her. "And on your hands – is that all from your nose?"

"Yes. Yes, all from the nose." She tried to smile, but he could see it hurt a little.

"Okay. As long as that's all, as long as you're sure there's nothing else. I want to help you so you can tell me."

"Thank you. I'm fine, really I am."

She could see he wasn't convinced. She stood up and started to open her dressing gown. He stopped her.

"If you say you're fine then that's okay with me. Please, there's no need."

There was a silence. They just sat for a while. The girl spoke first.

"What is your name?"

How odd that seemed.

"Paul," he said. "My name is Paul."

He held out his hand as if meeting her properly for the first time. She shook it with a gentle formality completely at odds with all that had gone before. It was a lighter moment in an evening devoid of those, and it raised a smile.

"My name is Anna," she said quietly.

Paul was sure it wasn't. It might be her working name, something easy for the Americans and the Europeans when they were booking their entertainment for the evening, but he accepted it without question.

"Hello, Anna. I am delighted to meet you."

She was still shaking his hand, holding it more tightly than he would have expected, and he began to feel a little self-conscious. She looked straight into his eyes with a renewed intensity he found unsettling. It seemed as if she was seeking a deeper understanding of who he might be. Perhaps assessing his conviction or searching for a sign that he was a man she could trust.

Whatever she saw in him, she seemed reassured by it.

"My name is Alisa," she said, and she gave his hand a squeeze before finally letting it go. A single tear rolled down her cheek.

"Hello, Alisa," he said. "It's very nice to meet you."

Chapter 12

MONDAY

It was the early hours of Monday morning, the first morning of five full days of the Secure Co. International Sales Conference. The situation felt a little surreal. A Russian escort was sitting in Paul's hotel bedroom in nothing more than a bathrobe, and a violent Russian enforcer, if Gary's insights were to be taken seriously, occupied the adjoining room. This was not how Paul imagined things would play out when he completed the conference registration forms in his office back in the UK. He'd committed himself then to what he fully expected to be a routine and essentially uneventful sales conference, albeit on the Côte d'Azur. This was turning into something altogether very different.

Alisa seemed calmer now. The tears had stopped, her emotions were a little more contained and her body language more assured. Paul sensed that she felt safe with him, and with a degree of confidence, at least for now, he was sure she was. His confidence was based entirely on the very real probability that the man in room 732 could have no idea his victim had been given refuge in the hotel bedroom next door. If nothing else, he'd got that much right.

His thoughts turned briefly to his next-door neighbour. What would he do next? Paul was unsure. But there was the distinct possibility he might not give the girl any further consideration, the entire incident being consigned to history, an alcohol-fuelled aberration and an irrelevance in the twisted and violent world he apparently inhabited. He'd taken what he wanted from the girl and then ruthlessly discarded her once he had no further use for her services. Paul knew that he'd been drinking heavily the previous evening. Maybe this was how he conducted himself with women in his own country. Would he see any wrong in what he did? Would he even remember what happened once he had exhausted what remained of the night to sleep it all off?

Paul helped himself to another bottle of mineral water from the minibar. He studied Alisa as he returned to the bedroom, taking a seat in the second armchair with the coffee table between them. The self-recrimination was starting to kick in now. Should he have got involved earlier? Could he have prevented the worst of it from happening if he had?

The girl effected a self-conscious smile as he took a long sip of cooling mineral water. There was no point in beating himself up about all that now.

Alisa shuffled in the chair, pulling her feet up onto the seat, wrapping both arms around her knees. She still looked a little lost in the huge bathrobe. She remained silent but there was a little more spirit in her demeanour. Whatever pain she was feeling, he was now convinced, the least part of it was physical.

Sunday had been a long day. A 4 am start, all the hassle of air travel and the fatiguing effects of the flight, a long walk in the sleep-inducing sea air, a few beers and a couple of glasses of wine; ordinarily that would have been more than enough to knock him out for a few hours of long-overdue sleep, without the dramas that unfolded in the early hours of the morning. It was 4.30 am local time, more than twenty-four hours since his day started, and he was completely exhausted. What next? What was he supposed to do now?

There was still the occasional noise from the room next door, but no voices.

Alisa was still sitting quietly in the chair. She inspected her hands where the blood, that so distressed her earlier, remained all too evident. The smears troubled her still and seemed impervious to her efforts to remove them.

"How are you feeling?" he asked. "Would you like a hot drink? Or a shower maybe? It might help."

"Yes please," she said, with an immediacy that took him by surprise. "Both please." It was as if she'd been waiting for permission.

"You go and have a shower and I'll make us a drink."

Alisa stood up slowly, hitched up the huge robe and made her way to the bathroom. Paul watched her go. She looked so vulnerable, so small. After a few minutes he heard the shower door open and then shut again, closely followed by the soothing, cleansing sound of running water.

He found some hot chocolate sachets behind the Nespresso capsules but there was no kettle. After firing up the Nespresso machine, he tipped the contents of the sachets into two mugs. The noise from the machine, as it came to temperature, was deafening, in contrast to the efforts they were making to stay silent and undetected.

Paul held off making the drinks until Alisa returned from her shower. There were only two sachets of hot chocolate on the hospitality tray and he wanted Alisa to have hers hot, as advertised.

While he waited, he picked up the second-hand newspaper he'd begun reading on the flight over from England. Was that really only yesterday? It was still folded quite clumsily in on itself, and the same headline caught his attention.

Russian Mafia Competes For Slice Of Illegal Weapons Trade In North Africa.

He read on from where he'd left off.

Grainy images, too graphic to reproduce in this publication, were briefly uploaded to social media before being removed. It is understood they were taken from inside the remote Siberian city and appear to show the aftermath of a multiple shooting, amid rumours that some of the victims were French nationals. While it is unclear what initially sparked the incident, a connection with the extensive organised crime interests in the city appears most likely.

He skipped a couple of paragraphs and read on...

Speculation has been growing regarding a possible attempt by the Papé crime syndicate to undermine Russian ambitions in North Africa. If so, attacking core revenue streams in the Russian Mafia's own backyard would be both bold and potentially very effective. However, the infamous French crime syndicate is by no means the only potential suspect in the alleged massacre. While the Russians' considerable Norilsk business interests give every impression of being legitimate now, their acquisition during the fall of communism has long been a source of internal rancour and, on several previous occasions, violent recriminations between powerful, home-grown criminal elements.

Since reports of the incident first began to surface, a compelling counterstory, attributed to a reliable but unnamed source close to Joel Papé's organisation, has started to emerge. These new claims lend a degree of credibility to the suggestion that members of the French syndicate did travel to the city, but with a very different agenda. The claim states that, far from trying to undermine the Russians in Siberia, a delegation travelled from Marseilles to Norilsk to complete a deal that would align the interests of both parties. The shootings themselves remain unexplained.

The truth of what actually took place in the derelict Siberian warehouse, and the identity of those involved, is unlikely to emerge anytime soon. The city is located deep inside the Arctic Circle, inaccessible for long periods in winter, and permanently "closed" to all outside journalists. Even the movement of Soviet nationals is strictly controlled, with access to the city limited by a stifling and politically motivated bureaucracy.

Official local media and the notoriously tight-lipped Russian security services are denying any incident has taken place at all, maintaining that any such reports are overstated and inaccurate...

There was more, but Paul was interrupted. He deposited the second-hand newspaper into the wastepaper bin under the desk as the bathroom door opened. Alisa, completely engulfed by the bathrobe once again, stepped back into the bedroom. A hand towel was expertly wrapped around her head in the style of a turban. Just her face peered out from a sea of white.

She instinctively knew what he was smiling at.

"Are you laughing at me?"

"A little, maybe."

He calculated that honesty was the best policy.

He pressed the button on the coffee machine and it fired up in earnest. With no coffee capsule to inhibit it, the hot water flowed readily into the mug. He stirred it and handed it to her before making his own.

Alisa sniffed at the chocolaty drink and gave a little sigh. It was far too hot to drink straight away and she placed it on the bedside table next to Paul's iPhone. She sat on the bed, her back resting against a pile of pillows, which she rearranged until she was completely comfortable. There seemed to be a theme developing, everything conspiring to make her seem even more petite than she really was. Paul hadn't appreciated just how big the bed was until he saw her sitting on it with her knees drawn up to her chin and her arms wrapped around them.

"How about now?" he asked. "Does that feel better?"

"Much, much better," she said.

Paul finished making the second drink and turned off the machine. Placing it on the other bedside table, he went to the bathroom for a quick wash. He was very aware he too would benefit from taking a shower. The effects of the adrenaline had caused him to perspire noticeably, and there were the girl's salty tears and several spots of blood from when he'd helped Alisa to her feet earlier. A long relaxing shower would be good, but a quick wash would have to do.

He turned off the bathroom lights and closed the door to kill the sound of the fan that continued to run. In the lobby, he paused again. There was no sound at all from the room next door. He bent down and pulled away one corner of the towel at the bottom of the connecting doors. The faint glow of light was still there but no discernible movement. He pushed the towel back into position. Turning off the light, he put his eye to the viewer in the bedroom door. There was no movement in the corridor either, but something else caught his eye.

It was an electric-blue dress still lying where it had been thrown. Silently, Paul opened the door, recovered the dress and then closed and locked the bedroom door securely once again. He hung it up in the wardrobe, which illuminated helpfully when he opened it. He could see it was badly creased and had a large dark stain on the front. He was confident the creases would all fall out the instant it was worn again, such was the fit, which was more than could be said for his crumpled-looking suits that were now hanging limply next to their more glamorous new companion. He returned to the bedroom and closed the lobby door silently behind him.

Alisa was still sitting on the bed just as he'd left her, except now she was cupping the steaming mug in her hands and watching him intently. It was strange. Paul felt vaguely uncomfortable in his own bedroom in her company. It was as if he'd entered her bedroom and not the other way around. He was intruding on her privacy, on her vulnerability, and he was suddenly very conscious he was about to spend what remained of the night with Alisa, without any form of consent through choice.

"Is it okay if I lie here?" He knew he sounded ridiculous.

He indicated the opposite side of the bed to hers. There was easily enough room for four people in the bed, six if they were all her size.

"Silly," she said, smiling.

He took that as a yes and lay down on the bed. He was still wearing his jeans and the polo shirt. He knew he looked awkward and ill at ease next to Alisa, and he couldn't completely dismiss the feeling that she hadn't finished gently mocking him quite yet.

"Aren't you going to get in?" she said, teasing him.

Her smile was so wide as to cause her to wince slightly.

"Well… yes, but I don't want to make you feel uncomfortable."

The notion was ridiculous. The embarrassment was all his.

"You won't, Paul. Honestly, I'm fine. Just get in. It's your room."

Paul hesitated.

"Are you sure you're all right staying here with me like this?"

His words sounded as awkward as he felt. The inference of the question was at odds with what was happening.

"No one is expecting me…" she explained, and then she paused.

Paul sensed her reluctance, as if the explanation could somehow betray her, perhaps blur the lines that he'd so consciously drawn between her two personas, Alisa and Anna. His silence compelled her to continue.

"No one will miss me, not until the morning… I was supposed to be with that *pig* until then. I have nowhere else to go, nowhere I can go."

And there it was; Alisa and Anna were the same person in that moment. No longer was she the total innocent in a dreadful episode, but to some extent she was complicit in it, a co-author of her own terrible experience. Alisa looked troubled.

"I really do appreciate you letting me stay, but it is your room, Paul. Don't let me stop you from getting some sleep. Honestly, I am feeling a lot better."

Paul felt her distress and dismissed the rest as inconsequential in the circumstances. This certainly wasn't the time to start apportioning blame.

"Do you mind if I…" He was wafting his hand up and down his clothed body, trying to communicate his predicament.

"Take them off," she said, grinning.

Paul got the sense she was still enjoying his discomfort, but he didn't mind that at all.

He climbed off the bed and grabbed a pair of boxers from the suitcase. Rather self-consciously, he stepped into the lobby to change, reappearing dressed in nothing more than a stripy pair of M&S's finest. It was a concession to his guest, as he usually slept completely unencumbered.

Alisa was almost in fits of laughter.

"I've seen it all before, you know."

Paul didn't doubt it for a moment. He climbed into the bed and pulled the duvet up to his chin. Alisa was miles away on the far side of the bed. It was genuinely huge.

"Aren't you going to get in?" he asked, turning the tables.

Alisa looked thoughtful for a moment and then smiled. He was comforted by the welcome change in her mood. It was good to see her smile. Her face lit up, and a little of her natural beauty shone through.

"But before you do, I have to admit I haven't necessarily seen it all before, so maybe you should just keep the robe on and save my blushes." He was only half joking; she looked so warm and safe swathed in the huge robe.

"Yes, you have!" she countered, totally at ease with the fact. "I was completely naked when you found me."

"I'm not so sure about that. I think it was Anna I met out there. I think Anna's probably a very different girl to Alisa."

Even Paul didn't entirely know what he meant. It just came out. Perhaps he was merely making the distinction, trying to emphasise that he wasn't judging her, that he recognised the girl for who she was and not for what she did. He was desperate for her to see him as a decent man and not to be mistaken for the type of man she usually met in hotel bedrooms. After all, Alisa had chosen to tell him her real name, an act of trust as far as he was concerned, an intimate confidence shared, and he wanted her to know he recognised that.

Alisa placed the mug of hot chocolate very deliberately on the bedside table and pulled the towel from her hair. Unconfined blonde tresses, still a little damp, cascaded across her shoulders and down her back. Purposefully she made her way across the bed, pushing a few stray curls away from her face as she approached him.

"You are a nice man!" she said, and kissed him lightly on the cheek. Her lips were soft and warm on his skin. He caught the scent of her hair as she moved towards him and again as she moved away. It was just an innocent kiss but it made his head spin. Returning to her own side of the bed, Alisa pulled back the duvet and, still cocooned in the luxuriant robe, climbed in.

Paul turned out the lights and within moments was asleep.

Chapter 13

Silvi was immediately aware something was wrong. A man was shouting in the hallway downstairs and Maria was screaming back at him. The apartment was cold and dark, the curtains drawn, yet a little of the early morning light seeped through. A ribbon of fluorescent yellow from the strip light on the landing crept under the ill-fitting door, warped through a combination of age and neglect. Her eyes adjusted quickly in the half light.

She stepped barefoot onto the raw floorboards and made her way across the room to where Alisa's bed was still made, cold and unused since the previous day. It wasn't a surprise; neither of them had intended to be at home that night. She took a deep breath; she was alone.

Maria's voice carried the full height of the building, four floors up to where Silvi and Alisa shared an apartment. Something was wrong and Maria sounded terrified.

Silvi ventured out onto the landing, drawing the door closed behind her. She could see Maria as she peered over the fragile bannister down into the gloom of the hallway. She was cowering in front of a huge man, four floors below her, the door to Maria's ground floor apartment open and still swinging on its hinges.

She recognised the man at once. It was Boris, the man she'd spent the previous evening with, the man whose hotel room she'd left so abruptly only a few short hours earlier.

The phone call in the early hours of the morning had changed everything. If it hadn't been for that she would still have been at the hotel contemplating the nature of the service that would soon be demanded of her. But that wasn't to be. The phone call was short and one-sided. Boris listened but said nothing in return. He slammed the phone down and told her to leave. The same man that now confronted Maria had kicked her out of his hotel bedroom without a word of explanation. Now, somehow, he'd found his way to their home deep inside the old town. But it wasn't Maria he wanted. It wasn't even her. It was Alisa's name he spat into Maria's face and it was Alisa alone that seemed the sole subject of his attention.

Silvi shuffled uneasily, unsure what to do. Boris was demanding to know where the "whore Alisa" was, and Maria was refusing to say anything meaningful at all. Silvi had no idea how Boris had found the apartment building, or what had motivated him to drag Maria from her apartment into the hall. Why was Maria being singled out by the Russian gangster if it was Alisa he was after? How could he possibly know there was a connection between them?

A sense of dread hit her. Her stomach churned at the prospect and her breath caught. Could Alex have given him the address? Could Alex have betrayed them and given up the one vestige of personal privacy they still held dear? Why would he do that to them, or to Maria for that matter? There must to be another explanation. Alex would never betray them to a man like him.

In the hallway below, Boris grabbed Maria. She hit out at him, wildly trying to break his grasp, but it was all to no avail. Boris's face was flushed with anger and his threats became increasingly intimidating. He forced Maria to the floor, raising his fist to strike her, pausing only to repeat his demands.

Silvi scoured the landing for something to throw at him, something heavy that would fall the full height of the building and smash down onto his huge head, but there was nothing. She wanted to shout out, to tell him to stop and leave Maria alone, anything to save Maria from getting hurt, but Silvi had been wary of Boris the previous night, and seeing him rage now, she knew that words alone would count for nothing.

Below, Boris hesitated, his fist still ready to strike, but he stalled, as if hammering it down into the defenceless woman at his feet was to be the last resort. Boris stopped himself, and in that moment Maria's plight seemed, somehow, less inevitable. Silvi wondered whether, if his victim had been a man and not a terrified woman who was so utterly at his mercy, would he have been so restrained? Silvi doubted it; a man would certainly have felt the full power of Boris by now.

Boris spat out his demands one more time and Silvi feared for her friend. But something told her that he wouldn't hit her, that his words were just threats and not the inevitable precursor to unrestrained violence. If he was going to strike, he would already have done it by now, and Silvi sensed that Maria knew it too.

Maria gave him nothing. Her features conveyed only contempt for her abuser. She knew the answer to some of his demands, but Silvi knew she would never tell him what he wanted to know. Maria knew exactly where

Alisa lived – of course she knew – but he would never get that information from her.

Boris tried again. His need to find Alisa was urgent; he seemed crazed, barely in control. He demanded that Maria tell him where he could find Alisa at that instant, but that much Maria didn't know. Even if she did, there was nothing he could do to her that would make her divulge such information to a man like him. Alex had confided only in Silvi and Alisa. Maria knew nothing of the arrangements for the previous evening. Alex had organised everything directly with them and left Maria completely in the dark. And now Silvi knew why. Maria would never have allowed Alex to send them to see such men. The unfortunate truth for the raging Boris was that Maria couldn't tell him where to find the "whore Alisa" because, quite simply, she didn't know.

Boris cursed Maria as she braced herself at his feet, but even he seemed to realise he would get nothing from her. Maria was tough and, in a way, he seemed to respect that. Boris lowered his fist and turned to leave, pausing only to spit on the floor at her feet. Maria didn't flinch.

He took two steps and then stopped dead in his tracks.

"The other girl, Silvi… where is she?" he bellowed.

He was standing over her again, tracking her across the hallway as Maria scrambled to get away from him. If only she could just get back to her own apartment and lock herself in…

"Where is Silvi? Which is her apartment?" he raged.

Four floors up, Silvi's blood ran cold. The walls seemed to close in around her, her legs turned to lead, and the sound of her heart racing pounded in her ears. She started to panic. In an instant, Boris had turned his attentions to finding her. How did he even know where they lived? How had he found Maria? None of this made sense. If Boris knew enough to find their apartment building, why had he gone after Maria at all?

"Which apartment?" Boris roared. Spittle flew into Maria's face as Boris bore down on her.

As Maria tried to crawl away from her aggressor, Silvi hesitated no longer. She knew she needed to get away. She ran back to her apartment and locked the door.

The house was old and the door solid, but Silvi knew Boris would make light work of it if Maria finally broke. She pulled a dress from the fully laden drying line they had so resourcefully strung across the tiny living area, grabbed a pair of shoes and the handbag she'd used the night before, and headed back to the apartment door. She slipped the dress over her head and then pressed her ear to the gap between the door and the ornate timber frame. There was no more time to be lost. She cautiously turned the key in the lock and stepped back out onto the landing once again.

She tiptoed to the back of the house, opened the window and stepped out onto the fire escape. She made her way barefoot down the metal steps and into the yard at the rear of the building.

But still she wasn't out of danger. The yard was a dead end and the only exit was through a passageway that came out close to the front doors. She recovered a small mirror from her handbag and tried holding it at an angle, her hand trembling uncontrollably, desperate to see around the corner to the apartment building's front door.

There was no sign of Boris. Silvi eased herself around the corner to the main entrance of the apartment building. Maria was still in the hall, but she'd managed to cover the short distance over to the front door of her ground floor apartment and perhaps to safety. Boris was nowhere to be seen. Maria spotted Silvi in the doorway.

"Go, go!" she mouthed, her eyes following the line of the stairs upwards as they rose from the side of the hallway.

Silvi couldn't bear to leave her there, but she knew Maria was strong. She needed to save herself now – Boris had a new target. Maria had given him nothing despite his threats. Surely he would just leave her alone.

Silvi could hear the devastation being unleashed as the Russian crashed around on the upper floors, making a lightning search of the building and inevitably making his way to her apartment, an apartment he would find all too soon. He would smash the door down or break the lock. Had she even bothered to lock it? She couldn't remember... He would see the collection of photographs that would unintentionally betray her, the electric-blue dress from the previous evening, the curtains still drawn and the bed still warm.

Suddenly, she heard the thunder of heavy footsteps slamming their way back down the stairs. He was four floors up but moving fast. Could he have already worked it out? Silvi and Maria needed to make their move.

"Go, go!" Maria mouthed again.

"Thank you..." Silvi whispered in response, but Maria was already gone, locking her apartment door and hammering the security bolts into place.

Still barefoot, Silvi made the most of her meagre advantage, her shoes in one hand and a tiny blue clutch bag in the other. There was no time to waste.

She just ran. She made no plan, her route erratic. She set out to lose herself in the maze of narrow streets that made up the old town. Right, left, right again; she just kept on running. Finally, she found herself in the town hall square. She wanted to be invisible. There were only a few people around, but every head was turned, every eye upon her. She could barely be more conspicuous.

She pushed on but her stamina was fading fast. Her breathing, mere gasps, was growing shorter and more painful. She made one more effort to put as much distance between herself and the Russian as her failing strength would allow. Eventually, she had nothing left. If he was behind her now there was little more she could do. She slowed and then stopped to catch her breath.

Her route was unplanned and manic, but she knew the old town and that alone served her well. There were more people in the square she now found herself in, mostly tourists eager to make the most of their day, but she was still very much the centre of their attention. At first, she just wanted to be anonymous, but now she was only too glad of their glances and the spectacle she was creating as all heads turned in her direction. Even if he caught up with her, what could he do to her now? There were just too many people around.

Boris was nowhere to be seen. She caught her breath again. She hadn't noticed the pain when making her escape, but now, as she tried to pull on her heels, she winced breathlessly at the damage inflicted by the cobbled streets. Her feet were bruised, cut and raw.

She made her way to the old flower market and the corner of Rue Louis Gassin. Alisa and Silvi often took breakfast at a restaurant there. But more importantly right now, she could be among people she knew. Not friends exactly, but right now people were good, familiar people even better. The restaurant was busy, as Silvi knew it would be.

Chapter 14

MONDAY

The morning came much sooner than was welcome. Paul had no idea of the time – his iPhone was on the opposite side of the bed and he missed it irrationally. The sun was seeping through the thin curtains and he reluctantly acknowledged it was time to get up.

The previous evening's events came flooding back, and they seemed all too incredible to be true. He rolled over in the bed and there she was, lying only a few inches away from him, as lovely as he remembered. He could make out her soft features and the contrastingly ugly bump on the side of her head; it was silhouetted slightly and looked even angrier than before.

He winced for her – *That's going to hurt when she wakes up* – and he made a mental note to leave her a couple of paracetamol from his washbag. He was sure they would help.

He lay there quietly for a while, staring at the ceiling, trying to decide what to do. Finally, he decided to do exactly what he'd planned to do all along. He'd told Alisa she could stay as long as she needed to and he still meant that, but he needed to get on with his day. He was only too aware that as soon as she awoke she would have places to be, other people to see, perhaps even friends to meet. Without a doubt she would leave his life as quickly as she'd come into it, and almost certainly with less drama. It would soon be over, an extraordinarily interlude in an otherwise uneventful life, a private interlude never to be shared – who could he tell? No matter how he rearranged the events in his head, he'd just spent the night in a hotel bedroom with a Russian escort. It hadn't been like that, of course, but who else would make the distinction between Anna and Alisa? He could hear them now: "Didn't call the police, ay…", "Stayed in your room all night, ay…"

He slipped out of the bed and selected some running gear from his suitcase. He could see enough without turning on the lights and dressed quietly so not to disturb her. There was a pen and paper by the bedside so he wrote a brief note.

Gone for a quick run.

He reasoned that if she wanted to slip away, he'd just given her that chance. He felt it was the right thing to do. He slipped into the bathroom and tore off a strip of paracetamol. He quietly set them down on her bedside table next to the half-full bottle of mineral water. He paused for a moment – this was probably the last time he would ever see her; she hadn't stirred at all.

*****

He felt energised. Paul hit the promenade along with hundreds of like-minded people and set off at a pace. He would run for seventeen minutes in one direction and then seventeen minutes back. That should be just over six kilometres and plenty for a workday. The Promenade des Anglais was perfectly flat, unlike his usual runs at home, so it shouldn't be too taxing. It was warm though, and that would add to the challenge.

He'd taken to running relatively late in life, conveniently convincing himself for a long time that road running would be too damaging to his knees. He'd taken it up two years earlier, when, at forty, he realised that he had to do something extra to keep off the pounds and to fight back against the twin perils of heart disease and diabetes that blighted the male side of his family. He enjoyed working out in the gym too, weights mainly, and also attended the occasional boxing class, pairing up and taking it in turns to batter the pads in a bid to stay lean.

The truth was, boxing aside, he hated cardio. He clung determinedly to the view that he was far too heavy-set to start running at his age and should just stick with the weights instead.

A good pair of running shoes and his increasing waistline soon put paid to that argument. In fact, Paul actually enjoyed it now. Getting fit and lean was a target he comfortably achieved and he felt all the better for it.

He returned to the hotel and cooled down outside for a while, pacing up and down on the hotel forecourt under the port-cochère. Once he'd regained his breath, following his sprint finish, he headed back inside the hotel and back to his room. His pulse quickened again, and he wondered if she would still be there. Paul had thought of nothing else throughout the run and was unsure how he'd react if she was gone. He already felt a little hollow at the prospect, a tiny void forming where something extraordinary and exciting had once been, no matter how fleetingly.

He passed the door to room 732 and there was now a do not disturb notice hanging from a small peg centrally located on the door. It consisted of a thick black circle with a red line struck through it, and a hand below that, with the palm held up in the "Halt" position. It was unambiguous in any language.

But what did it mean? The Russian could still be in there, or maybe he'd gone out and just didn't want anyone else going into the bedroom to witness the aftermath of his night of drunken violence.

Paul slipped the key into the electronic lock on his own bedroom door. Would it be "mild elation" or "abject disappointment"?

She hadn't gone; she was sitting in the same easy chair he'd guided her to in the early hours of the morning. How different she looked though. She was freshly showered, calm and completely relaxed. The table was covered with a selection of breads, croissant, fruit salad, coffee and a muesli of some description.

"Orange juice?" she said, beaming.

"Yes, please," Paul said calmly, although his heart was racing, partly from his exertions and partly because Alisa was still part of his day. He wasn't entirely clear as to the greater cause.

"I'm so glad you're still here," Paul said, betraying more of his feelings than he'd intended.

"I hope you don't mind. I thought you'd like some breakfast after your run and—"

"It's perfect," he said. "I'll grab a quick shower. Start without me if you like."

"I'll wait."

Paul shaved and showered in record time and, swapping the towel for the second bathrobe from the wardrobe, he joined her for breakfast. It was delightful. They ate, drank and talked about nothing of consequence, and when it was done Alisa tidied up while he finished getting dressed. Paul felt more at ease about her leaving him now. He'd got to know her a little better, and somehow spending breakfast together seemed to diminish, if only for him, the impact of the terrible events of the previous night.

As time ticked by, he knew he needed to ask.

"What happens now?"

"I don't know. I really don't know… I have to go, but I'm not sure what will happen to me after last night." She spoke calmly but something was wrong. She was apprehensive. "I can't thank you enough for all you've done for me, but I have to see someone."

"Can't they come to the hotel? If they meet you here, you could leave together. It might not be safe for you to go out on your own." He fought the compulsion to ask who she was planning to meet. It had nothing to do with him.

"I don't know where will be safe anymore, but I can't expect them to come here – it wouldn't be right. I can't ask them to do that, but I have to find out what happens now."

Paul was about to protest.

"It will be okay, Paul," Alisa reassured him. "I have to do this sometime. I have to go…"

Of course she did. He knew that, but it was hard to just let her disappear into the city and have no way of knowing what would become of her. Maybe he could give her his contact details and she could let him know how things worked out – that she was safe. Perhaps, later in the week, they could have a coffee or lunch maybe and set aside the circumstances of how they first met. But the notion was ridiculous; they came from very different worlds and their chance meeting was conducive to nothing more than bringing out the Good Samaritan in him. Any decent person would have done the same for her; a better man might have done more. Why would she bother with him once she was free of the hotel and the trauma she'd suffered there?

"My phone is still in *his* room…" Alisa blurted out, "and so are my shoes, my dress, my purse…" She was becoming distressed once more.

Paul was disgusted with himself. He hadn't even thought about her shoes or any of her other personal effects. She was still dressed in nothing more than a hotel bathrobe and had nothing else to her name. All this time she must have been preoccupied with her clothes, her belongings abandoned in the other room and how she would get home. He hadn't even considered it. Of course she was still in the room when he got back from his run – what else could she do? He was angry with himself. She didn't have a choice. Even as he'd been getting dressed himself, it hadn't even occurred to him.

"I'm so sorry."

Paul was fully dressed now: crumpled suit, white shirt and highly polished black shoes.

"I'm so sorry. I just didn't think."

There were tears now too, and Paul couldn't believe his stupidity. He felt like he'd let her down once again, though there was no intent on his part; he'd just been typically thoughtless. Sophie would have been merciless in her appraisal of his behaviour. Sneaking out earlier, without waking Alisa, suddenly seemed like entirely the wrong thing to do, but he couldn't change any of that right now.

"I have your dress. It's in the wardrobe," he belatedly remembered, and went to retrieve it from its hanger. He felt worse. Did she think he'd kept that from her? Why would he do that?

The dress was still creased and the large dark stain clearly visible. It was almost certainly dried blood from the previous night, and they both knew she couldn't wear it.

"I didn't tell you that I'd found it on the corridor last night because I didn't want to upset you again. I'm sure it will all wash out." But he doubted she would ever want to wear the dress again even if it did.

"It's just that I have to go. I have nothing to wear… and my purse… I have to get my purse."

Alisa dabbed the tears from her cheeks. She looked desperate. Paul draped the dress over the chair by the desk in a way that hid the stain from view and sat down on the bed in front of her again.

"I just didn't think about your clothes. I'm so sorry." Paul was frustrated, but only with himself.

"It's not your fault. You've been so kind…"

"Look, let's fix it! I can at least sort out some clothes for you," Paul said. "I've plenty of time before the meeting starts, so write down your sizes and I'll go out and get you something to wear. It's no trouble. I want to do it." Paul couldn't have sounded any more sincere.

"I have money. I will pay you back." Alisa's sincerity was equally as convincing.

Paul wasn't listening. He didn't want her money; he just wanted to sort things out. He grabbed the pen and paper from the bedside table and gave them to her. Alisa began to scribble down the details on a fresh page.

Paul was still frustrated with himself, but now he was preoccupied with the issue of her phone and purse. Clothes would be easy to resolve, but her personal effects in the other bedroom were a completely different issue. There must be a way to get them back, but no obvious solution presented itself for now.

"Don't worry, Alisa, I'm sure we can sort all this out."

Alisa still looked lost.

"I'll get you some clothes and then we can find a way of getting your things back, even if I have to beat that bastard to a pulp myself."

They both knew he couldn't, and she smiled at his contrived bravado.

"Can I have Zara jeans if you can find them? They're usually a really good fit for me." Alisa's smile was catnip. How could he refuse?

But Paul was surprised that, even now, under these extraordinary circumstances, there was to be no compromise to style. He really didn't understand women at all and perhaps he never would. As far as he was concerned, one clothes shop was as good as any other, and if there was a Zara store in Nice he would find it. It simply made no difference to him at all.

He picked up his iPad and sat on the bed next to her. He tapped in the passcode and then entered *Zara*, *Nice* and *France* into the search bar. The return was instant. He swapped the iPad for his phone and stood up to leave.

"Thank you," she said, and before he could take another step, she jumped to her feet and gave him a hug.

Chapter 15

MONDAY

"*Bonjour!*" The manager of the restaurant greeted Silvi as he had on so many occasions before: a kiss on each cheek and then a third for good measure. He pointed to a table in the morning sunshine.

"*Non, monsieur, ici merci.*" She indicated a table inside, towards the back.

"As you wish."

As Silvi made her way through the restaurant, she caught her reflection in the glass counter and felt self-conscious and exposed. She spotted a cap and a scruffy jacket hanging on a peg by the entrance to the kitchen.

"*Monsieur?*" she asked.

He knew what she needed and smiled in response. She grabbed them, and slipping into the jacket, she took a seat at a table facing the street. With the green dress all but hidden and her hair swept up and tucked under the cap, Silvi felt a little more secure.

After just a few minutes, a familiar waiter approached with a cappuccino and set it down in front of her.

"*Gratui!*" he said with a smile.

"*Merci.* Thank you, monsieur."

"Do you need anything? Are you okay?" the waiter enquired confidentially.

The manager was watching them from the pavement with a look of genuine concern on his face. Perhaps familiar people are just friends in waiting, she considered, her breathing slowly returning to normal.

"Thank you. I'm waiting for a friend," she said weakly.

The waiter took no offence.

"Anything you need… anything at all." Then he smiled and left her to her thoughts.

Now that she felt safe, her thoughts turned immediately to Maria.

Silvi wanted to call her. She needed to speak to her and know she was safe. Maria was so brave protecting her, but at what cost?

Silvi scrambled around in her tiny bag and retrieved her iPhone.

"Merde!" She only found her work phone among her usual clutter, but it would have to do. Her personal phone was still back in the apartment by her bedside where she'd left it. She hit the *Home* button. It was still on silent, a professional consideration to her date the previous night. She cursed herself for not changing the settings before she went to bed. If she had, she would have heard the missed calls, three in all, and a text. They had all been sent within a few minutes of each other, the earliest at six thirty-two in the morning, and all from the same number. They were all from Alex.

She opened the text.

Get away from the apartment. Giorgi and Boris are coming for Alisa. I need to go away for a while. I'll call you soon. Be safe.

She could barely believe her eyes. She read the message again, and then again to be sure. First, Boris turned up at their apartment, and now this. What was happening? The natural order of things, what rhythm there was in her life, was suddenly crumbling away, her routine inexplicably disintegrating around her.

She needed to prioritise. Maybe Alex had already spoken to Alisa or sent her a text message too, but she wasn't going to take that chance. She would call Alisa first, then Maria, and finally Alex.

The text message frightened her. Why would Alex leave so suddenly? He'd always been there for them and she couldn't imagine what could be so bad it would make him leave like that... no warning, no notice... and where would he go? What would they do without Alex to protect them? Everything had changed. Silvi began to shake. She felt confused, frightened and overwhelmed. Tears formed, causing her to blink and obscuring her vision. She couldn't see the screen clearly. She needed to pull herself together.

She was furious with herself too. If only she'd taken the phone off silent mode last night, or even looked at it earlier, she could have warned Maria, and that bastard Boris would never have got the chance to hurt her.

She tapped on Alisa's name in her favourites list and the phone started to ring. "Pick up, pick up, come on..." The message service kicked in.

"Merde!"

She tried again. The iPhone bleeped and displayed the "Low Charge" message. She'd rolled into bed the previous night and now regretted not plugging the phone in to recharge its battery.

The phone rang out and the answerphone service picked up once again.

"Merde!"

Silvi tried to steady her trembling hands and redialled. No answer!

She knew Alisa wasn't with either of the Russians. If she was, why would they be looking for her right now. So why wasn't she picking up? Something must have happened to her? Or… maybe Alisa still had her phone switched to silent mode too!

She decided to send her a text message just in case. Silvi copied Alex's words into a new message she created, edited it slightly and pressed *Send*.

Stay away from the apartment. Giorgi and Boris are coming for you. Alex has gone… I'll call you soon. Be safe.

She redialled once again and this time she decided to leave a voice message.

The answerphone kicked in for a fourth time. She waited impatiently as the voice invited her to leave a message or press hash for more options. It took an age… Finally, it was her turn to speak.

"Boris and Giorgi are after you. Don't go back to the apartment. Alex has gone! I'm having breakfast in the usual… I'll wait for you – call me!" And she hung up.

She could do nothing more to contact Alisa now.

Silvi rang Maria.

"Are you all right?" Maria asked urgently, before Silvi could even speak.

"Yes, I'm fine. What about you?"

"I'm sorry. I'm so sorry, but he just guessed about the apartment. I must have looked up and he just guessed." Maria was distraught.

"Did he hurt you?"

"Men can't hurt me anymore, little one. He's just a boy. If he comes back I'll kill him. I'll kill the bastard. He's a dead man if he hurts either of you." The warmth in her voice brought a tear to Silvi's eyes. "You must stay out of sight. They want to get to her very badly. They think you know where she is… Just stay out of sight and don't come back here whatever happens."

"I don't know where she is. I have no idea. She's not answering her phone…" There were a series of battery level warning bleeps in her ear. "Oh my God. I have to go. I've got no charge on this phone and I'm waiting for her to call me."

"Okay, I'll call you back if I hear from her. Stay safe, little one…"

Silvi could hear a series of loud bangs from Maria's end of the phone call. "I have to go, little one. Don't worry about me. Just stay safe…" And Maria was gone.

Silvi checked the phone in horror. Did the phone just die or had Maria hung up in a hurry? The iPhone displayed three per cent charge. She switched the screen off immediately. That was it. No more phone calls.

Chapter 16

MONDAY

Paul tapped *Zara* into the web browser on the iPhone. The address 10 Avenue Jean Médecin was returned as the location, an avenue Paul knew well.

Leaving the hotel, he turned left towards the Jardins Albert-Premier, reputedly the oldest park in Nice and located where the Avenue de Verdun meets the Promenade des Anglais. At the corner of the park he turned left and followed the Avenue de Verdun to the Place Masséna: the huge square at the very heart of the city where smart trams swept through at a ninety-degree curve. The carriages of a sleek, silver and bronze tram cruised past, quietly channelling its course from the Boulevard Jean Jaurès into the impressive Avenue Jean Médecin itself. The stunning square was the largest of its type in Europe, Paul recalled Sophie reading out to him from the guidebook, and he remembered how he would graciously acknowledge her insights with genuine enthusiasm as they strolled together arm in arm. The guidebook was never far away when travelling with Sophie.

The avenue was no less spectacular than the square. Arrow straight and lined with shops, banks and restaurants as far as the eye could see. The Avenue Jean Médecin stretched out in front of him, broad and completely pedestrianised save for a few choice routes that bisected it at right angles and the constant presence of the immaculate trams.

It was no more than a fifteen-minute walk from the hotel to the Zara store. He trawled the aisles until he found an assistant who spoke a little English and gave her the list.

"Jeans?" he said, apparently unhelpfully.

The girl was on a mission, and he followed her tamely around the store as she gathered up a few items.

"Wait, wait," she instructed, so he waited by the cash desk.

She returned a few moments later with several pairs of jeans, an assortment of tops, two pairs of shoes and a scarf for some reason that was never explained.

She proceeded to display them in combinations on the counter, but Paul was out of his depth. He had no idea what went with what and asked her to choose. Apparently, the scarf went with everything. She selected a slightly worn-looking pair of jeans and a light green top that, once again, he just didn't get.

"Wait, wait!" she said once more, and he waited obediently as bid.

She changed the shoes to a pair of what he imagined were fashionable trainers and declared her work done.

"Socks, maybe?" They weren't on the list, but since he was here...

"*Chaussettes? Oui.*" She was gone and then back in a moment.

"Socks," she confirmed, as she laid them out anatomically below the jeans, just overlapping the trainers. The green top and scarf were already in position. The performance amused a number of fellow female shoppers and a couple of her colleagues also gathered around. The assistant was warming to her task again.

"Wait, wait!" And she was gone again.

"This perhaps?" She produced a pair of girl's undies from a multipack of three and again positioned them according to standard anatomy on the counter. Paul knew she was only doing it for sport and everyone laughed. They laughed louder when he declared it a brilliant idea and said, "*Oui!*" Hilarious apparently.

"*Enfin!*" she said, and she was gone again.

The assistant returned with three belts and insisted Paul chose one. The crowd was fully engaged now, offering advice and encouragement. Another assistant appeared, somewhat mischievously holding up a short light-coloured skirt, principally for the benefit of the audience.

She laid it over the underwear and delighted in her work. It was a pale cream skirt, way above the knee if the jeans were anything to go by, resulting in a unanimous show of approval from the crowd. The original assistant took one of the belts from Paul, offering it up first to the jeans and then to the skirt, nodding at both combinations. It was clear that the belt went with both items, which made it the obvious choice.

The performance complete, he agreed to buy the lot and the crowd, as they say, went wild.

*****

He headed back to the hotel with a pair of jeans, a green top, and a pair of trainers. In addition to the original list, he had a pair of socks, a skirt, a belt, three pairs of simple white knickers in an opened packet, and the scarf. He was still smiling about the entire episode as he called into a pharmacy on the Rue de France and picked up a toothbrush, a lady's deodorant and a large packet of paracetamol.

The round trip took no more than forty minutes. When he got back to the room, he noticed the do not disturb hanger was still on the door of room 732 and another had appeared on 733. The housekeeper's trolley was outside the room at the far end of the corridor nearest the fire exit.

Paul decided to test a theory.

He quietly slipped the door hanger off the peg on 732 and placed it on the floor. He grabbed a towel from the trolley and dropped it in front of the door, covering the hanger as if the maid was in the process of resupplying the room. The housekeeper was nowhere to be seen. He knocked loudly on the door and then quickly slipped back around the corner, listening for any activity. He gave it a few moments, but there was no reaction at all.

Paul retrieved the towel and replaced the do not disturb hanger. He was convinced the Russian had gone, at least for now.

Alisa appeared to have taken another shower, as far as he could tell – there was a steamy residue in the lobby and he could hear the hairdryer in action in the bathroom. The door was ajar. The hairdryer stopped as he made his way clumsily into the bedroom with the shopping.

She joined him as he dumped the bags on the bed, spreading them out on the enormous expanse of duvet.

"So many things! What have you got?" Her eyes lit up and she seemed genuinely surprised.

"Wait till you see before you get too excited."

She took the first bag. The jeans and the top were greeted with a huge grin. "I love it!" she declared, holding the top and the jeans together.

Clever me, Paul thought.

Next the shoes. As they emerged from the box she flashed him a smile. "They're perfect!" she said enthusiastically.

The next bag contained all the bits and pieces. First there was the underwear; she looked at Paul as if to say, *"You clever thing, you!"* Or was it *"You dirty old bastard!"*? He couldn't be sure, but either way she reopened the box and pulled a pair out. With no more ado, she slipped them on under the tenuous modesty provided by the vast hotel bathrobe. Paul made a point of turning away. It was just a gesture, and he sensed her gently mocking him once again.

"Silly!" she said, grinning.

Next was the belt and then the scarf; she slipped the belt on and then lifted her damp hair and wrapped the scarf effortlessly around her neck. It looked great. She did a little twirl as if on the catwalk and shot him another approving smile.

"And I got you these too." Paul pulled out a thin polythene bag from his jacket pocket. Inside were all the items he'd picked up for her from the pharmacy. He looked around to check if she had taken the paracetamol he'd left for her earlier and saw the empty foil wrappers next to the empty bottle of mineral water on her bedside table.

"This is amazing!" Alisa declared. "Aren't you clever?"

Paul would tell her the story sometime – he was sure she would find it amusing – but for now he was more than happy for her to think him clever, at least for a while.

There was one more bag, and she peered in.

"What is this?"

She pulled out the little cream skirt. "Naughty man!" she said. "I think this is more for you than for me."

"I didn't even choose it – you had to be there…" Paul protested meekly.

She pressed her finger to his lips. "I love it!" she said, and gave him a gentle yet lingering peck on the cheek by way of a convincer.

Chapter 17

MONDAY

Conference registration started at 11 am, but the first business session didn't begin in earnest until two o'clock in the afternoon. In Paul's opinion, there was way too much opportunity in the agenda for delegates to engage in doing nothing much at all. Of course, it was intended that the time be spent catching up with old friends and networking for new ones, an occupation Paul would readily engage in if the venue was full of potential clients, but that simply wasn't the case at the company's own international sales conference. He would ordinarily begrudge this time on principle, given the make-up of the participants, but not today. It was all extra time he could better employ, so he decided to forgo all the corporate glad-handing and spend it getting to know Alisa a little bit better instead.

Paul knew he would have to make an appearance at some stage, and certainly no later than 2 pm, no matter how consuming a diversion Alisa turned out to be. He was required, by corporate convention if nothing else, to register formally and collect his name badge complete with its plastic pouch and obligatory lanyard. He had no doubt that the whole tacky ensemble would be Secure Co. branded in a completely gratuitous display of corporate vanity. With every delegate at the conference already on the payroll, what was the point?

Breakfast with Alisa had been leisurely and relaxed. Once the clothing drama was resolved, the time passed pleasantly between them. Alisa switched on the TV and was flicking through the options, settling on a French news channel. She'd already brushed her teeth with her new toothbrush, finished blow-drying her hair and then dressed, choosing the jeans over the skirt, which didn't surprise him at all. She was showing no obvious impatience to leave and, once again, she rearranged the pillows on the bed to her own comfort and seemingly settled in.

The conversation after breakfast flowed effortlessly. Alisa didn't raise the subject of the previous night and Paul resisted the temptation to interrogate her too overtly. They just chatted about things in general, eventually coming back to the loss of her purse, her phone and any number of other personal items in room 732. She put a brave face on things, but Paul could tell they were still very much on her mind. The phone seemed to be her highest priority.

He was only too aware of just how dependent he was on his own phone, and imagined a girl of Alisa's generation would be no less wedded to hers, perhaps even more so. Alisa had lost her precious purse too and that was clearly a big deal for her. Paul knew, from personal experience, that Sophie would all but lose her mind if the same happened to her. Sophie's entire world revolved around such things.

Paul checked his emails on the iPad and spent a good while deleting the spam and responding to the rest. It all felt very natural, Alisa was on the bed catching up on the local news and Paul was tapping away in the comfort of one of the armchairs.

He entertained no pressing desire for her to leave and had no intention of rushing her but, as the time approached for him to go downstairs to the conference, he needed to know what she planned to do next. The conference session would drag on until at least five o'clock that evening, maybe even later, and he very much doubted Alisa would be hanging around until then.

"Right!" he started, interrupting her viewing. "I have to go down in a few minutes. Do you need anything before I go?"

Paul assumed his intervention would bring matters to a head. He'd told Alisa she could stay as long as she wanted and that was still true, but now, even though she had everything she needed to enable her to leave, she still seemed far from ready to go. As much as he enjoyed having her around, there had to be a reason for her obvious reluctance and he just wanted to know what it was.

Perhaps she was clinging to a forlorn hope that, somehow, they might still be able to recover her missing belongings from room 732, but Paul was sure they both knew that wasn't going to happen. Maybe she was merely waiting for him to go to the conference so then she could quietly slip away with the minimum of fuss, and that he could readily understand.

Alisa appeared to have something else on her mind.

"Paul, can I borrow your phone? I need to send an email." It was as if the idea had only just occurred to her, and maybe it had.

"Yes, of course you can. Don't you want to ring them instead? I don't mind. I'm happy to let you have some privacy if that's what you need?"

"No, it's not that. I can't believe it, but I just don't know Silvi's telephone number. I never call her that way. I just dial her by name from my mobile. It's really silly of me, I know."

It hadn't occurred to him before, and it wasn't something he ever thought about, but the truth was that he didn't have many telephone numbers committed to memory either. Once the number was entered into his phone he just dialled by name too – everybody did. The only telephone numbers he could immediately recall to memory were the office direct dial and his parents' home telephone number; to his enduring shame he was only too aware which one of those he used most frequently. Alisa wasn't being silly at all.

"But you do know her email address?"

"I don't remember her personal email. It's the same as her phone number really. I just email her from my contacts list, so I have no idea what it is from memory. But I can find another email address for her on the internet. I just need to check it first. There are some random numbers in the address and I can never remember what they are. It's not an email address I would normally use, but I'll be able to contact her if I can look it up. Is that okay?"

Paul tapped his passcode into the iPhone and handed it to her. Alisa opened the web browser and started typing. Paul was at her side.

Silvi, Nice, escort, France. And then she hit *Return.*

"Shit! I wasn't expecting that!"

Alisa grinned.

"It's okay, we can delete it all afterwards." She seemed amused by the alarm in his voice.

Alisa selected an option that appeared halfway down the page. There was an "Age 18 Only" warning message with an option to enter or leave the site. Paul was amazed to see it was all in English. He was familiar with the old maxim that French was the language of love, but it appeared, with a few exceptions, that the language of sex was most definitely English.

Alisa tapped *Enter* and the screen refreshed, showing images of a young girl, in her early twenties perhaps, in all manner of revealing outfits and provocative poses. He wasn't surprised to see it was the same girl that Alisa had entertained the Russians with in the restaurant the previous evening.

Across the top of the web page were a series of tabs: *Home, Gallery, Availability, Contact* and, more intriguingly, *Rates, Reviews,* and *Services.* Paul perched on the edge of the bed and watched as Alisa navigated her way to *Contact.* The screen refreshed again, just a couple of images this time, along with a mobile telephone number and an email address.

"You can call her if you like!"

Paul pointed at the telephone number displayed on the screen, as if he'd just solved a riddle.

"It's not Silvi's number. It goes through to Maria, who looks after the bookings for us," Alisa replied, waving her hand dismissively. It was as if it was the most natural thing in the world. Paul realised he was going to have to adjust his mindset. For Alisa, such things were completely normal and utterly mundane.

Alisa skilfully used the copy and paste function, lifting the email address and populating the *To* field on a new email template on the phone. She hit the *Home* key and then *Settings*.

"I take it you have an iPhone then?" Paul remarked, clearly impressed with her mastery of his precious mobile phone.

"I *did*!" she said, barely able to conceal her frustration, but her concentration was on the job in hand. It wasn't the time for small talk or to mourn the loss of her personal effects.

Next she selected *General* and then scrolled down the options menu to *International*.

"Excuse me for asking, but what are you up to?"

"You'll see…" she said, looking up from her work. "You do trust me, don't you?"

"Of course, but you'll have to reset it again. I've no idea what's going on now."

"Don't worry, you'll be fine. I am a professional, you know." And she flashed him another killer smile.

That much Paul did know.

Next it was *Language* settings, and then finally she scrolled down to an option he couldn't read but presumed was Russian.

"*Da!*" she said by way of confirmation.

She hit the *OK* option and the phone screen went blank. A series of alien hieroglyphics and a rolling bar appeared in the middle of the screen.

"The problem with Silvi is that she can be really lazy… she speaks very good English," Alisa explained, "but she barely reads a word of it. I am working on that with her but she's such a terrible student." Alisa stared intently at the screen as she spoke. "Nearly done…"

The phone was in the process of changing settings. A few moments later it was done.

"Good!" Alisa declared. She seemed happy with her work.

Returning to the email, she started typing.

"We manage our own emails," she said by way of further explanation. "So this will go directly to Silvi. The phone number on the website goes through to Maria but she changes it quite regularly. When we get too many timewasters… you know how it is…"

"Not really…" Paul offered flatly.

"Maria just takes care of all of that for us. We use private phone numbers to call each other. It just keeps things completely separate. But it's no big deal to change our phone numbers. We do it all the time."

Paul nodded absently and watched her work. He didn't feel the need to offer

Alisa any privacy as she typed; they both knew he couldn't read a single word of the email she was busily composing.

He was also more than a little unsettled by the fact that his iPhone had been rendered into a completely unfamiliar object in front of his eyes. The process had taken a matter of a few seconds in the hands of a virtual stranger who was clearly an iPhone expert. He felt lost without it and more readily understood Alisa's distress at losing hers.

Alisa sensed his disquiet.

"It's okay," she said reassuringly. "I'm just telling Silvi to email back her mobile phone number to this email address so I can call her... and..." She paused to look up at him. "And I've told her that the email address belongs to a friend – you!" Alisa quite rightly judged that Paul would take some satisfaction from that assessment of their relationship.

Finally, Alisa seemed content with the email, and Paul, for his part, appreciated the explanations and the vote of confidence the finished article apparently conveyed.

"Here!" she said, pointing to a completely incomprehensible section of text. "It says you are my hero... and that I know she would like you!"

Paul nodded his appreciation.

"Silvi's the girl you were with last night, isn't she?" Paul asked, and then he braced himself for Alisa's reaction. Perhaps he should have mentioned that he'd seen them both on Sunday night at the pizza restaurant, and certainly before now.

"You saw us last night? Where?"

"I was with some colleagues in the restaurant when you and Silvi turned up. You created quite a stir you know..."

"Really, I can't imagine why!" she said, with a very precise understanding of exactly why.

Alisa hit *Send*.

"All done. Now all I have to do is wait."

Alisa reset the phone and handed it back. Paul was more than a little relieved to see the hieroglyphs replaced with characters from a more familiar alphabet.

"What will you do now?" Paul asked.

Alisa was thoughtful for a moment.

"Can I stay a little longer, until you come back up from your meeting? Silvi will have emailed her phone number to your phone by then so I can call her. But I can't get in touch with her until I have her number, and I can't get that until you come back upstairs with your phone. Then I will go, I promise."

Paul did his best to look as though he was agonising about his decision, but there was never any doubt. Then he surprised himself.

"Why don't I just leave you the phone? I don't need it while I'm downstairs. It would need to be on silent anyway, and I was planning on taking the iPad to make notes."

"Really!" Alisa looked stunned. "That would be amazing. I promise I'll leave it when I go…"

Suddenly the folly of his offer crystallised in his mind. He was having second thoughts. Was he really about to leave his precious iPhone with a girl he barely knew, an escort, a girl with an aversion to law enforcement and a girl whose world had just been turned upside down. It was a huge leap of faith.

Alisa appeared to instinctively sense his reversal.

"It's okay, Paul, that's too much to ask. You hardly know me. I can wait until you get back."

It was Paul's turn to fix Alisa with a stare.

"Its fine, Alisa. I trust you to do the right thing."

"I will leave it. I promise."

It didn't need saying. Paul realised in that instant that he would never have offered it in the first place if he harboured any doubts on that score.

"I know you will. Besides, I can always track you down on your website," he joked. Paul wasn't totally sure she had one.

"Of course you can."

And now he knew. With a realisation that did him little credit, he knew he would have to take a look at some stage. He didn't doubt it was wrong, but he couldn't help being intrigued. *Rates*, *Reviews*, and *Services*, in particular, left him inappropriately curious. He was more than a little unsettled by what he might find, but he'd take a look anyway and then delete his cookies and history files in a symbolic act of contrition and good housekeeping.

But it was decided. Paul would lend Alisa his iPhone and leave her unaccompanied in room 733 to await Silvi's response to her email. Alisa was all hugs and smiles now and utterly genuine in her appreciation. It was a still a huge leap of faith, but he felt suitably reassured by the genuine depth of her gratitude.

Paul lingered momentarily at the bedroom door. In all likelihood *this* would be the last time he would ever see Alisa, and he knew he would miss her despite the brevity of their acquaintance. He left her holding his iPhone in one hand and blowing him a kiss with the other.

"The passcode is 5555," he said, positioning the do not disturb sign on the bedroom door then closing it silently and securely behind him.

Chapter 18

Silvi had sat in the café for what seemed like an eternity. It had been no later than 9 am when she arrived and it was now twenty past two in the afternoon. Her hosts kept the coffee coming and wouldn't accept any payment from her. They were aware of her distress and determined to look after her.

"Anything to eat? You must eat," they insisted, but she couldn't.

Bread, cheese and a small salad arrived anyway, but it remained untouched on the table in front of her.

From her seat, she maintained a clear view of the restaurant entrance, the busy tables on the pavement and the street beyond. To her left, a series of three French windows opened up onto the bustling flower market, with its brightly coloured stalls and a constant stream of browsers in a relentless ebb and flow.

Remote and anonymous, yet surrounded by diners, she felt safe and comfortable in the familiar surroundings. Time dragged on. She passed the hours agonising about what had happened earlier and what would happen next. Being safe was enough for Silvi right now, but even that would count for little if anything happened to her friend.

She knew she'd have to leave the sanctuary of the café eventually; she couldn't just sit in there forever. For now, though, it seemed the only option, having committed to be there and given Alisa the only clue she would need to find her. There was no choice. She needed to wait for her friend, but once they were together, she knew she would feel better. Alisa was the sensible one; she always knew what to do.

Silvi checked her phone every fifteen minutes and the charge level dropped to two per cent, but there was still no contact, no calls, no messages, nothing at all.

The cheese started to dry out and the salad wilt. She sparked up the phone once again. Still no text messages, so she tapped the email icon just in case, and a few emails landed. She begrudged each one of them the inevitable charge they drained from her dying phone battery. Among the current batch to download was an email from a paul.smith@SecureCo.com. It had been sent at five to two, which was about half an hour ago. She was about to delete it with the rest of the spam when she noticed that the first few words of the message displayed below the sender's email address were in Russian. Not unusual in itself, but the email was from a guy called Paul Smith.

She berated herself for not having checked her emails earlier. She instinctively knew it was important. It had to be something. A wave of hope washed over her momentarily and then her anxiety peaked once again, the full weight of it bearing down on her. She fought to hold back the tears and began fumbling hopelessly with her dying iPhone. Quickly, she tapped out a reply, including her mobile phone number. She pressed *Send* and immediately shut the screen down to conserve power.

Who the hell was Paul Smith? She mused, but he didn't sound like a Russian hit-man, and for now, those were credentials enough.

Moments later the phone rang. Silvi wept when she heard the comforting familiarity of Alisa's voice. There was no time to waste and no battery life to squander. She quickly confirmed her location and hung up.

Chapter 19

MONDAY

It was five to two when Paul finally collected his personalised and, as predicted, fully branded name badge. Paul had already missed lunch and made his way directly to the conference hall on the second floor, eventually spotting Gary and Doug among the crowd in the lobby. The place was buzzing. Delegates from virtually every country in Europe were mingling with a substantial cohort from the States. Doug and Gary were pressing the flesh to good effect, and Paul determined to remain civil when anonymity proved impossible.

"You must have slept well. I haven't seen you all morning," said Gary as he paddled his way over.

"Really, I was out running this morning. I must have missed you out there."

"Unless you were running through the breakfast room, mate, there's no bloody chance." He was all smiles and looked decidedly well fed. "It's great up there by the way. Doug and I are planning on skipping the *do* tonight and having a bit of dinner on the terrace on the third floor. Do you fancy it?"

"I don't see why not. I haven't got anything else planned." The thought saddened him a little.

Doug excused himself from a very large German gentleman he'd been making small talk with and joined them.

"Afternoon, Paul, Gary." He greeted them both warmly. "Shall we go in, show a bit of willing maybe?"

They joined a steady trickle of delegates as they made their way into the conference hall. It was a large room, air-conditioned, with pumping music playing and subdued lighting. Paul was aware that he would almost certainly be asleep in minutes if it wasn't for the thumping bass line. The beat and tempo, he was forced to concede, was highly effective in generating an atmosphere of dramatic anticipation.

The agenda was electronically displayed on large screen TVs at intervals along the length of the hall. There would be an opening speech by Donald Ferranti, followed by presentations from some of the principal players from the US, and finally, a motivational speaker to get them all fired up. The whole session was due to end at 5 pm and it couldn't come soon enough for Paul. He just wasn't in the mood and was desperate to be elsewhere.

In an attempt to appear engaged, he fired up the iPad. It was open on the memo application, as if he was genuinely intending to take notes. As a prop, it worked fine; if there was nothing of merit to record, it would provide some measure of distraction. He adjusted the volume to silent mode and waited.

They sat patiently, anticipating the storm that would surely break.

The volume of the music increased as the lights dimmed. The pounding beat was punctuated by a series of coordinated flashing lights. A cloud of swirling dry ice billowed up from the rear of the stage and out over the audience. A booming over-amplified voice introduced the celebrity facilitator. He bounced confidently onto the stage all smiles as he energetically applauded his audience for the enthusiastic welcome he had confidently predetermined *he*, himself, would receive. The American section of the crowd reacted as one; the Europeans displayed a less effusive cultural reserve.

Even spot-lit and centre stage, Paul didn't recognise the presenter, but his relative anonymity did nothing to dent the confidence of someone who was clearly supercharged by his own carefully manufactured celebrity status. He was loud and enthusiastic and lamentably uninformed. He fired off the obligatory welcomes, mispronouncing all but two of the more straightforward names on his VIP list, and then cracked a few one-liners that became somewhat lost in translation. His lack of any real understanding of the company and its products did nothing to dissuade him from reeling off any number of tired old jokes, the same jokes he almost certainly used week after week. Undeterred, and with a well-practised flourish, he finally introduced Donald Ferranti to rapturous applause. Paul dutifully joined in. It was the high point of his involvement.

Paul tapped on the iPad and the screen illuminated. More by way of his usual habit than for any other reason, he hit the *Email* button and waited for it to update. The download response time was excruciatingly slow, but it made steady progress. Eventually the usual spam landed, plus a few more emails that would need some attention in due course.

One message caught his eye in particular. It was from <u>Silvi.angel787.</u> <u>nice@msn.fr</u>. It was timestamped 14.21, and he could immediately see that it had already been opened. Paul clicked on it. It felt like the wrong thing to do, but he did it before his conscience had the time to make a compelling case not to. The text was in Russian but the telephone number was numeric.

He rebuked himself for his actions; reading the email felt like nothing less than an act of betrayal.

Paul just sat there for a while looking at the text and wondering what it might say, what he might learn about Alisa, or Silvi for that matter. If only he could read it. He knew it was wrong, and that it was totally contradictory to his earlier compulsion for mutual trust, but he felt compelled – he needed to know.

Paul was on a mission now. He completely blanked out the presentation booming out from the stage, which was no small feat given the intrusive volume. He was totally absorbed in his quest to read Russian. Putting his principles aside in a heartbeat, he copied and pasted the Russian text in Silvi's email to the memo pad. It seemed a sensible precaution. His devices were synchronised with the office-based file server. If Alisa deleted the email on the iPhone, it would disappear from the iPad the moment the device refreshed. Then he quickly scrolled down to *Sent Items* and waited for it to update. It took forever. The iPad's current internet connection was a desperately meagre mobile phone signal. After a short while, a number of old sent messages appeared, the most recent from August. It was clear there was the best part of a months' worth of them to download before it would get to the more recent ones and then finally to those sent earlier that day. He rarely needed to access sent messages on the iPad, and the folder only updated when called on to do so. None of this was going to be easy.

Paul turned his attention to the speaker, but it wasn't long before he dismissed him as a distraction. He checked the progress on the iPad. It was slow, very slow.

After a while, all sent messages up to 10 September had downloaded; eventually the email addressed to Silvi.angel787.nice@msn.fr appeared. Paul opened it without hesitation. There was a short delay before the text appeared, but when it did he immediately copied and pasted the entire email to the memo pad.

Paul's heart was racing, and a bead of sweat formed on his brow. Was it guilt, or anticipation? Perhaps a little of both. He took a deep breath. He now had the text of both messages safely copied: the one Alisa had sent from his phone to Silvi, and the response from Silvi to her. Discovering their content would be more difficult and, given the download speed, painfully slow.

Paul took a break and tried to re-engage with the presentation. There was a video playing on a huge screen that formed part of the backdrop to the stage. Paul had no idea what the film was about or who the man was who was standing at the lectern being wildly animated as he delivered a theatrical commentary.

"Who is that again?" Paul asked Gary.

"Not sure, something to do with product development, I think."

For all Gary's attentiveness, he seemed no better informed than Paul. He zoned out instantly as Gary stared blankly back at the screen.

With his attention turned back to the matter in hand, he entered a search for "Russian to English translation". Eventually a full page of options displayed on the search results. One was for Google Translate. Paul selected it and waited. Slowly it began to refresh, again washing down the screen in a painfully slow progression.

When the Google Translate page finally downloaded, Paul pasted the Russian text into the *Translate Message* box.

Пожалуйста, позвоните мне срочно, потому что что-то страшное случилось вчера вечером, и мне нужно поговорить с вами. Я не смею покинуть отель.

Присылайте ваши мобильного телефона для текущего адреса она принадлежит человеку по имени Пол. Он в порядке я ему доверяю А х

It was almost instant. The translation appeared in the adjacent box, but it was in yet another foreign language, French. There was an option to change the language setting and Paul selected English.

The result was again, almost instant, and to his amazement it was entirely credible. His fears that it would come back with nonsense or something vague and generic were immediately allayed.

Please call me urgently, because something terrible had happened last night, and I need to talk to you. I do not dare to leave the hotel.

Send us your mobile phone number for the current address it belongs to a man called Paul. He's okay I trust him. A x

The translation was reassuringly close to what Alisa had told him she'd written and, while there were some contextual anomalies, those clever people at Google had created software that returned a plausible result. Paul noted that there was no mention of him being a hero, and he berated himself once again for betraying the trust that, until only a short while ago, counted for so much.

Not really a hero then! he acknowledged to himself silently.

He felt quite the reverse in fact. Duplicitous at best; disgusted with himself at worst. On the upside, it lifted his spirits considerably to read in her own words that she did actually trust him. The irony wasn't lost on him.

But, while the translation was credible, the message itself didn't seem to make much sense at all. Why was she so scared to leave the hotel? Paul could understand her not wanting to run into the Russian again; that did make sense. But why would Alisa be too scared to leave the hotel in the daytime and with dozens of other people milling around? Surely she would have asked him to accompany her if she was that nervous? They'd had plenty time during the morning to leave the hotel together. There must be more to it; something about all this just didn't add up.

Paul copied Silvi's message into the *Translate Message* box and hit *Return*.

It froze. "Shit!" Paul's frustration was evident and audible. Gary and Doug both looked over.

"What are you doing?" Doug was looking down at the iPad.

"Nothing, the damn thing just froze!" Paul hit the *Home* button to clear the screen.

"I'm not surprised..." Doug said, but he looked very surprised. "Was that Russian?"

I bet the bastard reads it fluently! Paul thought, and then he felt bad. Doug had done nothing wrong, but the frustration of googling on a paltry signal was taking its toll.

"It's just something I'm working on," Paul said in a bid to deflect Doug's attention. He closed the iPad down completely.

Doug's focus returned to the stage, where the facilitator was back in full flow. He was introducing the motivational guru with a CV that was taking an age to relate. How long had he been at this? It was four minutes to four and they were down to the last speaker on the agenda.

He discreetly fired up the iPad again, conscious that Doug might be a little more curious from now on. He would have to be more guarded if he wanted to avoid awkward questions. Doug was bound to look over the instant Silvi's message translated, and it would, no doubt, be totally incriminating in some unrecoverable way.

Paul started again. Google Translate appeared at the first time of asking, but it loaded as agonizingly slowly as before. At least he knew it worked. As soon as it appeared, he copied Silvi's message in to the *Translate Message* box and hit *Return*.

"Fuck it!" It was in French.

Doug was back on his case.

"Are you all right?"

"Yes, fine. Sorry, I just have this one last thing to do. Then I'm finished."

Paul sensed Doug's growing frustration with his behaviour but, to his credit, he affected a smile that implied he was satisfied with Paul's clearly inadequate explanation and then, conspicuously, returned his attention back to the speaker.

Pacing around on the stage, the motivational guru had just told a gag the English-speaking element in the audience seemed to thoroughly enjoy. Paul couldn't help noticing there were a far greater number of vacant expressions in the room than those convulsed in mirth. He wondered if he had, in fact, missed out on anything at all.

Turning his attention back to the iPad, Google Translate had completed its work but infuriatingly reset itself to the local language. It was just one more irritation and the cause of his latest indiscretion.

Clever Google, Paul thought as he scrolled up to the *English* option and hit *Return.*

Это плохо, мой друг. Алекс ушел, и они ищут для вас. Не возвращайтесь к квартире. Позвони мне и оставаться в безопасности.

Again, it was almost instant. *Google! Bloody amazing!*

This is bad, my friend. Alex is gone, and they're looking for you. Do not go back to the apartment. Give me a call and stay safe. K x

But the translation only raised more questions, all without answers. Who the hell was Alex? Why had Alex gone? And gone where? More importantly, what did that actually mean for Alisa?

Paul took a moment and then read the translation again.

Who exactly was looking for her? If it was the Russian from the previous night… that didn't seem to make any sense either. It was one of the Russians that threw her out of the bedroom in the first place. Why would someone who was so desperate to find her now do that only a few hours earlier?

And… who the hell was *K*?

There were no answers – just more questions.

Paul was certain now that there was far more going on than he knew about. Something terrible must have happened, and it was obvious that he didn't know the full story… not even close. He felt compelled to get back to the room, back to Alisa, and he needed to get there right away.

"I have to go!" Paul blurted out. He felt he owed Doug that much of an explanation. "Gary, let me out…" he snapped, as he leapt out of his chair with no regard for the speaker or his audience. He made no effort to do it quietly; he just got out of there as fast as he could.

Moments later, he was cursing the lift. "Come on, come on…" Paul knew he must have appeared demented to the conference support crew assembled in the lift lobby, but the lift was unrelenting in its reluctance – its arrival was painfully lethargic.

"Doors opening." The doors reminded him of the search returns on the iPad – agonizingly slow.

"Come on! Come on!" Paul was frantic as he finally entered the lift. "Damn it!" The light for the fourth floor was illuminated on the control panel. Paul hit the seventh.

"Fourth floor, doors opening," the lift announced. It seemed so apathetic it was almost slurring its words. Paul could see the faces of two men on the fourth floor as the doors slowly parted.

He put his hand up and shouted "*Non!*"

They stepped back, more in surprise than anything else, and Paul punched the *Door Close* button as he glared out at them from the lift car.

It was excruciating.

"Doors closing."

The doors closed and the lift rose once more.

"Doors opening."

He forced himself through the gap the instant he could, then sped off down the corridor. Paul's heart sank as he rounded the corner. The maid's trolley was outside the door once again and the do not disturb hanger was missing. Its twin was still in place on the door to room 732, but Paul knew she was gone; he just knew it.

He swiped the lock and entered the room. Alisa had gone, and for the first time since he'd rescued her from the corridor in the early hours of the morning, he was back in his hotel bedroom and completely alone.

Chapter 20

MONDAY

There was no trace of Alisa in the bedroom; nothing at all to indicate that she was ever there. The breakfast trays had been cleared away and the bed expertly remade with the pillows and cushions plumped and perfectly positioned. The shopping bags were gone and the room smelt fragrantly of fresh linen and scented polish. Room 733 had been aired and meticulously cleaned, professionally serviced by a maid who had done a first-class, five-star job.

The bathroom was as new. Masses of fluffy white towels, each folded with military precision, were hanging neatly from the rail. The complimentary toiletries had all been diligently refreshed and arranged too; nothing was out of place. Then he spotted it. The pink toothbrush he'd so thoughtfully bought for her was still there. It alone hinted at her presence, as it rested next to his in a glass tumbler on the top of the vanity unit. It was a small thing, but at least he knew Alisa was real enough from that one tiny intimate detail.

In the wardrobe, his dinner jacket and a single crumpled suit hung limply as before. A pair of large white dressing gowns hung at their side, once again securely bound by the peevish stricture of their own belts. The electric-blue cocktail dress was gone, but there was just a hint of her perfume on the dishevelled items that remained. On the floor, in the corner of the wardrobe, a small Zara shopping bag lay in the shadows, apparently discarded. He leaned in and opened it. Alisa had left the skirt behind; that didn't surprise him, on reflection. Maybe she hadn't really "loved it" after all. The discovery saddened him a little, but he couldn't explain why it did; the feeling seemed ridiculous. It wasn't as if he'd chosen it for her himself in the first place.

He sat on the bed feeling exhausted and exhaled heavily. On the nightstand on the far side, he spotted his phone. It was plugged in and apparently on charge, with the pad and pen neatly arranged next to it. Alisa had left his mobile phone, just as she'd promised. He knew she would – he'd trusted her – but it was still a source of comfort to see the precious device at rest on the bedside table. He was forced to concede that taking the time to recharge his iPhone was a nice touch; repaying his kindness with a small but charming act of consideration. He walked wearily over to the easy chair and sat down, dropping the iPad onto the bed.

He didn't really know what to make of things. But the plan had worked, Alisa had made contact with Silvi and then, between them, they had sorted something out. The truth was that, in reality, it didn't have anything to do with him anymore, but even so, the content of the two email messages still troubled him.

Who is this Alex person? Who or what is he to Alisa?

The message was clear enough. It said he had "gone", but gone where, and why?

The questions just kept on coming…

Who is it that's actually looking for Alisa? And how do they know where she lives?

Paul didn't imagine professional escorts gave out that kind of personal information too readily. Could it be someone other than the two Russians from the restaurant who were searching for her, the incident the previous night merely a coincidence? That seemed too unlikely. How much bad luck can one girl have?

There had to be much more to all this, so much more to it than Alisa just getting roughed up by a violent client, but Paul could only find questions. He was furious with himself before for not doing enough, and now he was certain he should have just called the police when he had the chance. Why did he listen to her when he knew all along that calling the police was the right thing to do? But she was terrified at the prospect. *"No police,"* Alisa had pleaded with him, but why did he listen?

Paul wasn't thinking straight. He took a moment. The only reason he knew Alisa's predicament was more complicated than he initially thought was because he'd translated two emails he had no right to read. If Alisa wanted his help she could have waited for him to return from the conference. It was that simple. Alisa had made her choice and what happened next was nothing to do with him at all.

As Paul unplugged the phone from the charging cable, he noticed a few words scribbled on the notepad at its side. Alisa had left a message. He picked it up with a sense of relief.

The message said "Call Sophie", and below those two isolated words Alisa had scribbled a large *X* for a kiss. His heart sank and his mind raced.

"What? How could Alisa know anything about Sophie?" Paul was baffled for the moment.

Could Sophie have called and Alisa answered? That wouldn't be good for him, but he was strangely sanguine about that possibility. He hadn't given Sophie a thought all day, and now he felt bad about that too. If Sophie had spoken to Alisa it would just bring things to a head sooner rather than later as far as their relationship was concerned. If Sophie got the impression he was seeing someone else, Paul knew he, and everything to do with their relationship, would be consigned to history the moment he got home. He'd just spent the previous night with a Russian prostitute, and no matter what the circumstances might have been, that would take some serious explaining to Sophie. In truth, he wasn't sure he had the appetite to try.

Paul picked up the iPhone and checked it. There were no phone calls from Sophie. The most recent call in the phone's history was an outgoing call to the number in Silvi's email. There were no other calls made that day, nothing in or out, and, reassuringly, Alisa hadn't bothered to delete the call to Silvi's number either. Emails then? How did she know about Sophie? The last few emails included the incoming email from Silvi and an outgoing one from his own phone to her, but nothing from Sophie.

He checked the phone's diary and then it became obvious. He must have inadvertently set the "Call Sophie" alert to repeat daily at 2 pm. It would have flashed up on the screen while Alisa was waiting for a response from Silvi and then cleared automatically when she used the phone. That was it; the explanation was that simple.

He was still no closer to understanding what had happened to Alisa, and calling Sophie was the last thing on his mind.

*****

The conference would be wrapping up for the day about now and he considered heading to the bar. He could do with a beer, but he just couldn't face the prospect of meeting up with Gary and Doug. He hadn't exactly covered himself in glory earlier, and he couldn't yet find the motivation to come up with a plausible excuse to explain it.

As he mulled things over, he unconsciously plumped up the cushions, just like Alisa had, kicked off his shoes and flopped down on her side of the bed.

Paul closed his eyes and immediately he could see her flying through the air, crashing into the wall and lying naked, slumped in the corridor. He could see her sitting in the armchair sobbing and desperately rubbing the blood from her hands. Next, he saw her swamped by the massive bathrobe, and then standing at the end of the bed effortlessly wrapping the scarf he'd bought for her elegantly around her slender neck. She performed her catwalk twirl, and as she spun, her hair revealed the angry weal disfiguring her otherwise delicate features. She was smiling now, happy in that moment, yet still broken and lost all the same.

Paul shook his head, opened his eyes again, and climbed off the bed. He needed to get her out of his mind. He still couldn't face the bar, or the bonhomie that went with it, but he could, as a last resort, raid the minibar instead and hang the expense.

In the bedroom lobby he noticed the towel was gone from the bottom of the connecting doors. He hadn't registered that earlier. Who notices things that *aren't* there? He noticed it now, but at least that did make sense. The room had been serviced, and no self-respecting housekeeper would leave a towel on the floor of a serviced hotel bedroom.

Paul held his breath for a moment and listened. There wasn't any sound from the room next door but he still felt compelled to stuff a towel back into position. He went to the bathroom, grabbed a towel and then changed his mind.

If that bastard comes back, I want to know about it.

Instead, and surprising himself, he silently unlocked the dividing door and opened it fully. The only thing separating them now was the second door, which was, he assumed, locked from the opposite side. There was no way of knowing for sure, but he gave it a push anyway. It didn't move. He listened again but there was no sound. He stepped out into the corridor. There was no one around and the do not disturb hanger was still in place.

He braced himself and banged loudly on the Russian's door. Silently he stepped back into room 733 and began wrestling with his bedroom door in a bid to speed up its closure, but the powerful door mechanism fought back. In the end, he just let it close at its own speed until it got to the last few centimetres. As it did, he slowed it down even more to prevent the tell-tale click of the lock securing. He was alert all the time for any reaction in room 732, but there was none.

Paul closed and locked the dividing door again.

No point taking too many risks, he reasoned.

The minibar was beckoning again, and this time there would be no distraction. He grabbed an 8 euro bottle of Peroni and initiated a search to locate a bottle opener. It could be anywhere in a hotel bedroom: possibly attached to the side of the desk, in the bathroom, on the tray with the Nespresso, in the minibar, near the minibar. He'd encountered virtually every conceivable variation over the years. On this occasion, it was on the shelf next to the safe. He opened the bottle with a flourish and for no good reason tapped 5555 into the number pad on the safe door. The motor whirred as the bolts drew back and the door popped ajar. He looked inside and immediately realised that some of his cash was missing, and a credit card too.

He was confused for a moment and then the truth of what must have happened hit him, and it hit him hard. He couldn't bear to think it, but it was all too obvious. Alisa: there was no other possible explanation.

Alisa had stolen from him and then disappeared into the city like a common thief. The anger and disappointment that bore down on him was shattering. How could he have been so stupid? It was the only logical solution. It had to be her, but he instantly recognised there was no one else to blame but himself.

It was he who had given her the passcode, and he'd done it all too willingly. How could he have been so unbelievably naïve? He'd done it on nothing more than a sympathetic impulse, but that same code was also the passcode for his iPad, his briefcase, the bedroom safe and any number of other items, including all but one of his credit cards.

Looking back with the benefit of hindsight, he could barely believe how casual he'd been about giving it to her. It was the passcode of an idiot! No one with any common sense would use such a simplistic combination, and they certainly wouldn't give it willingly to a complete stranger. But he'd done precisely that, and, what was worse, he'd been routinely lazy and indiscreet about such security for years. He could hardly be surprised that his stupidity had finally caught up with him.

Alisa had stolen from him, but he couldn't find it in himself to blame her. Alisa was frightened and desperate, or at least that's how it appeared to him, and he'd been foolish, his judgement thoroughly compromised by nothing more than a pretty face. He couldn't allow himself to condemn her even now.

He checked again and found there was no mistake. He'd deposited two credit cards and 400 euros in the safe. Now there were only 200 euros left and one of the credit cards was definitely missing.

Alisa had been smart about it too – clever, sneaky. She'd left some of the euros and one of the credit cards behind.

That's what clever thieves do! he thought. *They work on the principle that you might not notice just some money missing, or just one of the credit cards.*

Perhaps Alisa believed Paul was *idiot* enough to think he'd left the credit card somewhere else, or better still, that he just didn't have it in the first place.

Paul couldn't believe it.

How could she be so calculating? Who would go to the trouble of cracking the safe and then only take some of the spoils?

Paul's head was spinning.

"A smart, sneaky hooker, that's who!"

The words caught in his throat. He couldn't allow himself to believe that of her, but there was no other explanation.

It wasn't really about the money or the credit card either, he would just cancel that, and in truth, he would hardly miss a mere 200 euros. It wasn't any of that. What hurt most was the betrayal. He'd been there for her, he'd helped her, he'd chosen to trust her, he'd taken her in, kept her safe and showed her compassion when she needed it most, but despite all that, a petty theft had been his reward.

He slammed the safe door shut and paced the room. He seethed inside but still fought the truth of it. He checked once more. There was no mistake, yet his mood changed again. Disappointment and sadness replaced much of the anger, and he slumped onto the bed, closed his eyes and downed the Peroni in one.

"Fuck it!"

The first Peroni tasted sour, the next one not so much.

He switched on the TV. It was still tuned to Alisa's news channel. Paul stared at it. He couldn't be bothered to turn it over. What would be the point?

He picked up the message pad and read the words out loud once again.

"Call Sophie."

But he couldn't bring himself to dial the numbers. He didn't feel like phoning Sophie – how could he? Perhaps he didn't deserve her either. After all that had happened the previous night, it wouldn't be right anyway, and what was worse, far worse, he still couldn't get the stunning Russian escort out of his mind.

Chapter 21

It was with little enthusiasm that Paul took the lift to the third floor.

As the lift doors opened with the usual irritating announcement, Paul found himself staring aimlessly into a large lobby with a long corridor leading off directly ahead. On the right were a series of small conference rooms with Secure Co. branded signage over each door: Workshop 1, Workshop 2... six in all. Paul hadn't properly consulted the agenda since signing up in August, but he now resigned himself to the prospect of spending much of the following day in one of these rooms. He hadn't been in the right frame of mind for the conference on the first day; given the course of the afternoon's events, he wasn't sure he could face it at all tomorrow.

But that was another day!

The bar and restaurant were located on the opposite side of the corridor to the conference rooms, which in turn were bisected by a lobby that led out to the third-floor rooftop patio. It was huge. The swimming pool and a row of sun loungers filled one side, while the rest was set with dining tables that were for the most part unlaid.

The real action was at the front of the patio. Six steps led up to a raised terrace that afforded panoramic views over the bay and the promenade itself. It was packed with diners, in contrast to the lower section, and the waiting staff buzzed around attentively.

Looking back from the terrace, a series of balconies rose six floors up on each of three sides of the patio, the bedrooms they served enjoying magnificent views. But despite the vista, it occurred to Paul that he was still content with his own room, other than the issue of the connecting door; the sea view rooms would no doubt carry a substantial premium, and there would be no escaping the constant bustle from the terrace below.

On the fourth side of the terrace a series of monumental columns rose, perhaps eighty feet into the air, supporting a portico that framed the dining area below. It formed a stunning edifice when viewed from the promenade and was a valuable and impressive legacy of the conservation efforts of the hotel's developers.

Paul approached Gary and Doug with some trepidation. "Evening, gentlemen…"

"Everything alright, mate?"

Gary was shaking Paul's hand and looking concerned. Gary was one of the good guys, Paul reluctantly forced himself to concede.

"Yes, yes, fine really – just something I had to do. I'm so sorry. Was it a big issue?" Paul cringed, anticipating the response.

"Caused a bit of stir," Doug said, putting his menu down on the table.

Paul could tell that both of his new colleagues took a dim view of his behaviour during the afternoon session.

"Don't worry about it, mate. I told everyone you were German," Gary joked, and even Doug smiled.

"Sit, sit, I'm bloody starving. We were just about to order. We weren't sure if you were going to make it." Gary shoved a menu into Paul's hand as Doug signalled to the waiter that they would need a few more minutes.

"That's all right, let him come. I'll look while you're ordering. Are we having starters?"

"Damn right," said Gary, and he promptly placed his order with the smartly attired waiter who arrived.

The food was good and the company better, but it was difficult for Paul to join in with the conversation when it turned to the conference. He'd barely attended during the first day and had no real appreciation of what was on the agenda for the following morning.

He was certain, with some measure of regret, that Doug's opinion of him was deteriorating hour by hour, and he only had himself to blame. He'd excused himself early from dinner on the first night, behaved outrageously that afternoon and now he was late down for dinner as well. Not a word from him by way of explanation did little to ease the situation. All the same, Doug's opinion mattered to Paul, and once he'd rationalised everything in his own mind, he determined he would come up with something credible and make every effort to set the record straight.

They skipped dessert for the second night in a row. Perhaps eating in at the hotel didn't equate to a night out and therefore didn't merit pudding; Gary had been adamant on the subject the previous evening.

They ordered coffee, to be accompanied by a rare single malt, which Doug ordered after studious consideration of the list. Paul insisted they were charged to his account; it was a token gesture, but the least he could do under the circumstances.

It was a pleasant evening, but as the terrace started to empty, Paul reluctantly decided it was time to take his leave. He would be the first to retire once again, which could be considered bad form in some circles, but putting it down to an early morning start in order to accommodate his run seemed reasonable enough.

No one argued. It was a worthy excuse.

Before turning in, he took a brief stroll down the promenade. It helped to clear his mind and afforded him a little time to reflect and get things into a better perspective.

Chapter 22

MONDAY

A do not disturb sign was hanging from the peg in the centre of both bedroom doors, entrance to rooms 732 and 733 similarly embargoed. Paul
swiped the lock on room 733 before it struck him. He hadn't left the do not
disturb hanger on his bedroom door when he'd gone to dinner with Gary
and Doug. Could he inadvertently be on the wrong floor? He stepped back,
scanned the corridor for clues, but nothing useful presented itself. He hadn't
visited any other bedroom floors during his stay but, he assumed, in common
with so many modern hotels, each floor would be almost indistinguishable
one from another. The room numbers on the bedroom doors were 732 and
733. It was definitely the right floor.

Paul depressed the door handle and pushed. The lights were on, the curtains drawn and the sound of a French news channel from the TV filled the
room.

Alisa was sitting in her usual chair, her hair damp and hanging limply
over her shoulders and cascading onto the oversized bathrobe, which, once
again, swamped her tiny frame. She appeared to have showered again, and
Paul wondered if she would ever truly feel cleansed of all that happened to
her in the room next door.

Before he could speak, Alisa jumped to her feet.

"Paul!" she exclaimed.

She lifted her robe as she ran across the bedroom and greeted him in
the lobby. Paul just stood in silence, letting the bedroom door close noisily behind him. She enveloped him in her arms, pressing her head against
his chest, squeezing herself to him. It was the most intimate and enduring
moment they'd shared, and Paul instinctively returned her embrace. His surprise was complete – what the hell was going on?

"What are you doing here?" It sounded harsh. It was an expression of
surprise as much as a question, and both emotions were tinged with a little
anger. Paul tried to bend his knees slightly to look into her eyes. He needed

answers and he knew he would find them there. Alisa resisted and just held onto him ever more tightly, avoiding his gaze.

"What's happened, Alisa? What is it?"

He could sense the fear in her; any confidence she'd regained earlier in the day was gone. She seemed profoundly relieved to be back but there was a renewed vulnerability in the way she clung onto him. Why had she come back? Was it merely to apologise or to make amends in some other way? Despite the theft, was it possible that returning to room 733, and to him, was somehow a more palatable option than whatever else awaited her outside the relative safety of his hotel bedroom? Whatever her motives, he was suspicious of her now and a tightening knot clawed away at his stomach. He hated feeling this way about her, but she'd stolen from him – how else was he supposed to feel?

"I'm sorry," she said without looking up. "I didn't know what else to do."

The consuming note of fear in her voice melted away his anger temporarily, but the aching knot in his stomach tightened, and the suspicion remained. There had to be a good reason, an overwhelming need for her to return.

One last chance. With the anger gone, he would give her that.

Paul led Alisa back to her armchair and perched on the bed opposite. A can of tonic water and two glass tumblers sat on the coffee table. A bedroom key card and a couple of tiny gin bottles lay empty and discarded on the desk; the minibar had clearly provided a measure of solace in his absence.

"I thought you were gone for good. I didn't expect to see you again."

"I needed to come back," she said. "I left you a note."

Paul was confused.

"I saw that, but it didn't explain anything. I've been worried about you."

He decided to wait before challenging her about the theft. It would make him feel so much better if she addressed the issue first.

"Yes..." she whimpered, "I left you a note."

But the only note he'd seen was a scribbled reminder to "Call Sophie", and that was no explanation at all. Alisa appeared to register his confusion.

"I left the note in the safe for you. I didn't want the maid... anyone else to find it." She looked up. "Did you see it?"

"No, I didn't...?"

Alisa didn't elaborate; she was already distracted by her own thoughts.

"Something's happened, Paul, something terrible," she said. "I nearly didn't come back. I didn't want to involve you any more than you already are. It's not fair on you... but you are already involved in a way, and I had to come back. I had to explain, and I just don't know where else to go."

Alisa's voice trailed away, as if, for that moment, she'd absent-mindedly lost her thread.

Her mood darkened. He sat silently and waited.

"Paul," she started, and then she stopped abruptly. She took his hand in hers, just as she had the previous night, and Paul couldn't help but feel the depth of her anxiety as she squeezed her fingers around his. Her nail varnish was chipped and worn and she seemed all too conscious of the damage. She tried to hide it from view, curling her fingers around his ever more tightly.

"Would you like another drink?" Paul asked.

There was a small measure of liquid remaining in one of the glasses on the coffee table, the second was empty. Without looking up, Alisa slowly shook her head. "No, thank you." Her drying hair fell away as she moved, revealing the full extent of the bruise on her temple. It still looked raw, but the swelling was starting to settle.

"I'm going to have one – are you sure?"

Alisa shook her head again.

Paul rose from the bed and entered the bedroom lobby. He retrieved the last Peroni from the minibar and then took a moment to collect his thoughts. With the wardrobe door open, Paul was temporarily out of Alisa's line of sight. He tapped 5555 into the safe.

The money was still missing, as was the credit card, but there was a note. Paul had missed it before; he simply hadn't seen it. It was resting quite conspicuously on top of his travel documents, but he hadn't bothered to check them earlier. Belatedly he checked through them now. Everything was present and correct as far as he could tell.

He shut the safe and, with the note in his hand still unread, returned to Alisa.

"Paul, I have to tell you something. I've done something terrible and you will never forgive me."

"It's okay, Alisa, you can tell me anything. I'm not going to judge you. Why don't you just take your time and tell me everything."

Still she struggled.

"It's only a few euros," he said.

"No, no, it's not that. It's worse, so much worse."

There were tears in her eyes as she finally looked up. She fixed him with a dead stare, a look implying a deep sadness and enduring, haunting pain. It felt as though Alisa was peering deep into his soul, as if searching, once again, for that nice man she'd met on a previous night. Would he still be there for her even now?

"Alisa, it's okay." Paul returned the intensity of her stare. "Take a deep breath and just tell me. I want to help. Start from the beginning and tell me everything."

Suddenly there was a loud noise from the balcony.

Paul jumped to his feet as he heard the patio door opening behind the curtains. The net curtains were slid aside but the intruder was still obscured.

"What the hell?" Paul was instantly braced to fight, thinking it must be the man from next door. He'd worked it out and climbed the balcony to get to Alisa. Paul determined that the *bastard* was going down; he didn't care how big he was. He knew there was only so much he could do, but perhaps he could give Alisa a few precious seconds to get away.

"No! No! It's okay, Paul. Don't! Stop!" Alisa shouted.

But he was already at the curtains as they started to part. He was set to engage the intruder with the most devastating punch of his life; he needed to make it count.

"No, STOP!" Alisa screamed.

Paul stopped dead.

The curtains twitched and parted... and Silvi stepped through.

She was slightly shorter than Alisa, and younger too, no more than twenty-three years old, wearing a green version of the skin-tight dresses they'd both worn the previous night. If anything, it was even shorter. Her long, straight blonde hair was to one side, flowing in a single sweep around her delicate neck and over her left shoulder.

"I'm sorry. Are you okay?"

Silvi said nothing. She seemed too shaken to speak. Alisa uttered a few comforting words in Russian and the second girl beat a hasty retreat back through the curtains and onto the balcony.

"What's going on? I didn't know she was here. I could have killed her!"

"Paul, I have to tell you what happened." The tears were rolling down her cheeks now.

Paul slumped down in the second easy chair with the coffee table between them. The bottle of Peroni was still in his left hand and the note, now crumpled into a ball, in his right. He planted the bottle firmly on the coffee table, taking a moment to calm down. He unfolded the scrap of paper and ironed it flat on his knee as he caught his breath. Somehow, now seemed as good a time as any to read it.

"My nice man," It began. *"I have taken some money. I will pay you back, I promise. I have to see Silvi and I will come back when I can. Thank you for everything."*

At the bottom of the page there was a large *X* for a kiss.

Paul stared at the note for a long time. A lump formed in his throat, replacing the aching knot that had previously clawed away at his stomach. How could he have doubted her so readily? She never intended to steel the money.

She only took what she needed, and only then because there was no other choice. Alisa possessed nothing to call her own – he should have been more aware of that. Everything she had with her on that dreadful night was lost to her, abandoned and completely out of reach in the other bedroom.

"I will pay you back," Alisa reiterated, with all the conviction in the world. "All of it, I promise… but…"

"It's okay, Alisa. I'm not worried about the money. None of that matters. Just tell me what's going on."

Paul didn't care about the money. He smiled broadly and Alisa relaxed. He genuinely didn't care.

"I am intrigued though," he said, smiling. "How did you get into the safe? I know it was locked."

"It was," Alisa acknowledged, looking a little sheepish at the admission.

"Well?" But Paul suspected he already knew the answer.

"Well… since you ask," she said, her resolve returning, "I saw you put your code into the iPad earlier, and then you gave me the same passcode for the phone. It doesn't take a genius to work it out, and under the circumstances I thought it was worth a try… Don't you think?"

Paul winced a little in acknowledgement. He was being gently rebuked, with some justification, by the very person who had just cracked his safe and stolen his money.

"Yes, I do think…" He smiled, flushed with the embarrassment of his own stupidity.

"I just tried 5555 and it worked. I was just lucky I suppose!" she confided nervously. "Or you are just lazy," she suggested rather more firmly.

Paul was only too aware which of the two propositions was the more accurate.

Chapter 23

MONDAY

He'd given her a few minutes. Alisa seemed a little brighter, but he had to know.

"Just tell me what's going on, Alisa. If I'm going to help you I need to know everything."

Alisa took a deep breath and began.

"It all went so badly wrong last night... I was so scared Alex would be angry with me. But it wasn't just Alex. I was too scared to leave the hotel this morning too. I'm sorry. I didn't even want to leave this room. I just didn't know what to do. I needed to speak to Silvi. At least then I could find out how angry Alex was about everything. Alex is good to us, Paul, but he has a temper too and I know I've made a terrible mess of things."

"Who is Alex?"

"We work for him sometimes... he's a friend."

"So how can a friend possibly be angry with you? That monster next door attacked you. How can Alex be angry?"

"I know, but it's complicated, Paul. You don't know these people." Alisa shook her head as if to dismiss Alex's part as inconsequential. "I know now that he's not angry. He's not the problem."

"Okay. So what is?"

"Silvi told me not to go back to our apartment and that Boris and Giorgi were looking for me. They're both terrible men. They're no better than animals, Paul."

"But I don't understand. Why would one of them let you go last night if they're looking for you now? That really doesn't make any sense to me."

"It does make sense. He had to let me go. It wasn't as simple as that. Giorgi didn't just let me go. I made him! But things have changed since then, and now they want to get me back. I think they'll kill me if they find me. I was lucky to get away from him when I did. I was lucky you were there to help me."

"But why? I still don't understand."

Alisa's shoulders dropped. She placed a trembling hand over her mouth. The vitality seemed to drain from her and she began to shake, her whole body suddenly afflicted. Alisa was clearly terrified, but terrified of what?

"What is it? Is it because they think you'll go to the police?"

She bit her lip and looked up at him. Her hands were in her lap now and she was wringing them together as if still trying to excise the blood that had troubled her so deeply the previous night.

"No," she said.

"It's okay, Alisa. You're safe now. What is it?"

"They wouldn't want me going to the police, but it's not how you think. It's not just about what happened to me anymore."

"So, what is this all about?"

Alisa shifted uncomfortably in her chair.

"They just don't want the police to know anything about them being here in Nice."

"I get that, but if it's not about you, what is it about?"

Alisa shifted uncomfortably again.

"Paul, they have business here. They're here to do something terrible."

"I never doubted that…"

"It is all business for them… and Alex is helping them. The police are the last thing any of them need right now. But it's all gone terribly wrong and they've found Silvi and Maria as well and it's all my fault."

"Okay, but one thing at a time, we can get to Silvi and Maria in a minute. What happened in that room, Alisa? Why did he hurt you?"

"It's hard to tell you. I don't want you to think badly of me. I know you don't approve of what we do, but last night wasn't normal and everything went wrong, and now Silvi and Maria are involved as well."

Paul was suddenly very aware that Silvi was still on the balcony.

"What about Silvi? Why is she out there on the balcony?"

"She's sort of spying on next door. Giorgi's balcony door and curtains are still open, so she's waiting to see if he comes back."

"And has he?"

"No, not so far. We've been here since eight o'clock and we've heard nothing. I need to get my things back, Paul – I just have to. I can't leave any of my things in that room." Alisa took a deep breath. "I need my phone and my purse at least, and I'm scared about what might happen if I don't get them back."

"We can worry about that later."

Alisa offered her hand across the table. Paul instinctively took it. She closed her trembling fingers around his once again and he looked reassuringly into her pale blue eyes. He'd forgotten just how beautiful she was. But her beauty was a distraction now, and he wasn't sure about her any more. There was still a nagging suspicion and he knew she was holding back. She smiled back at him, and he became all too conscious that his own resolve softened instantly under her touch. He was feeling manipulated, but there was so much more he needed to know. He removed his hand from hers in a bid to restore his ebbing sense of control.

"One thing at a time, Alisa. We will find a way."

Alisa sensed the change in his mood and continued.

"The two men we were with last night," she started, "it wasn't normal. They're in Nice to do something terrible. They're bad men, violent, vicious men, Paul. Alex is helping them. He doesn't want to be involved, but he has no choice. He booked the hotel rooms for them and he gave them a car to use while they're here. He has to give them anything they want."

And that included you and Silvi, I suppose, Paul snarled silently to himself.

"Who exactly is this Alex? Is he your boss? Is he your pimp?" He could barely contain his disgust. "Was he the other man with you at the restaurant last night?"

"Yes, he was with us. He introduced us to Boris and Giorgi last night. We'd never met them before. We sometimes work for Alex, but he is not really our boss. He works for another man, a terrible man that makes him do terrible things. We live in one of Alex's apartments and he looks after us. Alex is not so bad really, and we're safe when we work because he's a powerful man in the city. If it wasn't for Alex we wouldn't be able to work at all. It just wouldn't be safe."

"Safe?" Paul exclaimed indignantly. He made no attempt to disguise his frustration at the suggestion that Alisa's so-called friend Alex was keeping them safe. Nothing about his brief acquaintance with Alisa, or Silvi for that matter, gave him any confidence that either of the girls were even remotely safe.

"We are our own bosses really," Alisa added with mix of pride and indignation. "But we do Alex favours sometimes, and in return he helps us too."

Paul instinctively dismissed Alisa's defence of Alex's involvement and recalled Gary's reading of the situation on Sunday evening in the pizza restaurant. He'd been right about everything so far: a couple of Russian Mafia thugs in town up to no good, the local fixer entertaining them with a couple of his best girls. Gary was insightful, to say the least.

"Paul, you have to understand… Alex said these men were important to him, so we said we would see them as a favour to him."

"Did you really have a choice?" Paul asked without even trying to hide his scepticism. Alex was quickly becoming the target of a deepening contempt.

"As I said, sometimes we do him favours, and Alex promised to get them really drunk so they would be less trouble. But with men like them, Paul, you never really know if they will just go to sleep or turn into monsters."

Alisa took a long drink of her gin and tonic and Paul finished off the Peroni. He took a deep breath.

"So?"

"So…" Alisa began, "Boris and Giorgi did get drunk, really drunk, and we kept them out as late as possible, but eventually they wanted to come back to the hotel. Silvi told me that Boris just went to sleep when they got back to his room. That was good for her, but I wasn't so lucky.

"Okay. What happened?"

"Silvi told me that Boris was woken up by a phone call in the middle of the night. She didn't hear what was said but she could tell that something was wrong. Boris told her she had to leave straight away. He told her to go, so Silvi just went home."

"Okay, but I meant what happened to you?"

"I will tell you, but it's important." Alisa had something else on her mind. "I think Giorgi must have phoned Boris while I was in here with you."

"That makes sense I suppose…"

"Silvi was lucky really. She had an easy night with Boris."

Alisa seemed to drift away a little. She seemed distant and distracted by her own misfortune. She took another drink and swallowed hard, trying to retain her composure, but she was getting to the difficult part and Paul could sense it. There were tears in her eyes once again. Paul made a conscious decision to ignore them for now, and his apparent indifference seemed to compel Alisa to carry on.

"When we came back to the room he was very drunk. He wanted sex, Paul, and I said I would give him…" She faltered.

"It's okay, I understand what you do, but don't worry about that, just tell me what happened."

"I said I would give him…" She made a gesture and Paul understood immediately. "But the pig wasn't happy with me. He got angry. I hated him. I didn't want to have sex with him."

It was Paul's turn to shift uncomfortably in his chair. Alisa seemed only too aware of his disquiet.

"It's what we do," she said, in an attempt to normalise the conversation. "It's no big deal. Mostly we don't mind. It's just work for us, but not with him. It's not like that generally because the men we see are older, more sophisticated, and certainly not animals like those two. Giorgi is not the sort of man who can afford to pay for my company usually."

Alisa seemed to take some comfort in that fact but instantly became uncertain about Paul's reaction to it.

"It's okay, Alisa, I don't need to know *those* details." He shifted again.

"It's not like you think, Paul. Not every man can pay so much, so we only see rich men. They are older perhaps, but they are not pigs and they can be very sweet and treat us well, and then it's fine. It's just a job, that's all. These men don't want trouble, just some fun. They want to be entertained. Sometimes they just want someone to talk to. But Giorgi was just a drunken pig and he became very angry. He was so strong and I just couldn't stop him."

Alisa paused again.

"Paul…" Alisa started, but she could hardly get the words out, "We do things… I know you know what we do but it's hard to tell you."

"It's all right, just tell me what happened." Paul tried to reassure her, but it was hopeless and the tears were coming in earnest now. He relented and tried to comfort her, but there was little he could do.

"What the hell did he do to you, Alisa?"

Alisa couldn't speak. She tried to gesture.

"It's okay. I think I know what you're trying to say, and I understand. You had no choice, you had to. I do understand that, Alisa. Please don't upset yourself. It's all right, I'm not judging you."

"It's not all right," she blurted out.

Alisa seemed angry with herself.

"I do have a choice, and I choose to do these things. I make good money but I am not proud. It makes me sad to tell you."

She grabbed his hand again and gripped it tightly.

"It's not okay!" she said, sobbing.

Paul had no intention of pulling away this time.

"He hurt me, Paul. I was so scared," she said finally. "He really frightened me."

She couldn't go on, and the tears rolled in a steady steam down her cheeks.

"I know he did. Alisa…" Paul tried his best to console her, but as Alisa sobbed, Paul just looked on helplessly.

Finally, she found her voice once again.

"He was forcing me. I couldn't breathe," Alisa continued. "I thought he would let me choke. I thought he would let me die like that. I couldn't breathe at all. He was an animal. I hit him and he hit me back." Her hand went involuntarily to her face. "Here, he hit me here, and I couldn't breathe." She wiped her tears away and then grabbed Paul's hand once again.

"I'm sorry. What must you think of me?" She was raising her left hand to her neck. "It wasn't like this," she cried. "He didn't choke me like this…"

She wrapped her trembling fingers around her throat by way of illustration. She was inconsolable. But there were no marks on her neck that would indicate she'd been throttled. A man as powerful as Giorgi could do it easily, but not without leaving a mark. There would be bruises maybe, a tell-tale redness for sure. She moved her hand slowly to her mouth, just two fingers pressed to her lips. She could barely speak.

"It was like this… I couldn't breathe. I just couldn't breathe… He forced himself on me and I thought I would die like that."

Paul went to Alisa. He realised what the evil *bastard* had done to her.

"He forced my mouth open and he wouldn't stop," she cried. "I thought he would kill me like that. I was so scared."

"Alisa, it's okay, I understand. You don't have to say any more. That's all over now. You must know he can't hurt you anymore. I promise you that."

But still she sobbed.

"You're safe here with me. He can't get to you now."

Her head was bowed, her tears falling relentlessly on her lap. After a few moments more, she found her voice again. Her demeanour suddenly changed. She spoke with an intensity that came from deep within her. It surprised Paul as she fixed him with a stare, a powerful consuming stare fuelled by an inner strength he would never have imagined her capable of.

"I stabbed him, Paul. I stabbed the *bastard* in the leg!"

There was a moment of silence while Paul processed the full meaning of Alisa's words.

"I stabbed him!" she repeated, and she seemed relieved to get it all out in the open.

No sooner had the words been formed than the fleeting strength that propelled them from the depths of her distress suddenly subsided and a desperate vulnerability overwhelmed her once again.

"Come here," he said, gently taking her in his arms. "That's the bravest thing I've ever heard." And he held her tightly as she sobbed, and the full emotion of all that had happened to her spilled out.

"It's all right, Alisa," Paul reassured her after a while. "It's going to be all right." But he had no realistic expectation that it would.

Time slipped by without a word passing between them. The room was silent save for the occasional sob and sniffle, but slowly Alisa regained her composure. She wiped her eyes on the sleeve of her gown.

"Are you going to make me leave?" she asked pitifully.

"Of course not. Why on earth would you think that?"

"I don't know, but I wouldn't blame you."

"I'm not going to make you leave."

Alisa slumped back in the chair.

"I can stay?"

"You can stay."

Paul paused to let her wipe her eyes again. "But there *is* just one more thing I need to know." He effected a smile in a bid to break the mood.

"What is it?" Alisa asked, regarding him nervously.

He maintained the smile. It was time to change the direction of the conversation for a while.

"There was a credit card in the safe, Alisa, but I can't find it anywhere. Do you know what happened to it?"

The relief on her face was instant.

"Come with me," she said, with a little steel back in her eyes.

She led him into the bedroom lobby. She squeezed his hand and pointed at the tiny green LED on the wall. Then, as if to emphasise her point, she switched on the lights and cupped her ear to the reassuring hum of the air-conditioner that gurgled away unnoticed overhead.

"There!" she said, with a smile that lit up her soft features and banished the tears.

Sitting in the energy-saving device by the bedroom door was the missing Visa card. A temporary replacement for the key card she liberated before leaving his room to meet up with Silvi.

"I always intended to come back, Paul. Always!"

Chapter 24

THREE MONTHS EARLIER
NORILSK, SIBERIA

The man jumped from the train into a deserted and desolate wasteland, and a fresh covering of snow broke his fall. The icy winds clawed at his skin and the crisp fresh air filled his lungs. The contrast was stark: the dark foul-smelling claustrophobic gloom of the railway carriage replaced by an unending mono-chrome landscape under a leaden sky.

There was little hint of nature to give the land definition. All around him the frozen ground was strewn with the debris of decades of industrial neglect: machinery, piles of waste and crumbling abandoned buildings, all ravaged by yet another unforgiving winter.

He took in the scene. It was familiar, enduring, depressingly constant, and nothing much had changed with the passing of time. Behind him, the train crawled noisily away in the direction of the dilapidated unmanned station. He knew it wouldn't stop. The freight transport would just rumble through en route towards its final destination, the city's freight yards another five kilometres to the east.

Knee-deep in the snow he waited, scanning the platforms for life. There was none. But unmanned or not, the station wasn't his destination – the marshalling yard was as close as he would get.

As the last few wagons passed, he settled on his haunches, low against the biting wind and static in the bleakest of landscapes. The ageing diesel locomotive laboured onwards. Fifty carriages, maybe more, a combination of rusting tanker wagons, open tops and the putrid enclosed rolling stock that had been his refuge for the journey. Each battered wagon was now en route to receive their first payloads of the season, the weather having finally relented. It would be twenty-four hours before that same train headed back to Dudinka. Twenty-four hours was all he had.

He already knew the journey back would be worse than the one he'd endured on the way in. The locomotive would labour again, struggling to cope under the massive increase in weight, each wagon fully loaded from the stockpiled output of the winter's smelting and mining operations. Finding shelter among it would be a challenge.

As he waited, his breath formed crystals in the air that billowed wildly on the arctic wind. A few chilling minutes later he was completely alone in the marshalling yard, still half a mile from the station and as anonymous as he'd hoped. He scanned the route just travelled for signs of life but there were none.

In the distance, the city was waking up. He pulled his collar close and plunged his double-gloved hands deep into his pockets. Heading out across open land, he braced himself against the freezing gusts and made his way to the road, a narrow single-lane strip of tarmac visible only as a grey shadow as it cut its way through the vast snow-covered wastes to the north.

It was late June, the start of the all too short summer season, and still the thermometer barely passed zero. The journey was slow, bitterly cold and hideously uncomfortable, but the money was good. He'd agreed to make the journey back to Norilsk this one last time; he'd already determined he would never return again. If it hadn't been for the job, he would never have returned at all.

The winds had caused the fresh falls to drift, and he waded through them towards more open ground, where the going would be easier. As he left the drifts behind, the snow crunched angrily under his boots as he walked. It was frozen and compacted like concrete, and it had a permanence that implied it might never thaw at all. The road was still covered with a thick icy crust, stained and soiled, still supercooled by the all-pervasive permafrost that left the land bleak and lifeless.

The industrial plants continued to take their toll too. The air was tinged with a hint of sulphur and laden with a fine corrosive grit. It irritated his eyes and scoured the exposed skin on his face. Nothing much could live in such conditions, the soil long since rendered poisonous from years of acid rain and unending falls of dangerously contaminated acrid dust. Nothing had changed; nothing had changed at all.

He paced up and down under the soft haunting glow of a solitary street light. Incongruous in its setting, it was miles from anywhere. There seemed to be little point to it other than to mark out a single location in an otherwise featureless stretch of carriageway. "Wait by the street light," had been his instruction, but standing out in the open in the middle of nowhere was the last thing he intended to do.

It was a dangerous secretive place, with access to the city itself strictly controlled and monitored. Norilsk was a "closed city", its existence denied, a national embarrassment, an industrial schism in an ancient wilderness.

He needed to stay unnoticed, but once in the city itself he knew it would be almost impossible. He didn't care for scrutiny, but in such a place, it wasn't so much *if* he was being observed, but *who* was doing the observing that really mattered. He self-consciously stepped away from the light, taking cover in the lee of a huge earth-moving machine. It was a mere carcase, way beyond any possibility of repair and long since abandoned.

There was daylight but it was subdued and reluctant. He knew the quality of it would get better as summer went on, perhaps for six weeks more, before finally giving way to months of darkness, an unnatural all-consuming perpetual night-time. The seasons were brutal, a period of constant daylight followed by months of unrelenting gloom. Even now the sun was so low on the horizon it shone pitifully, barely visible through the pall of smog that belched from the chimneys that gave the city its only reason to exist.

The streetlight buzzed in the silence and flickered in the half-light.

He checked his watch. Twenty minutes before his lift was due to arrive.

He studied the grey outline of the city in the distance, the ghostly scare he'd once called home. That hadn't changed much either; it was just as he recalled. It was a truly vile place. Norilsk was nothing more than a godforsaken Siberian outpost, bleak and isolated, its history as bleak as its setting. He knew its origins well enough, built on the agonies of thousands of forced labourers, all victims of the Gulag and the unwilling founders of Stalin's industrial dream city in the north.

The result was nothing less than a dystopian landscape made nightmare by its grotesque proportions and impossible, life-reducing living conditions. It was still the most polluted and coldest city on earth, and to him it appeared to be just as much a prison now as it had ever been. His own childhood had slipped neglectfully away amid its filthy, crumbling tenements.

There were no walls even then, no fortifications or guards, but even so, there had been no possibility of escape. The city was so remote, so removed from the rest of the country, stripped from the nation's conscience and embargoed to keep its appalling legacy hidden. There was nowhere within a credible distance to go and, then as now, no legitimate means to get in or out.

And now he was breaking back into the nightmare. He didn't have the papers, the state ID card or any of the other numerous bureaucratic approvals required to make his journey, but who on earth would really care? Who, that mattered, would even know?

TUESDAY

Chapter 25

It was nearly one o'clock in the morning. The minibar was out of stock of most of the supplies. A couple of brandies, a red wine and three bottles of cloudy beer that gave Paul a headache just to look at them were all that remained.

"Right!" He called the room to order and the girls snapped to attention. "Let's get your things back. I have an idea."

Alisa stared at him blankly as Silvi jumped to her feet.

Paul had been occupied by the thought of it. It was Silvi's sudden appearance through the curtains that gave him the idea. It was straightforward enough. Simply nip over the glass divider between the two balconies, through the open patio door and then back again the same way. But Paul needed to be sure the room was empty. He'd tested his conviction that it was empty on two previous occasions, and Silvi hadn't seen any sign of Boris during her surveillance, but it just made sense to check once more and be certain.

He instructed Silvi to resume her vigil on the balcony once again. Alisa and Paul stood in the bedroom lobby with the door to the bedroom shut and the lights off. Paul bent down and removed the towel. There wasn't a sound, no movement, nothing at all from the room next door.

"I have to be sure," he whispered. "I'm going to knock on the door and wait in the corridor…"

"It's not safe. What if he's in there?"

"I'm sure he isn't, Alisa, but I have to know. I would rather find that out when I'm in the corridor than when I'm on his balcony."

"I can't ask you to do this…" she whispered as emphatically as she could. "We have to find another way."

"You're not asking me. It's entirely my own idea and there's no other way. Now, just wait here and listen. I'll be back in a couple of minutes."

With that, Paul stepped out of the bedroom and closed the door behind him. The do not disturb sign was still hanging, suitably undisturbed, on the hook in the centre of 732's bedroom door. Paul braced himself and, standing to the right-hand side of the door, knocked loudly. He immediately rounded the corner and waited for any reaction. There was none.

Back in the lobby with Alisa, she confirmed the same.

"Right, stay here and listen for any movement in the corridor."

Paul extinguished all the bedroom lights except for one, and it cast a series of eerily disembodied shadows about the room as he moved, which did nothing to calm his nerves. He slipped through the patio doors and joined Silvi outside.

"Okay!" he said, peering in to the gloom and over the balustrade of the seventh-floor balcony. "Let's get this done!"

Silvi helped Paul quietly reposition the table next to the glass divider. He placed one of the chairs next to it and the other on top. Silvi giggled as he pulled a pair of his running socks over his shoes.

"Shhhh!" he whispered, with one finger pressed to his lips. "It'll be quieter."

Paul wasn't sure how successful such stealth tactics would be. This wasn't exactly his day job, but it seemed like a sensible precaution.

Using the chairs and table as oversized steps, Paul climbed to the top of the glass divider and then dropped himself down on the other side. It was disconcertingly easy, as long as he disregarded the fact that he was on the seventh floor and the somewhat difficult relationship he endured with precipitous drops. Paul chose to perform the feat with his back to the balcony edge, and on that basis the plan worked well enough.

He approached the sliding door. It was unlocked and slightly open, easy enough to make his way through. Before entering, he took the further precaution of moving the table on Giorgi's balcony to mirror the position of the one on his own. If he needed to make a break for it, at least he could use it to help him get back to the relative safety of his own bedroom. It seemed sensible, but the ease with which he'd gained access to 732 afforded him very little comfort on that score.

Stepping inside the room felt strange. It was oddly silent, brooding and somewhat unsettling. Paul drew the curtains shut, stepped across to the bedside and switched on the lamp with the back of his hand. *No fingerprints*, he thought, feeling vaguely ridiculous but compelled all the same.

Nothing. The room remained dark. He immediately realised he would have to activate the energy-saving device by the bedroom door before he'd get any light at all. He eased himself through the bedroom towards the lobby. He could see the faint orange glow that located the unactivated master switch on the wall. Even before he slipped the credit card out of his pocket and into the device, he already knew what the room would look like. If he knew anything about hotels at all, his instincts told him the room would be identical to his own in every respect, except it would be mirrored precisely.

There were no surprises as the LED on the wall turned green and the single lamp by the bedside began to glow meekly. The air-conditioning unit hissed into life too. The gloom slowly lifted as the bedside light gradually warmed to its task, increasing its output marginally, imperceptibly. Paul hated low-energy lighting; there was something irritatingly reluctant about it.

With the single lamp casting a modest glow across the room, he quickly swept it for signs of anything that might belong to Alisa. Her handbag, mobile phone and shoes were the main items, but he was looking for anything that might give away the fact that she'd ever been there at all. He was unsure about underwear and had never thought to ask. How would he have couched the question without sounding weird in some way? Alisa hadn't put underwear on the shopping list, so he wasn't sure what he was supposed to think. He sensed himself getting distracted.

He found a shoe and the handbag straight away. He'd seen the handbag before, once in the restaurant on Sunday night and again that evening. Silvi had an identical one in the bedroom next door. The handbag was open, its contents spilled across the floor on the far side of the bed. It appeared to have been searched in haste and then discarded without care.

It was uncomfortable, somehow invasive, picking up her personal items and stuffing them back into the bag with so little regard. Some of the things he didn't want to recognise and made a concerted effort to do it more by instinct, blindly pushing them back into their discreet refuge. But it was hard not to register the condoms, the pump-action bottle of lubricant, a small vibrator, a pair of latex gloves, lipstick, a tiny deodorant, mints and a few other items pertinent to her trade.

Under the bed, he spotted a small dark cylindrical object and retrieved it. It was pepper spray.

Where the hell was that when it was needed?

He tucked it back into the handbag and tried to fasten it shut, but it just wouldn't close.

Paul gave the handbag a shake and tried to adjust some of the objects to free up some space. As he adjusted the contents he noted there was no cash or credit cards. He could only assume that, of the two of them, and despite his earlier conviction to the contrary, it had been Alisa who had been robbed that night.

Giorgi did at least leave her something: a slender pink leather wallet which surfaced from the depths of her handbag and was now stopping the clasp from closing.

It was no more than a credit card holder and contained nothing except a passport-sized photograph that was hanging out of it, only held in place by a single corner. Giorgi appeared to have taken everything else of value and dislodged the tiny photograph from its place of safe keeping in the process. The smiling faces of two children beamed happily back at him from the tiny image – both boys, aged between four and six, he calculated at a guess. They were clearly brothers. They shared similar features and the same light brown hair, one boy probably a couple of years older than the other.

There was no phone.

Paul sat with his back against the bed for a moment and surveyed what he could see of the room. He still held the picture of the two boys in his hand. He knew it would be precious to Alisa and gently eased it back into place. He would make no mention of it when he gave Alisa her personal effects back. The photograph was personal and intimate; it was none of his business.

It was a surprise though. He couldn't help but speculate. Could these two young boys be Alisa's sons? Why wouldn't they be? Could they be the reason Alisa was far from home, sacrificing herself to give her absent children a better life? Mothers do extraordinary things for their children, so it wasn't much of a leap to imagine that Alisa was doing all she could for hers. He found the prospect both humbling and unsettling in equal measure, yet it seemed like justification enough. And after all, who was he to judge?

But he still needed to locate the phone. He was going to need more light.

Then it came to him as a revelation. He was gone. After all the sneaking about, the precautions and the listening at cracks in the joinery, the Russian was gone. There was nothing of his in the room – no clothes, no suitcase and no personal effects. Alisa's abuser had deserted the scene of his crime, and there seemed little prospect of him coming back.

Emboldened by the realisation, Paul turned on more lights. He checked the wardrobe and found it empty. Back in the bedroom he opened the drawers and again there was nothing. By the side of the desk he found the other shoe, hold-up stockings and the smallest pair of knickers he'd ever seen. He stuffed them into his pocket, feeling like some sort of sex pest and dreading the door opening, the local gendarmes catching him in the act.

But where's the phone? There was no sign of it.

He pulled back the bedclothes but again there was nothing. He looked behind the chairs, the curtains and under the bed. There was no phone. Finally, Paul was forced to consider the possibility that the Russian had taken that too. If Giorgi had Alisa's phone, he could have access to everything: her phone numbers, contact details, emails, text messages and even her diary. Paul had briefly experienced for himself just how vulnerable he felt when handing over his iPhone to Alisa. He practically ran his business from it, and now he was certain that hers was gone for good.

Alisa probably relied on her phone every bit as much as he did. It would be just as vital to her, and probably a great deal more sensitive to her clients, given the nature of her business. He understood completely why she was so desperate to get it back. Paul just hoped she was more security conscious with her passcode than he was.

He made his way around the bed on his hands and knees. By the desk he noticed a large dark stain on the carpet. It looked sinister and he felt compelled to take a closer look. He removed the latex gloves from Alisa's handbag and put one on as far as it was possible. They were a small and Paul's hands were a medium at least. He drew a single finger through the patch of carpet; he was sure it was blood. It wasn't entirely unexpected, but it was a problem.

No matter how forensically Paul removed all trace of Alisa being in the room, the presence of so much blood would demand further investigation by the hotel and inevitably the police. They would check the CCTV footage and see her arriving with Giorgi. The cameras would capture their route through the hotel, including, as they headed down the corridor together, towards his bedroom. They would record him leaving at some stage in the early hours of Monday morning, almost certainly carrying an injury and quite possibly his luggage too. And later in the day they would see the same girl leaving the hotel, inexplicably wearing completely different clothes. They would have no choice but to investigate.

Paul was certain there was no CCTV on the short leg of the corridor between rooms 731 to 735, but the approach from the lift lobby, the lift car and reception were all covered by the little black domes that saw and recorded every movement. Alisa being thrown into the corridor had resulted in total inaction on behalf of the hotel. That footage alone would be a witness to the abuse she suffered, but with no CCTV images available of that incident, all evidence would be against her. They would soon identify Alisa's movements from the rest of the footage, and it wouldn't take much detective work to identify her; she had a website, for Christ's sake. Paul assumed, with some confidence, that the local gendarmerie would be more than competent enough to track her down. Then again, how bad an option would that really be under the circumstances? Paul considered that he would take the French police over two Russian hitmen every time.

The solution was obvious: he would have to clean it up; it was the only logical option that came to him. He was tired and confused, appalled by everything that had happened and disgusted by what confronted him. If he could just get rid of the blood, there would be nothing suspicious for the maid to report.

Paul switched on the bathroom light and pushed open the door. His stomach churned and he nearly threw up on the spot.

The bathroom was covered in blood. There was a large pool of blood on the floor and yet more down the side of the bath and over the shower screen. Dark sinister smears soiled the basin and bloody fingerprints marked the taps where it appeared Alisa's victim had tried to wash himself down. Several towels were covered in yet more blood that had formed crusty stains as they dried, a putrid towelling heap stuck together and dumped in the bath. Most disturbing of all was the bloodstained fruit knife on the vanity unit.

A picture began to form in his mind. He knew Alisa had stabbed Giorgi in the leg in close proximity to the desk where she would have been able to reach for the knife – she told him that much herself. Giorgi must have thrown her out into the corridor before retreating into the bathroom to tend his wound and perhaps even remove the knife. That would take some doing, real guts. Not everyone would possess the mental or physical strength to do something like that, but Giorgi was all muscle and testosterone, and Paul had little doubt he was capable of it. What choice did Giorgi have? If he turned up at a hospital with a knife wound the police would be informed as a matter of procedure. That wasn't an option for a man trying to keep a low profile. But he would certainly need to remove it, and that meant he'd need help or he would have to do it himself. Either way, the gruesome patches of congealed blood on the towels in the bath could only be the result of his efforts to control the bleeding. Then there was the discarded knife on the vanity unit near the bath. The picture forming in Paul's mind took on a greater clarity. There was just so much blood here. Whether Giorgi had help or did it himself, he must have sat on the side of the bath as he tried to staunch the wound once the knife was removed. The face cloths were missing too. Paul could only speculate, but maybe they were used as improvised dressings before Giorgi called Boris for help. Paul retched at the thought of it.

There was no wonder Boris had dispensed with Silvi's services so prematurely; things had seriously spiralled out of control in Giorgi's bedroom.

Given the state of the bathroom, it was now no surprise to Paul that room 732 had been vacated. Other than the blood, there was no sign of Giorgi ever having been there at all. He'd left in a hurry too. There was no attempt made to clean things up. He'd just gathered his belongings and left, putting the do not disturb sign on the door to buy himself some extra time.

But how much time did he have? There was no way of knowing how many nights Alex had booked the hotel for, and that was yet another problem. He wasn't around to ask. Alex had abandoned the girls and left them to face all this *shit* on their own. Paul's contempt for him plumbed new depths.

Paul was certain that a do not disturb sign wouldn't deter the maid from her duties if Tuesday morning was checkout day. Paul checked his watch. It was already the morning. It was already Tuesday, and daylight was only a matter of a few short hours away.

As Alisa unlocked the connecting door and slowly pulled it open, Paul tried to reassure her.

"It's okay," he said. "He's gone. He's gone for good. There's no way he's coming back... ever."

Alisa didn't look reassured and peered nervously into the room. Paul gently prised her hand off the door handle and guided her back to the chair that had become her refuge.

He called Silvi in from the balcony.

"Things have changed, Silvi. We need a plan B."

Chapter 26

THREE MONTHS EARLIER
NORILSK, SIBERIA

The man already knew the car was approaching, a plume of exhaust fumes giving it away long before the vehicle itself came into view.

He stamped his feet and shook two disposable hand-warming pads into life inside the confines of his pocket. Carefully he stuffed one of the warming pads inside the palm of each extreme cold weather mitt and over the thin lining of his inner glove, the chemically induced heat bringing his fingers slowly back to life.

As the car approached, he removed one of the bulky mitts, opened his backpack and recovered his weapon. His Heckler and Kock semi-automatic pistol had become his gun of choice recently. He checked the magazine as best he could and then snapped it back firmly into position.

The growl of a worn-out diesel engine broadcasted the arrival of his lift, fully fifteen minutes late. He slipped the heating pad out of his left mitt and wrapped it around the trigger guard as he waited. Moments later he discarded it altogether.

He removed the thin glove from his right hand, checked for free movement on the trigger safety catch, and shoved his ungloved hand, complete with loaded weapon, into the pocket of his padded jacket.

The car drew to halt at the side of the street light and idled noisily in the silence.

The windscreen was clear; he could see the driver was alone, sitting unmoving in the seat. He revved the engine impatiently and then leaned across, releasing the passenger-side door and pushing it open.

His pace quickened in recognition of the invitation and the potential relief from the cold, but he remained wary and alert.

"Get in before we both freeze!" the driver bawled.

He approached the car, his hand still inside his jacket pocket, the gun aimed directly at the driver.

"Relax, my friend. Just get in the car," the other man urged impatiently. He hesitated.

"Just get in and shut the damn door or I'll leave you here to freeze! There's no one else coming to get you. I doubt you'd survive the walk back to Dudinka." The driver laughed at the prospect.

He climbed in and slammed the car door shut. The car performed a U-turn before heading back in the direction of the city.

"You can take your hand out of your pocket my friend... I'm not your enemy."

The driver appeared relaxed and confident. There was no obvious threat, so he complied without acknowledgement.

"So..." the driver said, "they tell me you know our targets. Is that correct?"

"Yes," he replied dispassionately.

"So, I take it there *is* more than one target?"

"Yes," he replied again.

"Two targets then?"

"Yes."

"You don't say much, do you?" the driver snarled.

"We're not here to talk... and I'm not your friend. This is just business, so why don't you tell me how this is going down."

The driver looked pissed off.

"I should have just left you to freeze where you stood," he said. "But you're right, we're not friends." The driver laughed loudly, a contrived laugh at odds with the fragile tension that existed between them.

He floored the accelerator and the car lurched forward before slewing sideways on the ice. Little was gained by way of forward momentum and the passenger was left grasping at the dashboard to steady himself. As the revving engine settled, the driver steered expertly into the skid and the snow tyres regained their grip once again. The cold metal of a gun barrel was at his temple.

The passenger froze.

The driver laughed again, relaxed his grip on the gun and let it fall away from the side of his passenger's head.

"You're right, of course. We are not friends. But I am not your enemy either," he said calmly. Then he placed the gun on top of the dashboard in front of him. He raced through the gears and hammered the throttle again. The car sped away as if on rails.

It was the passenger's turn to ask the questions.

"They tell me you know the location... Is that right?"

The driver nodded sagely.

"They tell me you know when the exchange is going to happen… Is that right?

"Yes, my *friend*. I know these things." But he didn't elaborate further.

After a short silence, the driver drew the car to a halt at the side of the road.

"They call me Roman," he said, and offered his hand and a smile.

He reluctantly shook it, feeling vulnerable with his own hand so far from his weapon.

"I know," he said. "I know what they call you."

A silence followed. The passenger offered nothing in return: no name, no greeting, nothing to resolve the antipathy that still remained.

The driver studied the road ahead impassively for a long moment and then turned to face his passenger. Roman's expression had changed again. He looked all business, and there was nothing friendly in the way he regarded his passenger now.

The passenger settled further into his seat. He knew Roman hadn't survived as long as he had in his duplicitous world by being a genial host. He was a professional assassin, a stone-cold killer, a calculating and accomplished murderer, and accepting any pretence to the contrary could be a fatal mistake.

He surveyed the grey outline of the city ahead as the driver regathered his weapon and placed it out of sight. Norilsk held nothing but bitter memories for him. It was an unhappy place where adults worked long hours, drank strong liquor and indulged themselves to ease the mind-bending drudgery of it all. There was little else to pass the time. Kids were an inevitable, and in his experience, a wholly unwanted, by-product of existence in such a town. The act of perpetuating life in this a place was, to his mind, irresponsible and self-indulgent. Norilsk was no place to start a family, no place for a child, and the last place he wanted to be.

"You will do exactly what I tell you. Is that clear?"

He had never doubted it. Norilsk might well be his home town, but he was only too aware that it was, unquestionably, Roman's world they would be operating in.

"Let's get this done. I don't want to be in this stinking shithole any longer than I have to be."

"Fair enough," Roman said coldly. "Show me the file."

He grabbed his backpack from the footwell of the car and pulled out a manila envelope. He handed it to Roman. The driver removed the contents and studied them without a word. Finally, he pushed them back into the envelope and handed it back.

"I know him. That man is Joel Papé. He's a very serious mark. This is big, my friend. There will be repercussions after this one." Roman let out a long breath. "Anatoly told me he would get Papé to come here. I didn't believe that would happen. Anatoly's a dangerous bastard to know, don't you think?"

"I'm not paid to have opinions," the passenger snapped back in response.

"Anatoly pays well, my friend, but watch your step with him. I've worked for him on many occasions and I wouldn't turn my back on that bastard, not for a second."

"I'm not interested in any of that. Anatoly is paying us to do a job, and that job is Papé. Let's just get on with it."

The driver shrugged.

"Okay. The second target then? Is there another file?" he demanded.

"No."

"Who's the second target?" Roman growled impatiently. "Don't test me. I can be dangerous too."

The passenger ignored the implied threat.

"Whoever hands Papé the money. I assume you already know the deal is a fiction."

"I had my doubts."

"Whoever hands Papé the money is the second target," he repeated, regarding Roman coldly. "That's why we need to wait until the exchange takes place."

"Fine," the driver growled. "I'll take the first target. Papé is mine. You take the money man. Agreed?"

"If that's how you want it to go down, that's fine with me."

"That's exactly how I want it," Roman said with a finality that the junior man had no intention of challenging.

Roman started the car. His expression softened again.

"Hungry?" he asked.

"Yes," the passenger answered flatly.

Roman slammed the old Volkswagen into gear and pulled away, leaving a cloud of noxious exhaust fumes trailing indiscreetly behind them.

Chapter 27

There was never any realistic prospect of asking Alisa to go back into room 732. Paul couldn't expect her to confront all *that*, having just witnessed her reaction when he first opened the connecting doors. It was late, it had already been another very long day and Alisa looked shattered; the sight of all that blood would be just too much.

"Alisa… why don't you get some sleep? We can sort this out."

Paul handed her the handbag, which she immediately clutched to her like it contained everything she valued in the world.

"My phone?" she asked.

"I'm sorry, your phone isn't there, but I've got your shoes and… well… these." Paul discreetly handed her the thong. She took it from him somewhat sheepishly. "If you had any credit cards or money, I'm afraid they're gone too."

She opened the handbag and began searching through its contents. She opened the little pink wallet, pulled the photo from its refuge and ran her finger across the tiny image. Without a word, she slipped it back inside, but her face betrayed its significance to her. It was safe now and restored to her, and she appeared to take some measure of comfort from that.

Suddenly she became agitated again. She shook her head, a look of anguish on her face.

"The letter from my mother?" she said. "Where's the letter?"

"There was no letter. I searched the entire room and there was certainly no letter."

"Then that's how they found Maria. I can't believe it. It's all my fault. They found Maria because of me."

Paul didn't understand why a letter would mean that, but Alisa was distraught.

"We get our families and friends to write to us at Maria's address," Silvi explained with a sense of sadness. "Sometimes we have to move around if

142

Alex needs the apartment. He always finds us somewhere to stay, and we've even stayed at his house on a few occasions, but normally we just use the flat. But Maria never moves. She's been there for years, so she takes our post in for us. When Alisa's family write to her, it is always at Maria's address. Maria just passes the letters on to us when they arrive."

"So, this letter would have Alisa's name on it but Maria's address?"

Silvi exchanged glances with Alisa for confirmation. She nodded.

"So that's why Boris went after Maria at the apartment. He just assumed Maria lived with Alisa."

Both girls looked shattered now.

Finally, something made sense. The letter explained how the Russians found the apartment but not how Alex knew the girls were in danger in the first place. But somehow Alex did know, and he'd tried to warn them. But how or when he found out they were in danger still wasn't clear.

Did Alex think to warn Maria too? Why would he? He wouldn't necessarily know Boris had discovered their address from a letter in Alisa's handbag, and would he have understood the significance of that, for Maria, even if he did?

Paul's mind was racing again.

The room was warm, subdued and felt reassuringly safe. Alisa was worn down by the drama of the last two days and she'd had her fair share of the minibar. The recent revelations and the loss of the letter seemed to have drained her of what little reserves of energy she still possessed. She looked utterly broken as she lay on the bed. Silvi pulled the covers over her and spoke a few soothing words in Russian that seemed to mean the world to her.

"I hadn't even read it!" Alisa was baleful and desolate. "Maria only gave it to me as I was leaving on Sunday evening. I would never take a private letter to an appointment, never…" Alisa's words trailed off to a whisper.

She was still clutching the handbag to her, the photo safely returned and tucked away in its tiny wallet. Paul could readily understand why she would never take personal correspondence to an appointment – that made sense – but he suspected the photograph of the two young boys went with her everywhere.

"Get some rest, Alisa. It won't take us long to have a tidy-up next door."

Silvi was at his side, and with no comprehension of the horrors that awaited her beyond the connecting doors, she backed him up. She said a few more reassuring words in Russian, kissed her friend tenderly on the forehead and tucked her in.

*****

Paul waited in the lobby for Silvi to join him. He closed the door and switched on the lobby light.

"It's not pretty, Silvi. Are you okay with this?"

"Yes, let's just do it." Silvi seemed reassuringly confident.

"Are you okay with blood?"

"Of course," she said. "No problem."

He opened the adjoining doors and led her into room 732. Paul picked up the blood-smeared latex gloves he'd deposited on the desk earlier and started to pull them on.

"Do you have any of these?"

She nodded. Silvi opened her handbag and retrieved an identical pair.

"How bad is it?" she asked.

"It's bad!"

Silvi looked a little less certain now…

"Put the gloves on," he suggested calmly.

She did as she was asked and Paul opened the bathroom door.

"It's really bad."

Silvi was clearly shocked at what she saw. She took a deep breath and Paul could see the distaste on her face, but there was no faulting her resolve.

"I've seen worse," she said.

"Really?" Paul was incredulous.

"No… not really! What do you think I am?"

Silvi was making jokes, even now, and he had to admire her spirit.

"I'll start in here. You have a go at that mark on the carpet. We'll use the towels and then I'll get rid of them in the morning."

What was the worst that could happen? Alex's credit card might get charged for the cost of replacing the missing laundry, but Paul considered that would be a small price for him to pay in the circumstances.

Silvi set to work. She filled a glass with warm water and grabbed a roll of toilet tissue and one of the clean towels.

In the bathroom, Paul removed the shower attachment from its cradle on the bath and put the bloodstained towels to one side. They were dry now and there was nothing to be gained from letting them get wet again. As he worked he was surprised just how quickly the blood rehydrated as he sprayed the showerhead liberally over the worst affected areas in the bathroom.

The shower attachment reached the basin and that took only a few minutes. He was soon rubbing it down with a clean towel, polishing it to a standard that would satisfy even the most fastidious housekeeper. The bath and the shower screen were just as easy; with the bulk of the blood rinsed away, a quick wipe with the clean towel was all it took.

The floor was more of a problem. The blood was thick and congealed, and he began the chore with a fistful of toilet tissue in an attempt to wipe up the very worst of it. He flushed the soiled paper down the toilet in batches. Every now and then Silvi popped in, nodded her approval at Paul's efforts, refreshed her water and flushed away a fistful of toilet paper of her own.

As he worked, his white running socks acquired a pink tidemark that began to creep up and over his shoes. He'd forgotten he was wearing them, and the sight of the blood seeping into his trainers revolted him. He removed the socks and dried the soles of his shoes on a bath mat that was hanging, still clean, from a rail beneath the main towel rack. The mat quickly turned a pale pink, and he was forced to catch his breath as the distastefulness of the chore briefly overwhelmed him.

He stepped back into the bedroom to find Silvi working her way towards the lobby, tackling a series of blood spots he hadn't noticed before on the carpet. She renewed her warm water again and went straight back to it. He searched the bedroom drawers for the standard-issue plastic laundry bag he'd previously spotted in one of them.

He stuffed the bloodstained towels and his socks into the laundry bag and put it in the lobby.

Back in the bathroom, he spotted the stainless steel gully set into the marble floor immediately under the vanity unit. He renewed his efforts, using the showerhead to wash the highly polished surface and manoeuvring the pink liquid towards the gully. He flooded the floor with warm water and rubbed the more stubborn stains with yet more toilet paper. Several more flushes and the dwindling supply of tissue had done its job. It was just a case of rinsing it all away and then allowing the floor to dry. The water ran away with the minimum of effort, and after twenty minutes of work the bathroom floor looked clean – certainly free of bodily fluids and completely clear of blood in particular.

Paul allowed the marble floor to dry and, with another fistful of white toilet paper, he buffed it thoroughly to remove any remnants. There wasn't even a hint of pink left on the paper and he considered his job done.

Silvi had done a fantastic job too, but she was still concerned about the large patch of blood by the desk. Paul took a moment and watched her as she worked. She was kneeling on the carpet in high heels, a figure-hugging cocktail dress and her long blonde hair tied up to keep it out of the way. She was such a pretty girl. How had it all come to this?

Silvi looked up at him, catching him staring at her as he indulgently watched her toil. She managed a smile, a gentle rebuke that brought him self-consciously to his feet. But beyond the distraction of her smile he could see she was struggling. Paul knelt down next to her and pressed his fingers into the carpet. It was nearly dry but a residue of revolting pink liquid still stained the latex of his glove. What more could they do? They were running short of toilet paper and only one clean towel remained.

Paul took a moment to consider their options.

"Do you fancy a coffee?" he asked.

Silvi looked stunned.

"Why not!" she replied, and got to her feet.

In the bathroom, he filled the water container from the Nespresso machine and then returned to the bedroom, where Silvi was waiting for him. He switched the machine on to warm up the water. While he waited, he gave the troublesome patch on the carpet one more thorough blotting with what remained of the toilet tissue.

Silvi sat silently on the bed, and in a role reversal, she watched Paul work for a while.

"Do you work out?" she asked.

"What?" he replied. He sensed he was being teased again.

"Nothing, I was just wondering," she said, grinning.

The Nespresso machine gurgled as it came up to temperature.

Paul made two lungos and passed one to Silvi. He took a sip and savoured the strong rich blend as it slipped down his throat, and then he paused, anticipating the hit of caffeine that would surely come.

"That's good!"

"Well… do you?" she persisted, with a huge grin on her face.

"Drink your coffee. It's been a long day."

Silvi raised the steaming cup to her lips and smiled at him provocatively.

What he did next took her by surprise, but she caught on immediately. Paul knelt down next to the stain on the carpet and poured what remained of his coffee onto the damp patch.

"If there's going to be a stain, Silvi," he said, "it may as well be a coffee stain."

Silvi took a hit from her own cup and then sprang up from the bed and followed suit. Paul popped another capsule into the machine. They had eight to go at, but Paul reckoned four or five would easily do the job.

Finally, he stood back to admire their work. He knew only too well that, despite their best efforts, any forensic examination of the room would easily reveal the true nature of the stain and, almost certainly, the full extent of the blood-letting in the bathroom as well, but it would have to do. No obvious sign of blood meant there was no obvious reason to call in the police. That would be a good result and, in truth, there was little more they could do anyway.

Silvi disappeared into the bathroom one last time. She re-emerged having flushed away yet more toilet paper and depositing the last of the bloodstained towels in the laundry bag.

"Have you forgotten something?" she asked.

"I don't think so."

She didn't say a word but produced the cleaned, yet still potentially incriminating, fruit knife.

"Well…" he said, "apart from the murder weapon itself, I think I had it covered."

They added the latex gloves to the contents of the laundry bag and Paul slipped the fruit knife into his pocket. He didn't think discarding it with the towels was a good idea. Instead, he intended to leave it somewhere to get lost among the rest of the hotel's cutlery. He made a mental note to be particularly selective about the sort of knife he used for the duration of his stay.

Their work done, it was time to get back to his room. He looked around one last time; he intended to leave it looking as normal as possible.

Silvi picked up the laundry bag and closed the adjoining door into Paul's room. Paul remained in room 732. He needed to lock the second adjoining door from the Russian's side and then leave the way he came. As he closed the door, Silvi pulled hers open once again.

"Wait!" she said.

She slipped her hand through the gap and passed Paul a partially used toilet roll from room 733.

"I thought it would be better than there not being any tissue left at all," she said.

He took it without comment.

"Oh!" she said, "…and then there is this!"

She leaned past him and, with a cheeky grin on her face, pulled his credit card out of the energy saver. She closed the adjoining door and plunged him into darkness.

Silvi somehow knew he'd forgotten about that too, and Paul breathed a sigh of relief.

He deposited the toilet roll in the bathroom and then made his way across the bedroom by touch to the balcony doors. It wasn't a problem as he was so familiar with the layout of the room, but all the same, he made an extra effort to avoid the coffee stain they'd so painstakingly manufactured. Paul had certainly had enough of blood for one day, no matter how well disguised it was.

He drew back the curtains in room 732 in readiness for the morning and stepped out onto the balcony. He mounted the table and then, using the improvised steps, let himself down on the other side. He used the winding-pole for the balcony's sunshade to slowly manoeuvre the table on the far side of the glass screen back into its original position.

He was satisfied that the maid would find room 732 in an entirely acceptable condition, notwithstanding the unavoidable conclusion that the previous occupant was, at the very best, a clumsy, caffeine-addicted, towel-stealing incontinent. Paul knew he could readily live with that as an outcome.

Chapter 28

THREE MONTHS EARLIER
NORILSK, SIBERIA

The car was well hidden in a dilapidated storage shed, one of many derelict buildings that made up the decommissioned smelting works. He remembered it from when he was a child, a vast industrial complex now broken and ruthlessly plundered for scrap. It was located on the sprawling eastern side of the city and was notorious for its staggering CO_2 emissions. Norilsk was one of the most polluting industrial centres in the world, and even back when he lived here it was reputed to have produced a hundred thousand tonnes of sulphur dioxide every year and two per cent of the world's entire CO_2 emissions annually. He had no doubt that Station 28 Industrial Smelting Unit, as it was "affectionately" known back then, had played its full part, but even that couldn't save it from closure. Perhaps it had become uneconomic or the stats were just too much of an embarrassment for it to continue. Either way, it had been shut down, only to be replaced with even larger factories that continued to pump out a seemingly endless supply of pollutants.

He checked and reloaded his weapons.

He took a deep breath, the hint of sulphur ever-present, then wiped his hands on his jeans and settled in.

As the minutes passed, he visualised his means of escape, the way back to the car and the various routes he could take to get back out to the main road. It was important to have options,

He watched Roman coolly setting out the tools of his trade. The powerful semi-automatic assault rifle and a Glock 19 9mm pistol, both meticulously checked and positioned at his right hand. Those guns were his trademark. Roman would take the principal shot with the rifle and then use the Glock for close protection as he withdrew. Neither of them was planning on hanging around.

They were both in elevated positions: ten metres up on an overhead gantry littered with packing cases and abandoned equipment. Roman was fifteen metres away to the left of his position. Both men had good cover from the ground yet still maintained a clear line of sight to the kill zone, which was no more than thirty metres in front of them. Roman had instinctively chosen the perfect spot to take his shot. It was difficult not to admire the cold, detached way he went about his business.

It wouldn't be long.

He didn't feel nervous, just a sense of anticipation. He couldn't claim to have the vast experience of his mentor but he knew how to handle a gun, and with Roman at his side he felt they held all the cards – elevation, good cover and the element of surprise. And Roman was exactly the sort of man you would want at your side. He knew him by reputation. He was highly respected in the profession, brutally efficient when required to be, and the go-to man if you could afford his legendary fee.

But this was a big payday for both of them, and there was the promise of more work to come if both targets were successfully dispatched. There was even a bonus for getting the second man.

But Roman had his flaws. He was predictable in some ways; he'd insisted on taking responsibility for the principal kill. Joel Papé was the head of the French syndicate, the obstacle to Anatoly's ambitions in North Africa and the man identified in the file. Roman regarded him as having the highest profile of the two targets. That was predictable.

The junior man was more than happy to be delegated the secondary target. That suited him just fine. The second hit was the bonus shot as far as he was concerned and, in reality, the one shot he already knew he alone had to take.

His earpiece crackled into life.

"It's on!" Roman hissed into his mic.

Two men entered the vast empty shed with semi-automatic weapons drawn. He studied them closely as they approached a table set out in the middle of the kill zone. They appeared alert and on edge.

As he watched Roman settle into his final position, he opened his backpack and recovered the second of his two weapons: the Glock 21 Gen 4 handgun. He fixed an Osprey 45 Suppressor to the barrel, slipped off the safety catch and set it down out of sight. Roman was already lining up his shot.

Two more armed men appeared, a third immediately to their rear. The first party to the exchange had arrived on cue and now they awaited the arrival of the others. He looked over to Roman, who signalled his intent. The last of the five men to arrive was unmistakably the man from the file, Joel Papé, the principal target and now the sole object of Roman's unfaltering attention.

One of the next men to arrive would be the money man and ostensibly the second of their two targets. He raised his primary weapon in readiness. It was already clear that there would be a battle once Roman took down his man, and both he and Roman instinctively checked their weapons once again.

He did the maths: five men in the first party, perhaps five more in the second; two targets and eight more potential kills to consider. The odds weren't in their favour, but Roman was the experienced operator; he was the legend and he looked utterly unfazed at the prospect.

Outside the vast shed a car cruised sedately to a halt. Four men appeared at the entrance. They didn't falter, striding purposefully towards the first party. The lead man held a briefcase. He was all smiles and confidence. Two men stopped short of the table as the man with the briefcase and the fourth approached.

His earpiece crackled into life once again.

"That's Viktor with the briefcase, and Dimitri on his left," Roman whispered. "I know them both. Viktor is Anatoly's second in command. If he's the money man, if he's the second target, Anatoly is even more of a bastard than I thought he was."

He clicked his mic once in response.

"I would happily kill them both for nothing," Roman growled into his mouthpiece as he minutely adjusted the sights on the rifle.

He recalculated. Two targets, seven additional potential kills – the odds had improved marginally.

In truth, and in his experience, albeit limited, once the shooting started and the first kill hit the deck, there was no way of knowing what would happen next. The two parties to the exchange would be as likely to open up on each other as combine their resources to rationally seek out the source of the original shot. All trust would be gone in that instant. All sense of control lost. Rational thought cast aside as each man went for his gun. Who aimed at who would depend entirely on the strength of any genuine trust that might have previously existed between them. Instinctively they would suspect each other, one seeking defence in revenge, the other taking all measures to protect themselves from the bullets and recriminations that would surely follow. All this would take place in the blink of an eye, a few desperate moments, the split-second it would take for the first man to die and the others to react.

Only time would tell, and that time was now.

No sooner had Roman pulled the trigger than the first target was down. Papé hit the concrete floor in a heartbeat – all life extinguished. The bullet entered his head just above his eye, blasting the back of his skull away in a sickening explosion of blood, brain and bone.

Fifteen metres to Roman's right, he reached for the silenced pistol in the same instant, bringing it to bear and pulling the trigger before Roman had time to react. His aim was good. The legendary assassin hit the deck as lifeless as his own target had only a few fractions of a second earlier.

All hell broke loose below him. Viktor and Dimitri had prepared well. Roman's shot was their cue. They opened up with a withering, accurately directed and sustained fire – it all happened before Papé's men could respond. With Papé down, the two parties turned on each other, firing at will, but the Frenchmen were too slow off the mark. Viktor's four-man team fired first and with lethal accuracy, taking their visitors down in a hail of bullets. A few rounds headed in Roman's direction but nothing went back in return.

High up on the gantry, he watched the one-sided battle unfold, unnoticed by the men below. The silencer had successfully disguised the direction of his own shot as he knew it would. It was audible, for certain, clearly heard by the frantic men below him as they dived for cover or took aim in reprisal. But the source of the shot that had taken Roman's life was baffled, distorted and disrupted. The muted sound of the single stifled discharge bouncing off the corrugated roof and walls of the huge shed, its source completely lost and made irrelevant in the melee that followed.

Boris had planned to use the confusion to make good his escape. No one would ever know there was a second shooter on the gantry, just as Roman would never know that, for Boris, there had only ever truly been one high-value target. Not even Viktor had known about that.

With Roman dead and Boris intent on escape, the only remaining threat to either of the parties to the exchange was now entirely and exclusively from each other.

With both his designated targets down, Boris quietly exited the vast shed the way he'd entered it, leaving the men below him committed to a private war all of their own.

The money man, Viktor, had always been safe from him. Once Papé had been dispatched, it was only ever about Roman. Boris didn't know why Roman had to die. It wasn't his place to know and he didn't much care either way. They weren't exactly friends.

Boris had entered Roman's brutal and dangerous world now, and he would learn from the master's mistakes. In the short time he'd spent with the man he had seen glimpses of what made him so extraordinarily successful at his job. He exuded an aura of quiet confidence and was supremely professional when it came to the kill, but there were weaknesses too. He died at the express instructions of his own paymaster and at the hands of a man he considered to be a colleague.

Boris felt no remorse for his actions – why should he? Roman had killed so many times before. The man knew too much, perhaps. Maybe he'd crossed a line or broken an unwritten convention of some unholy murderous code. Roman had spent years working exclusively for men who routinely traded life for cash without sentiment. How could he possibly have expected to remain immune to their capricious violence?

Boris would certainly learn from Roman, and he determinedly committed the experience to memory, allowing it to sear indelibly into his consciousness – a salutary lesson never to be forgotten.

The next job was already agreed. He could almost feel the warming glow of the Mediterranean sunshine on his face as he fired up the Volkswagen and set off for the city once again. It was a two-man job, but even that held no fear for him. It was a simple task and, unlike Roman, there was at least one man Boris knew he could trust completely.

With both targets dead and his bonus earned in full, Boris left Norilsk forever and without a single shred of regret.

Chapter 29

TUESDAY

Alisa was asleep in the gloom and Paul saw no reason to wake her. He tip-toed through the bedroom and slipped into the lobby. Silvi was sitting on the floor, her back to the bathroom wall with two miniature brandies in her hand. Hers was open.

"Thanks," he said, sliding down the wall to sit beside her.

She broke the seal and passed him the tiny bottle.

"Cheers!"

"*Ypa!*" she said. "It's Russian for cheers."

"*Ypa!*" Paul replied as they touched bottles.

Silvi took a good sip of the warming spirit and placed her head on his shoulder. It was a welcome end to a traumatic evening, a night he would never forget – surely the calm after the storm. Silvi's perfume wafted over him. She'd managed a quick spray since getting back, anything to get away from the smell and unpleasantness in the other room.

They sat there for a while not speaking, and the peace was soothing. She settled a little deeper into his shoulder, taking his arm in hers, and he thought she might fall asleep right there and then. Paul looked at her in the mirror on the back of the wardrobe door and was a little surprised to see her eyes wide open, fixing him with a smile. She looked relaxed, peaceful, and there was a little sparkle in her eye. Paul had a drink and rested his head on hers, feeling her soft golden hair against his cheek.

Time stalled pleasantly for a while, and not a word passed between them. Eventually, he became aware of her looking at him with a little more inten-sity, her pretty features captured, reflected, in the mirror.

"What?" he asked in a conspiratorial whisper.

She was looking at him with mischief in her eyes.

"What is it?" He was clearly missing something.

"Nothing," she said, but her smile broadened.

Paul studied her for a moment – her head on his shoulder, her arm wrapped tightly around his – and then he realised. She caught his gaze at the very moment he noticed and the game was up. Paul turned away in mock embarrassment, but she caught him at the instant she intended. Her reflection permitted, perhaps invited, a tantalising glimpse of her legs way above the hemline.

She was daring him to look, teasing him, her legs slightly parted. The grin on her face confirmed that he'd fallen into her trap, and it amused her greatly. She knew he couldn't resist, no man could, and she revelled in the moment his eyes were drawn to the smooth curve of her inner thigh and beyond.

"Naughty!" she said, mocking him, and Paul died a thousand deaths.

"I'm sorry. I wasn't…" He protested his innocence.

"I know, I know!" She was beaming. "Very naughty!" she said again. Her smile was broader still and she made no effort to protect her virtue. She didn't move, and now he was locked in a battle of mind over matter. He took a distracting drink of brandy, playing for time. It was a game to her, and Paul had no doubt she had played many like it before. He was certain her win rate would be spectacular.

Her face lit up with delight; she knew he was struggling. Silvi waited, anticipating his failure. It would only be a matter of time before he let himself down again. It wasn't long. He could feel his gaze falling. He was powerless to stop it and he could tell Silvi was all too familiar with such weakness. Silvi started to sway her right leg shamelessly. She was teasing him again and he was helpless.

"You looked!" she declared. Silvi was triumphant.

"I didn't!" he protested again, but he had.

She knew men well enough and Paul was evidently no exception. He was Alisa's "Nice" man all right, but deep down he was just like the rest, and he sensed that Silvi knew it too. Paul knocked back the rest of his brandy. The bottle held more than he thought and he struggled to choke back a cough.

"I'm going for a shower," he announced, defeated, "and then… I think we should get some sleep."

Silvi watched him stand and let him go without a word. In the bathroom Paul chastised himself silently.

You're nearly old enough to be her father. You should be ashamed of yourself!

He turned the shower on, stripped and stepped in. The warm water washed over him and he savoured its cleansing power. He realised then just how grubby he felt. It came as a shock, and he urgently set about the soap, scouring away the filth and grime he had come to associate with room 732.

The bathroom door opened. It backed on to the shower and he could only see Silvi through the mirror over the vanity unit. The roles were reversed now, and he saw the humour in what she'd done. He was naked, exposed and trapped; she was fully clothed and in full control.

Paul felt hopelessly self-conscious. He turned to face the wall, the water cascading down his back, his head turned to see what she would do next.

She entered the bathroom, kicked off her shoes and stood at the basin in front of the shower. She started to wash her hands, her face and then her neck. He couldn't take his eyes off her. Her green dress clung to her young body and her hands seamed to glide sensuously as she groomed. She knew what she was doing, making him pay in full measure for his indiscretions.

She looked around to see him staring at her, still with his back self-consciously turned towards her. She picked up the pink toothbrush.

"May I?" she enquired.

"It's Alisa's. I'm sure she won't mind."

Paul's breath was short and he couldn't disguise it. He couldn't believe the effect she was having on him. It was way past three o'clock in the morning, it had been one a hell of a day and yet Silvi still retained the power to seduce and arouse. She applied a little toothpaste to the brush and proceeded to bend over at the sink rather more than was truly necessary.

The green dress rode high on her thighs and her firm rear began to wriggle provocatively from side to side as she brushed. She never took her eyes off him. She fixed him with a reflected stare and watched him, awkwardly smiling back and acknowledging the full extent of her win. Touché. He was forced to accept he was entirely at her mercy. Silvi was clearly enjoying teasing him and she was playing her hand well.

She put the toothbrush down and turned to face him, leaning back against the vanity unit. She put her hands up to her head and ran her fingers through her hair, the little green dress riding up higher still. Things weren't getting any easier. Silvi loosened her hair and shook it down, a few stray curls falling seductively across her face.

She bit her lip and peered up at him through the golden veil of her unkempt mane.

"Show me!" she said, her voice deep and seductive.

"What?" There was no way he could turn around now; the game was up and he was completely exposed.

"Turn around, let me see!" That voice again. She pushed herself away from the vanity unit and stood opposite him. She was irresistible, seductive and utterly in charge. He couldn't explain what possessed him, but he did as she commanded. Paul stood there, naked and compliant, as she knew he would.

Silvi bit her lip again, looking him up and down.

"Why Paul!" she exclaimed suggestively. "You are full of surprises…"

Silvi stepped confidently up to the glass shower door and placed her hand on it at a height just below his waist, and she lingered there for a moment. He was transfixed. He would have stayed there until she told him otherwise.

She stepped away from the glass and pulled the shower door open. The water continued to cascade over his shoulders and down the full length of his body, and now it spilled out onto the bathroom floor. She took hold of the hem of her dress and, in a single continuous movement, pulled it slowly over her head.

She stood there naked, her figure stunning. Silvi reached out once again and brushed her fingers gently down his chest, down over his stomach and beyond. Paul tensed at her touch and stared into her eyes, which never wavered in their gaze.

Still holding him captive with her smile, she eased him forward until the water flowed down his back. Silvi entered the shower and dropped to her knees, taking him into her mouth.

She was soft and gentle at first, building and controlling – he was completely under her spell. He should have stopped her, he could have said no, but as his breath shortened and the sensations started to overpower his senses, the words were simply lost.

The shower engulfed them both now. Her hair lay flat against her head, his hands resting on her shoulders as she moved effortlessly, indulgently, relentlessly. She took both his hands in hers and held them. Then Silvi's gaze turned to the mirror and he obediently followed it there, the intimacy of her actions heightened, exaggerated by their very reflection. Her eyes narrowed and her breathing became short, coming in controlled gasps. Then she sighed, as if her pleasure was mirroring Paul's exactly. She saw him looking at her, transfixed, studying her, and now she knew she had him completely. Deliberately she changed tempo, more slowly but deeper, longer, her reflected features conveying her hunger for the moment.

He could hardly get his breath, her passion taking control of every part of him, and still she teased him. And then she changed the rhythm again, more sensuous, more intimate, deeper still. It wasn't going to be long.

"Oh my God!" he called out.

She seemed renewed, her gasps conveying her desire. He could barely stand, but he braced himself on the glass, a crushing wave of pleasure about to wash over him. Still she continued, her technique changing again, there was an increasing intensity in the way she held him but somehow softer too, more slowly now, yet unrelenting, her breathing matching his, low moans accompanying every stroke. It was too intense, but he didn't have the energy to stop her or even the slightest intention of trying.

Finally, she released him, but her hand seamlessly took over. The same rhythms, the same stroke as before as she slowly rose to her feet. He could feel her body pressed firmly against him, his skin alive to her touch. Silvi's breasts brushed his stomach and then his chest.

He felt her lips at his, her hot, minty breath on his face. She kissed him. It was sensuous and intimate. She ran her tongue across his lips. Paul's mouth opened involuntarily and she kissed him deeply.

Now she placed her cheek by his, her mouth slightly open, brushing at his lower ear, and all the time her perfume was drawing him closer to her. Gentle moans again, as if the full extent of his pleasure was entirely mutual. Her hand was working faster now. A sigh, and then she pulled him fully to her, as if their bodies could merge into one. Her skin was against his, her hair damp and fragrant, her slender fingers caressing the back of his neck. All the time her other hand picking up a pace as Silvi's intent became more urgent and inevitable. Moments later he was racked in release, his senses flooded by a consuming tide of pleasure that completely overwhelmed him.

And now she was done. All he could do was hold on to her, braced against the cool marble wall. He kissed her on her cheek as she slowly relinquished her absolute control. As he gathered his thoughts, she raised herself once more to his ear.

"My turn..." she whispered.

He was still coming down, the fatigue and receding waves of latent pleasure still causing his mind to drift. He opened his eyes, taking her in fully as she stood wet and naked in front of him. He would have given her anything...

"You want me to...?"

"The shower, silly. It's my turn for the shower – out, out!" She grinned and shooed him out of the cubical with a gesture of her hands.

As he stood there, naked, spent, shattered and dripping wet, he could see her in the mirror still. She was beaming again. She placed two fingers on her lips, kissed them and planted them on the glass, level with his mouth. And it was over.

Wrapped in a bath towel, Paul stood in the lobby, feeling rebuked by his own image in the full-length mirror on the wardrobe door. The bathroom door was shut and he was momentarily alone with his thoughts, his conscience kicking in fully fifteen minutes too late. Now it taunted him with the obvious but untimely conclusion that recent events should never have happened at all.

How could he have been so weak? Silvi was so young and he should have known better. Paul knew he hadn't taken advantage of some naïve innocent, but he still felt bad all the same. She'd initiated everything, reeling him in, using all the skill and guile of a woman many years her senior. But age had nothing to with it. Even given her tender years, her experience of men was almost certainly greater than most women he'd ever met.

Silvi appeared to instinctively know what made men tick, and she'd worked him out for sure. Maybe all men are fundamentally the same, he considered as he struggled to justify his own frailty. Right now, Paul couldn't imagine any man, worthy of the title, who could have readily resisted her charms. Or perhaps he was just being disingenuous, willing to embrace an unflattering gender stereotype in his compulsion to excuse himself?

It was a performance – utterly compelling, but a performance all the same. Was he just another job to her? Is that all it was, just another day at the office? He was tormented by the thought. It was inconceivable that she just wanted him; that would be ridiculous. A man with an ego far greater than his would still struggle to convince himself of that.

Paul hated the thought that Silvi had just paid him in kind for helping her and Alisa. The thought had occurred to him at the time but, to his eternal shame, he'd discarded it at the same moment he'd lost his moral compass.

Paul imagined that Silvi, and Alisa for that matter, would have a different relationship with sex than most women. How else could they do what they do? But that didn't make him feel any better either.

Silvi and Alisa still needed his help, and maybe it was just an easy way to lock him in. But if men were so transparent to her, Silvi must have known that no such sacrifice was required on his account. He was already locked in and committed; Paul needed no such inducement to stick around. But, then again, perhaps it was because Silvi knew men so much better than they actually knew themselves that she felt she needed to.

He was merciless in his belated, self-inflicted guilt. But wasn't he the weak, naïve one in the piece? Silvi knew exactly what she was doing; he'd given her no encouragement. Maybe it was so much simpler than that.

Perhaps, after all his introspection, Silvi was just amusing herself and it was just a distraction from all that had gone before. Although the physical pleasure was all his, he had no doubt she enjoyed the control, the manipulation and seeing him helplessly under her spell. Perhaps it was nothing more than that.

What troubled him most was Alisa – what would she think of him now? He felt at the very least that he'd betrayed her trust, and not for the first time. He'd crossed a line, and what made it worse still, it was with Silvi, her closest friend. Whatever his relationship was with Alisa, he'd convinced himself it was, at the very least, predicated on trust, and he'd jeopardised it once again with his own petty weakness.

He slipped under the duvet. Alisa was fast asleep, seemingly miles away on the far side of the vast bed. The bedside lamp was still lit and he lay there facing her in the half-light for a moment. She looked lovely, restful and oblivious of so much that had unfolded in the early hours of that morning. He was glad she hadn't woken up; he wasn't sure he could look her in the eye right now.

Paul was still lost in his own self-indulgent musings when Silvi came to bed. They hadn't discussed sleeping arrangements, it had never occurred to Paul, and he doubted that neither Alisa nor Silvi had given it a second thought.

Silvi climbed under the duvet next to him, fresh and naked, her hair still warm and fragrant from the dryer. Without a word, she switched off the light and snuggled up like it was the most natural thing in the world.

Paul placed his arms around her; it felt like the right thing to do. She seemed to mould herself to him, her head on his shoulder, her arm across his chest, her leg over his, gently forcing her foot between his calves.

Despite the intimacy, there was nothing sexual in her embrace, and Paul felt a powerful, compelling responsibility to protect her.

He was tired, so tired, but sleep evaded him. He was feeling somewhat overwhelmed by the events of the last forty-eight hours, and it didn't help that, although it was Silvi he held in his arms, it was Alisa he couldn't get out of his mind.

The evening drew on and sleep remained stubbornly elusive. He lay staring at the ceiling listening to Alisa and Silvi sleeping soundly in his care. It was only when he resolved to be utterly honest with himself and Sophie as soon as he returned home, that he was finally able to close his eyes and allow much-needed rest to come.

Chapter 30

TUESDAY

The curtains were still drawn, yet the morning's early light seeped into the room as the sun rose on another glorious morning on the Côte d'Azur. There was movement from the far side of the bed and Paul became aware of Alisa at his side. Silvi was still fast asleep. She hadn't stirred all night; neither of them had. He felt a sudden and urgent need to move, to change position and rearrange his aching limbs, but he was still pinned and fixed in place by Silvi as she slept on.

"Morning, sleepy," Alisa said. She was up close and personal, having made her way across the huge bed. "You snore. Did you know that?" she growled with mock authority. "I'm not letting you sleep on your back again if you're going to snore all night!"

Paul considered the implications.

"Firstly... I don't snore," he protested, "and secondly, I take it you're planning on sticking around then?"

"Maybe..."

Paul took a moment to consider whether the prospect of the girls staying another night was, in fact, the bad idea his instincts were telling him it was. Alisa, perhaps sensing his dilemma, smiled sweetly, and his instincts were dismissed in a heartbeat.

"Are you hungry?" he asked.

"I'm starving."

Alisa seemed energised. She bounced out of bed and headed for the curtains. Paul couldn't help but notice that she'd shed the bathrobe at some point during the night and now stood naked and silhouetted in the half-light. He turned away before she could become aware of him staring at her as she busied herself, fussing about in the gloom.

"You better give room service a call. I can't move. Silvi's got me in an armlock."

"Just wake her up," Alisa suggested firmly. "She gets grumpy if she sleeps too much."

With that, she threw the curtains wide open, allowing the brilliant morning sunshine to flood the room. As Paul's vision adjusted to the light, she scooped up her bathrobe and slipped it on before turning around.

"Can you pass me a pair of boxers from the suitcase, please?" Paul was suddenly aware of his own predicament.

"Come and get them!" she said, teasing him.

"Please?" he pleaded, and he tried to look as pathetic as possible. The look clearly came naturally, and without any further teasing, Alisa foraged for a few moments until she came up with something she appeared confident fitted the bill. She threw a fresh pair of "M&S specials" as hard as she could towards his face, and Paul reacted just quickly enough to catch them before they landed.

He untangled himself from Silvi, who grumbled a little but otherwise just resumed the position minus him. Under the duvet, he wrestled his way into the boxers before scrambling out of the bed on Alisa's side. She watched his performance with an undisguised look of amusement.

"You're going to have to get over all this shyness with us around, you know."

Paul fought back. "I don't see you parading around naked," he ventured, with a conviction that carried sufficient weight to imply he hadn't noticed her nakedness earlier.

"Of course not. What kind of girl do you think I am?"

It was obvious she enjoyed his all too evident discomfort, as the question sparked all manner of responses in his mind.

Paul picked up the bedside phone and ordered continental breakfast for three, which was, he noted to himself, something of a first for him. It was going to be forty minutes to an hour before it was ready, which wasn't particularly "five star" as far as he was concerned.

"Paul?" Alisa sounded serious. "We really did appreciate your help yesterday. We both did. This whole thing has been very frightening for us. I know it's all my fault and I don't know how I can ever repay you for all the kindness you've shown us."

Paul's mind drifted back to the shower incident in the early hours of the morning. It occurred to him that the slate had, in all probability, already been cleared. He cast the thought from his mind.

"Honestly, I'm happy to help." Paul was sincere.

"I know! I do know that, but even so... I wish we'd met under different circumstances."

The ambiguity and context haunted him for the moment. The only realistic way he would have been likely to meet her under different circumstances was if he was one of Gary's "thousand pound a night hooker types". It wasn't only the funding that was an issue. It just wasn't his scene.

"Breakfast isn't going to be ready for ages," he said, changing the subject. "I'll go for a quick run and then we'd better get Silvi some clothes. There's no way either of you can go back to your apartment, and she can't walk around town in that green dress. She'll stick out like a sore thumb."

Alisa looked unsure about the analogy but grasped the concept.

Paul grabbed some socks, his trainers, a t-shirt and a pair of lined running shorts from the suitcase, and headed for the lobby to change. At the door, he stopped, turned to face Alisa, whipped off the "M&S specials" and pulled on the shorts.

"Not so shy now!" he said, laughing, his face flushed red from the skirmish with his own insecurities.

"Why, Paul!" Alisa exclaimed with a feigned demure, "You are full of surprises!"

He was immediately transported back to the shower incident in the early hours of the morning once again. He needed some air. On his way out, he palmed the fruit knife from room 732, picked up the laundry bag stuffed full of soiled towels, and headed for the lift, closing the bedroom door securely behind him.

*****

When he got back, Alisa and Silvi had made themselves very much at home. They were each enveloped in oversized bathrobes and relaxing in the armchairs awaiting his return. A familiar selection of breakfast items was laid out across the bed, on the coffee table and still more on the desk. There was a tempting and plentiful supply of food but nothing had been touched.

"Start without me, ladies. Please don't wait. I'm just going to get a quick shower."

"Paul?" Alisa called after him. "Before you go…"

Paul stopped.

"Yes," he said.

"I was just wondering…"

"What?"

"I was just wondering if you might like… well I was thinking… would you like some company?" She could hardly contain herself. Silvi had obviously told her everything.

"Ha ha, very funny!" Paul said, cringing, uncertain how to react. "It wasn't my fault, she made me," he protested in an attempt to make light of things.

But it was already obvious to him that the very issue that had kept him awake for a good part of the night was of little consequence to the girls; just a bit of fun and nothing more.

"He's quite right," Silvi said, jumping to Paul's defence, a massive grin on her face. "I made him. He didn't stand a chance!" Silvi was giggling uncontrollably.

The two girls were completely at ease with it all, and he realised, there and then, that he needed to stop judging them by his own narrow view of the world. He felt a little envious that they were so comfortable with matters that seemed to confound and unhinge people far better adjusted to life than he was.

"One at a time then please, that's all I'm asking," he said, his bravado just a mask for his deepening embarrassment.

"Are you sure about that?" Alisa countered, as tears of laughter rolled down Silvi's face.

Paul wasn't sure about anything and retreated alone to the bathroom.

He showered and dressed. He selected the least creased pair of suit trousers, an open-neck shirt and a pair of highly polished black shoes. He left the jacket in the wardrobe and joined the girls for breakfast. The smell of freshly baked croissant and the last of the Nespressos filled the room, the aromas reminding him just how hungry he really was.

They worked their way through the bread and cheese, assorted pastries and fresh fruit in no particular order, washing it all down with freshly squeezed orange juice, a pot of English breakfast tea and strong coffees individually brewed to order.

"Right, we need to get Silvi something to wear," Paul announced as he polished off his lungo.

It was agreed, Alisa was to put together another shopping list. Clothes, a few essentials and anything else they could think of between them to assist in changing their appearance. It was obvious that Silvi couldn't walk around in the little green cocktail dress, and both girls needed a few personal items that couldn't be borrowed or improvised from the meagre pickings of his washbag.

There was no way Silvi and Alisa could hide away in the hotel forever either, so changing their appearance just seemed to be a sensible precaution and something they could be working on while they decided what to do next. Boris and Giorgi had only ever seen Alisa and Silvi in their professional guise, so plain and simple was the order of the day as far as Paul was concerned.

Silvi tried to call Maria, but her phone went straight to voicemail. It was still early, and under normal circumstances that wasn't particularly unusual,

Alisa explained. But things were far from normal. According to Alisa, Maria would routinely switch the phones off until midday, if only to catch up on some sleep after manning them into the early hours. But after everything that had taken place in the last twenty-four hours, both girls were decidedly uneasy that they were still unable to contact her, even this early in the morning. Surely Maria would be as desperate to be in touch with Silvi and Alisa as they were to speak to her? Silvi was going to keep trying.

Alex was more of an immediate concern; his phone number was completely unobtainable.

"Alex is always on his phone. It's never switched off," Alisa declared with a note of genuine concern in her voice. "He runs his entire business from that phone. I've never known him to switch it off, or for it to be unavailable for that matter. Even if he doesn't answer straight away, it always goes to voicemail."

"But not today," Paul observed. "Anyway, what exactly is his business? What else is Alex into?"

They declined to elaborate, simply choosing to ignore the question, but Alisa was a little more forthcoming about his work ethic. Whatever Alex was into, he conducted business almost 24/7 and, according to Alisa, his contacts were not the sort of people that even he would keep waiting. They were both becoming increasingly convinced that something terrible must have happened to him.

"Or he's still working with them?" Paul considered.

"There's no way he would do that now. Not after what's happened. He would never do anything to hurt us." Silvi was adamant, but Alisa held her counsel.

"Under the circumstances," Paul offered thoughtfully, "no matter what has happened to Alex, even if he does get in touch, just don't tell him anything. He'll understand if he cares about you. We can't take the risk that he might still be working with them. I imagine Boris and Giorgi can be very persuasive when they need to be. We have to at least consider the possibility that he might not have any choice about what he does next."

"He's not working with them!" Silvi snapped. "He sent me the text message and he called me three times. He tried to warn us!"

"Even so... for now, just promise me. No texts and no emails... not until we know for sure."

Silvi stayed silent.

"I'm just asking you to be careful, that's all... and Alex will understand. If he cares about you at all, Silvi, he *will* understand." Paul concluded his reasoning, but it was Alisa's nod of agreement that swayed the argument.

Silvi wasn't convinced at all, but Alisa was on board. Reluctantly Silvi accepted her friend's lead.

With nothing much else to do for now, Alisa and Silvi were to remain in the hotel room, and Paul, with no great enthusiasm, resolved to go to the conference after dropping off the shopping list with the concierge. He harboured mixed feelings about leaving them, but he was in Nice on business of his own and was keenly aware he'd already missed way too much of the event. It was about time he re-engaged with his original agenda.

Silvi's phone was on charge, courtesy of his invaluable charging cable, and she agreed to text him immediately if there were any developments.

He set his phone to vibrate and headed for the lifts.

Chapter 31

TUESDAY

In the hotel lobby, Paul handed Alisa's shopping list to a concierge he hadn't met before.

"Good morning, sir." The concierge smiled as he diligently scanned the list. His eyebrows rose disconcertingly at a number of the items, but finally he nodded his agreement.

"*Oui, monsieur*, that is not a problem." But there was a problem. Something was clearly troubling him. The concierge looked Paul up and down; he was discreet but his concern carried just enough authority to warrant a query.

"What is it?" Paul duly enquired.

"The sizes, monsieur, are you quite sure?"

"Yes absolutely," Paul confirmed with no intention of explaining.

"Of course, sir..." But there was still something. "How would you like me to pay for the er... the items, monsieur?"

"Sorry... With this this, if that's possible?" Paul took a credit card from his wallet and handed it to the concierge.

"*Merci, monsieur.* I'm sure we can do that for you..." There was clearly another query coming.

"It's 5 5 5 5," Paul said.

"Of course, sir." He was unfailingly polite, yet his tone implied that the simplicity of the PIN wasn't entirely unexpected. The concierge was totally unfazed by the request but still held obvious reservations, perhaps not least among them his guest's somewhat ambitious estimation of his own personal statistics.

"By midday... is that possible?" Paul asked.

"Maybe." He gave a Gallic shrug to emphasise his predicament. "It is difficult, sir... so many *items*. It may take some time." But there was a lack of finality about it that implied that the task might be accomplished if the motivation was right.

"Of course."

Paul took out his wallet once again. Inside were a few fifties and a twenty. Paul went for the twenty.

"The hotel is *very* busy, sir," the concierge advised as he scanned the contents of the wallet.

"Of course." Paul took the hint. He removed a fifty and handed it to the concierge, who did a plausible impression of being surprised by his generosity.

"Midday, sir, that is no problem at all."

*****

It was seminar day, as Paul had suspected. He was completely unprepared, having still neglected to consult the agenda. With no knowledge of which of the presentations he was supposed to be attending first, he merely opted to join Gary and Doug, escorting them into whichever seminar room they were heading towards.

The first seminar was tediously entitled "Data Capture and Interrogation". The speaker was American and predictably enthusiastic about his subject. Gary and Doug were appropriately engaged once again, but Paul found himself checking his phone every few minutes and was totally unaware of the topic at hand.

The previous night had been long and eventful and he was fighting a losing battle to stop his mind from wandering, from drifting back to Alisa and Silvi, to the room next door and the state of the bathroom. The half-gloom of the seminar room did nothing to aid his concentration. He felt isolated from the present and almost entirely lost in his own thoughts. It had been an extraordinary couple of days and Paul was forced to admit he'd completely lost his focus.

It was 11.45 am when the phone vibrated.

The session had broken at eleven-thirty and Paul realised he was sipping a cup of coffee he didn't recall pouring in the first place. He was standing in the third-floor lobby outside the seminar rooms, and Gary and Doug were nowhere to be seen. He'd been somewhat distant all morning and perhaps they'd just given up on him. He couldn't really blame them if they had.

It was a text. It simply read:

They have Maria. We need you.

The phone number on the screen was Silvi's.

*****

168

When Paul got back to the room Alisa was already in the lobby, tears flooding down her cheeks. Silvi ran over with her phone held out at arm's length, presumably for him to read the message displayed on the screen. The text was in Russian, a point seemingly lost in their distress. He allowed the door to shut behind him and stepped over the shopping bags that lay abandoned in the lobby untouched. The concierge had clearly earned his tip.

"The text is from *my* phone," Alisa managed to say. "They've got my phone, Paul."

"Okay, what does the message say?"

Silvi was the most coherent.

We have your bitch Maria. If you go to the police we will kill her and then we will find you and kill you too. Stay away from the police and we will let her go when it is done.

"When what's done?" Paul barked. "What the hell is going on?"

Silvi withdrew the phone and tapped on an attachment linked to the message. She presented Paul with the phone once again.

The text was accompanied by a single video file. Now open, it revealed the image of a woman – he presumed it must be Maria – tied to a chair. Silver tape was stretched taut across her mouth, her head was bowed and her lank hair hung across her face. Tears streamed down her cheeks – the woman looked haunted and desperate. As the short clip came to an end, the image zoomed in before freezing on a close-up of her eyes. The terror captured within them gripped him monetarily. He sensed her pain, her vulnerability.

Paul took the phone and studied the final image closely.

There was little in it to give away the woman's location. It looked like a basement perhaps or a garage, certainly a place of utility. What detail there was gave few clues: white walls, a dark unfinished floor, a basic metal chair, but nothing else to distinguish it.

"Is this Maria?" he demanded. Matters were escalating. He needed to know exactly what he was looking at.

"It's all completely my fault," Alisa said, sobbing. "All of it!"

Silvi nodded confirmation to Paul's question but couldn't bring herself to say the words.

"Do you know this place? Have you seen it before?"

He doubted they would have, but it was worth a try.

Alisa couldn't answer. Silvi shook her head in despair.

He tried his best to calm the girls. Both were distraught. They each seemed to be blaming themselves for their part in Maria's predicament. Alisa clearly blamed herself for everything, but Silvi wouldn't allow her friend to shoulder the guilt alone.

"I heard the banging on Maria's door at the other end of the phone when she hung up yesterday," Silvi said while sobbing. "I knew something was wrong but I didn't do anything about it. I was too scared to even consider what it might mean for her. Boris must have gone back for her after I ran away, after I abandoned her to those pigs."

"It's not your fault, Silvi. None of this is your fault. There's nothing you could have done to help her."

Silvi took no comfort from his words.

"Think about it… there's nothing you could have done to stop Boris from taking her. He could have taken you hostage as well if you'd stayed to help. You did the right thing, Silvi." He turned to Alisa. "And you mustn't blame yourself either. The only people to blame for all this is Boris and Giorgi. No one else."

But Silvi wasn't listening. The colour drained from her cheeks as the memory of the previous day suddenly jolted back in detail.

"'I have to go, little one. Don't worry about me. Just stay safe.' That's what Maria said to me just before she hung up." Silvi was shaking now. "Maria knew Boris had come back for her and she still put my safety first, ahead of her own."

Paul guided the girls into the bedroom and very deliberately placed Silvi's phone down on the desk.

"Sit down, both of you."

They did as they were told. He sat on the bed opposite them.

"Right." Paul was short on patience. "Alisa, I know there's so much more to all this. You need to tell me everything you know. Don't leave anything out. You have to tell me right now."

"Tell him!" Silvi urged her. She obviously knew more than she'd let on previously, but now Silvi looked angry with Alisa too. "Tell him. You have to."

"It is all my fault. I should have told you before. I'm so sorry. Poor Maria, they're going to kill her! Maria is going to die because of me!"

Paul sensed Alisa's hopelessness deepening with every syllable. Silvi shook uncontrollably. What comfort they had found in each other's company had deserted them completely.

"No one is going to kill anyone. They're just trying to frighten you." He reassured them with no basis for any such analysis. "They're just bullies, that's all. Don't worry about them, just focus on Maria. Tell me everything you know, right now, then we can decide what we need to do next."

Paul tried to sound confident, but he knew he'd been out of his depth since the early hours of Monday morning. This latest revelation would merely determine by how much.

Finally, Alisa began.

"When I was with Giorgi in that room there was a file on the desk. He was drunk and he went to the bathroom. He took ages and I just started looking around to pass the time. I looked inside it…" She paused to look at Silvi.

Whatever else Silvi did know, the file was as much news to her as anyone else.

"What about it? What did you see?" Paul said urgently.

Alisa could barely look at him.

"The file. What was in it?" he demanded.

"I know why they're here, Paul. I've seen it. I shouldn't have looked, I know that, but I couldn't ignore it once I had."

"Okay, so there was a file. What did it say?" His patience was wearing thin. Alisa's reluctance and vulnerability was fast losing its charm.

"But they will kill you too. If they think you know, they will kill you – both of you."

"No, they won't, Alisa. That's not going to happen. Forget them. What was in the file?"

"They're going to take a girl and kidnap her. There were photographs, and there were photographs of a man too. I think they're going to kill him as well."

"Why would you think that?" Paul demanded. Now that Alisa was finally talking, he was convinced she was being melodramatic. How could she possibly know they intended to kidnap or kill anyone? It was all too unlikely, all far too far-fetched. Alisa was unravelling in front of him and it seemed her imagination was running wildly out of control.

"There was a big red cross on the photograph. It was over his face. They're really bad men, Paul. Alex knows some very dangerous people, but these two are the worst I've ever seen him with. Maybe they will kill Alex too." Alisa paused again.

"Okay, let me get this straight," he said calmly in an attempt to play down Alisa's wild interpretation of the file's contents. "You think they're going to kidnap someone and kill a man because of a red cross on a photograph. Is that it? Have I got that absolutely right?"

"Paul," she said, with tears still in her eyes. "They're not scared of me going to the authorities because of what happened between me and Giorgi. It's because I know why they're here in Nice, and they think I took some photographs last night that would prove it to the police if they got hold of them."

"Alisa… why would he think you have their photographs? When Giorgi threw you out of his bedroom you had nothing! You were naked! How could they possibly think you have any of their photographs?

"No, no, it wasn't like that. He didn't know about the photographs then, but he would have found out that they were missing later, after I got away from him"

"Okay." Paul took a deep breath. "Take your time, Alisa, and tell me exactly what happened."

"When he came out of the bathroom he was very aggressive. I told you what happened, what he did to me, and then I stabbed him in the leg to make him stop. He threw me out of his bedroom and that's when you came to help me."

"But how does he know that you've seen the file? Why would he think you have their photographs?"

"Because I hid some of them while he was in the bathroom. I knew he was a pig and I didn't want anything to happen to the girl in the photograph. Paul, I took the photos and I hid them. I was going to wait until the morning and then tell the police where they were. It's not easy for me to speak to the police. They would be more interested in what I was doing in the hotel in the first place, and I didn't think they would believe me anyway. I don't know what I was going to do really, but if I called the police in the morning and told them where they could find the photographs in the bedroom, I thought they might take me seriously. But after what happened, I couldn't go to the authorities. After I stabbed him I was too scared to tell the police anything."

"It's okay, Alisa, I understand that."

Alisa was in full flow now.

"I suppose they didn't want to stay in the hotel after what happened. But when he threw me into the corridor he wouldn't have known anything about me hiding the photographs. They would only have found that out when they next looked in the file. That's why I was scared to leave the hotel. I thought they might come back to look for them… or for me. That's why they're trying to find me. When they realised some of the photographs were missing, they would know that I was the only person that had access to them last night."

"I don't understand why you didn't just tell me all this in the first place?" Paul could feel his frustration building. "Why didn't you just tell me?"

"I was scared, Paul. I didn't know what to do. I didn't know how much I could trust you. If you hadn't helped me that night I don't know what would have happened to me. How could I tell you that I'd just stabbed a man in the leg or anything about the photographs? You would have just turned me away or called the police yourself. I couldn't have blamed you if you did. You didn't know anything about me. Why wouldn't you call the police? I just didn't think I could tell you."

"Okay. Okay… Let's not worry about that right now."

"And now they've taken Maria," she said, sobbing again. "Before this, it was just about me. They only wanted to get me. I didn't want to tell you or Silvi about the photographs in case they came after you too. It wouldn't be fair. And after I stabbed him, Paul, I couldn't go to the police either. I stabbed him. I could have killed him."

"It's too late for all that now. We're all involved, so we may as well know it all. And trust me, I'm certain you haven't killed Giorgi. He's very much alive so we need to know everything. Is there anything else?

"I wish you had killed the bastard!" Silvi contributed unhelpfully.

"Look, no one is dead and no one is going to die, so let's get that straight, and they aren't going to go to all the trouble of kidnapping Maria just to kill her either, are they?"

"But the man with the red cross?"

Paul didn't have an answer for that.

"One thing at a time. Let's just deal with the photos first. Alisa, where are they now?"

"They will still be in the room, I suppose. I pushed them between the bed base and the mattress. They must still be in there."

"Right, I'm going next door," Paul declared, instantly getting to his feet. He headed directly for the balcony before the girls could say another word. Paul was in no doubt the photographs were important. He'd work out exactly how important later.

It was straightforward enough. He would climb the balcony one more time, straight over the glass dividing screen, go in through the patio doors and grab the photographs. Once he'd found them, he could use the bedroom door like anyone else and Alisa could let him back into 733 without the drama of scaling the balcony on the return trip. Simple!

Paul faltered for a moment. As he scanned the distant balconies for potential witnesses, the possibility of an unintended and life threateningly rapid descent to the square below snapped sharply into focus. They were on the seventh floor, and without the blanket of darkness to mask the drop, the altitude was that bit more intimidating. At least it was a one-way trip.

Fuck it! Paul thought. *What's the worst that can happen?*

Alisa and Silvi followed him onto the balcony and just stared at him in disbelief as he regathered his nerve.

"What if somebody sees you?"

Paul was past caring. It had taken only a few moments to get over the glass partition the previous night and he knew he could do it again. If anyone saw him, and if he was challenged, he would pass it off as a bit of middle-aged bravado for the two girls he was currently entertaining in his hotel bedroom. Paul didn't much care about having to defend that either right now. His conscience was clear on that score anyway. The Silvi incident was just two consenting adults having fun. No money changed hands and, even if it had, he was all but single anyway.

"There has to be another way, Paul," Alisa protested.

"We're out of time, Alisa. If the maid services that bedroom, she'll find the photographs and then who knows what will happen. If the images are as incriminating as you think they are, the police will be involved for sure. The way I see it, you're linked to those guys, whether you like it or not, and then there's the blood. Clearing up all that blood will have been a complete waste of time. Boris and Giorgi have long gone, and you'll be left answering all the difficult questions. It will be you that's in deep shit if the police link you to that bedroom. They'll start with you and then what? If they start asking questions about Boris and Giorgi, what are you going to do? What are you going to say? 'No comment' isn't going to cut it. Think about it. Think about the consequences. If Boris and Giorgi find out you're talking to the police, what do you think they'll do with Maria? What do you think they'll do to you? We can't wait. If there's any chance of keeping you out of this mess at all, we need to do it now. We don't have a choice."

He pulled the table next to the partition once again, climbed up and dropped himself over onto the far side. He quickly got inside the room and easily located the photographs wedged between the mattress and the bed base, exactly as Alisa had described. He snatched them from their hiding place and headed for the door and then froze. The instant he took hold of the door handle he heard the electronic bedroom lock swiped from the other side and the door handle started to depress.

There was no way he could make it back to the balcony, let alone scale the glass partition to make his escape. Paul dived into the bathroom and closed the door. There wasn't time to switch the lights on. He just stood there, motionless in the darkness. A clawing chill swept over him as the hairs on the back of his neck bristled. He recalled the horrors he'd encountered the first time he'd entered that room. He imagined the blood, the knife and the red tide mark enveloping the white sport socks he'd used to cover his shoes. He shook the thought from his mind as he heard someone enter the bedroom.

It couldn't be the Russians. Surely they wouldn't come back after all this time? It must be the maid. Paul had nothing to lose.

"*Pardon!*" he called out without any great understanding of the correct vocabulary. His Franco-Russian accent was almost certainly appalling, but it did the trick.

"*Pardon, monsieur,*" came the response, and he heard the maid withdrawing from the room. It was now clear to Paul that Tuesday was the day that the Russians were due to check out, the day that even the do not disturb sign lost its authority to conceal the events and aftermath of all that had happened in room 732. The truth was, he'd recovered the photographs with just seconds to spare.

A few short moments later, Paul was out in the corridor. The maid was nowhere to be seen and Alisa let him back into room 733. Paul breathed an uncertain sigh of relief: mission accomplished, but what next? What precisely was he supposed to do next?

Chapter 32

The first of the A4-sized photographs was of a girl, tall and beautiful, poised and elegantly dressed, her long brunette hair immaculately coiffured. Her features looked Russian, and Paul couldn't help wondering if all Russian girls were attractive, or perhaps he was just fated in some way.

The second photo was of the same girl getting into a car, looking more casual this time in fitted jeans and a designer top, but still glamorous and certainly expensive.

The third photograph was of a man. He was tall, athletic and in his late-twenties. It appeared to have been taken covertly, the man striding out in a black suit, a tieless white shirt, and completely oblivious to the attentions of the photographer. He had shopping bags in one hand and something small dangling from the other. It appeared to be a key fob; Paul looked more closely – a BMW key fob to be precise. The car in the previous picture was a sleek black BMW saloon; surely that was a link? A thick marker pen had been used to draw a large and somewhat disconcerting red X across his face. Its meaning was far from conclusive, but it was unsettling all the same.

The next image was of the girl sitting casually in an al fresco restaurant enjoying the sunshine with a couple of friends. The man in the open-neck shirt was sitting alone at a table some distance from the girls, dark shades in place, the newspaper neatly folded and an espresso-sized coffee cup at its side. Paul recognised the restaurant immediately – he'd been there before.

The final image was of the same restaurant, and according to the date and time stamp in the bottom left-hand corner, it had been taken ninety minutes later than the previous photograph on the same day. The girls were gone, just the man in the open-neck shirt remained. He looked relaxed, very much at ease, shades still in place but jacketless, the paper refolded but clearly well read, and a cappuccino-sized coffee cup had replaced the espresso.

"That's the girl!" Alisa declared, as she handed Silvi the first image. She seemed to be relieved that the photographs confirmed her story. "Look on the back. It's got her name written on it."

Paul turned the first picture over. The name Katia Shapiro was scribbled in blue ink.

"I know her!" he said, somewhat enthusiastically.

"How? Who is she?" Silvi found her voice.

"I don't *know* her exactly," Paul replied, a little less enthusiastically. "But I've seen her before, in a magazine downstairs in the foyer. There's an article all about her."

"What does all this mean?" Silvi was holding the picture of Katia Shapiro getting into the car. On the reverse were a series of numbers accompanied by dashes and yet more numbers. At the top of the page someone had written the phrase "*1er* étape", or was it "*1er* étage"? Further down, and in different handwriting, there was the word "*зарезервированный*" in what Paul immediately presumed was yet more Russian.

Paul was focused on the numbers for now.

"These have to be dates, and these could be times," he suggested, and he passed the photo to Alisa. She nodded her agreement.

"And this?" Paul pointed to the Russian text at the bottom of the page.

"In English, it means… 'reserved'," Alisa said confidently.

"What about this?" Paul moved on to the French phrases at the top of the page.

"It's either means 'first floor' or 'first stage'. The handwriting isn't clear. It could be a *p* or maybe a *g*. I'm not sure. But it is either 'first floor' or 'first stage', I am certain of that." Alisa angled the page as if to get a better insight, but she still couldn't decide.

"Okay, we're making progress."

Paul was comfortable with the consensus as far as it went, not that any of it made much sense. Just more questions: the "first floor" of what? The "first stage" of what? What was being "reserved"?

"This is Alex's writing, isn't it, Alisa?" Silvi sounded convinced.

"Yes, definitely."

There was no room for doubt any more in Paul's mind. Alex was definitely helping Boris and Giorgi. If Alisa's interpretation of events was to be taken seriously, it was entirely possible that he was assisting them in nothing less than a plot to kidnap Katia Shapiro. The girls looked devastated by the prospect. They clearly knew what Alex was, the people he mixed with and the murky world he inhabited, but the prospect of him being involved in the abduction of an innocent young girl certainly left them shaken, if only fleetingly.

"Could he really be mixed up in all this?" Paul asked. "Really?"

Alex was clearly a more complex individual than he'd imagined – one minute a hero to the girls, the next the villainous architect of a plot against another girl no less innocent than either Alisa or Silvi. How did this man manage such contradictions?

Paul moved the conversation on.

"So… if Alex has written down the numbers and the French text, who's responsible for the Russian writing at the bottom of the page?"

The girls stared blankly at the script.

There was clearly no way of knowing the answer, so Paul moved on again.

"What is it about the photos that made you think this girl is going to be kidnapped?"

The photos seemed odd, definitely suspicious, but there was nothing to suggest to him that kidnapping was the obvious conclusion.

"He told me, or at least he said things when he was hurting me. I told you about it…" She looked more quizzical than convinced.

"No, I don't think you did. What did he say?" Paul's voice sounded weary and resigned. *"We need to know everything,"* he'd said earlier, yet still the revelations came.

Alisa looked hurt.

"He was drunk," she said. "As I told you, he was really drunk, and he called me Katia when he grabbed me. I thought it was strange, but I'd already seen the photographs by then and I already knew the girl was called Katia Shapiro."

"You didn't tell me that, Alisa." Paul let out a sigh of frustration. He was losing his patience with Alisa and now he didn't care if she knew it.

"He just grabbed me and told me that he was going to…"

Alisa stopped.

"Go on…" Paul demanded, with no patience left. "Come on, Alisa all of it…"

"He called me Katia and he said he would…" She took a deep breath before finally letting it all out.

Paul knew he was pushing her hard now and sensed the dam was about to break. He'd left her with nowhere else to go. There was no choice now. She was compelled to tell it all in detail, even if it meant reliving it once again. He sensed her gathering what reserves she might still possess, steeling herself to face the full horror of what happened to her. He knew it was harsh, but he stayed silent, forcing her to continue, and now the words spilled from her lips as the raw pain of it all clawed at her emotions.

"He said he would screw me like the whore that I was. Paul… he said he would send me back to *my father* in pieces. I know he meant Katia's father, but I was so scared. He said it would mess with *my father's* head if I went back to him with my face spoilt. He said he was going to rape a pretty little rich girl and then cut my face to teach *my father* a lesson. He said I was a spoilt bitch who needed to experience some of life's brutality for myself. He talked to me as if I was Katia Shapiro. He forced me to strip. He pushed me to the floor, onto my knees. He grabbed my hair and held me down. I couldn't move because he was too strong. I was so scared I couldn't get away from him. He thought I was her… he kept on calling me Katia. He forced my mouth open as he tore at his belt, at his trousers. I couldn't break away. Then he forced me to…" Alisa paused. She couldn't go on.

"Oh my God, Alisa, I'm so sorry. I had no idea." Paul suddenly felt terrible. "Look, take your time. Let's take a break. I'm so sorry…"

Silvi was at her side. Alisa had been through so much and Paul knew he'd pushed her too far.

"He said all those things to you…" Silvi said, sobbing. "I had no idea. Why didn't you tell *me*?" Silvi flung her arms around her friend.

No one spoke for a moment. Alisa finally filled the silence.

"I didn't think I could ever say the words," she said.

Paul was devastated for her and appalled with himself.

"I'm sorry, Alisa," he said. "I just had no idea…" He stepped out on to the balcony to give the girls a moment to themselves. Silvi caught his eye.

"It's all out now, Paul. It's better this way," she reassured him, but it didn't make him feel any better.

After a few minutes Paul stepped back into the room.

"I'm going to get one of the magazines from reception. It might be useful, and it will give you both some time together, without me…"

Alisa held out her hand and Paul took it gladly. She gave it a squeeze.

"It's okay. I just need a moment," she said. "It was all so horrible."

"I know and I'm sorry. Take as long as you need."

Paul picked up his iPhone as he left the room and checked it out of habit.

There were several text messages from Gary. The terrier just couldn't leave things alone. The first message was blunt and straight to the point. **What happened? Why the emergency exit again?** Paul knew he meant well, but it was all too intrusive. The second text struck a similar tone. **You were off before I could catch up with you. What's going on?** And then a more conciliatory note in the third. **We'll be done by four thirty at the latest. Perhaps we should all meet up later?** Paul didn't respond to any of them.

Immediately below Gary's messages, the "Call Sophie" reminder was displayed on the screen once again. Paul dismissed them all with a single click of the *Home* button and headed for the lifts.

Chapter 33

It was a full half hour before Paul headed back to the room. He'd read the article twice, in full, and was now desperate to take a closer look at the photos. The girl in the magazine and the girl in the photographs were unquestionably the same person.

He grabbed a bottle of mineral water from the minibar. He offered it first to the girls and then took a long cool draught for himself.

"Maria is the priority," he declared as he gathered up the images. "But we do need to find a way to warn this girl Katia. We can't go to the police, but we can at least warn Katia Shapiro about the danger she's in."

He laid the photographs out in a considered order on the desk.

"Right now, we don't know how to find Maria, at least not yet, but we do know they're holding her to stop either of you going to the police. Based on what you've told us, Alisa, and the photographs, we know this is all linked to what they're planning to do with Katia Shapiro."

He held up the first image as if to emphasise his point.

"So, to help Maria, it might help us if we understand what these bastards have got planned for Katia. Are you up to going through the photos again?"

"I think it might help," Silvi added.

Alisa nodded and wiped her eyes with a fistful of soggy tissue.

He started with the first image, but it offered very little other than to identify the girl. Her name was written on the back, but that was it.

Paul turned to the second picture. It showed the girl about to climb into the black BMW. The car was outside a magnificent building, which, for now, he didn't recognise. Could the location be significant? Or was it just the girl that caught the photographer's attention?

"Where do you think this was taken?" Paul said.

Alisa was on a different tack.

"There were lots of pictures like this one," she said. "Her getting into the car..."

"Really?" That seemed odd to Paul. Why would anyone take lots of pictures of the same thing? In the digital age taking multiple images of the same subject was entirely routine, but why would they print them all out? Multiple printed images of the same subject must mean something.

Alisa handed him the picture with the times and dates written on the back. Paul sparked his iPhone into life and brought up the calendar.

"Look… if these are times and dates, all the dates are Fridays and the times are within twenty minutes of each other. Alex must have been watching her for weeks."

"The other photographs – were they always in front of the same building?" Paul asked.

Alisa looked studiously at the image.

"I'm not sure. I think so. I remember wondering why anyone would take so many pictures of the same thing. I think it must be the same place."

"What about the car?"

"Yes, always the same, a black car."

Alisa appeared absolutely certain about that, but just being sure about the colour left room for doubt.

"It's a black BMW 5 Series with blacked-out windows. Can you be sure it's the same car?"

"I think so. I'm not good with cars, but it was always black."

Paul moved on.

"What about the clothes?"

"No, they were different. She was wearing different outfits in every photograph. She has some amazing clothes. They were definitely different each time."

Trust a girl to spot that! Paul thought, but it was a good result all the same. Different clothes meant different days as far as he was concerned.

He silently summarised their progress. Alisa had seen multiple photographs of the same girl, on different days, getting into the same car, outside what was possibly the same building. That had to mean something too.

"Could it be a fashion shoot of some kind? That could explain the different outfits?" Silvi asked casually.

That seemed unlikely. The photographs weren't posed as far as Alisa could remember. They were similar in style to the photo of the man with the red marker pen daubed across his face – covert and taken from a distance.

"So, we can rule that out." Paul moved on. "What made you hide this picture in particular?" he asked Alisa very directly.

"I don't really know. It was on top of the pile and it had the writing on it, so I thought it might be more important."

Paul was confident her instincts were right. The writing was on the reverse of the picture, which, in turn, was on top of the pile. It seemed to him that it may well be summarising the content of some of the other images. There were ten dates and ten times listed.

"Can you remember how many pictures there were like this?"

Alisa shook her head.

"Roughly?" Paul didn't want to give her any clues.

"I'm not sure…"

"Fifty perhaps?" Paul suggested finally, the deliberately high number was intended to provoke an instinctive response.

"More like ten or twelve," Alisa confirmed.

Paul was comfortable with that. He felt they had arrived at a plausible explanation for all the similar photographs, but he still needed to know where they were taken.

Silvi jumped in.

"But if she is the daughter of a billionaire, wouldn't she have some protection? A bodyguard maybe." Again, Silvi had a good point.

"She does – look, the guy with the bags. He's not a personal shopper, is he?" Alisa said, seemingly much brighter now. "He could be her bodyguard though." She pulled out the photograph of the man with the increasingly ominous red ink *X* across his face.

The man looked fit and athletic; he wasn't a meathead like Giorgi and Boris, all brawn and no brains. The guy in the photo looked smart, intelligent and confident. If Paul had been the billionaire father of a beautiful twenty-something, this guy was exactly the sort of individual he would put in charge of her safekeeping. On second thoughts, he was a little too good-looking for any daughter of Paul's, imaginary or otherwise.

"Are we sure he's not just the boyfriend?" Silvi suggested.

"No way!" Alisa was adamant. "Look at the photograph – he's driving the car and she's getting in the back. There's no way he's the boyfriend."

The front windows of the BMW were fully wound down in the image, and Paul could see right through the car, with the driver clearly visible at the wheel. It was the same man.

Beyond the car, on the wall of the building, he spotted five gilt letters individually affixed to the stone façade and spelling out the word "HOTEL"; it was barely legible, but they were there all the same. Maybe those few letters could prove vital, one small piece of good fortune, a lucky break he was only too aware they desperately needed. If the car had been parked even slightly differently, "HOTEL" would have been completely masked from view.

Paul turned to the photograph of the three girls in the al fresco restaurant, the athletic-looking man sitting at a separate table nearby. That wasn't the behaviour of a boyfriend either, but it was exactly how you might expect a chauffeur-cum-bodyguard to act.

"He's the chauffeur!" Silvi decided.

"Yes, but I still think he might be personal protection as well. If she was my daughter, and I had Shapiro money, I wouldn't be taking any risks."

Paul tapped the photograph as he considered the implications.

"Wouldn't the chauffeur just stay with the car?" he asked.

The truth was they didn't really know, but despite his relaxed demeanour in the restaurant, he still looked alert and engaged in the first image, becoming rather more casual in the second. At the end of the day it didn't matter – chauffeur, bodyguard or both – he definitely wasn't the boyfriend, and it seemed obvious to Paul now that Boris and Giorgi had quite literally marked him out for special attention.

"He's hot too," Silvi commented unhelpfully.

Paul ignored the intervention and moved on.

"According to the article in the magazine, Katia Shapiro spends her Friday afternoons in the al fresco Häagen Dazs restaurant in Monaco" – Paul held up the image as confirmation – "and then goes shopping with her friends."

"So?" Alisa chipped in.

"So... If they're looking to snatch her, they would be looking for the right opportunity. If she has a routine, that just makes it easy for them. If we're right about the time and dates, they already know where she's going to be on Friday afternoons and roughly what time she's going to be there. So... if I had to guess, and I suspect that is all we can do, one of these locations is where they're going to do it. All we need to do now is to work out where the other photograph was taken, and I think I have a good idea where it might be."

Paul picked up the picture of the girl getting into the BMW. He told them to look at the wall of the building, through the open front windows of the car.

"Can you see what it says... right there?"

It was tiny and the girls strained to see it. But there was no doubt it said "HOTEL".

Result!

"Do you recognise it?"

They hesitated.

"It's not in Nice," Silvi finally concluded. "We know all the hotels in Nice."

Paul suddenly felt a little uncomfortable.

"All the good ones anyway," Alisa added, sticking her tongue out for effect.

It made him smile, but he still found the girl's professional familiarity with the city's hotels unsettling.

"It's definitely not in Nice!" Silvi looked confident now.

Paul grabbed his iPad and handed it to Alisa.

"Why don't you get on the net and search for images of all the top hotels in the area? It's so distinctive you might find it from there. Start with the Hôtel de Paris and the Hermitage in Monaco… call it a hunch."

Alisa immediately set to work.

As Alisa tapped away, Silvi caught his eye for a second time. She'd already worked out that Paul was pretty confident he knew where the hotel was, and whatever he was doing now was just mind games, a distraction for Alisa as she diligently searched the web for confirmation.

Silvi looked at herself in the mirror and flicked her hair over her shoulder with a flourish. She disappeared into the lobby and came back with a small flimsy plastic bag from the shopping the concierge had delivered to the room earlier in the day. She rummaged around for a few moments, eventually picking out a tiny sachet.

"Say *adieu a Silvi la blonde* and *bonjour a Kira la rouge…*" And she sashayed her way to the bathroom without a backwards glance.

Alisa looked up and smiled as she passed. They performed a low-five as if all was well in their world.

"*Je sais que vous aurez l'air beau, mon ami,*"[1] Alisa replied, and blew her a kiss.

Paul was none the wiser but realised he loved it when the girls spoke French. It wasn't the greatest revelation of the day, and even the mysterious *K* signature on Silvi's return email had just been explained. Things were starting to fall into place. Kira was evidently Silvi's real name, and yet one more little secret was shared.

Alisa put the iPad down. Her eyes were alight, the glint complementing the smile that suddenly illuminated her face.

"I've found it," she said. She was calm and composed at first and then burst with excitement. "I've found it!" Alisa jumped up and grabbed him. "Look… It's the Hotel Hermitage in Monaco… Your hunch was right!"

"Who's a clever girl then?" he said, grinning.

"I am!" she said, looking up at him. Then "*le penny*" dropped. "You knew! You already knew!" And she hit him softly on the arm.

"I was only guessing, but I had a fair idea it would be one of them."

"You already knew!" she repeated.

---

1. *I know you'll look beautiful, my friend.*

Alisa was still holding him. She fell silent and looked into his eyes once again.

"It's going to be all right, isn't it?" she asked, her words still tinged with fear. "Things are going to work out and Maria will be all right?"

"Of course it is," he said. "Maria is going to be fine."

Alisa placed her hand on the back of his neck and gently guided him to her. Her lips touched his in a slow and gentle kiss. It wasn't passionate but it was intimate, and Paul felt utterly exposed by it, as if she could know him completely from that simple brief embrace.

"I'm not sure I deserved that," he said, and then he silently rebuked himself for saying anything at all.

"You will never know just how much," she said, placing her head on his chest, her arms under his, with her hands pulling him closer to her.

"I'm sorry about earlier. I didn't mean to upset you…"

She looked up momentarily.

"Shuuuush," she whispered. "Just hold me."

He felt the damp warmth of her tears as they flowed, and the gentle rhythms of her distress.

"No more tears, Alisa. We need to be strong now…"

"Just hold me…" she said sobbing.

And he did.

Chapter 34

"What do you think?" Kira made her grand entrance trailing yet another written-off hotel towel behind her. She stood in front of the mirror and groomed her freshly dyed hair indulgently. She couldn't help but notice the less than enthusiastic reaction.

While Paul doubted blonde was her natural hair colour, red was certainly not her best look. But despite Kira's obvious reservations too, she did look very different. Looking different was the priority, and right now she looked nothing like the blonde he first saw when she was working as her alter ego, Silvi, on Sunday night. That difference was all that mattered. The all-new Kira was a good result whichever way he looked at it.

She sat at the end of the bed regarding herself in the mirror. Then she teased her hair into various configurations in an attempt to reduce the impact, but nothing seemed to work.

"Anyway," she said, "I think I know how to find Maria..."

The comment was casual but it stopped Paul dead in his tracks.

"How?"

Paul and Alisa looked stunned at Kira's sudden announcement.

"Well, I was thinking... What if we could find Boris or Giorgi – that would help, wouldn't it? They might lead us to her... What do you think?"

"Yes they might, but I think they'll be keeping a low profile right now." Paul wasn't sure where Kira was heading. "But go on."

"But if we could find them, that would give us a chance of finding Maria," Kira persisted.

"Yes, a good chance, maybe. We might be able to follow them. We've got nothing else. What do you have in mind?"

"I know where they might be at eleven o'clock tonight," Silvi declared. She stopped teasing her hair and turned to Alisa. "You do too," she said.

Alisa looked blank.

"How?" Paul was incredulous.

"Alisa has an appointment tonight at the Negresco. Don't you…?"

Kira waited for confirmation. Alisa nodded slowly as her friend's insight started to crystallise in her own mind too. Paul got it immediately but found himself momentarily distracted by the relaxed manner in which the girls reconciled their duplicitous lifestyles.

"Boris and Giorgi have Alisa's phone, so they'll have her diary too," Kira went on. "They've already sent us the text message, so we know they have access to it. If they've gone through the phone, they'll know she has an appointment tonight at the Negresco and what time she has to be there. If they know all that, they might try and find her there. I know they've taken Maria as a hostage, but if they could get their hands on Alisa too, they might even think they could get their missing photographs back. What do you think?"

It was a revelation and a genuine breakthrough. Paul was in no doubt the phone would have been searched forensically by the Russians by now, and if they did that, they would definitely know about her appointment.

Paul did his thinking out loud.

"They'll have accessed all the texts and voice messages you sent to Alisa too, and anything that Alex might have sent as well." Immediately he regretted the indiscretion, but he needed to know.

"Did you mention the hotel in any of your messages?"

Kira shook her head. "No, definitely not." She was adamant.

Alisa's face dropped and the colour drained from her features. He sensed both girls stiffen at the prospect.

"No, we didn't mention the hotel, but what about Alex?"

Paul didn't care about Alex, but he could see the girls did, and they were piecing it together for themselves. Alex might be up to his neck in all this, but he did send the text messages. His instincts were to warn the girls, and for Paul, that did buy him a little credit. But if the Russians knew he played a part in helping the girls evade them on Monday morning, there was every possibility they could have turned their unpredictable attentions on him as well.

But Alex wasn't Paul's concern. There were more pressing matters than Alex's welfare for him to consider. He wasted no time fretting for the Russian fixer and moved the conversation on.

"What time is the appointment again?" Paul asked, deep in thought. He needed to plan.

"Eleven o'clock, for two hours," Alisa confirmed.

Paul died a little inside as the more prosaic implications of the appointment hit him hard. There was no question of Alisa going to the appointment.

Paul had already decided that wasn't going to happen. He knew it would have to be he and he alone that would go to the Negresco. It was the only option that made any sense and the only option that, while still risky, was even remotely safe.

Paul had no great love for Maria. After all, she was complicit with Alex in trading the girls as far as he was concerned. Maria bore her own measure of guilt, but even so, he wasn't going to leave her out there and alone, a hostage to two brutal Russian gangsters capable of such violence, even against women. There was no doubt that the affection the girls felt for Maria was genuine enough. She was innocent too in her own way – just another vulnerable cog in the same wheel that was, through no fault of their own, spinning wildly out of control.

"I'm going to need a car." Paul was thinking out loud again.

"I can borrow a scooter. It will be easier to hide, more manoeuvrable, and you'll be able to follow them on that." Kira seemed delighted with the plan and totally untroubled by any real appreciation of the dangers. Her enthusiasm was infectious and the plan was instantly agreed.

While the girls busied themselves with the rest of the shopping bags, Paul took some time to think things through.

If he waited at the Hotel Negresco, he could easily identify the Russians if and when they turned up looking for Alisa. That in itself wasn't too risky. Neither of them had seen much of Paul, unless they could remember him from the restaurant on Sunday night. He doubted that. Their full attention had been taken by Alex and their lovely, if temporary, companions, Anna and Silvi. There was always the incident in the corridor when Giorgi first ran into him, but that was a lifetime ago. Paul doubted the Russian would remember him from that brief yet close encounter and, given the circumstances, he was fully prepared to take that risk anyway.

The truth was they had nothing else. They couldn't go to the police and they couldn't just let it happen. The priority was Maria, but they still needed to find a way to stop the Russian thugs abducting Katia Shapiro. There was no way he was going to allow Giorgi to carry out his vicious threats on that poor girl, and if anything, that one revelation alone made him more determined than ever.

At the end of the day, they would either turn up or they wouldn't. As far as Paul was concerned, there was nothing else they could do. As things stood right now, it was their best if not their only opportunity to find Maria, and on balance, they had absolutely nothing to lose.

Chapter 35

TUESDAY

Kira phoned ahead but still insisted on going with Paul.

The scooter belonged to her "special friend", according to Alisa. He was the suspicious type, not a man who took too kindly to strangers. Kira also argued, not unreasonably, that she knew the city far better than Paul did and he would struggle to find the tavern in the old town without her help anyway.

Paul failed to find a significant flaw in her logic and, with all arguments to the contrary lost, Paul and Alisa were left with little choice but to agree. He knew he needed to check out the Negresco before tonight. It was broad daylight, and the city would be packed with tourists and local people going about their business – just how dangerous could that really be?

Kira accepted a few tweaks to her new look, and although she bore little resemblance to the vision in blue from Sunday night, she was still very much a vision, only this time in jeans and t-shirt with her hair scooped up and coiffured in a medium shade of strawberry.

The bedroom door closed with a reassuring click and the do not disturb sign was once again left swinging from its peg.

*****

Paul sat at a table outside while Kira went inside to speak with her friend. He watched as she was greeted warmly and then as she disappeared deep into the gloomy recesses of the tavern. He felt a little out of place. It was a congested, decaying part of the historic quarter, where narrow streets and passageways connected courtyards and tiny squares, many with churches and ancient water fountains at their heart. Kira had been right about the old town being a maze. He would certainly have struggled to find his way without her.

Her friend's bar was tucked away, almost lost within the street scene, and not the sort of place tourists would normally frequent. A few might wander by, delighting in the brooding nature of the place. They might even declare it fascinating, authentic or even atmospheric, but all such descriptions would be little more than romantic euphemisms for what was, for the most part, a dark, foreboding inn half-sunken in a crumbling façade.

There were few people inside, and none but him sitting at the disorderly jumble of tables in the street. Paul doubted warm sunny afternoons were its peak time for business, not that any sun penetrated this far into the old town. It was cold, damp and menacing, more a place of the night, most likely frequented by a handful of locals and even then, Paul speculated, only by locals of a particularly sinister persuasion.

Five minutes later, Kira returned with a set of keys and two crash helmets, one in pink and the other in white. They both looked small, but it was obvious Paul would be getting the pink one, which was marginally larger than the first.

Kira led the way.

At the rear of the building, a scruffy timber door gave access to a dark cluttered courtyard. There were four scooters amid the boxes and packing cases that filled every part of it. There was barely enough room to reverse the oldest of the four battered-looking machines out onto the street, but Kira struggled manfully. Paul, for his part, held the creaking door open, supporting its weight for fear it would collapse from its rusted hinges before the manoeuvre was complete.

It was a tired relic of a scooter and in desperate need of a clean, but it started first time, whining and screaming as Kira piled on the revs to prevent it from stalling.

"It's temperamental!" she shouted over the din.

She put her helmet on and got on as if it was second nature, revving vigorously just in time as the motor coughed and spluttered.

"Get on," she ordered. "I'll show you how it's done." She glanced back, indicating the vacant passenger seat behind her.

Paul hesitated. He needed to drive.

"Get on," she insisted. "Or I'll go without you." She revved the engine again, and a plume of black fog spilled from the exhaust.

"You need to let me drive," Paul began saying, but there was no point arguing with her. Kira was stubborn, he already knew that, and it was obvious she was used to getting her own way.

No sooner had Paul straddled the machine than she was off. The motor screamed with the exertion and a foul cloud belched out in their wake as they tore down the road. As they twisted and turned through the maze of the old town, the streets became increasingly crowded and harrowingly narrow. Yet they made good progress, with Kira expertly picking a route. Apart from the nerve-shredding nature of her Franco-Russian driving, he was forced to concede, if only to himself, that Kira was a demon operator and he did feel very confident with her at the controls.

Eventually they hit the Promenade des Anglais and a few minutes later they were outside the flamboyant old hotel itself. The Negresco was imposing and unmistakable, a landmark hotel in a spectacular location. Kira slipped the scooter between two parked cars, killed the engine and kicked the machine expertly onto its stand.

"We'll take a look around outside to start with," Paul suggested.

He carried both helmets while Kira fixed her hair.

They took what he considered might pass for a leisurely stroll around the outside of the hotel. It occupied an entire block on the Promenade des Anglais, with a terrace running its full length facing out to sea. Congested one-way streets flanked the hotel on either side. The entire building reminded him of an enormous wedding cake: iced in white, with touches of pink and a watery green; its roof being particularly ornate, fashioned in the belle époque style he recalled Sophie relating from a previous visit.

Kira seemed agitated. There was something on her mind and Paul sensed she wouldn't be able to hold it in much longer. She was merely waiting for the right moment.

"I think I should drive tonight. It will be safer. You can't do it all yourself, and besides, you don't know your way around the city like I do." Kira was laying out her agenda.

"It's too dangerous!" Paul protested.

"I knew you would say that. That's why I wanted you to see me drive first. I'm good on a scooter. It's not as easy as it looks and they will never recognise me in a helmet... not at night, not dressed like this. They just won't."

She had a point, but he wasn't going to let it happen no matter how much she protested.

"We'll see..." he said. "Let's just do what we've come here to do for now. I need to have a look around inside." Paul changed the subject and headed back to where the scooter was parked.

There was limited on-street parking outside the hotel, and certainly no spaces available right now. The scooter was wedged, somewhat inconsiderately, between two parked cars that were already virtually bumper to bumper. Paul imagined that the few parking spaces provided would be constantly busy, considering the twin attractions of the promenade and the hotel itself. After a moment's consideration, he decided that he too could slip the scooter between parked cars when the time came and, with that settled, he headed for the front doors.

The main entrance to the hotel was located at the right-hand corner of the building and, according to legend and Sophie's guidebook, constantly marshalled by a phalanx of notoriously arrogant concierges. With helmets in hand, Paul and Kira strode past without giving them a second glance, totally resistant to any attempts to gain their attention.

Once inside, the mood changed completely. The atmosphere was overwhelmingly traditional, yet its rather flamboyant claim to be one of the world's foremost hotels appeared to be a marketing proposition that somewhat flattered to deceive. While it was still an elegant property, its glory days appeared long gone. Faded grandeur and a surreal carousel-themed restaurant did still set the hotel apart, but the vast lobby and its famous oval hall lacked any real warmth, merely hinting at the glamour of its halcyon days.

Paul pressed on. It would only be a matter of time before one of the ornately liveried lobby porters offered him the sort of assistance he had no need of, or challenged his purpose for being in the hotel in the first place, the scruffy helmets doing little to legitimise their visit.

He familiarised himself with the layout of the ground floor and then identified a seat from where he could see the main entrance doors, but there really wasn't that much of a choice. While the reception lobby was spacious, the seating options were sparse. On the positive side, from the only seat that struck him as suitable, he could see the lifts and there was an uninterrupted view down the full length of the lobby all the way down to vast oval hall and, beyond that, the bizarrely themed restaurant. For such a large reception area, there were surprisingly few places to sit. That one spot would have to do.

He was confident that if the Russians did turn up they would be impossible to miss and easy to observe, but he recognised a problem immediately. There was only that one suitable location, and it placed him at a huge disadvantage. There would be no way he would be able to get out of the hotel, fire up the scooter and follow them all on his own.

But this was it. There might not be a second chance. This was their one and only opportunity to find Maria, and even that was by no means certain. Reluctantly, he concluded that Kira would need to be outside with the scooter, with the motor running and ready to go the instant he jumped on the back. As much as he didn't want to admit it, she was an accomplished rider and, yes, she did know the city far better than he did. Despite his resolve to the contrary, she would win the argument after all.

Kira knew what Paul was going to say before he could find the words.

Now all they needed to do was convince Alisa, and they both knew she wouldn't like the idea one bit.

They spent a little longer outside the hotel trying to imagine where the Russians might park, how they might plan to take Alisa if she was foolish enough to honour her appointment. Would they wait until after the appointment itself or simply snatch her from the street before she could make her way into the hotel?

They would need a vehicle either way, and given the parking issues, that presented its own set of very real problems. The challenge of parking a scooter was nothing compared to guaranteeing a space suitable for a car or a van. So how would they do it? Did they have a plan at all?

Paul satisfied himself that they had seen all they needed and, given the newly agreed order of things, he submitted to Kira driving them back to her "special friend's" shadowy little bar in the old town.

They drew to a nerve-jangling stop next to the table he'd occupied earlier. There was still no one sitting outside, but the windows to the bar had been thrown open and the tables and chairs rearranged. The bar was gearing up for business, and the furniture was now neatly aligned on the damp, grease-stained pavement that fronted the building. The aroma of strong cannabis, unrefined tobacco, and stale beer wafted from the openings and now mingled with the choking exhaust fumes that constantly belched from the scooter.

Paul could see Kira's friend taking an order from a distinctly dodgy-looking character standing at the counter, a large and no doubt vicious dog at his heels. He threw Kira a casual wave as she removed her helmet and then he returned to his task.

"What do you think?" Kira demanded, looking rather pleased with herself.

Paul placed his helmet next to hers on the seat. She fussed with her hair and waited for his verdict.

"Well…" he said, "I think you're full of surprises too!"

She beamed back at him with a hint of Silvi in her eyes.

"I'm hungry. Shall we get some food?" he suggested.

"*Oui!*"

They ordered pizza to take away, some salad that came in little plastic boxes, a bottle of rosé and two cans of Coke Lite for the driver.

They sat for a while waiting for the food, not saying much at all and just watching the world go by. More tables were occupied now, the streets becoming increasingly busy as the afternoon drifted on.

Finally, Kira let out a sigh.

"It feels strange, don't you think… everyone just carrying on as normal, as if nothing's out of place."

It seemed to disturb her a little. Paul shrugged.

"Maybe…"

"It was pure luck, you know," she said reflectively.

Kira seemed to become distressed for the first time since he'd met her. Throughout all that had happened, all that had changed in her world, the revelations, the blood and the all-consuming fear that still gripped Alisa, she had appeared so strong, seemingly unfazed by any of it.

"There was no great design to all of this, Paul," she said. "There was no plan or order. It was purely a matter of chance that Alisa sat opposite Giorgi on Sunday night and not me. Do you think things might have been different if it was me that had got to that table first? It would have been me sitting down with Giorgi. I could have been the one alone in that bedroom with *that pig.*" The prospect of it clearly troubled her.

"I don't know, Kira, who can say… Perhaps."

"When we do these things, Paul, I'm sure you know… there's always a risk."

"That much I do know," he replied quietly. "But you're not alone now… you do know that?"

She sighed again.

"A city full of people…" she mused. "Look at them all… Yet I've never felt more alone in my life…"

*****

Later, Kira drove them back to the hotel. She deployed her considerable charms to persuade the concierge to allow her to leave the scooter under the porte-cochère. He was powerless to resist and Paul knew the feeling well.

Back in the room, Alisa, the brunette, had tidied up a little. The breakfast things were gone, the shopping bags were back out in the lobby, and the bed was made, in a fashion. Yet another towel, stained in various shades of brown hair dye, was reduced to nothing more than a cleaning rag. Its demise, however, was not entirely in vain, having played its full part in Alisa looking very different, yet just as lovely as ever.

The room hadn't been professionally serviced all day, with the inevitable result that they were running short of just about everything. Paul called room service and ordered fresh towels, toiletries, a top-up for the minibar and Nespresso capsules – the latter items being particularly essential fare.

He checked his phone. Gary's name loomed large. He'd called twice and left yet another text. He dismissed all three. The message to "Call Sophie" reappeared as well. Having been away from home for the best part of three days, it occurred to him that Sophie had made no obvious attempt to contact him either. He dismissed that too, but with a deepening a sense of sadness. Perhaps things were far worse between them than even he had imagined.

Paul rummaged through the chaos that was his briefcase and recovered a crumpled piece of A4. According to the agenda, he was already missing a Wild-West-themed evening complete with burgers, beans and a bucking bronco. As for tomorrow, it was the snappily entitled "Intruders in Innovation" lecture, followed by a Q&A with the Secure Co. board. None of that featured in his plans for the next twenty-four hours, and with that decided, there was nothing left for him to do now but wait...

Chapter 36

More than ten hours had elapsed since they received the text. It was entirely possible that Maria had been a hostage since early Monday morning, and Paul was only too aware the clock was ticking. They needed a break, and tracking down Giorgi or Boris would be a start.

The evening was fresh, and a stiff breeze blew in from the sea, disturbing the palms that lined the promenade, their ceaseless rustling pleasantly masking the sounds of the traffic hurrying by. The scooter was parked where they'd left it, and the concierge got a peck on the cheek for his consideration.

Paul set off on foot, and a few moments later he was overtaken by Kira. He watched nervously as she, with all the confidence in the world, rode off in the direction of the Negresco, an ominous trail of black smog in her wake.

It was late into the evening, but he wasn't at all surprised to see that there was no sign of Boris or Giorgi as he made his way towards the hotel.

Giorgi was wounded, he knew that, but just how badly? It occurred to him that it would be Boris he would be trying to spot, but that alone could be a mistake. He reminded himself to be guarded about making assumptions about the two Russians; he mustn't make the error of underestimating what either of them was capable of. Wounded or not, Giorgi was a tough man and, for all Paul knew, he could be sprinting up behind him at that very moment. He cast a nervous glance over his shoulder. Giorgi was nowhere to be seen, at least for now.

As he approached the hotel, he could see Kira on the pavement, the scooter tucked away between two parked cars as planned. The hotel terrace was busy with late diners chasing down their meals with a coffee, a brandy or just partaking of a nightcap before retiring to bed. The promenade was still teeming with strolling couples and others taking in the late sea air. Kira didn't look out of place, conspicuously consulting her phone in the habitual way young people do these days.

Paul's phone vibrated in his pocket as a text landed. It was from Kira and copied to Alisa, who was staying in touch with developments courtesy of Paul's synchronised iPad.

Here OK, it read. Kira's written English was basic at best.

Paul smiled in acknowledgement as he approached.

He marched past the concierge for the second time that day. This time he looked more credible and, minus the pink crash helmet, he barely registered a flicker on the face of the inscrutable concierge on guard at the door.

It was 10.30 pm, still half an hour before Alisa was due to make her entrance. He still had plenty of time to settle in and await their arrival. He headed straight for the solitary seat in the vast hall that he'd identified earlier and then stopped dead in his tracks. It was already occupied. Once again, he needed a plan B.

It never occurred to him that anyone would want to sit there. The limited seating provided in the huge lobby seemed to be more by way of display than to serve any material requirement of the hotel's guests. There were no alternatives, so there was nothing else for it, he would have to keep on walking and find a suitable spot further down the hall, deeper into the hotel and even further away from the entrance.

Paul felt himself unreasonably indignant about the man's lack of consideration. Why on earth would anyone want to sit there? The seat was solitary, isolated and looked hideously uncomfortable, a typical "signature piece", an artistic whimsy of an indulgent interior designer. The chair was spot-lit from above and entirely conspicuous in its setting. Who on earth would choose to sit there?

The answer was obvious enough once it occurred to him. Could the inconsiderate stranger have chosen that very spot for exactly the same reasons he chose it himself? Could there be another Russian in town? Could this stranger be working with Giorgi and Boris, and if he was, just how many more could there be?

Paul had no choice but to stand at the side of the hallway roughly halfway down. He could still see the front doors and the access to the lifts, if not the lift doors themselves. It would have to do. He pulled out the iPhone and called Kira with the news. He heard her take a sharp intake of breath but she didn't respond at first, he sensed she was just gathering herself. They both realised at once that it was on.

"What do you want me to do?"

"Just stay on the line," Paul said calmly.

He studied the man for a while. He was a completely different proposition to Giorgi and Boris. He was short, overweight and nervous. He wore a dark suit with a grey shirt under his jacket, and a receding hairline indicated a man of advancing years – late-fifties at least – with a ruddy face and an unpleasantly sweaty complexion. But how could Paul be sure he was with them? He couldn't just walk up and ask him, and he couldn't just stand there and stare at him either.

"Kira," he whispered into the phone.

"Yes." Her response was immediate but still breathless.

"If this guy is with them he must have a car somewhere, or one of the others could be driving. Maybe it's parked up somewhere nearby. Be careful, but try and see if there's anyone sitting in any of the parked cars near the hotel entrance. Stay on the line while you take a look."

"Okay, what are you going to do?"

"Just wait – that's all I can do for now. Have a quick look around and put your helmet on – they mustn't recognise you – and tell me if you see anything."

"Okay..." It was another breathless whisper. Kira was starting to flap.

10.47 pm.

A few more minutes passed and nothing happened. He saw the man check his watch, but that didn't mean anything. If Paul had been sitting in that chair, self-consciously lit up under a spotlight, he too would be all too conscious of the time. What was he doing? Why would he choose *that* chair? No one in their right mind would want to sit in that ridiculous seat, and yet that is exactly what he'd planned to do himself.

Kira was back on the line.

"I can't see anyone in the parked cars. What do you want me to do now?"

"Just stay on the line and let me know if you see anything – anything at all."

A young waiter passed by. He was carrying a silver tray with two glasses and an ice bucket with a bottle of Bollinger sticking out of the top. Paul couldn't help wondering if it was destined for the "client", perhaps setting the scene with an expensive bottle of bubbly – an expensive indulgence that would, eventually, end up as flat and unsatisfying as the rest of his evening. Paul had no sympathy for his loss either way.

Now that was more interesting. Two young girls walked arm in arm across the lobby engrossed in conversation. They were completely oblivious to the attentions of the man in the dark suit seated awkwardly under the spotlight. His eyes moved feverishly from the girls to his lap and then back again. He was consulting something he was holding discreetly out of view. The girls paused at the entrance to the bar and were soon joined by two young men who gallantly escorted them into the saloon. All interest from the man in the spot-lit chair waned immediately.

Paul was sure of it now – he must be working with Boris and Giorgi. Surely, the man in the dark suit was at the hotel waiting for Alisa.

10.53 pm.

As the minutes ticked by, the man became less discreet. More hotel guests entered the lobby, this time from the lifts, but he took little notice. It was only when they entered through the magnificent front doors of the hotel itself did his interest pique once again.

Suddenly he was on his feet. He held something in his hand. It was an image, but Paul couldn't be sure of what. Whatever it was, it was previously keenly guarded, masked from view, carefully protected and consulted with the greatest of discretion. Now it was held up and in full view as a large group of hotel guests made their way across the lobby. They dispersed variously to the lifts, the bar and passing Paul, two couples made their way to the restaurant. He was in no doubt now. There could be no other logical explanation. He must be looking for Alisa. Paul raised the phone to update Kira. The phone was dead.

Paul pressed redial. Kira answered at the first ring.

"I had to hang up," she gushed. "Alisa sent me an iMessage and I just wanted to let her know what was happening." Kira was still flapping, but she sounded scared too.

"It's okay. Are you all right?"

"I think so, but I've just seen a car go past and it's the second time I've seen it. I think it's just going around in circles!"

"Okay, what sort of car is it?"

"Silver, I think."

Seriously! How can girls be so shit at identifying cars! But Paul managed to maintain his poise.

"Okay, it's silver. How many doors?"

"I don't know… four I think. I can check next time."

"Try and get the registration number and write it down."

"Okay, next time it comes around, I will."

It was 10.58 pm, and Paul wondered how many more circuits it would make even if it was them.

"See if there's a hire company sticker in the back window. Anything that you think might help us identify it later. Does it have any bangs or scrapes? Is there anything unusual about it?"

"Okay, I'll try. I not very good with cars, but I think it's a BMW," she said, perhaps more to please Paul than with any genuine conviction.

"Okay, as soon as you have something, text it to Alisa so she knows what's going on, and get the details of that car over to her. It might be useful." Paul paused and lowered his voice. "Look, Kira, I really do think this could be them. You have to be careful – promise me you will be. If you get scared just get out of there. Make sure the scooter is running and just be ready to go at any moment. Don't wait for me if anything goes wrong. Just get out of there…"

"I will, I will," Kira said, breathing hard.

"I think this guy has a photo of Alisa. I mean Anna – you know what I mean. He's checking it against all the girls as they come by."

"He could have downloaded it off the website," Kira suggested.

Paul hadn't even considered where they might have got it from. Maybe he just wasn't cut out for all this cloak-and-dagger stuff. He still hadn't been on Alisa's website himself, but he had no doubt the Russians would have been. It would be easy enough for them to cut and paste an image from the internet, and Paul was now increasingly convinced it was an image of Alisa that the man in the dark suit was consulting for reference.

"Okay, okay, I'm going to hang up. Send a text to update Alisa and then ring me back straight away. Then we'll stay on the phone… alright?"

"Okay."

"And Kira, have you got your helmet on?"

"No. Not yet."

"Put the damn thing on and keep it on."

"Okay, I will." And the phone went dead.

A few minutes passed and the phone stayed silent.

It was three minutes past eleven and Alisa was already late for her appointment.

Paul could feel his adrenalin kicking in. Something was going to happen and it was going to happen soon. A single bead of sweat ran down his right temple. He wiped it away as he saw the man in the dark suit get to his feet. Paul's heart leapt. This was it.

Ring me back, ring me back! Paul thought, silently trying to force himself to stay calm.

Seven minutes past eleven.

Alisa was now seven minutes late and Kira still hadn't phoned back. She was supposed to ring back straight away, so something must to be wrong. *What's happened? Could she be in trouble?* Paul checked the phone for the thousandth time. It was still on silent and set to vibrate, but there were no missed calls. *What's gone wrong? Something must be wrong!*

The man in the dark suit rose from his chair and stepped anxiously from one foot to the other. He made no pretence now. He was just staring at the front doors. He had the piece of paper in his hand and consulted it incessantly, not trusting to his memory even for a moment. All were scrutinised. It was invasive, too obvious, and the clerks at the reception desk began to take an interest in his activities.

Paul was only too aware of his own frailties in the endeavour, but the guy in the dark suit was something else. He didn't seem to have a clue, or maybe he just didn't care. He seemed to be even more nervous than Paul; he was barely holding it together. Just as Paul thought he was about to lose all self-control, the man sat back down and rocked nervously backwards and forwards in his spot-lit chair.

Finally, the phone buzzed and Paul discreetly picked up the call. He heard Kira at the other end of the line but it was muffled. He couldn't hear what she was trying to say. Suddenly he spotted the man in the dark suit plunge his hand deep into his pocket and fetch out a phone of his own. He started to dial. Could he be about to call the whole thing off?

"Are you okay?" Paul didn't bother to quiz her about the delay. It was enough that she'd finally made the call. He strained to hear what she was saying but still couldn't understand. Kira was muffled, distant and completely inaudible. Paul could hear the laboured gurgling of the scooter as it idled, and he realised, at his insistence, she was calling him from the relative anonymity provided by her helmet. He just couldn't make out her words...

He heard movement. Kira was desperately trying to get the phone closer to her mouth. Suddenly she was back on the line.

"The car's come back. It's right next to me!" she managed to say.

Paul assumed she must have removed her helmet, and that it was the proximity of the car that had caused the delay in her calling him back. With the helmet off, he feared for her safety now more than ever.

"How many men are in the car?" he asked urgently. He needed to know.

"One. He's on the phone right now," she replied. "I've sent the details to Alisa." She paused again.

"Can he see you?"

"No..."

"Have you got your helmet on?"

"Sort of... I had to lift it up so you could hear me."

"Okay, Kira, I think this is it. I think this guy is going to make a move."

There was no response from Kira.

"Kira?" Nothing. Paul turned his back to the man in the dark suit to get a little more power into his voice without drawing attention to himself.

"KIRA!" It was still no more than a loud whisper but it did the trick. Kira was back on the line.

"It's BORIS!" she said, gasping.

Paul could hear the fear in her voice. It was Boris driving the silver BMW. He was parked up next to Kira and he was on the phone to the man in the dark suit. In that one word – that name "Boris" – he could hear her anguish.

"It's Boris!" she repeated. "He's right next to me."

"It's okay, Kira, stay calm. Has he recognised you?"

"No, I don't think he even knows I'm here."

"Right, get your helmet back on. Keep the motor running. I'm coming straight out. It's going to be fine."

He heard rustling from the other end of the line as Kira began to manoeuvre the helmet back into place.

Now he had Boris in his sights, Paul no longer needed to wait for the man in the dark suit to make his move. Paul would get to Kira and then they would follow Boris no matter what the other man did.

He turned his attention back to the spot-lit chair. He was gone! He scanned the lobby just in time to catch a glimpse of the man only yards away from the front doors of the hotel. In the few seconds he'd turned away to speak to Kira the man had finally called off his surveillance and made for the exit. He was getting away and there was little Paul could do about it. The man would hit the street in the next few moments, yet Paul was still deep inside the hotel. Just as he'd dismissed him as no longer a priority, it had all gone wrong. The man would be out of the hotel, across the pavement and into Boris's BMW before Paul could make it to the front doors.

"Kira, the man's heading your way. He's short, fat and wearing a dark suit. You should see him any minute."

"The car's moving, Paul…"

He could barely make out her words as she struggled with the helmet.

"Kira… Kira… KIRA." The phone went dead. Paul increased his pace.

The man in the dark suit was now completely out of sight. Paul barged past the first concierge and lunged for the exit doors, only to be met by another ushering a middle-aged couple into his path.

"*Monsieur!*" The concierge scolded him as Paul crashed his way through them.

Finally he was out on the street, and the cool air hit him. It was sobering. A car door slammed and then the sound of a powerful engine pierced the night. It was a silver Mercedes. Paul was momentarily disorientated. Was this the car? Could she have got the make of the car wrong? Could the car be a Mercedes and not a BMW after all? Of course she could. *"I'm not very good with cars."* She had said so herself. The one thing he knew for sure was that the car was silver and that, at least, he could rely on. But what was he to do now? Where the hell was Kira? Paul scanned the parked cars for the scooter, but it wasn't where she'd parked it earlier.

Then he heard the scooter revving angrily. She was dead ahead and only twenty yards away from him. She must have moved closer to the hotel so he would have less distance to cover to reach her. Paul picked up his pace again now that he had direction. Kira was staring directly at the Mercedes, but she didn't appear to have noticed him approaching at all. She was entirely focused on the car.

Suddenly there was a guttural roar from the scooter and she was off, trailing a smog of exhaust fumes behind her as he stood helplessly at the side of the road.

"Shit, no, no… Kira!" Paul watched as she wrung every ounce of power out of the ageing machine. She hadn't waited. Kira had seen the silver Mercedes pull away from the pavement and set off in pursuit without a backwards glance.

What now?

Paul grabbed his phone and stared at the blank screen. He could call her, but there was little point. She wouldn't be able to hear the phone anyway, and even if she could there was no way she could answer.

A taxi then… Paul scanned the street, but there were none to be seen. Kira was powering away down the promenade. Even if he could flag a taxi down it was too late. Kira was on her own now, and there was nothing he could do or say to change it.

He felt shattered. He feared for Kira, but what more could he do?

His only comfort was, at least for now, that it was Kira who was doing the pursuing and the Russians would have no idea she was on their trail.

This wasn't how he'd planned it, and he cursed himself for allowing Kira to talk him into letting her drive the scooter in the first place. The truth was, there had been no choice. If things had been different and he'd been alone, as originally planned, he would never have got out of the hotel in time. There was no way he could have observed the man in the hotel lobby and then made it to the scooter in time to follow them. There was even less chance of him doing it discreetly enough to follow them undetected.

It was bad enough that everyone for a hundred yards was staring at him, his head in his hands, breathing heavily as an irate concierge approached him at speed. Paul dismissed him with nothing more than a look. There must have been something in his demeanour that told the concierge that now was not the time to confront him.

If only Kira had waited a few more seconds, he would have been with her.

He cursed again as he made his way across the street in the direction of the Palais de la Méditerranée. Just a few more seconds!

As helpless as he felt, at least they were still in the game. Kira just needed to hold her nerve and stay safe. Alisa would be distraught again and she would blame him. If only he hadn't turned away at the critical moment. If only the concierge hadn't been in the way. If only Kira had waited just a few more seconds.

WEDNESDAY

Chapter 37

Alisa didn't blame Paul at all. She was in no condition to articulate an opinion on anything. Waiting alone and isolated in the hotel bedroom had clearly taken a heavy toll on what remained of her nerves. She looked resigned, desolate – everything was falling apart. Her world had turned upside down and now Kira had disappeared into the night too.

"We need to stay focused, Alisa." Paul tried to sound reassuring. "Kira is smart and determined. She shouldn't have gone off like that, but there's nothing we can do about it right now. We have to trust her to do the right thing."

Alisa just stared at him blankly, emotionless and fatigued.

"The car," Paul demanded in an attempt to snap Alisa out of her malaise. "Did she send you the details of the car? It might not be much but…"

Alisa seemed to re-engage.

"The car!" she exclaimed, suddenly reanimated, as if the mere mention of it had sent an electric charge through her body. "It's Alex's car, Paul! They're using Alex's car!"

"Let me see…" Paul held out his hand for the iPad. "But you told me that Alex was going to lend them a car, so what's wrong with that?" Paul didn't understand her anxiety. It seemed logical under the circumstances.

"*A* car yes… but not *that* car. Nobody gets to drive *that* car. It's his pride and joy! … And if he's gone away, he would need his car – wouldn't he?" Alisa enlarged the picture on the iPad and handed it to Paul. "Look…"

The screen displayed a photograph Kira had taken of the silver Mercedes and then emailed to Alisa.

Resourceful girl, Paul thought. The image was dark and grainy, but Alisa was in no doubt about whose car it was.

Paul stared at the image. He hadn't fully appreciated the top-of-the-range Mercedes CLS AMG Coupe in which the two Russians had made good their escape. "You're sure that's Alex's car?" he asked urgently. "You're absolutely sure?"

"Yes, yes, it's his car. He loves that thing more than anything. He would never leave that car behind." Alisa was adamant. "You don't know him, Paul. He would never let them use that car. Never! If they have that car, something terrible must have happened to Alex."

"Maybe…" Paul wasn't so sure.

He hit redial and waited for it to connect for the thousandth time. Kira's phone went to voicemail yet again.

"Fuck it!" he exploded. *Why the hell didn't she just wait for me? Why doesn't she answer?*

"What do we do now?" Alisa was ashen-faced. "They've taken Maria. They've got Alex and now they've got Kira too…" she said, weeping.

"No! You don't know that. Have a little faith in her."

The truth was, Paul had no idea what it all meant or what would become of Kira. Things certainly didn't look good for Alex, but he was the least of Paul's concerns right now. It was still all about Maria, but Kira's disappearance simply added to the issues that continued to mount. Alisa began pacing backwards and forwards at the end of the bed. He could see the pain in her eyes and knew she was starting to lose what little grip she still had left on her emotions. Paul needed to stop her descending deeper into a despair that was beginning to haunt her.

"What do we do now?" Alisa repeated. She was sobbing uncontrollably. "It's all my fault."

"We wait. That's all we can do."

Paul sat her down on the side of the bed. "We wait…"

He pressed redial once more.

"But what if—"

Paul didn't allow her to finish.

"We wait!"

As Kira's phone went to voicemail yet again, he fought the urge to scream out in frustration. He needed to stay calm, if only to keep Alisa from falling apart altogether.

"Twenty minutes," he said. "If we don't hear from her in the next twenty minutes I'll call the police and give them the details of the car. You'll have to tell them where Alex lives if it comes to that. Do you think you can do that?"

"Yes."

"Good," he said calmly. "So, you need to keep it together. Kira is going to need us both to stay focused and do the right thing."

"But they will kill Maria… and Alex, if we go to the police!"

"Stop thinking like that… Twenty minutes and then we make the call… We have to."

"But Maria…" she wailed.

"Let's just give Kira a little longer…"

Paul slumped back in the chair and hit redial again. Alisa couldn't sit still. She paced the bedroom in a daze. It was all becoming too much. How much more could she possibly take?

The ringtone timed out and Kira's voicemail service kicked in once again. Paul boiled inside.

"But what if something's happened to her?" Alisa continued her fretting.

"It hasn't. Just wait…"

Paul hit redial again, and this time, finally, Kira answered the call.

*****

Twenty minutes later there was a quiet tap on the bedroom door. Paul raised his hand to Alisa.

"Stay here," he said, shutting the bedroom lobby door. He left the lobby light off and peered through the spyhole. It was Kira and she was alone. Paul eased the door open, letting her in, and then closed it immediately behind her.

She was buzzing with adrenaline.

"It worked!" She beamed and threw her arms around him in excitement. The lobby door flew open. Alisa grabbed her friend and hugged her tightly. Words were exchanged in Russian. Paul heard the rebuke in Alisa's tone and then the joy – her friend was back.

"I followed them all the way. I know where they are!" Kira looked pleased with herself, but this was no time for playing games.

"Just tell us," Alisa pleaded.

"Alex's villa…" she said excitedly.

"Shit…" Paul slumped down on the bed.

Alisa's legs appeared to buckle as she slipped slowly onto the floor at his feet.

It was all too obvious. If they had Alex's car they probably had him too. If they had him, then why wouldn't they have his home as well? Kira confirmed nothing more than he already suspected, but the confirmation took his breath away. Perhaps they really were getting closer to finding Maria. It made sense too. The Russians needed somewhere else to set up camp after they left the hotel, and Alex's villa would be as good as anywhere.

"It was Alex's car. Didn't you recognise it, Kira?" Paul said quietly by way of explanation.

"No, no I didn't. I didn't know." Kira flashed him a look, vague and distant. "I didn't know…"

Paul helped Alisa back to her feet. She was pale and subdued. In contrast, Kira seemed energised and a little manic.

Once again, there were more questions than answers.

"Did you see anyone else at the villa?"

"No," Kira replied.

"When you got there, where there any lights on? Any movement at all?"

"I don't know. I can't remember... Is it important?"

"We still don't know if they're holding Maria at that villa. Was there anyone else there?"

Kira shook her head.

"Are you sure?"

"I didn't see anyone else – just the car going into Alex's villa."

"You didn't see Giorgi?" Paul quizzed her.

"No."

"Alex?"

"No, no one else. I'm sorry. I came straight back." Kira reproached herself. "I should have stayed."

"No, you damn well should not. You did the right thing coming straight back. You should never have gone there on your own in the first place." Paul was still angry about that.

"I thought we were going to lose them. I didn't see you," Kira protested.

"I was only a few seconds away from you, just a few more seconds..."

Alisa's distress brought Paul back to the matter in hand.

"Okay... forget about all that. All that matters now is what do we do next."

"What can we do?" Alisa said, sobbing.

"That's simple," Paul said. "But we can't do anything until the morning."

"But—"

"In the morning, Alisa. We all need some rest."

As the girls took it in turns in the bathroom, Paul sat quietly considering their options.

He needed to prioritise. Alisa was the key to everything, but it was Maria and Katia Shapiro that were in the most immediate danger. Maria's plight was the most pressing of all.

Friday seemed to be important, the time- and date-stamped photos, the magazine article and the Friday afternoon shopping trip in Monaco; so much appeared to revolve around Friday.

If Friday is the day they intended to take Katia, Paul considered, *surely Maria will be safe until then.*

It was a leap, but he needed to start somewhere. Paul picked up Kira's iPhone and opened up the message the Russians had sent on Tuesday morning.

We have your bitch Maria. If you go to the police we will kill her and then we will find you and kill you too. Stay away from the police and we will let her go when it is done.

He focused on the last sentence. He doubted they would "let her go when it is done" – why would they? He certainly couldn't trust them to do that, but surely Maria had real value as a hostage until it was. That alone might keep her alive until then, no matter what they intended to do with her after that. And, if he was right about that, Katia Shapiro was safe until Friday too.

He read the magazine article again. Friday. It was all about Friday. At least they had some time. Time to think. Time to work something out. Time to find Maria and time to warn Katia of the danger she was in.

He changed tack for a moment.

Why not just go to the police now? He could just give the police the information they already had and let them do the rest. Alisa had begged him not to involve the police, but even that didn't matter anymore. The text and the video clip of Maria had changed everything. Maria's life was as stake and they'd threatened to kill Alisa and Kira as well if they involved the police. Could they just be idle threats? How could he know for certain? How could he take that risk? What if Maria wasn't at Alex's villa? What if the police found nothing? What if Alex was still working with them? So many questions.

There was so little to give the authorities, nothing concrete, and room 732 still cast a long shadow over Alisa's part in the whole fiasco. They needed more. He needed to go to Alex's home... but not tonight...

Paul picked up the bedroom phone and called the concierge. He ordered a hire car for first thing in the morning and hung up.

*****

Paul showered last and returned to the bedroom to retrieve a fresh pair of M&S specials, his mind racing but his modesty still a matter of some concern to him. As he entered the bedroom, the scene he encountered stunned him and made his temper flare. Kira was bent over the desk with a rolled-up banknote in her hand and three lines of white powder on the desktop.

"What the fuck! What do you think you're doing? Where did that shit come from?" He could barely control his anger.

"It's all right. It's only a few lines. Just to take the edge off..." Kira put her hand out to offer Paul the banknote. "It's okay. It's been a tough day, don't you think?" The offer to try some was still open.

Alisa said nothing. She looked at Paul as though he should have known better.

"Are you into this shit as well?" he demanded.

"No, I am not!" Alisa answered with a staccato indignation. "We're not a pair of coke whores you know!"

Paul was incredulous. How could it be him that was being rebuked? He couldn't believe it. Kira leaned over the desk a second time, snorted one of the remaining lines, and then dived on to the bed.

"Come on, Paul, it's only a little thing... Don't get upset with me. I just needed something—"

"—to take the fucking edge off... I know, I heard you the first time." He was furious.

Paul felt betrayed, let down. He had little experience with drugs, but he'd seen enough police dramas on TV to know cocaine when he saw it. "Look... What...!" He was searching for the words but nothing came. "Just give me a minute..." Paul turned on his heels and returned to the bathroom.

Leaning heavily on the marble top of the vanity unit, he stared into the mirror and exhaled loudly. What the hell was he getting himself into here? Hour by hour there were fresh revelations, new problems to confront, and now this. Paul remembered how he'd overreacted to the shower incident. The girls led very different lives from him, and things that seemed to be a big deal to him meant nothing to either of them. Was he doing the same thing now? It was *only a few lines* apparently!

What would he do about it anyway? Was he really going to kick the girls out and wash his hands of the whole sordid affair? Could he really abandon them now, just as the full enormity of what they faced had become so clear?

Paul hadn't expected drugs – Is that what it took to get them through the day? Alisa said she wasn't involved, but how could he believe her? She'd not actually lied to him before, but there was a growing history of partial disclosure and omission – was this just one more instance of that?

He was in turmoil now. He had no answers. He dropped the towel and slipped on the M&S specials before cleaning his teeth in an untypical frenzy. He rinsed and then stared at his reflection in the mirror for a moment. The image of a man losing control stared back at him, and there was that question again – what was he going to do about it? More importantly, what was he going to do about it right now?

The bathroom door opened. It was Alisa. She'd slipped into one of the huge bathrobes, and he saw, once again, the vulnerable girl he'd met on that first night reflected in the mirror in front of him. He didn't turn to face her; there was no need. She came up close behind him and slipped her arms underneath his, crossing them over on his chest. She laid her head against his naked back and he felt the softness of her hair against his skin.

"I'm sorry. It's my fault. I could have stopped her. I mean… I should have stopped her."

He could see nothing of Alisa now, just her arms and her delicate hands planted on his chest holding him to her. He could feel the beating of her heart and the smell of her hair, still fresh from the shower. He could forgive this girl almost anything, but he still couldn't find the words.

"It's not what you think. I know how it looks, but it's okay. I will keep an eye on her. I don't let it get out of control."

Her words were comforting in tone but they rang hollow. He so desperately wanted to believe in them. Despite her reassurances, it did nothing to convince him that it was anything less than it appeared.

"She's not as strong as you think, Paul. She struggles sometimes and it helps."

"Jesus, Alisa, it's not the answer. You have to know that," Paul finally said.

"I know. Come to bed. It's really late. Please don't be angry. I couldn't bear it."

Paul brushed a hand over his forehead as he let out another long sigh. What else was he going to do?

"Don't be angry," she pleaded again. "It shouldn't have happened. I shouldn't have let it."

He turned to face her, but he remained completely silent as she led him back into the bedroom. He wasn't angry any more. He wasn't sure it had ever really been about that. Anger was the very least of what he felt. The whole episode just made him feel so desperately, desperately sad.

Chapter 38

WEDNESDAY

Paul shifted uneasily in the bed, opened his eyes and began assembling a jumble of fragmented thoughts into some sort of order. He'd awoken suddenly from a fretful sleep, his mind racing and his heart pounding in his chest.

It was six o'clock according to the digital display permanently illuminated on the vast TV, a full eighteen hours since they'd received the text message. It seemed like an eternity ago, and now events began to replay themselves unbidden and in no particular order as he shook the sleep from his eyes.

Since that one single text message, Boris and Giorgi had remained totally silent. No further text messages and no phone calls. Just one chilling message with its haunting video and sickening threats. It was dictating everything they did, and that, Paul reluctantly acknowledged, was exactly how Boris and Giorgi would have wanted it. That realisation hit him hard, and he cursed his stupidity. The threats were unsettling and utterly compelling, but allowing Boris and Giorgi to dictate their response was surely the wrong thing to do. He felt his pulse surge, his chest tightening. But what should his response be? What should it have been? Why was he waiting for them to make the next move?

The bedside phone rang and Paul picked it up immediately. It was the front desk; the hire car had arrived. It was time to take the initiative.

Paul slipped into his jeans and polo shirt and headed downstairs to complete the paperwork. He left the girls to put the finishing touches to the day's new look. Jeans, t-shirts and trainers, nothing too eye-catching, although Alisa accessorised with the scarf he'd so *thoughtfully* bought her.

As he stood at the concierge desk, he felt a hand planted firmly on his shoulder. Even before he turned around, he knew it would be Doug or Gary and he cursed his luck. He just didn't have the time for either of them right now.

"Matey, where the hell have ya been?" It was Gary. "I tried calling ya… didn't you get my texts?"

"Hi, Gary, sorry about all that. Something came up I'm afraid. I couldn't make the dinner last night. I assume you had a good evening though?"

"It was great actually. Just a bit of fun really. Food was a bit crap, but they had a bucking bronco and a load of other Wild West stuff!"

Paul suspected that such delights would be right up Gary's street.

"It's the product launches today, mate. Should be the highlight if you ask me. Are you going to make it?" Gary's eyes were trained on the set of car keys the Hertz rep had just handed Paul. "I guess not," he said without waiting for a response.

"If you're taking notes, could I have a copy? I've got something I really must do. I'd appreciate it."

"Sure, sure no problem. Anything. Just let me know what you need."

"Thanks, Gary, you're a star."

"Don't mention it," Gary said, and then he closed in a little. "Listen," he said with a note of conspiracy, "if there is something wrong, you can rely on me you know – if you need anything, that is. I don't mean to pry, but it's obvious something's up." Gary's intuition was firing on all cylinders again.

"Careful what you say, Gary. I might just take you up on that sometime." Paul tried a smile.

"You're sure?" Gary asked very directly.

"I'm sure."

But Gary wasn't prepared to let it go just yet.

"Paul, honestly, just ask. I mean it, anything you need. I'm your man."

"Thanks, I appreciate your concern, but everything's fine. I'll let you know if anything changes though."

"You do that, mate… No problem." And he gave him an almighty slap on the back.

Paul was becoming increasingly aware that he'd misjudged Gary at their first meeting in London. He was definitely one of the good guys, and who knows, his help might be exactly what Paul did need. Gary seemed to have incredible instincts, and another more detached opinion might help him see things more clearly. It was abundantly obvious that Gary knew there was more to Paul's erratic behaviour than he was letting on, and he was unlikely to let anything go that easily. It was the terrier in him; he just wasn't the type to let things drop.

"…and you're sure?" he asked one more time.

"Absolutely!"

But Paul wasn't sure of anything. However, one thing was for certain

– what was about to happen would only fuel Gary's suspicions further. Paul was only too conscious of Alisa and Kira as they approached from the depths of the lift lobby. This wasn't going to help one bit.

"Are you ready, darling?" Kira rasped as she floated by, a vision, arm in arm with another of equal allure.

"Fuck me, mate. What the hell is going on?"

"It's a long story, Gary. I'll tell you all about it another time. I think I owe you that much."

"Trust me, mate, I'm all ears, but you owe me *nothing*." Gary's offer of support was clearly unconditional. "As I say, I'm here if you need me. I mean it, mate. I'm your man," he repeated. "Just ask!" There was an unshakeable sincerity in his voice, but his focus had strayed. He could barely take his eyes off the girls.

"Look… just keep things to yourself for now will you, *mate?*" It was a polite request wrapped up in a conspiracy. Paul tried the "mate" angle to appeal to Gary's discretion.

"Not a word, mate. Trust me, not a fucking word."

"Thanks, I'll catch up with you tonight."

"See you in the bar… six-ish?" Gary suggested, and Paul took his leave.

*****

The hire car was a blue four-door Ford Focus. It was perfect, it being completely anonymous in every regard. Alisa jumped in the passenger seat and Kira took her place in the rear.

Alisa took the lead in giving directions.

Joining the road, they kept to the right-hand lane. He took the first right and then another to bring them back full circle onto the promenades. From there, and as directed, he took the underpass that brought them out onto the opposite side of the carriageway heading in the direction of the old harbour. The road quickly skirted the port and made its way out of town, seamlessly morphing into the Corniche Inferieure, the lower of the three increasingly scenic routes that led out of the city to Villefranche and Monaco beyond.

A few miles out of the city they stopped at a set of traffic lights. There was a florist's on the right-hand side of the junction and a small supermarket on the left.

"Turn left here. It's about two kilometres up on the right." Alisa's instructions kept on coming.

As the villa came into view, Paul insisted they duck down out of sight.

Neither of them would be recognisable from Sunday evening, but it seemed like a sensible precaution.

Paul drove sedately towards the villa. It was five past eight in the morning.

"It's this one," Kira said, pointing in the direction of a large set of gates. "But the car's gone!"

So much for staying out of sight! Kira was still buzzing from the rocket fuel she'd snorted the previous night. Paul was preoccupied by the thought of it.

"Stop pointing – put your hands down," he growled.

Kira snapped back in her seat, realising her mistake.

"We'll go past it, turn around and then I'll park up above the villa. You two just stay out of sight."

He drew the car to a halt and turned off the engine.

"What are we going to do?" Kira said.

"WE? We are going to do nothing. You're staying here and I'm going to take a look around."

It was still early, but the sun was already beating down on the windscreen of the anonymous blue hire car. Kira was in full flow.

"We can't just sit here all day," she announced mid-sentence.

Paul shot Alisa a glance. She spoke to her friend sharply in Russian and Kira fell silent.

Paul used the ensuing silence to get things straight in his mind. There was no sign of the Mercedes and there was nothing to suggest there was anyone at home in the villa.

"Stay here," he said, opening the car door. Then he turned to Kira in the back seat. "Kira, I mean it. Stay in the car."

She pulled a face.

Paul walked past the villa in as casual a manner as he could effect, but he became increasingly aware that it wasn't a part of town where strolling from villa to villa was likely to be the done thing. The road was precipitously steep and uneven. There were no pavements and the scale and quality of the properties suggested that even the most perfunctory journey would be undertaken in a top-of-the-range 4x4 or high-powered sports car.

There was real wealth here, and it was obvious to Paul that Alex had done very well for himself one way or another.

He gained a vantage point between two large metal paladin bins. They were already foul-smelling, and he had no doubt they would work up to a real stink as soon as the heat of the day brought them up to temperature. The metal was already warm to the touch and flies buzzed angrily at the lids. Paul had no intention of hanging around. If a pedestrian was likely to attract attention, a man crouching between rubbish bins would probably spark an international incident. He suspected that one call from a resident in this neighbourhood would have the French equivalent of a SWAT team scrambled and heading to his location in a matter of minutes.

Notwithstanding the deteriorating ambience, he did have a good view of the villa. There was still nothing to suggest the house was occupied and there was certainly no sign of Alex's powerful Mercedes.

The main gates to the villa were constructed from steel railings at least eight feet high. They were supported by a pair of stone pillars with carved eagles on the top. The massive gates were finely crafted and ornate in part, but they appeared to be quite specifically designed for security first and foremost, and certainly to deter any attempt to scale them.

Beyond the impressive gates, the driveway approached the house at an angle and then dropped away steeply to a double set of garage doors that were, for now, firmly closed. It appeared that at least four cars could be comfortably accommodated under the villa, but there was absolutely no way of knowing if the Mercedes had been parked inside and out of sight. There was no doubt that security was important to Alex, and two dark CCTV camera domes covered the gates and the full length of the driveway.

A flight of terracotta steps led up to the elevated front door, with large stone pots to either side, each fully planted with statuesque topiaries and a flourish of red geraniums. The house was rendered in a soft pink plaster and a large tiled terrace ran its full length. At the side of the house, a second raised terrace, complete with swimming pool and sun loungers faced the sea, with stunning, uninterrupted views across the bay. It was a beautiful spot and appeared, at least to Paul, to be a fabulously expensive piece of real estate.

Business must be very good indeed for Alex! he mused.

He'd achieved nothing and was about to return to the car when he saw Alisa striding down the road. She looked no less conspicuous than he had barely ten minutes earlier as she marched straight past the villa and then headed directly towards him.

"Have you seen anything?" she asked.

"No... what the hell are you doing here? I told you to stay in the car. Is Kira all right?"

"She's fine... She's just a bit nervous that's all."

"That's not all!" he snapped. It was his first reference to the events of the previous night.

Alisa chose to ignore it.

"I don't think anyone's at home in the villa," she said confidently, changing the subject.

"How do you know that?"

"I rang the house and no one answered."

It sounded like a stupid thing to have done, but the logic of it forced him to consider the possibility that he might be overthinking things.

"You did what? Why would they answer the telephone? They're not exactly house guests."

"I didn't think they would…"

"So, what makes you so confident they're not there?"

"Because *they* would think it was Silvi calling Alex," she said. "I used Kira's phone and left a message for Alex that they wouldn't be able to ignore. The message said that we… me and Silvi," she clarified, "were back at the apartment and that I needed to speak to him as soon as possible. That was over ten minutes ago. If they were in the villa and they heard that, they would have reacted by now, don't you think?"

The conclusion had merit.

"Yes, I do," he conceded. "Maybe."

Paul checked his watch. Ten minutes wasn't long, but surely they would react sooner rather than later.

"Have you got the phone with you?"

"Yes."

"Let's call them again."

Alisa redialled and let the phone ring. The answerphone picked up the call once again.

"Okay, hang up. I'll take a closer look."

He approached the gates, leaving Alisa crouching between the stinking bins on the far side of the road.

There was no way to get over the walls that surrounded the property and the gates looked impregnable. He gave the leading gate a tug. *You never know your luck.*

There was a loud metallic click and the huge gates immediately started to swing open on their electric motors.

Paul's heart leapt before missing a beat. He must have been spotted by Boris or Giorgi, perhaps in glorious technicolour on the state-of-the-art CCTV. The image of Boris and Giorgi charging out of the villa and down the drive played out vividly in his mind. He cast a nervous glance towards the front door, but there was no movement at all from the villa.

He turned to see Alisa at the keypad on the right-hand pillar. She'd tapped in a code and could hardly contain herself.

"Very funny." He scowled as he regathered himself. *We've even stayed at his house on a few occasions* he belatedly recalled Kira mentioning a lifetime ago.

The house was reassuringly quiet. Paul glanced at the CCTV cameras as they approached. The LEDs on top of the mountings were strangely inert.

"The CCTV cameras have been disabled," he suggested with a degree of confidence.

"How do you know that?"

"I'm a professional too," he said. "It's my business to know."

Getting into the villa was the next challenge.

Alisa skipped ahead of Paul, much to his frustration, and headed up the steps to the front door as if she didn't have a care in the world. At the top she stopped, crouched down by the side of a large terracotta pot, and recovered a key, which she then held up for his approval.

"Impressive," he whispered. "But be more careful. We have no idea where they are yet."

"They're not here, Paul," she insisted.

"You can't possibly know that for sure. Now go back to the car and wait."

"No. This is all my fault. If Maria is in there, I'm coming in with you."

She ran to the front door with the key.

"Wait," Paul ordered, "I want to check outside first."

Paul made a brief inspection of the perimeter of the villa before he allowed Alisa to unlock the front door and let them in; he was in no doubt the property was empty.

Paul conducted a lightning search of the first-floor rooms, the kitchen, the lounge, a small study, and the sun lounge, which opened up onto the pool terrace with stunning views out to sea. It was a beautiful property, but it had been left in an ugly state.

There was mess everywhere. The kitchen was the worst. Every piece of crockery had been used but not a single item washed up or put away. There was broken glass on the floor, empty pizza boxes on the side, and a number of blood-soiled bandages were hanging out of the kitchen bin with little attempt to discard them with any care.

"They've not been gone long," Paul suggested to Alisa, who nodded her agreement.

He headed upstairs. The bathroom had been ransacked, the bathroom cabinet emptied of its contents. The bedrooms had been used too, the beds having been left unmade with yet more bloody bandages littering the floor. The covers were drawn back on one of the king-size beds and a small watery bloodstain soiled the sheets about halfway down. Perhaps even now Giorgi's leg wound was still giving him trouble.

"I'm going to take a look downstairs in the garages. Wait here," Paul said as they returned to the kitchen.

The house felt cold and lifeless, but it was more than that – he couldn't shake the uneasiness he'd felt from the moment he'd stepped through the front door. It wasn't just Gary who had good instincts. Paul's were telling him in no uncertain terms that something was very wrong.

Alisa shaped to follow but Paul stopped her with a task of her own.

"Find that answerphone and delete the call history and the messages," he said.

She immediately spotted the flashing light on the study phone and set to work.

The basement was accessed from the kitchen by a stone staircase. It was pitch-black on the stairs but a little of the gloom lifted as he descended further into the garages below; a thin sliver of light seeped under the garage doors. Paul located the light switch and the overhead fluorescents flickered reluctantly into life. He recognised the scene immediately. The initial flashing of the strip lights illuminated the stark basement in a chilling series of eerie staccato flashes before finally flooding the space with yellow light.

This was where the Russians had held Maria. There was no mistaking it: the white walls, the dark unfinished floor and the cold anonymous utility of the place. A metal chair was unsettlingly placed in the centre of the room. Maria's plastic bindings, now cut, lay discarded on the floor.

Maria was gone but the basement was far from empty.

Lying on the floor, next to the garage door furthest from the steps, was the prostrate figure of a man. He appeared lifeless at first, but there was a slight movement, the almost imperceptible rise and fall of his chest as he gasped for air. Paul could just make out the sound of his laboured breathing as each shallow draw clawed agonisingly at his throat. His face bore all the signs of having lost a one-sided fight with a heavyweight boxer – red, bruised, disfigured and caked in dried blood. A gruesome trail of blood extended the full length of the basement, scuffed and smeared where the man had either dragged himself or been dragged across the floor. He was barely conscious and his legs were tightly bound together. He'd suffered a savage beating.

Paul approached him with caution. He'd never seen a man so brutalised. He couldn't imagine how anyone could inflict so much damage on another. What kind of person could do something like that? Boris and Giorgi were foremost in his mind.

The man was lying in a coagulating pool of his own blood and could barely move, and a smashed iPhone lay in pieces nearby. Paul was at his side in a heartbeat. He knew the man desperately needed help, and he needed it right now.

The man was bound with plastic cable ties that pinched cruelly at his wrists and ankles.

Paul knelt down beside him, and now, looking beyond the blood and gore, he finally recognised him. Paul heard footsteps coming down the stairs behind him.

"No! Alisa, don't come down here... stay upstairs. I told you to stay upstairs!"

It was too late.

"Alex!" she screamed.

She threw herself to the floor, barely able to control her emotions. She reached out to touch his face but recoiled. The tears flowed down her cheeks once more and Paul felt he'd had failed her yet again.

He'd obviously been wrong about Alex. Whatever had happened before, no matter what Paul thought of the man, Alex had protected the girls when it mattered most and had paid a terrible price. Even now, his actions could potentially have cost him his life.

Alisa fell across the stricken man, pulling at his hands.

"Stop, stop, let me..." Paul tried to calm her.

She drew herself back to her knees and wiped the tears from her eyes, a smear of Alex's blood colouring her cheeks.

"Here, call the ambulance."

Paul passed Alisa his phone and she fumbled with it hopelessly.

"Calm down. He's going to be okay. We're in time. Just calm down and call the ambulance."

Alisa had to make the call. She knew the address and spoke the language. If she wanted to help Alex, she needed to calm down and get it done.

"Alex needs you to do this..." he urged her.

"I'm okay... I'm okay..." she wailed, and then took a deep breath.

Paul's attentions shifted to Alex. He tried to turn him to see the full extent of his injuries but the man resisted. He was certainly stronger than Paul expected, and he took that as an encouraging sign.

Still fight left in the bastard, yet!

Alisa was still struggling with the phone but Alex remained the centre of her attention. She whispered a few comforting words in Russian as she stared in horror at his injuries. Alex appeared to register her presence, becoming agitated and trying to utter a few words of his own.

Paul pushed her away.

"Make the call!" he said, and then reconsidered. "Wait, wait..." He grabbed the phone from her and checked the signal strength – barely one bar registered, and then there was the prospect of the police to consider. "Use the landline upstairs and don't tell them who you are. Not a word…" And he shoved his iPhone back into his trouser pocket.

Alisa suddenly grasped the urgency of the situation and headed up the steps. Within a few short moments Paul could hear her in animated conversation with the emergency services on the phone in the kitchen.

It was now or never. He needed to do what he could for Alex and then get himself and Alisa out of the villa and back to Kira. And what would she be doing right now? He could only hope, for once, that she was doing as she was told and had stayed in the car.

The emergency services would soon be on their way and the house would be swarming with medical teams and, no doubt, the police would attend in force too. The last thing Paul wanted was for any of them to get tied up in a full-blown investigation. Maria was still missing and getting involved with the police was the one thing that would almost certainly get her killed. The threat the Russian's had made to her life, and to Alisa and Kira for that matter, was only made more real by what Paul was witnessing in the basement of Alex's villa.

He set about releasing the bindings on Alex's hands. Alex remained unresponsive for the moment, drifting in and out of consciousness. Paul worked at the cable ties, but they were just too tight. He'd need a knife to release them, but then there was a reaction from the stricken man: he seemed to recognise that help had arrived. He was conscious, barely.

"Alex," Paul said, "Alex… what happened here? Where's Maria?" There was no response.

Alisa stormed back down the stairs.

"They're on their way…"

"Good… get back upstairs and find a knife."

She rushed back up to the kitchen without a word.

Alex tried to speak and Paul leaned forward close to the man's lips so he could hear his words. Alex grabbed him by the arm, the firmness of the grip unsettling him at first, but it was fleeting and Paul offered no resistance.

"Listen to me," he said. "He will kill the girls. You have to keep them away." He coughed a little blood from his throat and Paul retched. "I'm finished. Just get the girls away from here. Promise me…"

Paul promised instinctively.

"Where's Maria?" Paul demanded, releasing his arm from Alex's failing grip.

"Anatoly. They will take her to him. He will kill her… and he will kill the Shapiro girl."

"I know about Katia. How are they going to do that? I need to stop them."

Paul considered that he might sound ridiculous to the Russian gangster lying battered on the concrete floor. He wasn't even sure Alex would care what happened to the Shapiro girl anyway. Why would he? Alex had been helping Boris and Giorgi. He'd been instrumental from the start and they appeared to be working to his plan. But perhaps, after all this, Alex would reveal what he knew. He owed the vicious Russians nothing now.

Paul moved back closer to the man on the floor. Alex's breath was stale and metallic.

He was about to speak again when his strength seemed to fail. His arm went limp and his eyes drifted and then closed ominously shut.

Alisa returned with the knife.

"Get some water... quickly!"

Alisa was off back up the steps in an instant.

Paul grabbed Alex and shook him hard.

"Wake up, you bastard!" he shouted. "Not yet! You're not done yet!"

Alex opened his eyes slightly.

"Maria, where will I find Maria?" Paul demanded.

"Anatoly – he will have her. He will kill her for fun..." His words were slurred, barely audible. Who was Anatoly? Yet more Russians and even more questions.

Alex said something in Russian and let out a faint, bitter laugh... "Anatoly, fuck him!" he spat dismissively.

"How do I find him... this Anatoly?" Paul demanded again. He knew he was nearly out of time. Alex wouldn't stay awake much longer and the emergency services were closing in.

"He will never set foot on French soil. Not after Norilsk..." Alex spluttered.

Paul's heart sank. What did that even mean? Where would they take Maria? And... Norilsk? What had this got to do with Norilsk? He'd heard that name before. He'd read about it in the newspaper article on the plane. But what did any of that have to do with Maria? What did Norilsk have to do with anything?

Paul grabbed Alex firmly a second time.

"Where will I find Anatoly?"

"Barabus!" he spluttered. "Barabus!"

His breathing became shallow and he faded out of consciousness again. Paul knew he would get nothing more from him.

He could already hear the wailing of sirens. They were out of time.

"Alex, they're coming for you. You're going to be okay, but we have to go." Paul had no idea if Alex could hear what he was saying, but if he could, the imminent arrival of medical help might just give him something to hang on for.

Alisa was at his side with a tumbler full of water in her trembling hands.

Paul grabbed the water and let a few drops fall onto Alex's face. He reacted but his eyes stayed firmly shut.

"He's going to be fine, Alisa. We have to go."

"We can't leave him…"

"We have to go… Come on," Paul insisted.

Alisa bent over him and placed a kiss on his bloodied forehead. The truth was, Alex had saved her from Boris and Giorgi and she knew it. Paul sensed it broke her heart to leave him.

He grabbed the manual release on the garage door, pulled hard and then pushed the up-and-over door fully open. The light and heat of the early morning sun washed over Alex but he failed to stir. There was no reaction at all. Paul feared he might never stir again.

"Come on…"

Paul grabbed Alisa by the arm and bundled her out of the garage. He dragged her down the drive, over to the car and pushed her into the back seat, where Kira had, for once, obediently waited for them. She looked terrified.

"What's happened? What is it?" she demanded.

"Just take care of Alisa," Paul said without looking back. He fired up the car, eased it into gear and pulled discreetly away.

It was the police who arrived first, with the ambulance only a few moments behind them.

Paul calmly turned the car around and headed up the hillside. He drove away from the coast and towards the Moyenne Corniche as the girls silently consoled each other.

It hadn't been much, but Paul comforted himself with the knowledge that they'd done everything they could for Alex. And in a twist of fortunes, if he survived his injuries, it would be Alex that would be the first of them to be truly safe.

Chapter 39

WEDNESDAY

Finding Alex had been traumatic, and both Alisa and Kira were understandably distraught. Even Paul had to concede he felt an unexpected surge of sympathy for the man. But he knew, now more than ever, that he needed to keep them focused. They were no closer to tracking down Maria and they still needed to find a way to prevent Katia Shapiro from becoming yet another victim.

If he'd got it right and interpreted the photographs correctly, he was still confident that Maria was safe as a hostage until Friday. But now there was Anatoly to consider. Who was he, why would the Russians take Maria to him, and where?

"He will never set foot on French soil, not after Norilsk…" Alex's words were seared into Paul's memory.

But why? What did Anatoly have to do with Norilsk? Paul could recall some of what he'd read about an incident in the newspaper, but not the detail. The shootings, the denials, arms trafficking in North Africa, rival factions, Russians, and yes… suspected "French nationals". It all seemed so distant, but now it felt pressing, urgent and connected. He needed to read that article again and in full. He'd brought a copy of the magazine with them but not the newspaper – why would he? Could Alex and Anatoly be involved in all that? He'd never heard of Norilsk before reading about it on the flight, and now he couldn't stop hearing the name. Surely there was a connection? What the hell had he got himself mixed up in?

Once again he needed to prioritise. Everything came back to Friday, and everything came back to keeping Alisa away from the Russians. That alone would keep Maria safe until whatever it was was *done*. Finding Maria was the key now, and Katia Shapiro was their only link.

Paul was sitting in the car waiting at the traffic lights earlier when a possible solution seeded itself in his mind. He was distracted momentarily by the florist setting out a display of plants at the roadside. It seemed so ordinary and routine. Alisa was fretfully giving him directions to Alex's villa as pots of bougainvillea, plumbago and mandevilla were being diligently arranged in front of the shop. The window displays were a riot of colour, yet all appeared ordered and precise, the stunning display marred only by a large Interflora sticker in the window next to the entrance door.

As the traffic lights turned to green, it came to him. It seemed too simple at first, but perhaps he really was just overthinking things in his desperation not to make a mistake. After all, Alisa had phoned Alex's villa when he was only too prepared to wait. That was a simple idea, but it was that simple idea that could potentially have saved Alex's life. Paul's idea was no less straight-forward, but with a little good fortune, it too might go some way to achieving a similar outcome for Katia.

His big idea was nothing more complex than sending Katia Shapiro a bunch of flowers.

The girls were distinctly underwhelmed. Alex's plight continued to occupy their thoughts and they were just not ready to move on.

"Look, there's nothing more we can do for him now," Paul said in an attempt to break the malaise that had settled like a fog over the back seat of the hire car. "We have to find Maria and warn Katia to stay away from Monaco. We have to keep going otherwise all of this will have been for nothing."

Paul pulled the car over to the side of the road and switched off the engine.

"Why have we stopped?" Alisa snapped.

"Where exactly do you want me to go?" he replied testily.

"I don't know... anywhere... it doesn't matter."

"It does matter. That's my point. It matters a lot!" Paul snapped back. "I know finding Alex like that was hard for both of you, but the important thing is we did find him, and we got him the help he needs."

"Alex..." Alisa mouthed quietly, "what if he dies? What then?"

"Look... he isn't going to die. He was in a bad way, I know that, but you didn't speak to him, I did. There was plenty of fight left in him. He's very strong... you know how tough he can be far better than I do. Alex isn't going to die, but..." Paul hesitated; he knew the girls were in a fragile state, "if he does die – which he won't – how does that justify us just giving up on Maria and Katia?"

Paul awaited a response. None came.

"Well, does it?" he demanded.

"No, we have to try." Kira was the first to find her voice.

"You didn't see him, Kira, it was terrible..." Alisa still seemed haunted by the image of Alex lying on the garage floor.

"It was terrible," Paul conceded, "but that just makes it all the more important that we stop these bastards."

"Yes. Yes, we must." Kira tugged at her friend's arm, encouraging Alisa to come to the same inevitable conclusion.

Kira was on board and Alisa was slowly coming around.

"We can't afford to waste time right now," Paul said. "We have to do something. No one else knows what's going on. I doubt the police will even know that Maria was in the villa with Alex. They don't know Maria's missing, so they won't even be looking for her. At the end of the day, we're all Maria has right now, and we have to stay together on this. Alisa... I know this is tough, but if we want to get Maria back, we have to keep going."

"But what can we do?"

"Katia Shapiro is our next move. We have to find her." Paul was adamant. "She's our only remaining link back to the Russians and our only link to Maria." Paul waited for a response. The girls just looked at each other blankly.

"Agreed?" Paul asked.

"Agreed," Alisa confirmed.

"Good! Let's get on with it then."

Paul already knew Katia Shapiro lived on the Cap Ferrat from the magazine article he'd read, but he had no idea where. He handed Kira the iPad and his copy of the magazine from the hotel lobby.

"Get on the net and see what you can find out about her." Paul knew it was a long shot. "I doubt you'll find her address on there, but you might find something useful."

"I still don't get it. How are we going to find Katia Shapiro with a bouquet of flowers?"

"It's actually very simple," Paul said, running the idea through his mind just in case it wasn't that simple after all. "We go to the local florist and order a bouquet of flowers for a certain Miss Shapiro, care of the Cap Ferrat. We just leave it to their professional pride to get them delivered. All we have to do is stake out the florist's shop and follow the delivery van to the girl's home."

Alisa looked less than impressed with the plan.

"We'll google her first," Paul continued. "I imagine we'll get some hits from that but I doubt it will be that straightforward to find her home address. If we can't find her that way, then we can try the flowers."

Alisa clearly wasn't convinced. She seemed distant, distressed, angry even. Paul was only too aware that he'd virtually dragged her away from Alex's villa earlier in the day, and she still appeared to be furious with him for that.

"It's very romantic though!" she scowled, "You thinking of flowers at a time like this." The sarcasm wasn't particularly endearing. "Maybe we could get some lilies for Alex while we're at it!"

Paul couldn't help feeling a little hurt. He was doing his best.

"We should just ask someone," Kira butted in.

"Who would you ask?" Paul was sure it was the wrong way to go. "Who around here is going to point out the home of a Russian billionaire's daughter?" Paul was short on patience again. "Try if you want to – be my guest – but when the local gendarmes turn up looking for us, how on earth is that going to help either Katia or Maria?"

The girls just stared at him once again.

"What if Maria ends up like Alex, or worse…?" Paul applied a little more pressure.

"What could be worse?" Alisa snapped, the image of Alex's injuries still raw.

"Alisa, he's going to be fine." Paul desperately needed her to focus.

In truth, he had no way of knowing Alex's prognosis any better than Alisa did, but it was time for her to move on.

"Look, we're not going to approach the locals and ask them anything. We maintain a low profile until we get Maria back, or we find out where she is, and then we go to the police or speak to whoever you want." Paul turned directly to Alisa. "Don't forget, if the police get involved, eventually they'll end up back in room 732. We did our best to clean it up, but the evidence against you will still be all over that room if they look hard enough. Anything we tell the police will ultimately come back to that. And that links you to Boris and Giorgi—"

Kira broke in.

"The police can't get involved… if they do—"

Alisa interrupted her friend. She seemed to slowly be coming to terms with the full measure of the problem. "If they do," she said thoughtfully, "Giorgi and Boris will just abandon their plans for Katia and then they'll kill Maria. They said they would kill her… and then they said they would come after us too." Alisa looked shaken by her new-found clarity.

"None of that is going to happen, is it, Paul?" Kira tried to reassure her friend, who had, quite suddenly, grasped the magnitude of the situation.

"Not if we get our act together, but we all need to focus."

Alisa nodded.

"We google Katia first and buy the flowers if all else fails… Agreed?" Paul summarised.

"Agreed." The girls were finally as one.

Kira was already on the case. Twenty minutes later they had found nothing useful. There were plenty of society pieces, photos of Katia with assorted suitors and even one of her with her father, which was a big deal apparently. He was the reclusive type of billionaire, rarely seen in public, but clearly happy enough to be photographed with his daughter on this one occasion. Katia was anything but reclusive, spending much of her time in all the right places, her year indulgently split between skiing in Kitzbühel, partying in London, New York and Paris and relaxing – Paul couldn't quite work out from what – in Capri, Portofino and Mallorca.

There were plenty of references to her living in a villa on the Cap Ferrat, but they were still no closer to finding it.

"Flowers it is then," Kira conceded, and she closed down the iPad.

"How do you know the florist will know where she lives?"

"Look at her. She's a single girl, a very attractive single girl at that..." Paul began.

Alisa pulled a face as if to imply the billionairess wasn't quite the beauty Paul was painting her to be.

"She'll be getting flowers all the time," he continued. "All we need to do is find the nearest Interflora franchise and they'll do the rest."

The girls still looked sceptical and Paul tried to explain his logic.

"People send flowers from all over the world, and when they do, they use Interflora. The person sending the flowers arranges it locally, and then the florist most local to whoever's receiving them makes up the order and delivers it. That's how it works."

Or at least that's how Paul imagined it worked. Either way, in the absence of any better suggestions, it was all he had.

"Someone, somewhere, will have sent this girl flowers." He pressed on with his argument. "If they have, at least one of them will have used Interflora, and even if they haven't, who's to say the local florist isn't doing business with her on a weekly basis. If she's ever had flowers delivered from the local florist, we have a chance."

The mood in the car changed. The girls were all business now.

It was agreed. Alisa was going to place the order but it would be Paul's credit card that would suffer the cost once again. It hadn't really occurred to him just how much all this was actually costing, but it dawned on him now as the expenses continued to mount up. The girl's clothes, the staggeringly expensive minibar bills, the car rental and now a massive bunch of flowers for a girl he'd never even met. And it did have to be an impressive arrangement. Anything less and the florist might not be sufficiently motivated to take the sale and deliver it without having the full address. Alisa would be nonchalant about the whole thing, as if such details were trivial, and the florist would enthusiastically take up the challenge. At least that was the plan.

"The card… what shall I put on the card?"

Alisa's question was a good one. He hadn't given it any consideration. The flowers were only intended to get an address. After that, they just didn't matter, but the card did present an opportunity.

"Nothing too melodramatic!" Paul suggested. "We don't want her to think they've been sent by a stalker, and it has to make sense to anyone else that might open it. She might have domestic staff to do that sort of thing for her."

"No doubt," Kira offered indignantly.

Alisa proposed the wording and it was approved.

Give Monaco a miss this Friday. Love and best wishes…

"Fine, let's go with that," he said, only too happy to see Alisa fully re-engaged.

Paul started the car and headed for the Cap.

The florist shop Paul had in mind was on the Cap Ferrat itself. He remembered it from a previous visit, although he'd never been inside. The roadside display and the window arrangements had caught Sophie's eye then, and once again they confirmed in a dramatic fashion that this was indeed an emporium of some standing. A single drive-by revealed the presence of the Interflora sticker on the window.

He parked the car a short distance away and Alisa climbed out with Paul's Visa card tucked securely into her palm. She was to place the order in person so she could write the card herself, and more importantly so she could check that the bouquet would definitely be dispatched directly from the shop, a question she'd already rehearsed dropping into the conversation with the florist as Kira attended to her hair and make-up.

"No chrysanthemums… nobody likes chrysanthemums," Paul suggested. A previous offering of the aforementioned did not go down well with Sophie, although they were given with genuine intent. It was a schoolboy error apparently; perfectly all right if the flowers were for his mother, but certainly not appropriate if he intended to make any sort of meaningful impression on her.

Paul watched Alisa go in the rear-view mirror. She looked the part, elegant and confident. When he factored in that she was Russian, she looked perfect, every bit the local demographic.

Alisa came up with the cover story herself too. She was staying with her cousin for a few days and wanted to send her some flowers by way of a thank you, but she had no idea what the address was – she never bothered with that kind of trivial detail – could they help? Say 250 euros would just about convey the message and, with luck, inspire the florist accordingly.

"Hell, Alisa, surely a 100 euros would have covered it!" Paul spluttered as she relayed her Hollywood moment, adding a layer of detail they'd never actually discussed.

"You said it needed to be impressive… You old romantic you…" she said, mocking him.

Paul couldn't be mad with her. It was good to see her in a better frame of mind. She even managed to smile at her own joke.

"What's the earliest they can deliver them?" Paul asked, resigned to the burgeoning debt he would have to face up to once he got back to the UK.

"I told them she would be going out this afternoon and it was really important that she got them before she did."

"Vital, no doubt," Kira snarled, not so comfortable with the scale of privilege in evidence on the Cap.

"Because she is *so* local…" Alisa continued, ignoring her friend's irritation, "they said they would do it as soon as their van gets back, and that shouldn't be much more than an hour."

"Perfect… Then we wait," Paul declared.

Forty minutes later, the florist's door opened, as a white van, with a reassuring Interflora logo on the side, pulled up in front of the shop. A large display of flowers was immediately carried to the delivery vehicle by an attractive young girl in a smart tabard.

"That's Sophie!" Alisa shared incidentally. "She was really good about the address. She said she understood completely, that I must lead such a busy life, and that it was not a problem at all to get them delivered."

Alisa flashed Paul a glance.

"So…" she said, "is your Sophie as pretty as her?"

"Yes, prettier," Paul said. He didn't hesitate for an instant, and Alisa stuck her tongue out in response.

Paul started the car.

"Not yet. That's not our arrangement."

"How do you know that, it's huge?" Paul said, killing the engine once again.

"I asked *my* Sophie to make it up in only white flowers. That way we would recognise it if there were any other arrangements in the van." Alisa looked quite pleased with herself.

"Clever girl," Paul conceded.

"I know," she said, grinning. "And if you spend that much money on flowers you have to give these people a bit of a challenge… you know what us spoilt little rich bitches are like," she gushed. "And, after all, red is so last year, darling." Alisa's mood had lifted considerably.

The van started to fill up.

"That's ours," Alisa declared with unshakeable certainty.

"It's a bit small." Paul couldn't disguise his disappointment.

"It's the only white arrangement on the van, so let's go with it," Kira suddenly piped up from the back seat. The after-effects of the previous night's indulgence were clearly taking effect. Kira looked drawn and tired.

The flowers did look stunning, but a little on the small side given the 250 euro price tag. Paul was, not unreasonably, pissed off.

The van pulled away, heading further on to the Cap Ferrat. They had travelled less than a mile when the delivery vehicle stopped and the driver got out and retrieved the white bouquet from the rear doors. The van had clearly been loaded in reverse order, which was great news, as Katia Shapiro's surprise delivery was apparently the first one on the run.

Her villa, unsurprisingly, was surrounded by high walls with large wooden gates defending the only entrance they could see. CCTV was much in evidence, and it was immediately obvious to Paul why the Russians had decided not to try and kidnap Katia Shapiro from her own residence. Katia's villa, even more so than Alex's home, looked utterly impregnable.

The company logo of a security firm specialising in monitored surveillance systems was displayed at regular intervals along the white rendered perimeter walls. Powerful security lighting, no doubt with PIR sensors, covered the grounds and the approach to the gates. It occurred to Paul that such a property would, quite conceivably, have a panic room somewhere on the premises too. He'd seen brochures on the Secure Co. website. Typically, such high-value individuals would have a safe room complete with steel doors, no windows, secure and protected communications, perhaps some basic supplies – champagne and fois grais came to mind – and CCTV: lots and lots of CCTV.

Even if the would-be kidnappers got through all that, the getaway would be problematic. The various routes off the Cap Ferrat converge as they meet the mainland, becoming narrow and congested and easily sealed off by the authorities in the event of an emergency. Taking to the water would be an option, but the police would have that covered within minutes of any alert being raised. Then there was the additional problem of the private security patrols to consider. They looked like a paramilitary outfit, no doubt made up of special forces wannabes, but nonetheless, it was another complication to throw into the mix.

The Cap was probably the last place you would try and snatch the girl; it just couldn't be done with any realistic chance of success.

From the street, there was no view of the villa at all. In fact, the whole road was like it. There was just the merest, occasional glimpse of the beautiful properties that were all but hidden by a combination of security walls, fencing, vegetation and some of the most ornate gates Paul had ever seen. The Shapiro residence looked as intimidatingly elegant as any.

The van driver rang the bell. After a short delay, the gates opened and a man stepped out to take delivery of the flowers.

He was a short, stocky man in a dark suit, and Paul recognised him immediately. The last time he'd seen him he was climbing into the front passenger seat of a silver Mercedes CLS AMG Coupe with Kira in hot pursuit.

"I don't believe it!" he growled.

"What is it?" Alisa said, immediately aware of the look of utter dismay on Paul's face.

"Katia Shapiro's in far more trouble than we thought," Paul said nervously. "That man was at the Negresco last night. He's working with Boris and Giorgi."

There was no mistake. It was definitely the same man. His presence at her villa was just one more twist to add into the mix. How on earth would they to get to Katia with him on sentry duty? It just wasn't going to happen.

It had been a relatively straightforward matter to find the Shapiro residence, but it was going to be quite another to do anything about it. If the man from the Negresco opened the card that accompanied the flowers, Katia would never get to see Alisa's warning or even the beautiful floral arrangement that was attempting to smuggle it to her. At 250 euros that seemed a real shame, but far more importantly, things in general were starting to look very bleak indeed for the Russian heiress.

He could still try a direct approach, but the man at the gates would never allow it. Paul had to accept that just knocking on the door of Katia's impregnable villa, even under normal circumstances, was unlikely to have had much chance of success. Katia was evidently wrapped in a sophisticated and well-considered blanket of security, notwithstanding the current obvious flaw. But with the kidnap plot only two days away, a kidnapper on the payroll and the very real possibility that he would have read the card and no doubt fully appreciated its significance, a direct approach at her home was never going to work.

Paul's head was spinning once again. Could he have just made things much worse? The truth was he'd failed to warn Katia of the danger she was in, potentially increased the vigilance of the kidnappers and made Alisa and her friends even more of a target than they already were. Paul felt shattered for them all. He reluctantly put the car into gear and pulled away. They had achieved absolutely nothing.

Chapter 40

The mood was dark as Paul drove them back to the mainland and away from the Cap Ferrat.

Alisa and Kira sat staring silently out of the windows of the rental car, each lost in their own thoughts. Paul's thoughts turned to Alex and the few words he'd managed to extract from him before he lost consciousness earlier in the day.

Who the hell is Anatoly? Paul hadn't heard the name mentioned before, but he sensed at the time that Alex had a genuine fear of the man. Maybe it was just fear of what he might do to the girls, but it seemed so much more than that. The longer Paul considered it, the more convinced he became that Alex was actually afraid of this Anatoly himself, and in Paul's estimation, Alex wasn't the sort of man to be easily intimidated.

And then there's Barabus. Who or what is Barabus? Alex had been momentarily lucid, precise even, as he spat out his final words before drifting away. Perhaps the important question was not who or what, but where was Barabus? Despite Alex's attempts to be clear, Paul was still none the wiser.

He regarded Alisa through the rear-view mirror. She looked lost.

"Alisa..." Paul said, but she was still far away with her own thoughts.

Paul drew the car to a halt. Without a word, he stepped out onto the compacted gravel and took a few deep breaths before slowly breathing out again. It was a stunning spot high on the Grand Corniche, with panoramic views of a beautiful coastline in both directions. The early afternoon sun warmed him as he stared out over an unending view, clear to the horizon, where the crystal-blue waters merged seamlessly with the azure sky. A gentle rustling filled the air as the lightest of sea breezes played among the trees, carrying a therapeutic blend of mimosa, rosemary and pine.

Paul called the girls to him and reluctantly they stepped out of the car.

Alisa brushed her hair away from her eyes, shielding them from the sun. Kira took Paul's arm and stood silently taking in the view. After the claustrophobia of room 733, it all seemed so serene and too beautiful to be real.

"We should get out of the city more often," Alisa said, sighing.

Paul waited a little longer as the sun's heat softened her mood further, melting away the horrors and disappointments of the morning. He needed time to think, and this was as good a place as any. It was already two o'clock in the afternoon and they'd achieved nothing. Paul took in another deep, calming breath, savoured it's heavily scented energising effect for a moment, and then headed back to the car.

"Get in. We're going to Monaco," he said.

*****

From the Boulevard Princess Charlotte, he took the right turn onto Avenue Saint-Michel. The road dropped away from the main carriageway and then turned a sharp right to a set of traffic lights. While stationary for a while, Paul allowed himself a few moments to enjoy the familiarity of the scene. The magnificent fountains of the Boulingrins Gardens in front of them and the magnificent Casino Square beyond. To his right were the canvas sails and tall pines that shaded the al fresco Häagan Dazs ice cream restaurant. It had been a happy place, a place where he and Sophie had lunched indulgently between motor races, but now it seemed tainted, as he became increasingly convinced it would play a significant and darker role in whatever was to take place on Friday afternoon.

The lights sequenced from red to green. He turned right into the Avenue de la Costa and then an immediate left into Allées des Boulingrins. It was just the briefest of drives between the flanks of the elegant gardens and then a sharp turn to the right and the gently spiralling descent into the darkness of the underground car park itself.

Paul took a ticket and the barrier started to rise steadily in front of them.

"This is where it's going to happen," he said. "Or... at least if I'm right, this is where it begins."

The girls finally snapped to attention.

The car park was much larger that it appeared from above. The entrance was tight, a spiralling ramp that gave access to a series of colour-coded floors cut deep into the rock. Paul had already decided to drive around the entire place and check out every level. He descended deeper and deeper into the car park, navigating each floor before descending once again to the next. At the southern end of each floor, and furthest away from the vehicle ramp, was the pedestrian access to the surface.

Paul drew the car to a stop and recovered the photographs from the glove-box. He flicked through them and paused at the image of the chauffeur with the red cross daubed on his face. He tried to imagine what such an annotation could mean to a man in a world such as theirs. Although he could only guess, he recalled the brutal treatment meted out to Alex and was certain it could only mean something swift and violent for the unsuspecting chauffeur.

Paul had seen the aftermath of their methods, how effectively debilitating they could be, even on a man as streetwise and powerful as Alex. If they could take down a man like Alex in his own home, Paul shuddered to think what they might be capable of in the dark, silent, brooding depths of an underground car park.

He was convinced, now more than ever, that Boris and Giorgi fully intended to eliminate any potential threat to their plan the chauffeur could represent, and then, with him out of the way, they would have free rein to snatch the innocent girl at a time of their choosing. It all made sense: the chauffeur with the red cross, the photographs of the black BMW outside the Hotel Hermitage, the image of Katia sitting in the nearby restaurant with the chauffeur at a separate table in close attendance. The clarity started to give Paul a much-needed boost.

Whatever was going to happen on Friday afternoon, Paul was certain it would start with the chauffeur and end with the Russians snatching Katia Shapiro. After what he'd witnessed in Alex's basement, there was no way he was prepared to allow any of that to happen.

The car park was pretty much as Paul had expected. Each floor was, to all intents and purposes, identical. Paul noted the two CCTV cameras strategically positioned, one at each end of every line of car parking spaces. A pair covered each floor, their tiny red LEDs blinking brightly in the gloom. There were a few VIP parking spaces reserved on the first floor of the car park, but that was the only difference to distinguish the first floor from any of the rest. But it was enough. He turned his attention to the handwriting on the back of the photograph Alisa had translated back in room 733.

"It's *étage*," he announced gravely as they crawled slowly past a row of parked cars on the first floor. "It's not *étape*, it's definitely *étage*. I'm certain now. It's the first floor they're referring to and that means just there." He was simultaneously pointing at the Russian hieroglyphics on the photograph and nodding towards the sign fixed to the back wall of the car park. The illuminated sign was immediately above the VIP parking area.

Alisa checked the text again. Paul had stopped the car at the start of the line of VIP "Réservé" parking spaces on the first floor of the car park. The handwriting was bad, but the meaning was unambiguous. The words written in French were "1er étage" after all, and the Russian hieroglyphics were a simple translation: "Reserved". The meaning was clear to Paul. The chauffeur would park in a reserved parking space on the first floor of the car park, and that, more than anything else so far, did make absolute sense.

"If I were them..." he mused, staring intently at the ominous picture of the chauffeur, "this is where I would take him out." His tone was grave and thoughtful, as if attempting to make sense of his own deliberations.

Paul reversed into a "non-Réservé" spot just down from the VIP area. He was buoyed by the confidence that they'd just made a significant break-through but uneasy about what it might mean. With renewed purpose, they headed up to the surface via the steps. Paul consulted his mobile phone with a serious intent – it was no casual time filler on this occasion. There was no phone signal at all in the depths of the underground car park, the service only returning as they emerged into the sunlight. Paul made a mental note as the connectivity restored itself one meagre bar at a time.

It was a pleasant two-minute walk through the park to the Häagan Dazs ice cream restaurant, and it was exactly as he remembered it. The terraced patio was still shaded from the sun by mature pines working in combination with a series of canvas sails. The sails themselves were stylishly strung between white posts that leaned at angles to dramatic affect. The restaurant was served from an open-fronted cabin and had a chilled display cabinet running its entire length. All manner of ice creams, cakes, cookies and toppings were tastefully displayed, served by smart young staff in branded polo shirts and starched white aprons.

But by far the best part of the entire offering was the delicious and heart-stoppingly calorific ice cream sundaes and coupes. It was these that made the café such a magnet for tourists and locals alike. It was a charming spot, cool under the trees, and with possibly one of the most self-indulgent menus anywhere in the world.

The girls ordered, somewhat self-consciously from the selection of coupes, just a few scoops of ice cream, albeit beautifully presented, and a Diet Coke each. Paul went for the full monty: a salted caramel ice cream sundae accom-panied by whipped cream, a biscuit of some sort and loads of caramel sauce. He comforted himself with the promise that he would run it off in the morn-ing, with little genuine expectation that he would. A small beer completed the damage with no change from 60 euros.

The conversation was stilted at first, but the mood lightened as the events of the morning drifted away for a while. The dark cloud that had shadowed them since finding Alex was temporarily carried away by the cooling breeze and under the growing realisation that they had to focus on the here and now.

With their renewed sense of purpose, they agreed that they should do what they could to keep Katia Shapiro safe from Boris and Giorgi. She was the only link they had to Maria, and while there was no grand plan, if they could keep Katia safe, that would at least mean that Maria still had some value to the Russians.

Paul started to explain his thinking. The magazine article had been clear, Friday afternoons were spent with friends in that very restaurant, followed by shopping and then cocktails at the Hotel Hermitage. In the absence of any other information, Paul concluded they had no choice but to start there, and in any event, the photographs seemed to support the story.

"So, Katia will be here, somewhere in this restaurant and the bodyguard—" Paul began.

"Are you sure he's not the boyfriend too," Kira blurted a little mischievously.

"I thought we'd settled that." Alisa seemed exasperated with Kira; the distinction didn't seem that important in the scheme of things.

"I know, but he is hot, don't you think?"

"What has that got to do with anything?" Alisa gave her friend a withering stare.

"Nothing really. I'm just saying, that's all. If he was my bodyguard he'd soon be my boyfriend... he wouldn't stand a chance... would he, Paul?"

"No... I'm sure he wouldn't." Paul's first-hand experience had taught him that when Kira turned on the "Silvi" charm, resistance was utterly futile. "Can we move on?"

"Sorry..." Kira said, staring somewhat provocatively into his eyes. "Please do..."

"As I was saying, Katia will be here, somewhere in this restaurant—"

"But what if it rains?" It was Alisa's turn to interrupt. "They wouldn't want to sit out here then, would they? Al fresco ice cream just isn't as much fun in the rain, is it?"

Although the question was irritating, it was relevant. He hadn't even considered it.

"It won't be raining. It can't rain... can it? It's Monaco, not Skegness." Paul whipped out the iPhone and tapped Monaco into the weather app. He was relieved to see it was going to be wall-to-wall sunshine until Sunday, when a monumental thunderstorm was forecast.

"Right, as I was saying, Katia will be here, somewhere in this restaurant, and the bodyguard..." Paul could see Kira was about to spark into life again. "Okay. Okay... boyfriend... will be sitting here in the restaurant but some distance away from Katia and her friends, as in the photograph."

He placed the relevant photograph down on the table for them to see.

"She meets up with her girlfriends and he sets up camp at a table away from them. They go shopping... and then – once the credit cards are maxed out – they all head off to the Hermitage for cocktails. The chauffeur just waits here like in the second photograph, drinking cappuccinos and reading the paper."

Paul placed the next photograph down on the table, the chauffeur alone in the restaurant with the time stamp ninety minutes later than the first.

"When Katia and her friends are done, she calls the chauffeur in to pick her up from the Hotel Hermitage and take her home."

He placed the image of the BMW outside the Hotel Hermitage on the table.

"Look at the time stamp," he said. "It's the same day and just twenty minutes later. Just under two hours since the first photograph of the three girls in the restaurant."

Paul waited for Alisa and Kira to satisfy themselves with the observation.

"Now that's pretty much how I see it playing out. What do you think?"

"Sounds right to me." Kira was comfortable with the precis.

"How can you be sure about any of that?" Alisa was rather more sceptical.

"I can't be sure. It's a guess. But if you look at the photos and think about what Giorgi and Boris are trying to do, it adds up. They'll know far more than we do from their little fat mole on the inside, of course, but even so, with what we do know ourselves, it does make sense to me."

Paul turned to Kira.

"Listen... I need you to do something, but it could be dangerous."

"Everything we do is a little bit dangerous, Paul," Kira, said, grinning.

"I'm serious. You'll need to be very careful."

Alisa regarded Paul with a hard stare.

"You don't need to get the chauffeur to marry you or anything, but you do need to distract him. Do you think you can do that?"

Paul's question was greeted with the sort of look that needed no interpretation. Of course she could do that. She'd spent a good part of her young adult life manipulating and distracting men.

"Of course, that will be easy..." Kira looked inappropriately pleased with herself.

"When you have him under your spell, you need to find a way to steal his car keys. That bit is really important... and his parking ticket if you can... we'll need that too." Paul waited for Kira's explosion of indignation, but it never came.

"Easy... anything else?" she asked.

Alisa fumed quietly on the far side of the table.

"Yes… and this is very important. You can't hang around. You need to get out of there and get the keys to me straight away."

"No, it's too dangerous!" Alisa exploded.

"It's okay, Alisa," Kira said. "I can do this, I want to… If it helps Maria, I owe her that much"

Paul intervened.

"I know things haven't gone well so far today, but trust me, I do know one thing. This man with the red cross on his face is almost certainly the next casualty in all this. He's on our side even if he doesn't realise it yet."

"You can't ask her to do this, Paul. It's too dangerous!" Alisa was measured now, but insistent.

"Alisa… I can do this. If Paul says it's the only way, I can do it… I need to do it. I have to help put this right… for Maria."

Alisa was furious.

"It's my mess. I'll do it!" she snapped.

"That's just far too risky, Alisa," Paul blurted out without thinking it through.

"If it's too dangerous for me, it's too dangerous for Kira!"

"But it's not the same thing at all. If they get to you, it's all over for Maria. You have to understand that."

"I'm doing it, Alisa. Paul's right!" Kira was adamant.

Paul admired Kira's confidence in his plan, yet the full weight of the implications bore down on him just that little bit more.

"Listen…" he said, "I think I've come up with a way to sort all this mess out, but we need those car keys. I can't think of any other way."

Alisa was staring daggers at Paul.

"I just can't think of another way, Alisa."

There was no breaking the stare that fixed him now.

"He'll get them back eventually. It's not like we're actually stealing the car. There's a good reason we need his car keys. Please, Alisa… I'm doing my best here"

"You know it's not about the car, Paul."

Of course he knew.

"I can do it, no problem… It'll be fun." Kira was enthusiastically confident.

"How safe are you both right now? Really?" Paul asked. "You've barely left the hotel room in the last two days and then only in disguise and escorted by me." He should have found a different form of words but they let it pass. "It's not safe for either of you. But we're up against time. On Friday, they'll snatch Katia unless we do something to stop them, and then what do you think they'll do with Maria?"

Paul paused for dramatic effect. He had to win the argument.

"Alisa, you already know what they're planning to do with Katia when they get their hands on her. We can't stand by and let that happen."

Paul knew it was unfair to put that degree of pressure on her and chastised himself as she flinched and withdrew a little. There was no doubt he felt guilty for raising such a painful memory, but he needed to make his point.

"We have to stop them, and we have to get Maria back. I can't do any of that without your help... both of you."

Paul paused for a reaction. There was none.

"I know this much," he continued. "The chauffeur, bodyguard... boyfriend... whatever we think he might be to Katia... he is in the gravest danger too. We can't help him, but I know we can help Katia and Maria. We have to try!"

Not a flicker from Alisa.

"I'm not going to pretend it's not risky – of course it is. But we're talking about Kira seducing the chauffeur here. It's not as if he's one of those Russian thugs."

Nothing. Alisa just stared at him.

"Two things could happen," he went on. "The chauffeur works out Kira is trying it on, and she either talks – or more likely she flirts her way out of it – or he calls the police. The police won't matter by then. Whatever Boris and Giorgi are planning for Friday, it will already be happening, so the risk to Maria from police involvement will already be playing out. If they turn up and recognise her, that's far more serious, but she'll have an ally in the chauffeur. He might well be able to protect her. If I'm right and he's Katia's bodyguard, in a straight fight he might even have the measure of the Russians. Either way, he buys Kira some time to get away... and we *are* talking about downtown Monaco here. What could they really do with so many people around?

"Frankly, you're both in more danger sitting here today with just me for protection. What am I going to do if those two animals turn up? I can't protect you, but this guy... well, he probably could. If he's trained in close protection, he might stand a chance one-on-one with those guys. What chance do you think I stand?"

He held up the image of the chauffeur.

"He certainly looks very capable to me!"

Paul caught Kira nodding enthusiastically. The chauffeur was a fine physical specimen, a fact that certainly wasn't lost on her.

"Don't forget, we're talking about the Russians' big payday here too. They'll be totally focused on getting to Katia. They won't even know we're around. Even if they see Kira and recognise her, they have far bigger issues than the two of you to deal with, on Friday of all days. They're not going to allow themselves to get distracted by us. They'll have one single objective on Friday afternoon and that's Katia Shapiro."

Paul had nothing else to add.

"What if he isn't into girls?" Alisa said.

Kira's face dropped at the prospect. Her mind was exclusively focused on her target.

"Jesus, Alisa, I don't know. What if the bloody sky falls in?" Paul was exhausted. But he saw her smile return.

"He doesn't stand a chance… not even then." Kira was warming to her part and already knew Alisa was finally on board.

"So, Kira gives you the car keys, what then? What am I doing while Kira gets to flirt with Jason Statham all afternoon?" Alisa had run out of what ifs.

"Well… that's a bit of a work in progress at the moment," he said somewhat evasively.

"What are you going to do, Paul?" she demanded directly, with a note of genuine concern in her voice.

He had to admit Alisa's obvious concern for him felt good.

"Eat your ice cream," he said. "I have a few more things to check out first, and when I'm sure, absolutely sure, I'll tell you exactly what I'm going to do."

Chapter 41

Although Maria and Alex were never far from their minds, the diversion that Monaco provided was a welcome change, and the afternoon passed pleasantly enough under the circumstances. They strolled around Casino Square taking in the sights, with Paul strategically snapping away on his iPhone. Next, they made their way to the Avenue des Beaux Art, ostensibly to explore the boutiques and arcades on either side, but with matters far darker occupying Paul's attentions. He was resigned to the fact that Maria was lost for now, which left only Monaco and the threat the Russians posed to Katia Shapiro as his primary focus.

As they left the arcade, the magnificent façade of the Hotel Hermitage greeted them. Out in front, the sweeping Avenue de l'Hermitage was, as usual, lined with exotic sports cars and fabulous limousines.

This hotel has to be important, Paul considered, as Kira strategically posed for yet another photograph. He indicated for her to move a little to her right and then snapped away casually until he was certain he had all the angles covered.

The entrance was immediately recognisable from the stolen photographs, and Paul was certain he'd found the very spot Alex had used to take his shots of Katia leaving the hotel. He tried to zoom in on the iPhone to match the two images as closely as possible, but it was immediately evident that Alex owned a far more sophisticated camera, with a much more capable zoom facility than was available to him. Despite the photographic frailties of his smartphone, a brief comparison of the two images left him in no doubt – this was exactly where Alex had taken the shots. He could only speculate. Was it just a good place to take the photographs, or did it have a more particular significance for the abduction itself? Neither was immediately apparent to Paul.

He needed a closer look.

As they approached the hotel, sightseers buzzed happily among the glamorous cars or rested from the sun under the tranquil shade of the trees in the

244

Square Beaumarchais. It was an elegant place, and everyone seemed calm and at ease. There was vast privilege on display here but little edge to it, as the tourists mingled comfortably, casually rubbing shoulders with the "great and the good".

Paul noted that there seemed to be very little by way of security, just the odd camera here and there, but there was no significant show of force.

Then the atmosphere suddenly changed.

From nowhere, two large limousines swept around the cobbled Avenue de l'Hermitage and drew to a halt at the front doors of the grand old hotel. Security seemed to appear from all sides and the tourists were politely, but firmly, ushered to a discreet distance.

Paul watched in silence as a number of men dressed in traditional white Arabic robes filed out of the hotel and into the cars. They were whisked away with little ceremony and an effortless efficiency. The security dissipated as quickly as it had assembled and a more gentle rhythm resumed as the hotel guests, sightseeing tourists and concierges returned as if nothing much had happened at all.

There was security after all and lots of it, but like everything else of function in the city, it was finely crafted and discreetly deployed. Nothing was permitted to undermine the affectation of effortless glamour.

That was impressive, Paul thought.

As he crossed the square, a young couple were politely declined entry to the hotel for what appeared to be a minor dress code violation, a censure they took in good heart. It was business as usual, but while the demeanour of the concierges was consummately professional and faultlessly polite, Paul had seen there were limits.

The hotel had a certain aura, a grandeur that demanded respect. Tourists were clearly welcome, and an inevitable part of everyday life for the hotel, but entry was still robustly controlled. No shorts, ripped jeans or trainers, maybe? Paul was guessing. But the concierge tactfully distinguished between those who were eligible and those who were not. In their diligence, the stunning refuge of the rich and famous was preserved for exactly that.

The truth was, he didn't need to see inside the hotel. He'd seen all he needed to from across the street and a brief walk around the Avenue de l'Hermitage itself.

As the plan started to take shape in his mind, his confidence grew with the reassuring realisation that if he had got it right, there was no doubt it could be done. Not by force or through any overt display of aggression, but by stealth, misdirection and a little deception. He couldn't know with any great clarity just how the Russians intended to abduct Katia Shapiro, but a plan to help her was coming together all the same. There could be no mistakes, timing was everything, and in an ironic twist of fate, he knew for certain he could only get it done with a little help from the Russians themselves. Paul allowed himself a moment; it was help they would be only too willing to provide.

*****

Paul drove the girls back to Nice, choosing a route that took them past Alex's home. The police were still there in force and a ribbon of yellow tape had been drawn across the entrance. The huge metal gates were wide open, but two armed officers barred access to the villa to all but the police and their support teams. There had been a major incident, and it was no surprise to Paul to see the full weight of the Nice police force deployed in response.

"We need to find out how Alex is... which hospital they've taken him to," Alisa said, breaking the silence, the weight of activity at his home suddenly crystallising her concerns.

"It's too risky," Paul said. "He's in the best possible place right now. There's nothing more we can do for him."

"Can't we try?" Kira wiped a tear from her eye as they drove past the house.

"Definitely not... No way!" Paul killed the idea stone dead.

It was the most natural thing in the world for the girls to want to check up on Alex's condition, but just getting in touch with the hospitals was too risky. The police would inevitably take more than a passing interest in any of Alex's known associates, and "known" or not, if the girls suddenly popped up on the radar, they would be at the very forefront of any police enquiry. There was no doubt in his mind that once the police were involved, one thing would lead to another and ultimately back to the seventh floor of the Palais de la Méditerranée. Paul was still convinced the outcome of any forensic examination of room 732 would be bad news for Alisa, and he saw no reason to take that risk.

Paul's thoughts turned to possible lines of enquiry the police might follow. They would certainly be looking for the girl who called the emergency services from the villa to report the incident and then left without explanation; why had she left the scene and not waited for the ambulance to arrive? Paul breathed a huge sigh of relief; it had been a good move to use the landline. Making the call from his mobile would have resulted in the police crashing through the door of room 733 in a matter of hours.

They could also be looking for the man and young woman who fled the scene only minutes after the call to the emergency services. The failure of the CCTV system, either through fault or by design, was a mixed blessing. While it failed to record their presence at the villa, it also provided the same blanket of anonymity to Boris and Giorgi, who, in all probability, disabled the system in the first place.

Or perhaps someone had witnessed the suspicious behaviour of a man seen lurking between the rubbish bins, or, even more disconcerting, the blue Ford Focus that performed a U-turn and left the scene just as the emergency services arrived. The very real prospect of the police hunting down their blue hire car confirmed in Paul's mind that, if nothing else, they needed a change of vehicle. He'd already come to that conclusion for very different reasons and, as a result, he now had something very specific in mind.

Fifteen minutes later, Paul brought the car to a halt at the front doors of their hotel. The ever-vigilant concierge immediately opened both doors on the passenger side of the car and Alisa and Kira alighted. Paul emerged from the driver's side and offered him the keys.

"Monsieur?" the concierge asked in an ingratiating manner.

"Can you take care of the car please? We won't be needing it for the rest of the day."

"No problem at all, monsieur."

Paul watched, with no small measure of relief, as the blue Ford Focus disappeared in the direction of the multi-storey car park. It would be out of sight for the rest of the day and quite possibly until Friday when the hire agreement finally expired. He was sure they couldn't use the car again and he was equally certain he couldn't risk returning it early – that would be the wrong thing to do.

Valet parking was a cool 29 euros a night, Paul observed from the tariff on the concierge desk. The costs were continuing to rack up.

Chapter 42

Alisa set to work on the iPad, with Kira in close attendance. Their task was to locate not one, but two hire cars to replace the mothballed vehicle the concierge had valet parked in the multi-storey at the rear of the hotel.

The first of the new hires would be a simple matter. It needed to be anything other than a blue Ford Focus. It had to be sourced from any rental company other than Hertz, and it needed to be delivered to the hotel by no later than seven in the morning; all of that was straightforward enough.

The second one needed to be something much more specific. Paul scribbled down his requirements on the bedside notepad, tore off the page and handed it to Alisa. Paul's criteria were demanding, non-negotiable and totally unambiguous.

He left Alisa and Kira to their work, intent on a little research of his own. He scoured the room for his source material. The second-hand newspaper had provided him with a little light reading on the flight over from the UK, and it now took on a new and more immediate interest, but the bedroom had been thoroughly serviced in their absence and it had been diligently cleared away by the maid.

Undeterred, he turned to his new best friend: Google. Paul searched for "Norilsk gangland shootings" on his iPhone. It didn't let him down. Google immediately returned a number of articles and Paul settled himself on the bed to read them all.

Twenty minutes reading time elapsed but he gleaned precious little additional information. There were no further developments and no revealing insights into what might have happened, only rehashed versions of the same speculative report he'd read earlier. There was, however, one point of real note. Each article in turn dedicated a few unsettling column inches to the Papé syndicate's penchant for violence, and, in particular, for settling scores swiftly and with unrestrained brutality. The organisation was implicated in several notorious revenge attacks, including a number of murders, all of which remained unsolved. In one high-profile case, a local politician had simply disappeared altogether, and despite having been abducted from his family home in broad daylight, no one, not even his family, had seen anything at all.

The Papé syndicate appeared to be all but immune to police scrutiny, according to the journalist's insights. On the rare occasion any significant arrests were made, they were fatally undermined by procedural flaws or on technicalities expertly raised by a legion of high-priced lawyers. Any prosecutions that did stick apparently gave the distinct impression of being little more than token gestures, and invariably they resulted in a low-level gang member taking the fall. One rather robust article openly speculated that such arrests only occurred when wider political considerations demanded it, and only then, the prosecutions resulted in the detention of minor criminals at the wrong end of the food chain. The article suggested that those serving time were either settling debts they had no other means of paying down or perhaps taking the fall in order to profit from the sacrifice in the longer term.

Paul could only speculate how that same organisation might react to an incident such as the shootings in Norilsk. Few details had been given, but the inference was clear. French nationals had lost their lives, and the possibility that Joel Papé himself could be among the victims was a recurring theme throughout.

"He will never set foot on French soil, not after Norilsk..." Paul recalled Alex's ramblings as he'd fought his losing battle for consciousness. *Not after Norilsk...* Paul thought once again.

There was nothing else to be learned from the news reports. Paul cleared the search from his iPhone, checked on Alisa's progress and then started a completely fresh search of his own. He had a new agenda.

As the results of his new enquiry returned, he made a few notes before studying his options in more detail. French law enforcement seemed a complicated business to Paul, with a baffling array of agencies and departments to familiarise himself with. He knew he would need to call in assistance at some stage, and having the relevant agencies on speed dial just felt like a sensible precaution.

"I think I've found it!" Alisa said enthusiastically as she handed Paul the iPad. "It's going to be in Cannes tomorrow and available from midday."

"Nothing in Nice?"

"There's nothing even remotely close to it in Nice. This is the only option, but it means you'll have to go to Cannes to collect it from there."

Paul studied the image of the vehicle on the screen.

"It looks promising," Paul said. "You're sure there's nothing else."

"Nothing. I've checked everywhere."

With no other options, Paul made the only decision he could.

"Get on the phone," he said. "Book it for tomorrow, for two days."

Paul was sure he'd made the right decision, but travelling to Cannes was a problem. It played no part in his hastily devised plan to find Maria before Friday and was yet another complication to overcome. But he needed that car. If the plan he was quietly formulating for Thursday didn't go his way, the second hire car would be the key to everything on Friday.

He handed Alisa his iPhone and a well-worn credit card.

"You already know the pin number, I believe," he said without missing a beat. "And if we need to go to Cannes to collect it, we're going to need another driver for tomorrow."

Alisa didn't register the implications, just initiated the call to the car hire company as Paul got to his feet.

*****

It was 6.20 pm. The conference would certainly have finished for the day. Paul had no doubt where Gary would be. It was Gary who had suggested they meet in the bar around *six-ish* that evening, and although meeting up for a drink had never been part of his plan either, that was exactly what he intended to do.

"I need to speak to someone. I won't be long. Keep the door shut and stay in the room," he said as he headed for the door.

Back in the gloomy corridor once again, he immediately encountered a housekeeper and an elderly hotel maintenance engineer. Both wore crisp, liveried uniforms and well-practised corporate smiles.

"*Bonsoir, monsieur,*" the maid said as she slipped her master key into the lock of room 732 and stepped inside.

In her wake, the maintenance engineer struggled to manoeuvre an industrial-sized carpet shampooer into position, temporarily blocking Paul's progress.

"*Pardon, monsieur,*" he said, acknowledging Paul, the smile giving way to a grimace.

Paul stood patiently to one side as the machine was pushed and pulled into position. It was a large machine in a narrow corridor, the task demanding considerable effort.

"May I?" Paul suggested graciously, tugging the machine towards him in a bid to line it up with the bedroom door. Two more shunts and their combined efforts saw the mission accomplished. Paul headed on his way.

"*Merci, monsieur,*" the maid called after him from the confines of the bedroom lobby. "You are too kind, sir."

"You're welcome," he called back in his Sunday best French accent, tinged with perhaps a hint of relief. His carefully manufactured coffee stain was about to get the treatment, and Paul felt his mood lift appreciably as he took his leave.

*****

As the elevator slowly descended, Paul's mind drifted back through the day.

He couldn't get the final image of Alex out of his head. The Russian fixer had been left slumped, seemingly lifeless, on the concrete floor in his own basement. He recalled throwing open the up-and-over garage door and the early morning sunlight that flooded in, revealing the full gory extent of Alex's injuries. He appeared utterly helpless at first glance, yet the strength of the man, albeit fleetingly, had taken him completely by surprise. Alex had remained an intimidating figure despite his plight. But that wasn't what occupied his thoughts for now. It was the depth of Alex's concern for Alisa and Kira that was totally unexpected. There was no doubt his concern had been real. It had been inexplicably selfless, almost to the point of reckless. Paul was troubled by the contradictions. Alex didn't quite fit the stereotypical villain he was relying on to make some sort of sense of what was happening.

And just how would the police respond to a local gangster getting a savage beating from, in all probability, another perhaps slightly more dangerous gangster? Would they simply regard the incident as "business as usual" between feuding criminal elements and attach a lower priority to it than would otherwise be the case? Would they see the bigger picture? Could they possibly know about Maria?

There was certainly nothing obvious at the scene to imply there was more than one victim. It would be entirely reasonable for the police to assume it was Alex that had been tied to the chair. Even now, after all that had happened, it was possible, probable even, that the police had no idea that Maria was ever in the basement at all.

How could they know? Even if Alex had been in any condition to talk to the police, would he have told them about Maria? Men on Alex's side of the law, Paul assumed, were unlikely to confide in the police. But surely these were very exceptional circumstances. If Alex had been able, would he have told them about Maria and seek their help, or would he, like Paul, regard telling the police as just too risky for reasons of his own?

"Third floor," the lift intoned, and the door opened to the roar of boisterous laughter. He forced a smile as he stepped out into a stifling atmosphere of corporate bonhomie.

Gary was, somewhat predictably, sitting at the bar with a small coterie of fellow delegates around him. All but Gary were strangers to Paul. He was networking to good effect and clearly in fine form, cracking jokes and fiddling endlessly with his mobile phone.

Paul nodded in acknowledgement as he caught his eye between anecdotes. Gary immediately sensed the conspiratorial nature of the intrusion and wasted no time in detaching himself from his new-found friends. He followed Paul to a quiet corner and settled on a stool opposite him. Paul got straight to the point.

"Gary," he began, "remember this morning…"

"Of course, I remember this morning." Gary effected bemusement at the question. "I've only had a couple, you know. I'm not hammered yet."

"The thing is… as it turns out, I really could use your help," Paul said with as much gravity as he could manage.

Gary threw back his shoulders and took in a deep breath; his eyes were suddenly alight at the prospect.

"Of course, mate. What do you need?"

"First of all, you have to keep this to yourself. You can't tell anybody about it." Paul studied him closely for a moment. "Can you promise me that?"

"No problem. My lips are sealed."

"You have to know something else too." Paul fixed Gary with a stare. "This could be dangerous. Really dangerous."

Gary lit up once again.

"Danger's my middle name, mate," he quipped. "Silent and dangerous. I'm virtually a bloody Ninja." He started to laugh at his own joke.

"Look, I'm deadly serious here. These guys are really dangerous people. You have to be absolutely sure."

"I've already told you I'm in, mate. Just tell me what's going on."

"We need to find a woman. Her name's Maria."

"What the hell are you talking about? What bloody woman? Who the hell is Maria?" Gary's mood changed in an instant.

"Keep your voice down," Paul snapped. "We need to find her and I need your help first thing in the morning."

"Who is she, this Maria?

"She's a friend of the girls you saw me with this morning. The girls from the restaurant on Sunday night… do you remember?"

"Yes, of course. Were they the same girls as this morning?"

"Yes… didn't you recognise them?"

"No, not really. I just assumed you weren't into all that... after what you said and—"

"I'm not! It's not like that!" Paul protested, distracted for the moment.

"Okay, okay, I was only saying..."

"Well don't just say! I need you to concentrate on what I'm telling you." Paul couldn't help feeling a little relief that Gary hadn't recognised Alisa or Kira, but the frustrations of the day were starting to surface. "Are you still in?" he continued, with what he knew to be an unreasonable degree of impatience.

"You want me to help you find this Maria?"

"Yes. Maria..."

"So, what's so important about this woman?" Gary exhaled loudly. His brow furrowed. "Is she lost or hiding from you? Doesn't she want to be found? I don't get it."

"Something like that."

"Like what? Which is it?"

"She's missing. That's all I can say for now."

"And it's dangerous?"

"I'm not going to sugar-coat this," Paul said bluntly.

"Fuck me, mate!" Gary's concentration seemed to drift. "Fuck me!"

"Look, I can't go into too much detail right now, but I could really use your help."

Gary was still joining the dots.

"No wonder you've been acting like such a dick all week," he said, grinning.

Paul ignored the comment. He was only too aware of it.

"I really do need your help, mate."

"Okay, I get that, but what do you need me to do?"

"I need you look after one of the girls from this morning and spend the day with her. Do you think you can do that?"

"Are you serious?"

"I thought we'd established that I'm deadly serious." Paul allowed a little more of his frustration to vent.

The mood changed again.

"One of those girls from this morning?" Gary looked like a man who couldn't believe his luck.

"Yes."

"Of course I can do that. It would be my pleasure." Gary could hardly remove the smile from his face. The terrier was back.

"And you're going to miss the entire conference tomorrow," Paul added.

"Fuck the conference."

Gary's enthusiasm was starting to boil over.

"And I'm going to need your car keys too."

Gary's enthusiasm vanished in an instant and a renewed look of suspicion took its place.

"What the hell do you need those for?" Gary snapped. "You do know my car's in the long-stay car park at Gatwick Airport, right?"

"It's just the keys I need, mate."

"And they have to be mine? What the hell for?"

"It has to be your car keys and I can't tell you that just yet. It's better that you don't know."

Gary sat silent for a moment slowly shaking his head and sucking in air. He scanned the bar as if looking for a hidden camera.

"Is this for real, mate, or are you just winding me up?"

"It's real."

Paul waited as Gary weighed things up. He took a moment to take in the room himself. There were no cameras, just a sea of corporate types hitting the bar and massaging their own egos. Paul watched in silence as Gary studied the scene too. He appeared to be assessing his options: three more days of corporate bullshit or a little drama and excitement in the company of a lovely young thing.

"I get to spend the whole day with one of the girls?" he clarified.

"Yes."

"And it's dangerous?"

"Yes." Paul's frustration all too evident.

"And I can't tell a soul?"

"Yes. That's about it."

His brow furrowed once again as if deep in contemplation.

"Well?" Paul demanded quietly. "In or out?"

A group of over-imbibed Germans jostled past.

"I'm in, mate... never in doubt," he said with a huge grin on his face. "Right," he said after the briefest of silences, "you need a beer... stay here."

Gary set off for the bar and Paul stayed as directed. A few moments later Gary was back with a half of lager in one hand and a further three balanced quite professionally on a tray in the other.

"These wankers don't know how to pull a pint," he growled as he returned. "It's mostly froth, the cheeky bastards... And the price... don't get me started." Gary had already got himself started.

"I have to get back to the room, Gary, I'm sorry."

Gary looked disappointed for a moment and then affected a mild indignation.

"You've got to have a drink with me… I'm giving up so much tomorrow," he said, with a sweep of his arm indicating the tableau playing out at the bar from his all-new perspective. "It's the least you can do," he joked.

Gary gave him his best hangdog expression and Paul relented.

"All right… just the one." Paul sat back down. "And that's your last," he ordered, looking Gary squarely in the eyes. "You need a clear head for tomorrow. I don't want you stinking of booze if you're sitting in a car all day with Kira."

"What bloody car?"

"Enjoy your beer. I'll tell you all the details in the morning. Seven sharp in the lobby."

*****

While Kira showered, Alisa sat on the bed next to Paul.

"I took this…" she said.

She plunged her hands into her jeans pockets and pulled out a fistful of high-value euro notes from each – nothing smaller than a twenty, but mostly fifties and hundreds.

"I got it from Alex's house. I know where he keeps some cash for emergencies… you know the sort of thing."

"Not really, no." Paul stared down at the cash in disbelief. "You've been carrying that lot around with you all day?"

"I just took it. I forgot about it… after we found Alex."

She had several thousand euros in each hand and Paul couldn't imagine any emergency that would require that sort of cash to resolve it, but then he had to admit he didn't live in Alex's turbulent world. He was apprehensive about it though. The last thing he wanted to do was to owe someone like Alex that kind of cash, but he took it from her and counted it out.

"I don't know… I don't like the idea of taking his money."

"You haven't. I have. And he will understand. It won't be a problem. I'll pay him back when this is all over."

She picked up the first pile of twenties.

"I want you to have this. It's to replace the money I borrowed and for the clothes for both of us. It's the least we can do to pay you back."

Paul shook his head slowly and gently pushed her hand away.

"No, I won't take his money, not for that. Really, I don't want it back. I would have gladly given you the money if I'd been here to ask. Let's just forget about all that."

"But all the clothes!" Alisa protested. "It's too much."

"The clothes in particular, they're a gift from me to you and Kira. I'm happy to do that. Please, just don't give any of that a second thought right now."

Alisa was going to protest further but stopped herself. With so much money lying in neat piles on the bed, arguing about a few hundred euros didn't make much sense to either of them. In the end, Paul was persuaded to put Alex's emergency funds to work. If the current situation didn't count as an emergency, Paul had to concede he couldn't imagine what threshold would have to be met to warrant the qualification.

Much against his own better judgement, Paul had started to warm to Alex. For one of the bad guys, he certainly had a few good points, and he was starting to develop a degree of respect for the concern he'd shown for Kira and Alisa's welfare. If he used the money exclusively to help his precious girls, Paul was confident, from what little he knew of the man, that he would see nothing too wrong in that.

"We should take a 1000 euros each and put the rest in the safe," Alisa suggested. "We can always get some more out if we need it."

Alisa got to her feet and walked to the bedroom lobby with the remaining cash in her hand. She tapped 5555 into the safe and placed the money inside without a word of protest from Paul. Alisa accessing his bedroom safe had somehow become completely routine. His world had been turned upside down by Alisa, and the strangest things were suddenly normal and mundane.

"I suppose we all know the code then, do we?" There was something of a resigned smile on his face.

Alisa smiled back somewhat sheepishly.

"I told Kira. I hope you don't mind."

Surprisingly, he realised he didn't mind at all.

Room 733 had become a little claustrophobic again, and having accepted the principle of putting Alex's money to work, he was readily convinced that getting a decent meal qualified as a sensible investment. After all, they had eaten nothing but ice cream since breakfast.

Alisa chose one of the better fish restaurants that lined the flower market, and before too long they were settling back into room 733 for an early night.

Alisa turned off the news channel on the TV as she finally came to bed, and Paul watched her as she pulled the duvet up to her chin and settled down, her face turned to his.

You really are very beautiful, he thought.

"*Doux rêves, mon Nice homme.*"[2] She smiled and slowly closed her eyes.

---

2. *"Sweet dreams, my Nice man."*

Paul was in the middle of the bed, as had become the custom, with the girls snuggling in on either side. Neither he nor Kira slept until, once again, she moulded herself to him, her head on his shoulder, her arm across his chest, her leg over his, gently forcing her foot between his calves. Her breathing slowed, and before too long she was fast asleep in his arms.

In the dark, Paul's reflections drifted back to home, and as one day slipped silently into the next, his thoughts turned to Sophie and the first time they were in Nice together. He saw them both standing arm in arm at the viewpoint of the Quai Raubu Capeu, where so many couples before them had spent the last few moments before sunset, staring indulgently out to sea. As he closed his eyes he could almost feel the sun's gentle warmth. He recalled the mellowing red glow of the approaching dusk as it consolidated into a flaming yellow haze. Time seemed to stall, the sky becoming a brooding canvas as the day melted into the horizon.

Paul remembered how Sophie had gently pulled him to her as the sky burned red about them. He remembered her turning to kiss him. He recalled her tenderness, a tenderness that had seemed sadly remote of late, yet the memory of it transported him back to those early days, as their love for each other had taken root, and on that first night in Nice, it began to blossom into something he thought would last a lifetime.

Their lips had met in a soft lingering embrace as the dusk settled. It had all been so completely perfect. But, as Sophie slowly pulled away, her hair was burnished golden by the dying embers of the fading sun, and it was only then he realised it was Alisa's smile that met his gaze. In that moment, and with so many miles between them, he knew for certain that nothing would ever be quite the same again.

THURSDAY

Chapter 43

The alarm went off at 6 am. Maria had been missing for over forty hours and Paul's sleep, such as it was, had been as fretful as ever.

Before too long they were busying themselves in preparation for the day. Paul checked the phones for charge and headed for reception. Kira raided the hotel buffet for croissants, brioches, and even managed to stuff a selection of cheese and ham into some mini baguettes before smuggling it all away. Alisa discreetly liberated some small bottles of mineral water from the housekeeper's trolley on her way down to reception for good measure.

The plan was simple. Gary and Kira would park up outside the villa Shapiro on the Cap Ferrat and keep it under constant surveillance. It seemed like a sensible thing to do. Katia and her duplicitous "gatekeeper" were the only link that remained to Boris and Giorgi and therefore to Maria. No matter how tenuous that link might be, Paul was conscious it represented their only realistic chance of finding Maria before Friday.

The plan was not without risk, but Paul was comfortable that he'd been honest with Gary about that, at least up to a point. The girls were readily reconciled to any risks they faced and it was Gary's job as much as anything else to keep Kira out of harm's way. Even if Gary and Kira sat outside the villa all day and didn't see a soul, it still wouldn't change the plan that Paul was steadily formulating for Friday afternoon. He'd continue to plan for the worst but stay open to any opportunity that might present itself during the day.

As for Gary, it was entirely possible he would just spend a very enjoyable day in Kira's charming company, which wasn't exactly the worst assignment in the world. It was certainly a far more agreeable prospect than squandering the entire day at the Secure Co. "workshops" he would be missing back at the hotel.

And Kira did have to go with him, despite Paul's overwhelming reservations. Gary didn't know where the villa was or what the Russians looked like.

"Short and fat" and "wearing a dark suit" was about all they could manage by way of a description of the man he'd first seen at the Negresco; that was clearly nowhere near enough for Gary to recognise him with any degree of confidence. There was no way that Alisa could go. She remained the key to keeping Maria safe and Paul still intended to keep her as far away from Boris and Giorgi as possible. Taking her with him to Cannes seemed like the right thing to do; she certainly had no place on a stake-out that, if things did go well, might take her directly to the front door of the dangerous and unpredictable Russians themselves.

Paul skipped breakfast and waited for Gary in the hotel reception. It was 6.55 am.

Gary arrived wearing a smart suit, a white shirt and even a tie. His jacket sleeves had been expertly tailored to the right length and Paul wondered why he hadn't taken the same trouble with his other suits.

"Morning, mate," Gary called out.

"Bloody hell, Gary, it's not a date, you know!"

"I just want to make a good impression, that's all."

The first of the two new hire cars turned out to be a red Opel Corsa, which had been conveniently deposited at the front doors of the hotel. Paul had completed the paperwork as he waited and then heaped another hire charge onto his long-suffering credit card. He handed the keys to Gary.

"Where are the girls? Which one am I looking after?"

"Powdering their noses, I suspect. They'll be back in a minute. You're with Kira… but you'll probably find that she ends up looking after you. She's headstrong, but this could be dangerous, so you'll have to be firm with her. It's your job to keep her safe. No risks… No risks at all… agreed?"

"Yes, of course, don't worry about it. I've got this under total control, mate." He patted Paul heavily on the back. "Has anyone ever told you, you worry too much?"

Paul admired his confidence, but recent experience had taught him that events tended to spiral out of control with an unsettling regularity.

"We're only going to keep an eye out," Gary reassured him. "Like you said, if we see anything, I'll call you and then get Kira away. Don't panic about it. I'll keep things nice and calm."

Gary suddenly became preoccupied as he spotted the two girls approaching from the lift lobby. Kira was carrying a heavily laden white plastic laundry bag in one hand and a small light blue handbag in the other.

Kira was wearing her dark blue jeans, a close-fitting t-shirt and trainers, with her long rose-tinted hair flowing behind her. Alisa had chosen the cream skirt, an equally snug-fitting t-shirt and the trainers; her newly brunette mane was rather more artfully sculptured than her friend's, with a few strands delicately teased out at the temples.

"Christ…" Gary muttered under his breath. "Where the hell did you find these two?" The question was entirely rhetorical, that much he already knew, but his jaw had dropped, and Paul made a point of pushing it closed with the back of his hand.

"Gary, focus!"

"So, this is Gary," Kira purred, looking him up and down provocatively.

"Hello, Gary," Alisa said, sounding disarmingly demure.

She held out her hand and Gary didn't know whether to shake it, kiss it or curtsy. He did an awkward combination of all three.

"Just relax, mate," Paul suggested firmly. "This is Kira. You'd better get acquainted. It's going to be a long day."

"Hi, Gary…" Kira gushed and kissed him on both cheeks. "I am very pleased to meet you," she enunciated precisely, in a playful impression of her best Queen's English.

Alisa rebuked her friend in Russian and the introductions were over.

Before too long, Kira was happily chatting away with Gary, acquainting him with the goodies she'd pilfered from the breakfast room. She seemed readily at ease in the company of men and appeared to have Gary hanging on her every word. He gave every impression of being delighted with her foraging efforts and was clearly looking forward to spending the day with her. He seemed disconcertingly oblivious to the seriousness of the situation.

"You wanted these?" Gary said, handing over the Ferrari key fob with the BMW car key dangling below it.

"Thanks, Gary, you're a star," Paul said.

He pulled Gary to one side and his demeanour darkened.

"Don't forget what I said last night. This is a serious situation and these guys are dangerous. Don't let your guard down – not even for a moment – and remember, right now, this girl's safety is entirely your responsibility."

*****

On the hotel forecourt, they climbed into the Opel Corsa with Gary at the wheel. Nice railway station was their first destination. After dropping Paul and Alisa off, Gary and Kira were to head directly for the Cap Ferrat and Katia Shapiro's magnificent villa.

Gary pulled up at the side of the congested pavement outside the ticket office. Paul and Alisa climbed out of the back seat. He tapped on the passenger-side window and Kira lowered it in response.

"Stay safe, both of you," Paul said. He leaned into the car and took Kira by the hand. "And you..." He waited till he had her full attention. "Listen to Gary. Don't take any risks. Stay in the car, and do exactly what he says – promise me..."

She promised, and Gary appeared to grow in stature, a terrier-like twinkle in his eyes.

"Don't worry. We've got this covered, haven't we, Kira?" He was barely able to contain himself. "We're the A-team now. You go have your jolly day out in Cannes. Leave all the cloak-and-dagger stuff to us."

Before Paul could respond, Gary hit the accelerator and they were off, with Kira blowing kisses out of the window.

Paul turned to see Alisa staring into the distance.

"I hope I've done the right thing," he said vaguely.

"Don't worry," she said quietly. "He seems really nice. I'm sure they'll be fine. How long have you known each other?"

Paul didn't answer the question. How could he tell her, especially at a time like this, that he hardly knew him at all?

*****

Alisa used Alex's emergency funds to buy two one-way tickets to Cannes. They had just over ten minutes to wait until the train was scheduled to depart, which gave them plenty of time to get to the platform.

There were any number of trains running between Nice and Cannes. They'd only just missed the eight thirty-eight. If they caught the eight fifty-five, with a journey time of no more than thirty minutes, they would still reach their destination by nine thirty at the latest.

For Paul, the prospect of spending the day alone with Alisa was a welcome one, and it started well. The carriages were sparsely occupied despite the time of day. Blocks of empty seats faced each other with tables in between; all but a few were free.

Paul gravitated towards an empty section of the carriage on the side of the train that offered at least some prospect of a view of the sea as they travelled west towards Cannes. Alisa had consciously chosen to slip in beside him instead of taking the seat opposite. She instinctively took his arm as they both stared out of the window together, casually watching the villages and towns of the Côte d'Azur slip steadily by.

He placed his hand on hers, as if to reassure her, and she smiled sweetly, closing her fingers around his. Paul's mind drifted back to the early hours of the morning and to the reconstructed memory of his first night in Nice with Sophie four years earlier. He and Sophie had been a couple in the early throws of a genuine love affair, but this was very different. Why did it all suddenly feel so very real to him?

"You're very quiet," she said. "Is everything okay?"

"It's fine," he said unconvincingly.

She gave his arm a gentle squeeze and snuggled in a little closer.

Such a gentle act conferred an honest affection. It felt totally natural, yet there remained an unresolved ambiguity in her touch. It was becoming increasingly difficult for Paul, Alisa had never been far from his thoughts, her beauty and vulnerability captivating him from the very first moment he saw her in the restaurant. And now, as she laughed and smiled spontaneously at his side, he felt drawn to her as never before.

She was beautiful, seductive and utterly intoxicating, and he found himself regretting the brevity of the journey as the train slowly pulled into Cannes station. The time alone together had been all too short, a few fleeting minutes that had quickened his pulse and softened his resistance to her, but the allusion of her intimacy remained a mystery, an enigma still to be revealed. Paul wondered, with a growing sense of sadness, if he would ever really know the girl at all.

*****

The taxi headed south on La Croisette in the direction of the Avis car hire office, just a few short miles from the station. Alisa stared wistfully out of the window as they were driven along the beautiful tree-lined avenue that swept the full length of the beachfront in Cannes.

La Croisette was much like the promenades in Nice, but smaller, slower paced and less congested. It too was flanked by famous old hotels on one side and wonderful seafront restaurants and their exclusive private beaches on the other. Between the hotels, stylish bars and elegant boutiques showcased a who's who of the world's most exotic brands. It was, if anything, more dignified, more intimate and certainly more exclusive than Nice, with a beauty, scale and charm all of its own.

It was barely 10 am as Paul approached the desk at the Avis car hire office, with Alisa close at his side.

"*Oui, monsieur*, we have taken a deposit, that is correct, but how would you like to settle the rest of the account?"

"May we see it first?" Paul asked politely.

The girl behind the desk looked a little bemused.

"It is clean, monsieur. The car was returned a little early, so there is no problem…"

"All the same, could I see it first?"

The girl gave him a well-practised Gallic shrug.

"*Oui!* If you would like to check, I am sure that is no problem."

The cleanliness wasn't his concern, but Paul wasn't about to explain.

"This way, monsieur…"

The girl led them out of the office and into a large compound. There were several rows of cars prepared for hire, with the vehicle in question parked in the middle of the first row.

"May I?" Paul said, and held out an open palm for the car keys.

He unlocked the car and then stepped well back with the key fob still firmly in his hand. He waited for a reaction from the vehicle but nothing happened; the proximity locking option was evidently switched off. He nodded his approval and proceeded to the rear of the car. He opened the boot and studied the interior, much to the obvious frustration of the Avis representative. He lifted the linings and checked the side panels, and then inspected the underside of the boot lid itself. There was no manual release mechanism within the confines of the luggage compartment, and once again Paul nodded his approval. So far so good.

"*Monsieur?*" She gave vent to her mounting frustration.

"Just a minute please…"

Paul sat behind the wheel and started the engine.

The girl tutted loudly and glared at Alisa, looking her up and down with a certain disdain.

With the powerful engine idling, he pressed the boot release. The boot lid powered open and then closed again, clicking firmly shut at the second push of the same button. He tested it again with the car in "Drive" with his foot pressed down firmly on the brake. The boot remained stubbornly closed and Paul registered the distinction as if it was vital in some way.

He climbed back out and locked the doors. There was an audible bleep and a double flash of lights by way of confirmation. Standing in front of the hire car he pushed down heavily on the bonnet. Nothing! He pushed again, only this time with a little more force. A high-pitched alarm sounded immediately and the same lights flashed manically in response. Paul killed the alarm and smiled at Alisa, who looked as confused as anyone, but then broke into a grin as she realised she had done well. The girl from the office registered one last tut with no apparent inclination to disguise her growing irritation.

Satisfied, he handed the keys back to the girl, who changed her vexed expression to one of confusion.

"*Monsieur?*" she asked.

"Yes, yes, that's all good. When can we take it?"

"Now, monsieur, if you are ready." There was more than a hint of impatience in her voice.

"Yes, quite ready, thank you." Paul refused to be baited.

The price of the car hire was a mind-blowing 780 euros per day, and Alisa had booked it for two days as instructed. By the time the sales girl finished, perhaps exacting some measure of revenge for wasting her time, she had expertly talked him into a collision waiver insurance premium and a number of other costly add-ons. The final bill for the two-day hire was a cool 1780 euros, which Paul added to the burgeoning debt piling up on his beleaguered credit card.

With the paperwork complete, Paul called Gary for an update.

"Nothing much to report other than we're out of croissant," Gary joked, and then he added something Paul was never intended to catch. He could hear Kira giggling away in response in the background. It was obvious she was already weaving her magic; Gary was completely under her spell. Paul was only too familiar with the signs.

"Okay, fine... But you do need to stay where you are, and you need stay alert, Gary." Paul was still unsure about the strength of Gary's resolve.

"All day, mate... if we have to. All bloody day!"

"You might have to. Thanks, Gary, just stay where you are. All day is exactly what it might take. I'm relying on you."

There were more giggles, and this time Gary was giggling too.

"All day, mate... all bloody night if we have to." Gary was only half joking. Any time spent with Kira was a good time.

Smitten, utterly smitten. As long as Gary had Kira for company, he wasn't going anywhere.

Paul moved the conversation on.

"We've got the car already – it's perfect." Paul flashed Alisa a smile. "So, we'll get something to eat, pick up a pay-as-you-go and then we'll head back—"

Gary cut in.

"Take your time, mate. We've got it all covered at this end. There's no rush."

And to be fair, Gary was right. Friday was Paul's focus now. There wasn't any real rush at all. Paul killed the call and turned to Alisa.

"Do you fancy something to eat before we head back?"

"That would be lovely," she replied.

*****

Paul reversed the hire car into a space in a quiet part of the underground car park of the Palais des Festivals et des Congrès, the somewhat ugly pur-pose-built exhibition centre on the otherwise beautiful seafront. With no events scheduled, there were huge sections of the vast car park completely vacant. Each one of the hundreds of individual parking spaces was denoted by the presence of a small green light illuminating it from overhead. As Paul manoeuvred the car into position, the green light above turned to red.

He locked the car and they made their way out of the car park towards the shops and boutiques of the Rue d'Antibes. A new pay-as-you-go mobile was the first order of business.

Alisa selected a handset to replace the one she'd lost in room 732, and Alex's emergency fund paid in cash. The shop assistant diligently set up some basic functions, including a new email address, which Paul had casually requested, and then gave them both a brief tutorial. The phone still needed to be fully charged, but it was activated and operational before they left the store. The shop assistant had been fantastic, expertly packing it back into its box, and they left with Alisa carrying her brand-new Samsung Galaxy in a shopping bag contentedly swinging at her side.

It was a glorious afternoon and they strolled the full length of La Croisette lost in conversation, pausing occasionally to study a menu or to gaze out aimlessly across the bay. At the marina, they retraced their steps a short dis-tance and crossed over La Croisette, ambling casually past the shops, bars and glamorous hotels.

Alisa had once again, contentedly bound herself to his arm. It all felt so familiar, she seemed totally relaxed and, at least for now, completely at ease with Paul by her side. He occasionally caught a fleeting glimpse of her reflected in the windows of the boutiques as they wandered by. She had a seductive elegance, an inherent grace and each step had its own engaging rhythm that drew him closer to her. Her soft features seemed to glow in the sunshine and her thick mane gentle bobbed and swept at her shoulders as she walked.

Paul allowed himself to imagine, if only for a moment, what it might be like to be an ordinary couple, together through choice and in the early flush of mutual attraction, perhaps without a care in the world.

He determinedly shook the thought from his mind.

Finally, they stopped to admire an exquisite light blue summer dress. It was beautifully displayed in the window of a boutique so exclusive as to negate the need for price tags. Alisa loved it, and Paul was certain there were few girls that could wear such a dress to better effect. He could contain him-self no longer.

"Alisa…" he began, almost entirely against his better judgement, "there's something I need to tell you…" But whatever it was, the words just wouldn't come. "I think… what I'm trying to say…"

She just smiled softly. It was as if she already knew, but she allowed him to pursue his cause a little longer.

"Alisa, these last few days with you have been incredible." He struggled on. "It's true that we've only just met. I know we barely know each other, but I was thinking—"

"What were you thinking, Paul?" she purred, as her smile broadened.

"Well, I was thinking that maybe, once this is all over, perhaps…" He paused for a deep breath.

Paul was floundering hopelessly, and she took pity on him. She raised a single delicate finger to his lips.

"Let's eat," she said, with all the ambiguity in the world.

Paul was only too aware that he'd embarrassed himself. He couldn't imagine what had possessed him, what possible good could come from such a clumsy and untimely intervention. The words were all wrong, but Alisa seemed to grasp his sentiment instinctively no matter how imperfectly it was expressed. He berated himself for his naïve stupidity. Alisa would have heard it all so many times before. She had smiled charmingly, as if she knew what he was trying to say better than he knew it himself. She let him down gently, changing the subject and saving him from further humiliation, but he was mortified, and he'd said too much, no matter how sweetly she managed his discomfort.

They walked silently side by side, and maybe ten minutes passed without a further word exchanged between them. It felt like a lifetime to Paul. No longer was her arm entwined in his, as it had been for so much of the day. He'd broken a faith, and although he had no overwhelming sense of regret, he knew things were different between them now.

It was just past midday as they approached the Hôtel Martinez.

"There's a nice bar here… by the beach. What do you think? Shall we get something to eat… or…?" he suggested awkwardly.

"If you like," Alisa replied absently, still deep in thought.

As they crossed the road she took his arm again, and Paul felt a surge of relief at her touch. Moments later she placed her head gently against his shoulder. There wasn't a word said, but there was a new fragile intimacy in the way she held him now. A little of the ambiguity seemed to fall away, and he dared to hope she might return a measure of the growing and profound affection he knew he felt for her.

Chapter 44

"Two mojitos and the menu, please," Paul ordered.

They were early enough to have their choice of tables. Alisa was instantly drawn towards an intimate table for two at the front of the terrace. It enjoyed an uninterrupted view of the beach and the stunning panorama across the glorious bay. Soft chillout music set a relaxing mood and waves lapped languidly over the golden sands as they took their seats. A large canvas parasol protected them from the midday sun and a gentle cooling breeze provided natural comfort against the growing heat of the day. The circular island-bar behind them buzzed with quiet activity, and in front, a narrow pier reached out over the sea, bedecked with sun loungers each with a canvas parasol of its own.

"This is lovely, Paul, thank you so much," Alisa said as she took in the full extent of the view.

"I was actually planning on letting Alex pick up the tab."

He immediately recognised he'd missed the gentle nuance in her casual remark, and cursed himself for being so crass.

"No, really, thank you. You've been amazing..."

Paul sensed a *but* coming.

"About earlier," he interjected, "I didn't mean to make things awkward between us. It's just that I realised something about you... well, about me really." Paul sighed heavily. "I think you know what I was trying to say, and I'm sorry if I said too much." He was increasingly aware he was still speaking when saying nothing at all seemed to be the order of the day. "I know I shouldn't have said anything," he continued, wondering when he would find the common sense to stop. "I hope you can just let that go... I mean—"

"It's okay, really it is." Alisa saved him from himself for the second time in half an hour. She was at his arm again and smiled sweetly, empathising with his predicament. "To be honest, you didn't *actually* say that much at all."

Alisa picked up her napkin and placed it on her lap.

270

"Don't worry," she said. "You haven't said too much. It's fine. It was *nice* of you, *but...*"

And there it was... the *but* that he'd been dreading.

"*But* it's been a really difficult few days... things are just a bit chaotic... don't you think?"

"I know," he admitted reluctantly. "You're right. It's been crazy."

"Anyway, you barely know me!" Her eyes seemed to sparkle, changing the mood in an instant. "When you think about it, I'm hardly the sort of girl you can take home to meet your mother." Alisa grinned mischievously. "Can you imagine what your poor mother would make of me!"

Paul was certain she would fall under her spell just as readily as anyone else.

"She's pretty broadminded, you know... I wouldn't tell her everything, of course, but I have no doubt she'd start looking for a new hat the minute she met you..." Paul wondered if the humour would translate.

Alisa laughed.

"Too soon?" he joked.

"Maybe just a little..."

She rubbed his arm in what he took to be an act of sympathy and changed the subject.

"I've been here before. Did I tell you that?"

"I don't think you did, no... Was it recently?" he asked.

"It was some time ago... two years at least..."

Alisa seemed a little distracted by the memory. The menus arrived, and the waiter seemed determined to relate the specials of the day without regard to the flow of the prevailing conversation.

"Shall we order?" Paul suggested. "And then we can talk."

"I'd like that," she said. "We need to talk."

A few moments later, Paul ordered two sea bass and a bottle of rosé, which he could quite readily have consumed himself.

"I wanted to be a teacher..." Alisa began.

The normality of her ambition struck him.

"My parents saved up for years to send me away to study. I have a younger sister too. Did I tell you that?"

"No, I don't know anything about your family." And Paul wondered if it was a good time to mention the two young boys in the photograph.

"There's not much to tell really. My parents do what they can. My father tries, but it's hard for him to find work at his age, and everything's so expensive in St Petersburg these days."

Alisa leaned back in her chair and smiled as if something puzzling had just resolved itself unexpectedly in her mind.

"They decided I was the clever one – can you believe that?"

"Of course!" he replied earnestly.

"They sent me away to study, and when I qualified I was going to get a job and send money back home to make things easier." Alisa let out a sigh. "The plan was to work abroad for a while and then go home and teach in St Petersburg." She shook her head and a few stray curls fell across her face. "The way things have turned out, that's not really an option anymore."

"Why would you say that?"

"It's a shame," she said. "But it just hasn't worked out the way I planned it. Everything was such a struggle."

"A struggle?"

"I seemed to struggle with everything. It's easy for me to understand it now. When I can look back it's obvious, but at the time I suppose I was just out of my depth with everything. I struggled with the studying and I found it hard to be so far away from home. I missed my mum. Silly really, but it was a struggle just to survive in the city. I could barely afford to eat sometimes and… in the end it became impossible to study full-time and afford to live in London."

"You studied in England?" Paul was surprised.

"Yes, of course!" Alisa sounded mildly indignant.

"What did you want to teach?"

"English, silly!" She scolded him as if the answer was obvious. "I wanted to learn to teach English. Then I could either return home or teach Russian children English in London, or anywhere for that matter – maybe even here in France. I was always good at languages, don't you think?"

"I certainly do think. Your English is almost perfect."

"Almost!"

"Your English is amazing. You know it is."

"I'm nearly fluent in French too. I'd like to work in France. Nice is wonderful…" Alisa's voice trailed away for a moment as the reality of recent events came crashing back to her.

"Look… Nice is wonderful," Paul reassured her. "And it will be again. Anyway, you can always work in England if things don't work out for you here."

Alisa looked at him thoughtfully.

"Yes maybe I could," she said, as if agonising over the prospect. "At least if I did that my English would be *perfect*…" She flashed him a smile.

Paul acknowledged his rebuke with a shrug.

"It's the best way to learn – to live and study in the country at the same time. Don't you agree?"

272

Paul did, on balance, but being typically English and therefore typically complacent about learning other languages, he'd never given it much thought.

"I do!" he conceded after a moment's consideration.

"But that's where it all changed for me…"

"In London?"

"Yes, it all became impossible. My money ran out and eventually I decided to get a job and study part-time. Your country is so amazing, so many options. We just don't have the same opportunities in my country."

"What did you do?" Paul was dreading the answer. Lap dancing and escort work sprang instantly to mind.

"I worked as a nanny, which meant I could study in the evenings."

Paul contained his sense of relief.

"It was great at first… I went to a college in the evenings and everything was perfect."

"So what happened?" The question sounded more like an accusation. *So, what went wrong then?* flashed through his mind as a more direct alternative. He couldn't help presupposing that things had gone very wrong indeed. It might have been a little unfair, but, from Paul's perspective, Alisa was selling herself to strangers in yet another foreign country, hundreds of miles from where she wanted to study, and certainly no closer to realising her ambition to teach.

Alisa let the inference pass.

"Things were fine at first. I worked for a lovely family. They paid me well and let me have as much time off to study as I needed. They had two wonderful children, Michael and Robert, and I loved them both. It nearly broke my heart when I had to leave them."

The wine arrived, and Paul thanked the waiter as he poured a little into each glass and set the bottle down in an ice bucket at his side. Alisa waited until he was gone.

"I was stupid, Paul, so stupid. It should never have happened, but I was so young and so far away from home. Looking back, maybe I was just a little lonely too. I don't know how it happened. I've learned so much since then, but in the end, I had no choice. I had to leave."

"That seems such a shame."

Paul could see the sense of loss in her eyes. Alisa drifted for a moment and then re-found her thread.

"I used to travel with the children and Helen when they went on holidays. They were great times. The family owned a home in St Tropez, and sometimes we even came here, to Cannes, for days out. It was beautiful by the sea with the children – they loved it and I loved being with them. Chris would join us when he could, but mostly it was just me, Helen and the boys... and Helen was lovely to me too. She was like a friend, and I ruined everything."

"What happened?"

"It was so stupid... I can't believe what happened, but sometimes you just can't help the way you feel."

Paul took a sip of wine, swallowed hard, and waited for Alisa to continue.

"Over the summer, I took some exams for my English course. The last one was on a Friday, but it was the same day that Helen wanted to take the children to the villa in St Tropez. Chris said I could sit my exam and then fly out the following day to join Helen and the boys in France on the Saturday evening."

Alisa seemed troubled.

"I regret what happened so much now, but... I didn't plan it, Paul... neither of us did..."

"You don't have to tell me if it's going to upset you."

"No, it's okay. I want to." Alisa resettled herself in her chair and took a deep breath. "So... Chris was staying at the house in London that night, and when I came back from my exam he suggested we should celebrate. He was a handsome man and he made me feel special. He was always kind to me and I'd always liked him. He took me to a smart restaurant and introduced me to some of his friends. He's an important man in London. He knows a lot of people."

Paul instinctively knew where the story was heading.

"It was all very innocent at first."

And now he was certain.

"He treated me like a lady. He made me feel very special. No one had ever treated me like that before. It was all very exciting and I was flattered, I suppose. When we got back to the house he opened a bottle of wine, and then, before either of us knew what was happening, we were kissing. We made love in the sitting room. I know that sounds terrible, but it just happened."

"Alisa... I suspect *he* knew exactly what he was doing."

"I know it was wrong, but I really did think I was in love with him. Chris made me feel so special. I hated myself for hurting Helen, but we couldn't stop. He was my first true love... my feelings for him ruined everything."

"Alisa, he was the older man. You can't blame yourself. He was a married man too. He knew exactly what he was doing. It's not your fault."

Paul could see that the memory was still raw.

"I suppose I know that really, but I was caught up in the excitement at the time and I couldn't stop myself. He even said he would leave Helen. He promised he would leave her so we could be together. I told him he couldn't do that because it would hurt the boys and I couldn't stand the thought of that, so we just carried on. Then one day, without warning, he sat me down and told me I had to go. It was just like that. He told me he didn't care for me anymore and that he never had. I was just a bit of excitement to him, but that was all over and he wanted me to go."

There were tears in her eyes now.

"It's okay. Don't upset yourself, Alisa. It was a long time ago," Paul said, guessing a little.

"Yes, I know, but I still can't believe that he didn't love me at all. He hurt me, Paul. I was just a bit of excitement to him, never anything more than that. When the excitement was gone, everything changed."

"I can see that."

Paul tried to comfort her. He gave her hand a squeeze, which seemed woefully inadequate under the circumstances.

"He told me I had to leave England. He didn't want me anywhere near Helen or the boys. He told me that I'd poisoned his relationship with his wife. They were his words... that I was the poison..."

Alisa took a moment to recover.

"I'm sorry, Alisa, I don't know what to say..."

"He arranged for me to travel to France. He sorted everything out without me knowing anything about it. He planned everything. He paid for my ticket and drove me to the airport and flew out with me to make sure I was gone. I barely had time to pack, and I never saw the children again. I only have this to remember them by."

Alisa fumbled in her handbag and recovered the picture of the two young boys Paul had seen back in room 732.

"I'm so sorry, Alisa."

"He took me to Maria and told her she needed to look after me. He said she would help me complete my studies in France, and he would send all my certificates out to me when they arrived at the house, but he never did. I want my certificates. I need them. I worked so hard, Paul. He won't take my calls and never answers my emails. He's scared I'll tell Helen what we did, but I would never do that. I could never hurt the children."

Alisa dabbed her eyes, and her bottom lip began to tremble involuntarily with emotion.

"What hurt me most of all was not being able to say goodbye to Michael and Robert. What must they think of me, just disappearing one day without a word or a hug or anything?"

More tears, despite her best efforts to hold them back. Sensing her increasing distress, he moved the story on.

"What happened when you got to France?"

"Maria took me in. Chris was right about her. She was very good to me. She said I could stay with her until I sorted myself out. She let me share the apartment with Kira and said I could stay for as long as I needed to. Maria is a very special person. She has been a true friend to me... they both have. I didn't have any money at the time or anywhere else to go. I couldn't go back home without my certificates, without anything to show for all the money my parents saved and all that time I spent away from home. I couldn't do that, and Chris kept my passport so I couldn't travel back to England, or anywhere else for that matter. I didn't have a choice. I had to stay with Maria and Kira."

She took a sip of wine.

"I don't suppose I'll ever finish my teaching qualifications now."

"I'm sure you will," Paul said. "I can see it's really important to you."

Alisa just looked at him blankly.

"I know you will, Alisa."

She shook her head despondently.

"I don't know, maybe..."

"Can I ask you something?" Paul said.

"Of course. What is it?"

"Is that why you started working for Maria?"

Alisa was unfazed.

"Yes... well no. I didn't know what to do, and Maria just looked after me like I was long-lost family. She doesn't have any children of her own and she looks after both of us like we're her own daughters."

Paul wasn't comfortable with that image. What sort of doting mother would allow her surrogate daughters to work in such a trade. But he remained silent and allowed Alisa to talk.

"I had nothing, and she helped me without asking for anything in return."

"Is Maria Chris's friend? Is he still involved?"

"No! She hates him! He was a bastard to her and I think he frightens her still. He's been coming to Nice for years. I don't know the full story but something terrible happened between them, but she never talks about it. I know he used to come to Nice when Maria worked. He was a regular. Trust me, they have a lot of history. She once told me that Chris had promised her the world and then let her down terribly when she needed him most. He broke Maria's heart too. Chris can be a bastard! But he knew Maria would do what he told her to. Chris just gets people to do what he wants."

"You're better off without him... surely?"

"He can be very charming, Paul. You don't know him."

He already felt he knew him quite well enough.

"Does he ever get in touch with you?"

"No, never…"

"With Maria?"

"Sometimes, I think so… She hates him… but he still seems to have some sort of hold over her. He frightens her, Paul, and now I know him better, he frightens me too."

Paul poured a little wine into each glass and then pursued his earlier question.

"Was it Maria who made you start working as an escort?" He surprised himself with the directness of the question. He just couldn't accept Maria as blameless in all this.

"No, no, it wasn't like that. I wanted to… I decided to, I mean. Maria never wanted me to work, but it was an easy way for me to get some money. If Kira could do it, I thought I could too. Maria introduced me to Alex so I'd be safe. She's very close to Alex and she knew he would help me. Neither of them pushed us to work. They both know what working can do to you… maybe because of what it did to her… but I didn't see a choice at the time. Maria does what she can to keep us safe, and Alex is always there to protect us.

"That's ridiculous, Alisa," he blurted out. "No one is protecting you! Surely you can see that! You're completely on your own in this. Where are they right now, when you need them most? You have to stop all this… Alex and Maria can't even protect themselves!"

Paul became self-conscious and lowered his voice.

"It's never been safe for you. You've just been kidding yourself. How can it be safe? What you do is fraught with risk. With Alex in hospital and Maria God knows where, you have no one to protect you! No one!"

His words lingered in the air unanswered.

"I have you," she said after a while. "Please say you will still help me. I need you. Maria needs you."

There was desperation in Alisa's voice that cut straight through his self-righteous indignation.

"You know you don't have to ask me that, Alisa… surely you know that."

The waiter appeared at the table with two fantastic-looking plates of sea bass, a little pasta on the side and a large bowl of salad to share. The arrival of the food was diverting and Alisa regained her composure.

"Let's eat," he said, and forced a smile.

Paul topped up the wine again.

"Can I ask you something else?" he said.

"Yes, of course."

"The drugs incident the other night. Was that just Kira or do you do feel the need to 'take the edge off' as well?" Paul was dreading the answer.

Alisa gave him a broad grin.

"Things aren't that bad yet," she said. "I hate the stuff. I've tried it, of course, but I could never use it like Kira does."

"Does she use it a lot?"

"No. Not really, but she mixes with the wrong people. That's the worst part about it. I try to stop her, but the other night she'd already taken some before she got back to the room, and once she's had a taste, sometimes there's no reasoning with her. It's always the same when she meets those people. When she took the scooter back, one of her so-called *friends* gave it to her. Some of them are into very bad things – everything they do is illegal – but they just draw her in somehow. I don't know what she sees in them."

"The drugs probably," he suggested flippantly.

"I know, I know… she has to be careful. I've seen it go badly wrong before. A girl starts using it for fun. You'd be surprised just how many clients use it, and they encourage the girls to take it too. Kira takes it to stay up. You know how it is."

He didn't.

"To keep awake and keep going, getting high helps. The hours can take it out of you, and it's a quick fix. But I do know it's not the answer. I've seen girls destroyed by it. They start working for the next hit and then move on to some terrible things, drugs far worse than coke, and once they do, there's no way back for them. They end up working on the streets, run by bastards that couldn't care less about them. It ruins their whole lives. Some of them never get away from it. I won't let that happen to Kira."

Alisa placed her knife and fork deliberately on the table. She waited until Paul had done the same and then took his hands in hers. She looked him squarely in the eyes.

"This is not my life, Paul. I have plans, so much I want to do, but this is where I am right now and I have to make the most of it. Don't get me wrong. Sometimes it *is* fun. It can be exciting, and yes, I like the risks. I like a little of the danger that goes with it too. It's just the way I am, I suppose, but it's not my life, and when things get better, I will change it. I'll make sure Kira doesn't end up working on the streets to feed a drug habit too. That will never happen to her. I won't allow it, and neither will Maria."

Paul took a deep breath.

"I don't know how you do it. Where do you get your strength from? I don't think I've ever met anyone quite like you."

"I should think not!" She feigned a little indignation. "A nice upstanding gentleman like you!"

Paul drained the last of the wine from the bottle, giving Alisa the lion's share. He knew they needed to get back to Nice before too long, and being stopped for driving under the influence played no part in his overall plan.

Finally, he had to know.

"But, Alisa, how do you do what you do? I just don't understand why you do it…"

Alisa looked at him for a moment.

"It's really not that complicated," she said casually. "We separate it. I just keep things completely separate. Some girls don't need to, but that's how it works for me. I have clothes for work and clothes for me. Hotel bedrooms are my office – that's how it is. I can be two separate people really. It's quite easy for me, and it's not as bad as you think. It's exciting to me, a little bit dangerous too sometimes… but dangerous in a good way, I mean."

"I just don't get it. You're so…" He couldn't find the right word. "Surely you don't need to do this?"

"I know it's difficult for you, but it's no big deal really. I know you don't want to hear this, but it can be a real buzz. You think it is all one way, but it's not. We have our ways. The guys think they're in control, but they're not. We have our methods, you know, delaying tactics, things we do when we don't want to do what they want. It's a game, and the clients don't even know they're being played. And the money, Paul – we can make so much money…"

Alisa was right. He didn't want to hear it, and more to the point, he just didn't believe it. Perhaps the high-end clients, the "decent" guys looking for a bit of fun or a shoulder to cry on – maybe they could be controlled – but what about the coke-fuelled clients or the drunk, dangerous, violent ones? How could they be controlled, or was it the dangerous ones that added that frisson of excitement that seemed to somehow legitimise it all? Paul was appalled by the thought of it.

Alisa could see he was struggling.

"It's only complicated if you let the two sides of you get confused."

"And have you?" Paul asked bluntly.

Alisa was undaunted.

"Once, maybe… It was a long time ago and it can never happen again. It was ridiculous, but he broke my heart too. He crossed the line and I'll never let that happen again. It hurts too much. It makes what I do so much harder knowing that it could happen. I can be tough when I need to be, but I can get lonely too sometimes. I was in love with Chris and then this. It sounds ridiculous, but sometimes you just can't help the way you feel about someone."

Paul shifted uncomfortably in his chair.

"He really got to me, even in those few short hours…"

Paul knew only too well how that could happen.

"So…" she said, pulling herself to her full height and taking a sip of rosé, "I have to be two separate people. I'll never let that happen again. It hurt too much and I can't afford to feel that way… not again. I'm sure you understand how hard it could be for me if things become confused."

Paul feared he understood only too well, and wondered with a deepening sadness if "not crossing the line" applied just as much to him as anybody else. He wasn't even sure he knew which side of the line he was actually on in the first place.

"I understand. I'm sorry. I should never have asked."

"I don't mind, Paul. I feel I could tell you anything."

He felt a compelling need to check his phone. There was a text that read: **Run out of brioche. Send reinforcements.** He showed it to Alisa, who repaid him with an innocent giggle.

"So… we have a little more time then," she said, all smiles again.

"I suppose we do. What did you have in mind?"

Paul was surprised to see her staring back at him through a few brunette curls she'd permitted to tumble casually, perhaps a little provocatively, across her face.

"I don't know," she said. "Let's just get the bill."

She drained the last few drops of wine from her glass and then busied herself to leave.

Alex's emergency fund picked up the tab and they set off back towards the car.

It was another beautiful day on the Côte d'Azur and, to anyone looking on, they could almost pass for being just one more loving couple whiling away a leisurely afternoon. As they walked, Paul was once again drawn to the image of Alisa reflected in the windows of the equally glamorous boutiques as they strolled arm in arm.

All too soon, they took the steps down to the car park, leaving the sunshine and La Croisette behind them. Paul approached the ticket machine to settle the parking fee.

"Leave that for a minute," she said. "You can do that later."

"But…"

"Come with me," she insisted.

Alisa grabbed his hand and, walking backwards, pulled him gently towards the car. Paul slipped the as yet unpaid parking ticket back into his pocket. The car park was all but deserted, practically empty. There was a soft green glow from the overhead lights, an ocean of green as far as the eye could see. Alone, above the solitary hire car, a single red light reflected judgementally on the roof, washing down over the blackened windows and across the gleaming paintwork.

"Open the car," Alisa whispered.

Paul clicked the button as instructed and the car unlocked, its lights flashing twice in their compliance.

Alisa took Paul by the arm and steered him into the back seat. She closed the door behind them and, as the interior light faded to black, she kissed him. Then she took the lead and removed some of her clothes, instructing Paul to do the same. Moments later, they made love on the back seat of the hire car. It was awkward and clumsy yet intimate and loving. It was reckless and carefree, unplanned, unsafe perhaps, but unrestrained and deeply honest. Alisa was even more beautiful to Paul now than before, and in that moment, he knew he loved her.

When it was over, they sat silently staring forward beyond the front seats and out into the vast empty space of the deserted car park. There was no romance in this place, yet they had shared something intense, genuine and utterly real.

"Alisa…" he began.

She placed a delicate finger to his lips once again.

"Please don't say anything," she whispered as she straightened her hair and planted an affectionate kiss on his cheek. "You're such a lovely man," she said, "but things are never the same when the excitement ends. Trust me, Paul, it's never the same."

And all her ambiguity returned.

Chapter 45

THURSDAY

On the left-hand pillar, a flashing orange light heralded the opening of the gates to Katia Shapiro's imposing villa.

"Someone's coming. Get ready!" Kira announced. She sat bolt upright in her seat, tugging at his arm.

Gary couldn't speak; he couldn't swallow. He chewed furiously and dropped what was left of a baguette on his lap as he scrambled to start the car. The gates were fully open now, but there was no sign of anyone or anything coming out. Then, suddenly, a black BMW appeared at the end of the drive. It was stationary momentarily, then turned right and sped off in the direction of the main road. From there it was just a short drive to the junction, and then a choice between another right turn to St Jean village, or a sharp left that lead to the main highway and away from the Cap Ferrat.

"It's not him," she said, relaxing back into her seat and releasing her grip on Gary's immaculately tailored sleeve.

The BMW's front windscreen had a lighter tint than the rest of the car and afforded them a brief glimpse of the chauffeur at the wheel. He was clearly alone in the front of the car, but there was no way of knowing if Katia Shapiro, or anyone else for that matter, was sitting hidden from view in the back.

"We'll wait," she said, seemingly taking charge. "I doubt the guy we're looking for is getting the chauffeur treatment."

Gary concurred. "And he doesn't warrant a bodyguard either?"

She took a long drink from the bottle of mineral water so generously donated by the unsuspecting maid on the seventh floor of the hotel. They settled in for another wait as the huge gates closed securely shut.

Despite Kira's engaging company, Gary was becoming a little restless. There had been no other activity at the villa all morning. No one went in and no one came out. It was a test of his commitment and self-control not to chase after the BMW just to break the monotony. He decided he could sit still no longer.

"I think I'll just take a quick look. You wait here."

"Paul said we had to stay together, in the car... no risks! Remember?" Kira protested mildly, but it was nothing more than a gesture.

"Don't worry. I'll only be a minute."

"Just be careful, that's all..."

"How dangerous can it be? Paul worries too much," he said. "Just lock the doors while I'm gone. Okay?"

Gary clambered out of the car, dusted off a few crumbs and crossed the road. He crept down the side of the wall that ran the full length of the villa's grounds, taking a moment to compose himself before slowly approaching the entrance.

Where the gates were hinged to the huge pillars that bore their substantial weight there was a small gap that permitted a glimpse into the grounds. The view was restricted, but it was enough. Gary turned on his heels and ran back to the car.

"Open the door!" he shouted as he sprinted across the road.

He dived into the driving seat and started the engine as the flashing orange light burst back into life.

"Put your seatbelt on. He's coming out," he said breathlessly.

"How do you know it's him?"

"He's short, fat, wearing a dark suit, he's just thrown a couple of suitcases in the boot of a car and he looks like he's about to shit himself!" Gary was still breathing heavily.

The gates started to open. This time there was no delay. A white Audi A1 flew out of the drive and set off in the same direction as the black BMW.

"Well?" Gary asked.

"It's him! Get going!"

Gary slammed the red Corsa into gear and raced off in pursuit.

"Steady, steady. Not too close. Not too close," Gary said to himself, pre-empting the same advice that would almost certainly be coming from Kira if she wasn't so preoccupied fumbling with her seatbelt.

The Audi approached the T-junction and braked hard to avoid a white 4x4 making its way from the village. Kira clicked her seatbelt into place. In the distance, a silver vehicle hurtled towards the junction from the direction of the mainland. Gary covered the brakes. He was totally focused on the Audi and wanted to keep some distance between them, it was only then the silver car caught his eye.

A white Porsche Cayenne 4x4 passed sedately by, and the man in the Audi A1 prepared to pull away. But Gary's focus had changed; the silver car appeared to accelerate as it approached. It wasn't slowing down, there was a roar from its engine, and the sunlight flashed off its paintwork. The driver of the Audi had seen it too. He seemed unsure, and he hesitated as the silver car closed in at a furious pace. His chance to pull away was gone; it was already too late. The speeding silver Mercedes screamed to a halt, leaving a trail of rubber as it slewed across the road, screeching to a halt a hair's breadth from the A1's front bumper. Broadsided and trapped, there was no way forward for the Audi.

Even before the Mercedes had fully come to a stop, a huge man leapt out of the silver car and tore around to the driver's door of the small white compact. He had an exaggerated limp but it wasn't slowing him down. The Audi driver crashed the gears trying to find reverse and hammered away at the door lock in an attempt to secure the car. The huge man with the limp grabbed the door handle and pulled furiously. His frustration boiled over as the door held fast, and he began shouting a barrage of abuse at the terrified man inside. The driver, in his desperation, had at least managed to lock the car doors, but he still struggled to find reverse. The engine of the Audi revved wildly, the gears crashing and grinding to no effect.

"Who the hell is that?" Gary shouted.

The man was still pulling at the car door, but it just wouldn't give. The short fat Russian inside was reduced to nothing more than a blind panic. He tried again and again to reverse the car.

"It's them!" Kira shouted, and she recoiled back into her seat. "That's Giorgi!"

Gary had already eased their car to a stop; his foot was pressed down hard against the brake pedal and his knuckles had blanched white as he gripped the steering wheel.

"What do we do?" His features flushed crimson as his pulse raged.

"Nothing – we can't do anything." Kira looked terrified and slid down low in her seat.

The hire car idled at the side of the road as Giorgi began hammering on the Audi's window. It didn't give. With the window intact and the doors locked, it was stalemate. If the driver could just find a gear, maybe he could still effect an escape. The huge Russian reached into the small of his back under his jacket. The Audi rocked furiously on its suspension and the engine screamed in protest. Giorgi pulled out an enormous handgun and brought it to bear in a single movement. It was all over for the man inside the car. If Giorgi pulled the trigger, he was a dead man.

"Stop the engine!" Giorgi screamed, and Kira interpreted.

But the man trapped inside the car continued to hammer the throttle and grind the gears, albeit to no effect.

Giorgi adjusted his grip on the gun, but there was still a chance for the driver if he could just reverse the car. The gears engaged and the engine note changed, just as the butt of the gun smashed into the window sending small shards of glass flying into the face of the driver. But still the window didn't give. Again and again he smashed the gun into the glass. Then, suddenly, he was through. He shoved a massive paw straight into the car just as it started to move backwards. He grabbed the man by the throat with one hand and went for the car keys with the other. The car stopped dead.

The driver was frantic. It looked as though Giorgi was about to drag him straight through the shattered window, but instead he reached inside the car and unlocked the door.

The short fat Russian was dragged out of the car and into the road. He was helpless, overpowered, perhaps paralysed by fear as Giorgi heaved him to the back of the Mercedes. The boot had already been popped open. Boris stood him up at the back of the car and then smashed the gun viciously against the side of his head. He was a dead weight now, and Giorgi threw him into the boot of the car like he was nothing at all.

No sooner was the boot slammed shut than the Mercedes powered off. It executed a U-turn and headed back in the direction it had just come from. Giorgi climbed into the Audi and set off, following the Mercedes in close order.

"Fuck me... fuck me... Shit." Not so much the gentleman now, Gary was hyperventilating.

They were just twenty-five yards back from the junction. *"Not too close,"* he'd told himself, and that alone had saved them from pulling up immediately behind the Audi as the Mercedes had screamed to a stop. *"Not too close".* "Fuck me... He had a gun! Shit! He had a fucking gun!" Gary had all but lost it.

"Follow them, quick, come on." Kira was all business.

"You're shitting me... right?" Gary was incredulous. "He had a fucking gun!"

"Paul told you it was dangerous. Now come on, they're getting away."

"Seriously?"

"Come on, Gary, PLEASE!" Kira was desperate.

Gary reluctantly put the car into gear.

"Come on! Come on! Don't let them get away!" Kira insisted.

He could see his hands shaking and feel the sweat beading at his temples. What the hell had he got himself into? *"Let me know if you need any help, mate. I'm your man,"* he had all too casually told Paul the day before, but these guys had guns! No one said *anything* about guns.

"Not too close. You're getting too close." When it came to the crunch, it was definitely Kira giving the orders.

The Corsa was fully fifty yards behind the Audi but closing in fast. Both cars in front had slowed to an even pace, but Gary had failed to notice the change in their rate of progress.

"Slow down, Gary. Slow down." Kira was giving the all orders now.

Gary slowed the car to the speed limit and maintained his gap.

At the main road, the Mercedes and the Audi turned right. There were traffic lights ahead and Gary was busily calculating his approach – he needed to get this just right. He shot through at the last minute, keeping a reasonable distance between him and the cars up ahead.

"What if they split up? Which car do I follow?"

Gary wasn't thinking straight.

"Alex's car…" Kira bawled. "The silver one!"

"Who the hell is Alex?"

"Just follow the silver car, the one with the man in the boot!" Kira sounded exasperated with him.

It was obvious which car he needed to follow once she'd said it out loud. Gary immediately focused on the lead vehicle of the two.

"Who the hell is Alex?"

Kira didn't answer.

After a few kilometres, both cars dived right into a road leading down to a village. A signpost pointed to Villefranche. Gary had heard of it before, even read about in the blurb in his hotel bedroom. It was once a small fishing village but was now a hotspot for tourists, not least because it served as the deep-water port for cruise liners visiting Nice. Gary had never been there before but Kira knew it well.

"Slow down, it's a dead end… Don't get too close," she ordered.

There was little chance of that happening now. Gary was on full alert and, after all, he'd already seen the gun.

"No risks," Paul had said to him. His new *mate* had been absolutely crystal clear about that. Gary could barely believe he was now tailing a pair of gun-wielding psychopathic Russian gangsters, and a man with a potentially serious head trauma, into a dead end. There was absolutely no danger of him getting too close. But Gary just concentrated on the driving and kept his mouth shut.

To the right of the village lay an old fort that had been preserved as a museum. Bizarrely, its limited grounds were completely laid to tarmac and now served the town as an overflow car park. Both the Mercedes and Audi cruised in. Gary stopped short of the car park entrance.

"Go and see what they're doing!" Kira ordered.

"What? Are you mental or something?"

"Go, or I will!"

"Okay, I'm going. I'm going!"

Gary jumped out. He ran across the road and then walked past the car park entrance as if he was nothing more than a passing pedestrian. He glanced in to see the Audi being reversed into a gap at the far end of a line of car parking spaces. The broken widow was furthest away from general view and the car could probably stay there, unnoticed, for hours if not days. There was no sign of the Mercedes.

He watched as Giorgi uncoiled himself from the tiny Audi and then stood nonchalantly at the end of another row of parked cars, as if he was waiting for a lift. The Mercedes swung back into view. Gary spun on his heels and walked back the way he'd come. He saw the Mercedes stop to pick up the giant Russian and then head straight towards him as it made its way back to the car park exit.

Shit, shit, don't run, don't run, Gary implored himself, in a bid to stay calm. If he ran, they would instinctively know that something was wrong.

As the silver Mercedes cruised slowly past him he felt every muscle in his body tense uncontrollably, but he kept on walking. As it headed down into the port and out of sight, he picked up speed, dashing across the road and back into the sanctuary of the red Opel Corsa.

"Fuck me, that was close!" he exploded as he slammed the car door shut.

"That was brilliant, Gary! You were amazing. I thought they'd see you for certain but you were—"

"Fuck me!" Gary panted breathlessly. "I don't feel particularly fucking amazing."

"Come on, get going… we can't lose them now!"

"What?"

"Get going, come on!"

Gary did as he was told. He started the car and slammed it into gear.

"I've got a bad feeling about this, Kira. This is not going to end well."

"Just don't lose them – that's all," Kira ordered.

As they entered the port, it was obvious to Gary that it was market day. A variety of vendors had set up their stalls on a crowded terrace on their left. To the right was the customs building, painted in a soft pink, and a little further on there was a small square lined with shops and restaurants. There was a large pay-and-display car park behind the customs house, but it looked busy and congested. Gary immediately understood why the Russians had dumped the Audi at the fort.

He cautiously followed the Mercedes down to the quayside and Kira pointed out the secure pier on the far side of the customs house. It served the launches that buzzed in and out all day from the cruise liners. Several lay at anchor only a few hundred yards out in the bay, and the pier was crowded with day-tourists flocking ashore.

The quayside stretched out ahead of them, taking a shallow left turn after a few hundred yards, and then continuing onwards and out of view. The road along the quay was narrow and packed with pedestrians. Upmarket restaurants and bars lined one side, and a single row of dining tables, complete with parasols, were placed at the water's edge on the other. Tiny motor boats were billeted at the stone quay, and a few fishing boats were moored securely to a pontoon that bobbed gently in the swell. Out in the bay, dozens of yachts and pleasure cruisers were anchored, many of their tenders crowding the quayside as their owners came ashore for the indulgently expensive cuisine on offer. The bars were busy, but the restaurants were serving only a few late-afternoon diners.

The road was packed with hundreds of tourists, mainly cruise ship types, who strolled around as if the road was pedestrianised. It wasn't, and the Mercedes patiently manoeuvred its way through them. The silver car rounded the corner past the last of the restaurants and crawled to a stop. It was quieter there, away from the restaurants and out of sight of the crowd. Nearby, a narrow jetty reached out over the water with three small tenders moored alongside.

"Drive past. Don't stop until you get to the end." Kira gave her instructions from the footwell of the Corsa. She was staying out of sight. Even with her new look, she didn't want to come face-to-face with Boris or Giorgi.

"No risks... promise me..." Paul had demanded, and they had both given their word.

As soon as they were past, Kira popped back up again, and peering back between the front seats, she kept the two Russians under surveillance.

"Right... stop the car. This is a safe distance. We can watch them from here," she said, recovering her composure.

Gary brought the car to a halt. The two Russians were standing at the back of the Mercedes waiting for the chance to get their victim out of the boot of the car and they were staring directly at a red Opel Corsa. Boris and Giorgi knew they were out of sight of the quayside, where the diners and the tourists were going about their business, but the car that had just passed them was still very much in view, and therefore a problem.

"Get out and go around the corner," Kira demanded. "They won't do anything until you're out of the car and out sight."

"I'm not leaving you, Kira." Gary was adamant. "It's too dangerous."

"You have to or we'll be here all night," she insisted. "They're watching us. They know you're still in the car but they haven't seen me. They'll think you're in the car on your own. I can watch them from here. I'll be safe enough. Just lock the doors when you go."

"They don't give a shit about locked doors, Kira. You saw what they did! I can't leave you…"

"Yes, you can! They don't even know I'm here. We need to give them enough time to get that man out of the car. You need to go… Just go. Go. GO!"

Gary climbed out.

"Don't look back. Just keep going."

Gary did exactly as he was told. Kira held her position.

As Gary disappeared from their line of sight, Boris and Giorgi sprang into action. The boot was popped open and the short fat Russian was hauled groggily to his feet.

In a heartbeat they had manhandled their stricken victim on to the largest of the three small boats at the jetty. He was bundled forward into the bow and a large tarpaulin pulled over him. The boat pulled smartly away from the quayside with Boris at the helm, its dark blue pennant braced against the wind.

Gary was on his way back. He jumped into the car and fired up the engine. As he turned the car around Kira never took her eyes off the little boat as it made its way out of the harbour. Before too long, it picked up speed and headed for deeper water.

Kira watched as the tender approached a huge yacht moored some way out in the bay. It was a magnificent vessel. The navy blue hull seemed to melt into the azure sea and the white superstructure blazed in the sunshine. The tender approached and all but disappeared, swamped by the sheer scale of the vast yacht. Kira strained to see its tiny white hull as it finally came to rest.

Gary dialled Paul's number. He answered on the third ring.

"Are you on your way back, mate? I think we might have found what you're looking for."

Chapter 46

Boris tethered the tender to the pontoon as Giorgi pulled back the tarpaulin and helped Oleg to his feet. He was still reeling from the effects of his close encounter with the butt of Giorgi's gun, and with that and the relentless rocking motion of the tiny boat, he was completely incapable of standing unaided.

A huge door, hinged just above the waterline, had been hydraulically lowered to provide a landing platform and facilitate the launching and receiving of tenders. With the platform in place, it left a large opening in the side of the hull that gave access to the yacht's immaculate tender bay. Two large elegantly liveried tenders remained in place, fixed on their mountings, and a pair of dark blue jet skis sat alongside.

A two-man welcoming committee stood in the shadowy expanse of the vast open hull. Impassive and nonchalant at first, they merely observed, offering nothing by way of assistance. Boris and Giorgi hauled the stricken man from the tender.

As they moved awkwardly towards the opening in the hull, Anatoly's lieutenants suddenly became impatient, regarding their visitors with a professional suspicion. Boris recognised them immediately; they had all been on the same side in Norilsk, even though he suspected that neither of them had ever known he was there. The memory of it flooded back, the salutary lesson never to be forgotten. It was all still so raw – the shots, the blood, the stench of it. Roman had fired the first shot and dispatched Joel Papé, then, barely a heartbeat later, Boris had dispatched Roman himself. It was Viktor and Dimitri, the two thugs that greeted him now, who finished the job and ruthlessly executed what remained of the French contingent. All of it expressly at Anatoly's behest.

"Bring him. Come on, what's keeping you?" Viktor demanded, without even a flicker of recognition.

Neither Boris nor Giorgi responded, but they continued to bundle Oleg into the cool shadows of the tender bay.

"Not so fast, not so fast," Dimitri growled, extracting as much menace from each word as he could.

"Make up your mind," Boris snapped.

Viktor just grunted while the other remained silent, refusing to rise to the implied challenge to their authority. He held out his hand and arrogantly barred any further progress. Giorgi got the message first, reaching back, and for a second time in the day he recovered his weapon from the waistband of his trousers. This time he meekly handed it to the man in front of him and pushed past with Oleg hanging limply at his side. Boris handed over a smaller yet equally lethal looking handgun he'd removed, very deliberately, from a discreet holster under his jacket.

"Watch your step with these bastards," Boris muttered to Giorgi as they brought Oleg back to his full height.

Dimitri barged past them.

"This way, ladies," he snarled, and headed up the steps to the main deck.

Boris and Giorgi followed obediently, the weight of their charge shared equally between them. Oleg drifted in and out of consciousness, completely unaware of his predicament. Viktor brought up the rear, carefully disarming Boris's and Giorgi's relinquished weapons.

At the top of the steps they turned right onto the main gangway and then left to the rear deck where Anatoly was waiting to receive them.

"So, this is the famous Oleg," he growled, as Boris did his best to stand him to attention.

Anatoly was a slim man with jagged features, close-cropped hair and manic eyes.

"Drink, gentlemen?"

Boris and Giorgi declined. Oleg was incapable of expressing a preference.

Anatoly waved away the attentions of the female steward standing stiffly behind a well-stocked bar. "Go, go," he barked, as he studied Oleg. The girl dutifully shuffled away.

"So where were you going in such a hurry, my friend? The airport perhaps? Did you really think I would let you slip away like that?"

Oleg was unresponsive.

"Wake this man up!" Anatoly bellowed, glaring at one of his stooges.

Dimitri stepped forward, and without breaking stride, he slammed a well-aimed fist into Oleg's solar plexus. The entirely predictable result was to render him even more senseless than he already was.

Anatoly's eyes flared. He delighted in the pointless display of violence. There was already no doubt he was in charge, yet it was abundantly clear that the brutal display of authority was not entirely for Oleg's consumption alone.

Anatoly turned to look Boris squarely in the face.

"Again!" he demanded.

Anatoly's gaze never left Boris's impassive features. The second impact landed without either of them bothering to witnessing the aftermath. Anatoly's eyes widened at the sound of it. Boris got the message loud and clear.

Oleg collapsed, and Giorgi lunged forward to stop him falling to the deck. He winced with pain as he took the full weight of the unconscious Oleg on his injured leg.

"What happened to you? What's the matter with your leg?" Anatoly snarled. "Did Oleg get the better of you?" He was entirely focused on Boris, but it was clear that Anatoly missed nothing.

"It's fine," Giorgi replied flatly.

Boris had been very clear with Giorgi. He'd warned him about Anatoly and told him not to antagonise him, but even so, he feared his reaction. Boris needed Giorgi to control his instincts, to control his temper. They were functionaries to this man: mercenary and expendable. They were just hired muscle brought in to perform a task and nothing more. But Anatoly was difficult to read. There could be no show of weakness. But it was a challenge, even for a man of far greater wisdom than Giorgi, to find the right balance between strength and respect that could make all the difference. But Anatoly paid well, and now they had come this far, Boris wanted their payday. He willed Giorgi to stay calm.

Giorgi chose to say nothing at all. Instead, he used his immense strength to force Oleg ramrod straight from the foetal position his body had assumed.

"So, what are we to do with you?" Anatoly turned his attention back to Oleg. The question was entirely rhetorical. There would be only one man doing the talking.

"Boris, my friend, I trust all is in order?"

"It is."

"And the girl... you will have her tomorrow?"

"Yes, we will have her."

"Good, good." He approached Boris, his mouth only inches from the giant Russian's face. "This is very important to me," he whispered confidentially. "You understand?" The question carried a threat all of its own.

"Of course."

"Good," he growled, and turned his attentions to Giorgi.

"I asked you once before. Now tell me, what the *fuck* is wrong with your leg?" Anatoly's words were venom.

"It's fine," Giorgi repeated, trying for as much conviction as possible.

Anatoly stepped back, his brow furrowed as if deep in thought. "Really?"

Anatoly motioned to his stooge a second time, and then nodded at Giorgi's leg. Dimitri coolly pulled out a large handgun of his own and slammed it hard into Giorgi's thigh. It was a fearsome blow. Giorgi buckled as any man would, but he took it without complaint. A small dark patch started to form on his leg just beneath his wound.

Anatoly seethed. "Either of you lie to me again... I will kill you both where you stand." He spat the words directly into Giorgi's face.

Boris tensed. He knew it would take all of Giorgi's very limited will power not to snap Anatoly's neck right there and then.

"Boris..." he began, fuming. "You tell me everything is in order for tomorrow, and then I find your bitch here is a cripple. I should kill you both."

He walked back to the bar the crew member had been so diligently tending earlier and poured himself a large measure of vodka from a bottle caked in ice. He studied the two men as he let the liquor slip down his throat. He swallowed in exaggerated fashion and began to nod insanely. A treacherous smile curled across his lips and he began to laugh.

"I like you," he said, as if he'd only just come to the conclusion. "Yes! Yes, I like you two. You have balls." He laughed some more, and the two stooges joined in.

Boris cracked a smile of his own. He indicated that Giorgi should do the same. He duly obliged.

"Yes, I like you crazy bastards. You have big balls, yes! Yes!"

Boris knew this could go either way, but the maniac Russian seemed to relax a little. Anatoly had tested them in some lunatic way and, as far as Boris could tell, it was a test they had somehow managed to pass.

He was a sick, dangerous bastard, in Boris's opinion, and he decided there and then he would never get involved with him again. They would get the job done, get paid and then they would be finished with him for good. Boris had regretted taking on the assignment the moment it started to go wrong. There was no way out for now, but working for a madman wasn't going to make sorting out Giorgi's mistakes any easier.

"Come... let's have a drink together. Tomorrow is a big day." Anatoly enthused with all the bonhomie in the world. Boris knew better than to refuse his offer a second time. Anatoly was already pouring the shots.

"Tell me, how is my old friend Alex? I haven't heard from him for a while." Anatoly spoke as if he was merely shooting the breeze, but there was always an edge.

Boris didn't flinch.

"He's lying low until it's all over. He'll be in touch when it's done."

It was partly true. Boris knew Alex hated Anatoly as much as the next man, but Alex had betrayed them, compounding Giorgi's stupidity with Alisa. He'd helped the girls escape after the photographs went missing, and that had forced him to take Maria as a hostage. Alex's actions had made things so much more complicated for him. Yet Alex wasn't a problem to Boris right now. Even if he did survive the vicious beating that Giorgi meted out, he would certainly know to keep well out of the way until things settled down.

And that was another mistake, something else that Giorgi had got wrong. Giorgi beating Alex to a pulp in his own basement, while Boris himself was preoccupied with other matters, was a typically brutal and ill-considered reaction to Alex's betrayal. If Boris hadn't been so distracted it would never have happened. Boris regretted it. He knew he should never have left Giorgi alone and unsupervised in the basement once he'd seen the text message their fixer had sent to his girls. But right now, Alex wasn't a pressing concern. Oleg was an entirely different matter.

"Sit, sit," Anatoly ordered. "What else can I get you? Food maybe… maybe a whore before the big day? I have British girls, only the best! What do you say? Would you like to screw a British whore before we take our turns with the Shapiro bitch tomorrow?"

Anatoly smiled manically. He didn't do humour well, and there was nothing amusing in his tone, but everybody laughed, except for Oleg, who was incapable of doing anything at all.

"Thank you, but no," Boris said politely. "Really, there is no need…"

He had already had his fill of whores, British or otherwise, and politely declined their host's growing hospitality.

"You two…" Anatoly waved his glass in the direction of his two lieutenants. "Take care of Oleg for my friends." He turned to Giorgi. "Leave him… sit, sit." Anatoly indicated that they should both take a stool at the bar.

Giorgi allowed Oleg to slide gently to the deck as the two men moved in. The first was carrying a length of chain. Boris and Giorgi each took a seat at the counter as Anatoly assumed the role of barmaid. The stooges proceeded to wind the chain around Oleg's legs and fix it into position with a padlock.

Oleg started to cry out. It might have been the pain or the fear, but whichever it was, Oleg began to struggle. His cries were desperate.

"Here, here use this."

Anatoly took up a monogramed linen napkin from a pile on the bar. They looked like expensive, pristine white Egyptian cotton, with the name of the yacht embroidered in navy blue on one corner. He took a sharp knife from the counter and sliced through the hem on two sides and then ripped the napkin in half. The blade nicked his finger and blood seeped onto both halves of the fine cloth as he tore at it. He cast the monogramed portion to one side and threw the other to Viktor. Boris discreetly palmed the complacently discarded portion and stuffed it into his jacket pocket.

Dimitri rammed his portion of the cloth into Oleg's mouth as he screamed for help.

Boris regarded their victim with a degree of sympathy now. With what little sensibility he'd regained, he was terrified, and with good reason. Anatoly seemed indifferent to what was taking place, but Boris and Giorgi were only too aware. At least Oleg wouldn't be able to talk, not even to Anatoly. Oleg was a loose end; he knew too much. Using him to stake out the Negresco had been another mistake, his own this time, and as it turned out, a complete waste of time. But Giorgi had been injured and temporarily out of action and he needed a new face, someone the girls hadn't seen before. At the time he felt like he had no choice. But if Oleg revealed what he knew about the two girls or the stake-out at the Negresco, he feared Anatoly would kill them both for sure.

As their host casually poured each man another generous shot of frozen vodka, Viktor and Dimitri picked Oleg up and dropped him over the seaward side of the yacht.

"Callous motherfucker," Boris muttered to himself, and then he laughed outrageously at whatever evil bullshit the lunatic Anatoly had just come out with.

Chapter 47

Paul pulled into the car park at the rear of the customs building in Villefranche-sur-Mer. He could see the red Opel Corsa reverse parked into a space under the shade of a mature plane tree. Gary and Kira were sitting on a bench staring out over the bay. With the market stalls now packed up for the day, the car park was lightly occupied, and he manoeuvred the powerful hire car into a space next to it.

"Which boat are they on?" Paul asked urgently as he joined Gary and Kira at the sea wall.

"It's a yacht actually, and it's that one," Gary replied, pointing out the massive boat anchored offshore in the deeper water.

Paul stood quietly for a moment studying the vessel. The girls fussed about, chatting away in Russian, apparently exchanging details of the day's events. Paul only had one thing on his mind and focused on the yacht. There were signs of movement on the main deck, but the vessel was moored too far out for him to discern any real detail.

"Any idea what's going on out there?"

"Not really," Gary replied after a few moments.

The tender could still be seen moored at the side of the huge yacht. Dwarfed by its scale, the white of its tiny form was just visible against the mass of the dark blue hull.

"What now?" Gary asked.

"We wait, I suppose," Paul said thoughtfully.

Gary seemed agitated.

"What are we waiting for? We've found them. Mission accomplished. Let's just get the police." But the look on Gary's face suggested he already knew things were far from over.

"Walk with me a minute," Paul said, and he headed off away from the girls.

Gary followed him as he made his way to a patch of shade under an even larger plane tree at the far edge of the car park.

"I didn't tell you everything," he began.

"Damn right you didn't!" Gary exploded. "They've got guns, for Christ's sake. You never told me that!" Gary was justifiably furious.

"Keep your voice down," Paul said firmly. "Gary, I had no idea about that. You can believe what you like, but I am telling you the truth. I had no idea."

Gary drew a long breath. "It wouldn't have made any difference to you even if you had known, would it?"

Paul considered the question, but before he could articulate an answer Gary was back on his case.

"What the hell have these girls got you involved in? Do you even know what's going on here? Really know, I mean… for a fact and not just guessing! Have you got any idea what you're doing?"

"Which question do you want me to answer, Gary?" Paul replied with a note of irritation.

"Bloody hell, mate, all of them," he replied in a barely supressed growl.

"Look, I don't know anything for certain but I'm working on it," Paul replied. "As for guns… they make no difference to me at all. I didn't know about them, but it's hardly a surprise now I come to think about it. But I certainly wouldn't have involved you if I'd known these guys were armed. That wouldn't have been fair… but as for the rest of it… I have no idea what we're involved in if I'm honest… and no!"

"No! No what?" Gary looked confused.

"No to your last question. I have no idea what I'm doing. I'm making this up as I go, but I can't just walk away. Look at them, Gary. How can I just walk away?"

"Mate, I can hardly take my bloody eyes of them, but guns… This is serious shit!"

"I know. I'm sorry. If you want to step away, I completely understand. I've already asked you to do too much—"

Gary interrupted. "Let me get this absolutely straight" – Gary looked as earnest as Paul had ever seen him – "even if you'd known these guys were armed with enormous guns, and more than happy to wave them around, by the way, you would still be here chasing these mad bastards down. Is that right?" His instincts were spot on as usual.

"Yes, Gary, I would."

"Fair enough!" he said with a finality that closed the matter.

Paul had a growing respect for Gary. He was tougher than he looked.

"What else are you not telling me? Why haven't you gone to the police with all this?"

"We can't go to the police, otherwise I would have already done exactly that by now."

"Why not? Surely that's precisely what we should do."

"It's not that straightforward. Trust me, I wish it was! The main problem—"

"What 'main problem'?" Gary interrupted him with a look of a man who could barely believe he was still unaware of the "main problem".

"The main problem," Paul repeated, "is that the Russians have threatened to kill Maria if they get even the slightest inkling that the police are involved… and the main problem with that, Gary, is I don't doubt it for a minute."

"What? As in murder?"

"Yes… as in murder. And once they've done that, they've threatened to come after the girls as well. These guys aren't going to leave loose ends. You've already seen they don't mess about."

Gary shuffled uncomfortably from one foot to the other and took a deep breath.

"It's just a bloody mess right now," Paul summarised without emotion.

Gary exhaled loudly. "And you think these guys are for real?"

"I have no doubt these guys are for real – no doubt about that at all. At the end of the day, I've given my word to these girls and I don't intend to let them down now. They don't have anyone else to help them, and I'm not just going to walk away because things are a little bit *scarier* than I first thought."

"A little bit scarier! You didn't see the size of the bloody gun."

"Look, Gary, I'm going to get Maria back if it's the last thing I do. I could really use your help, but if you want out then I don't blame you. The way things are going, you probably should just walk away right now. You've done enough already and, as you say, these bastards are far more dangerous than I realised. Call me reckless if you like, but knowing what these guys are capable of just makes me even more determined to sort it out. I can't just stand by and let it happen."

Gary thought for a moment.

"I'm in!" he declared. "Let's sort these chickenshit bastards out!"

Gary offered his hand and Paul shook it vigorously almost by instinct. It all felt a little bit "Enid Blyton" but Gary was still in, and after everything he'd been through that day, that was a great result whichever way he looked at it.

"Are you sure it wouldn't be better just to go to the police," Gary asked. Ever the terrier, he couldn't let it drop. "I'm just checking, that's all. Have you really thought that bit through?"

"Yes, absolutely. We'll get the police involved as soon as we can, as soon as we know where Maria is. We need to find her first. That's critical."

Gary looked shaken, but Paul needed to know. "Are you still in?"

"Absolutely!" Gary declared without hesitation. "Never in doubt!"

Alisa joined them, taking Paul's arm and resting her head on his shoulder. Gary raised an eyebrow and shot Paul a knowing look.

"I see!" he said with a frisson of drama.

Gary could be a bit of a jerk at times but, despite that, Paul was still glad to have him around.

"What's the yacht called, I wonder..." Alisa thought out loud.

"Let's find out," Paul said, patting his pockets. "Who's got some one euro coins?"

Gary checked his pockets and came up with a couple.

Paul headed off to the corner of the car park, where he'd already spotted a coin-operated tourist-style telescope. "I take it you didn't see this earlier, mate?" Paul grinned as he pushed the first euro into the slot and began adjusting the focus. Kira and Alisa joined them, talking excitedly, asking questions and fumbling around for extra coins.

As the fog cleared in the eyepiece and the optics began to work their magic, Paul located the yacht in the distance. One more tweak and he could make out several figures on the rear deck in more detail. He could see five men on the lower deck and two female crew members on the deck above setting out cushions and generally fussing about. He maxed out the zoom and readjusted the focus, running the telescope up and down the length of the vessel.

"It's owned by some Russian gazillionaire apparently," Gary said.

Paul refocused on the lower deck. "How do you know that?"

"We asked a local."

"Did this local say anything else about it?"

"You'll have to ask Kira for the details. She did all the talking. But basically, no one knows that much about it at all. It's one of the biggest yachts around here at the moment, so it created a bit of a stir when it turned up on Sunday night. No one seems to know that much about who owns it either, but that's not particularly unusual apparently. What is a bit more unusual is that it's only ever the crew that come ashore. Normally these massive yachts drop anchor out there and then the glitterati hit the bars and restaurants, but not with that one. It just sits out there with the crew ferrying stuff in and out." Gary looked quite pleased with himself.

Paul rammed another euro coin into the slot.

"Did your local know if the owner is on board?"

"We didn't ask, but the 'word on the street' is that somebody important must be out there. If anyone goes anywhere near it, they get shooed off by heavies on jet skis."

Paul panned back to the rear of the yacht and focused in on the stern. There was a name, but at that distance it was still hard to read. He tried to bring each letter into focus one at a time. After the third letter, he already knew exactly what he was looking at.

He had found *Barabus*.

Chapter 48

Another hour passed before there was any definitive movement aboard the yacht. Finally, two large figures climbed into the tender and started heading back to the shore. Paul dropped another of the dwindling supply of one euro coins into the slot and tracked the route of the tiny boat through the telescope.

"It's them," he said.

He recognised Giorgi and Boris as they approached and then veered away out of sight. They were heading towards the jetty beyond the restaurants to where Alex's spectacular Mercedes was parked at the quayside.

"There are only two of them," Gary commented, deep in thought. "I dread to think what they've done with the poor guy they stuffed in the boot."

"Not our concern," Paul said coldly. He had other matters on his mind. "We need to focus on Maria and Katia Shapiro."

Paul stood up and stretched to his full height. His arms ached from gripping the telescope and his vision needed to reset. He turned to Kira.

"The village is a dead end, right?"

Kira nodded.

"You're sure about that? They have to come back out of the village in this direction. Is that right?"

"Yes, there's no other way out. They have to come back this way."

Paul considered his options and made his decision. "Right," he said, "let's get moving."

Gary took the opportunity to commandeer the telescope as Paul finally relinquished it. As he settled into position the money ran out and the viewfinder faded to black. Gary stifled a curse.

"Kira, Alisa, you need to stay here and out of sight for now." Paul was already heading back towards the cars. They followed in his wake. "When we've gone, get some food and water for later. I don't know when we'll get back, but just keep an eye on that yacht. I'll call you on Kira's phone when

301

I know what's happening… and pick up a local road map, as large a scale as you can. Make sure it's got a really good street plan of Monaco, just in case."

Paul took the Opel Corsa keys off Gary and gave them to Alisa.

"Take these," he said. "Gary and I will follow the Mercedes in the other car. It'll be safer than using the Corsa again. We can't risk them recognising it from earlier. We'll come back as soon as we can."

Alisa took the rental car keys in one hand and grabbed Kira by the arm with the other.

"Okay, stay safe, you two," he said. Paul effected what he hoped would pass for a reassuring smile. "Gary… you're with me."

Five minutes later, Paul pulled the second hire car to a halt at the side of the street just outside the car park entrance. There was still no sign of the silver Mercedes but he kept the engine idling in readiness. As Gary craned his neck to watch through the rear window, Paul adjusted the wing mirror to a better angle, his attention alternating between that and the rear-view mirror as they waited. He checked his watch. What was keeping them? A few long minutes slowly elapsed.

Paul knew they had just been given a second chance to find Maria, an opportunity he never expected to get. The plan to stake out Katia's villa was about to pay off, but where was the silver Mercedes? Why the delay? What could possibly be taking them so long?

Finally, the Russians appeared. The Mercedes approached and then powered away disconcertingly quickly. Paul slipped the car into "Drive" and pulled out behind them. Boris was driving, with Giorgi in the passenger seat at his side.

The silver Mercedes made its way up and out of the village, eventually pulling up at a set of traffic lights. Paul held back, with Gary giving him the benefit of his expert advice. Boris turned left and headed for Nice. Paul allowed a scooter to pull out in front of them, breaking the tail for a while, a tactic much to Gary's approval.

As the outskirts of Nice came into view, the Mercedes indicated a right turn and then suddenly pulled up at the side of the road.

Paul slowed up behind them, bringing the hire car to a full stop barely forty metres to their rear.

"What are they up to?" Paul muttered under his breath. He could sense Gary's stress levels rising. "Just stay calm, Gary. Let's see what they do next."

Gary stayed silent but calm wasn't an option. He was starting to fret.

Suddenly, the driver's-side door of the Mercedes flew open and Boris uncoiled himself from behind the wheel.

"Shit! He's coming this way." Gary's fretting intensified.

"Stay calm, Gary. Just stay calm."

The huge Russian strode down the pavement towards them.

"He knows we're following them. We need to get out of here! What are you waiting for? Paul, for Christ's sake, let's get going!"

"Wait, Gary. Just wait…"

Boris was closing in fast; just twenty metres separated them from the huge Russian. A few more paces and then he reached behind his back, brushing his jacket aside as he closed in.

"He's going for his gun!" Gary exploded.

"Just wait."

But Paul's heart missed a beat. He felt a trickle of sweat run the length of his back and his muscles tensed involuntarily. He knew Gary was faring no better.

"Get us out of here, Paul!"

He eased the car into reverse and prepared to hit the accelerator. If the Russian went for his gun he would stamp on the "Go" pedal and worry about the consequences later. Paul couldn't breathe, his breath shortening with Boris's every step…

He was so close now, but he wasn't even looking in their direction. Two more paces and his arm swung forward, a thick wallet held firmly in his vast paw. Paul let out a slow breath as his pulse began to ease. Boris turned right and stepped into a small general store without giving Paul or Gary a second glance.

"That was close, mate. Let's get out of here… This is crazy!"

"No," Paul snapped. "Stay here. I'm going to find out what he's up to."

"He's doing some shopping. What the fuck do we care!"

"We care a lot, Gary." Paul flashed him a look that said so much more. "Just stay here, keep calm and wait."

Gary said nothing. He was pale and sweating. His eyes were almost bursting from their sockets but he remained completely silent.

Paul entered the shop. He began scanning the shelves without ever taking his focus off Boris. The shop appeared to sell a little of everything – fresh vegetables, tinned goods, some bakery items, there was a small hardware section, a freezer cabinet stuffed with all manner of random items and a deli counter strewn with stinking sausages and other local delicacies. It was the toiletries section that held Boris's attention for now.

Paul manoeuvred his way down the aisle for a better view.

Boris seemed lost, picking items up and then placing them back down on the shelf again.

Paul watched him. *What the hell are you doing?* His mind was racing and the fear was starting to consume him once again. With every fibre of his body tensed, he ached to explode into action, to run and create some distance between them. But he fought the instinct and continued his vigil.

Boris made his choice. He picked up a colourful shampoo, a bottle of aromatic shower gel, a perfumed soap of some description, toothpaste and a pink toothbrush.

A pink toothbrush! The potential relevance of it all hit Paul in a wave. The sense of dread that was crushing down on him gave way to a little optimism. He was right! Or at least there was a very good chance he was right.

Boris moved to an open-fronted refrigerated cabinet and, without wasting any time, picked out two large pizzas the size of spare wheels. They were both the "Meat Feast" variety, each one large enough to feed a family. Then he set off in the direction of the checkout and stopped. He stepped back to the refrigerator and grabbed a third pizza – much smaller this time and topped with pieces of cooked ham and chunks of pineapple.

Pink toothbrush, lady's toiletries and a small pizza topped with pineapple. That sealed it as far as Paul was concerned. Boris was shopping, albeit somewhat stereotypically, with a woman in mind. Yes, there was no doubt the massive meat pizzas were for him and Giorgi, but the toiletries and the pineapple-topped pizza were almost certainly for a woman. Now all they needed to do was follow them to their destination and surely that would lead them to Maria. Paul waited no longer. He spun on his heels and headed back to the car. Gary was still in a state.

"What took you so long? What's going on? Why are we still here?"

"Look, Gary, the only reason we can't go to the police is because we have no idea where Maria is. Right?"

"Right."

"We're about to find out exactly where she is. If they head back to the yacht, with what he's just bought, it's a fair bet she's on board. If they head off anywhere else, I'm betting she's never been on that yacht in her life and, what's more, I'm pretty certain that Anatoly, the gazillionaire, has no idea there's a 'Maria' involved at all."

"How can you be so sure?"

"Boris has just bought a pink toothbrush and a girlie pizza. I'm damn sure that's not for either of them, so let's just stay calm and see which way this plays out. Okay?"

"Okay... But..."

"But nothing... Just wait."

The door of the store opened and Boris strode out and headed back to the silver Mercedes. Giorgi was still sitting in the passenger seat. He hadn't stirred, possibly nursing his leg and leaving all the domestic chores to his partner in crime. Moments later, the Mercedes eased back into to the light afternoon traffic. It continued on its way, away from Villefranche and away from *Barabus*. Boris and Giorgi were heading towards Nice.

Paul's mind was racing once again. *This is it!* All he had to do was to stay calm and follow them to wherever it was they were holding Maria. He was already working out what he would need to tell the local police to get them to leap into action. Alisa could help him with that, of course… and once the police had a location and some of the backstory, he could just sit back and let the gendarmes do the rest. The relief was almost overwhelming yet nothing was truly resolved, not yet. But one thing was for sure. Given the direction of travel, Maria was definitely not on board *Barabus* – he was utterly certain of that.

Chapter 49

Paul continued to tail the Mercedes at a safe distance, or at least it felt like a safe distance as Gary's fretting began to subside. After a couple of miles, Boris pulled off the road and cruised into the car park of a large, tired-looking hotel. The car drew to a halt in a parking space close to the main doors and both men climbed out.

"This can't be right," Paul complained. "They can't be keeping Maria here. This just can't be right."

The terrier was back. Gary was all questions.

"What makes you so sure Maria isn't already on the yacht?" he asked.

Paul stopped their car on a loose gravel verge immediately outside the entrance to the hotel car park. He kept the motor running and took a deep breath. Gary wasn't done.

"Surely a bit of shopping isn't enough!"

"Trust me, it's not just the shopping. Maria being on that yacht just wouldn't make any sense now," Paul explained impatiently. In his mind, that issue was already settled, and Gary's lack of insight was beginning to grate. He continued before Gary could ask his supplemental. "Look, Giorgi messed up with Alisa back at the hotel in Nice. Taking Maria was an act of desperation as far as I see it. She's just an insurance policy for them, a way of stopping the girls from going to the police – nothing more than that."

"So... how do you know she isn't already on the yacht?"

Paul settled back in his seat and looked Gary squarely in the eye.

"Why didn't they take her to the yacht straight away, Gary? Why not take her there immediately after they abducted her? That's exactly what they did with Katia's 'gatekeeper'. We know *Barabus* cruised into Villefranche on Sunday night. Why take the risk of holding her at Alex's house at all? Why buy a pink toothbrush and a dodgy pineapple pizza? The crew from the yacht have been ferrying stuff over to *Barabus* for the last three days according to

306

your local… pizza and a toothbrush? Really? Don't you think they would have all those basics covered by now?

"But there's more to it than that… it's the Anatoly factor." Paul shuddered a little inside. "I know you're not seeing this yet, but there's something about this guy. You didn't see the fear in Alex's face when he was talking about him. This is not the sort of man you let down. Boris and Giorgi are pondlife compared to Alex, and even he was terrified of the man."

Gary was about to interrupt but Paul raised his hand; he was in full flow.

"Just listen. You've asked the question, now let me tell you the answer."

Gary stayed silent.

"Boris and Giorgi are here to do a job. Everything points to that job being for Anatoly. The first thing they do when they get into town is monumentally screw it up. How do you tell a man that scares the shit out of someone like Alex that you've messed up the way they have? How do you tell Anatoly that you got yourself into a knife-fight with a hooker, given her all the information she needs to go to the police about the real reason you're in town, get yourself stabbed in the leg for good measure, and then, if all that isn't bad enough, you go and abduct an ageing ex-prostitute as insurance in an attempt to keep some control of the situation?

"Can you imagine how you would tell someone like Anatoly all that, and then what? What next?

"PS 'Dear Anatoly, can we stash our kidnap victim on your yacht while we sort all our other shit out…'

"I don't think so! And then what after that?

"PPS 'We'll get around to kidnapping the girl you're paying us to snatch when we can…'

"I just can't see him taking too kindly to any of that."

Paul took a breath.

"Look, Gary, you've got great instincts, right?"

"So they say."

"So, what are your instincts telling you? Is Maria on that damned yacht or not?"

Gary thought for a moment.

"Not," he said calmly. Then, after a brief pause, he looked Paul straight in the eye. "Is that a good thing?"

"Yes, it's a very good thing."

They sat silently for a few moments. Gary wore the expression of a man who was having second thoughts.

"But it is a leap, don't you think?" Gary said finally.

"Christ, Gary! Maybe, but what happened between Alisa and Giorgi wasn't part of any plan. Taking Maria was desperate, staking out the Negresco a farce. Beating the living crap out of their host and local fixer seems plain stupid, and leaving him to die in his own villa is hardly the act of professionals at the top of their game. And now they've pistol-whipped a member of Katia Shapiro's personal staff and left him on *Barabus* with Anatoly... and, according to you and Kira, he was in the process of making a run for it when they took him down. You didn't see that guy's performance at the Negresco either, Gary. He was a rank amateur and completely out of his depth. So... I ask you... really... Is there anything about all that that makes you think these guys are in control of the situation?"

"I suppose not," he conceded, but the terrier in him wasn't done yet. "Who is this Anatoly anyway? How does he fit in? Why does he want this girl Katia so badly?" Gary was still struggling to understand.

"I don't know, but the 'why' doesn't really matter, does it? They're here to abduct her, and that does matter. She's the real target. Alisa, Maria, everything that's happened to Alex... that's all just a sideshow. I'm sure none of it should have happened. The way I see it, it's only ever been about Katia... but why? The truth is, Gary, right now, I just don't know the 'why', and frankly, I'm not sure I want to."

"Why can't we do something to get them to call the Katia Shapiro kidnapping off? Make it too risky for them. Surely if they called it all off, that would be a good result?"

Paul fumed. "It would be a complete disaster for Maria, Gary. If they called it off, Maria would have absolutely no value to them anymore. If they didn't need her as insurance, they don't need her at all. I don't want to be too melodramatic, but I just don't see these guys leaving witnesses."

"Are you sure about any of this?"

"Actually, Gary, now that you ask... I am. I'm absolutely certain of it."

Paul turned his attentions to the rear-view mirror. There was nothing to see, just the tatty entrance to an unkempt hotel with a pristine silver Mercedes incongruously parked outside. He settled back in his seat once again.

An uneventful hour passed, and then a second.

"I've got an idea," he said eventually.

"So, what are we going to do?" Gary asked, a note of trepidation in his voice.

"Let's turn up the heat," Paul said. "Let's see what they do when we apply a little pressure of our own."

Paul quickly tapped out a message on his iPhone and sent it to Kira. Once done, he counted to ten and then rang the phone. Alisa answered at the first ring.

"This is what I want you to do..."

*****

Kira and Alisa jumped into the Opel Corsa for privacy. Alisa brought up the original text message they received on Tuesday morning from Alisa's stolen mobile phone. The chilling message, sent by the Russians two days earlier, was displayed on the screen once again.

We have your bitch Maria. If you go to the police we will kill her and then we will find you and kill you too. Stay away from the police and we will let her go when it is done.

The video clip of Maria tied to the chair – helpless, tearful and terrified – was still attached. It had a haunting quality now, and seeing it again sent Alisa's thoughts racing back to the basement at Alex's villa. She tried to dismiss the unsettling memory from her mind as she got to work.

She quickly translated the message Paul had sent a few moments earlier. She took some time to check the Russian text and, once satisfied, she hit *Send*. That done, all they had to do was wait.

*****

"So, what's happening?"

Gary had stayed silent as Paul gave his instructions, but now he wanted the full explanation. It wasn't unreasonable. After all, he was sitting in the same car as Paul, facing the same potential dangers, and had every right to know if Paul had just lit the proverbial blue touch-paper.

"Proof of life, mate, proof of life… oh, and a little bit of spice just to shake them up a bit."

Gary was about to ask a follow-up question but thought better of it.

They waited.

After a few minutes Gary became impatient.

"What are we waiting for exactly?"

Paul ignored the question but passed Gary the phone so he could read the English version of the text for himself.

Send proof of life within one hour or we will go to the police and tell them everything we know. Must include proof of date and time or no deal.

And then the spice…

Before we tell the police, we will send all the details to Anatoly. You have one hour.

Paul recovered the phone from Gary, who still looked a little lost.

"I have no idea who this Anatoly is… at least not yet," Paul explained. "But I reckon they're more afraid of him than they are of the police. If Anatoly doesn't already know about the issue with Alisa, the photographs and Maria, I think they'll have a serious problem with him when he finds out." Paul paused for effect. "One thing I do know is that Alex was genuinely scared of this guy. I think getting on the wrong side of Anatoly is the very last thing these idiots want to do."

"What's the plan then… I assume you have one?" Gary still looked confused.

"If Maria is here at the hotel, they'll be able to send proof of life, no problem. But then we'll know exactly where she is for certain."

"And we can make the call to the police?" Gary suggested with a degree of apprehension.

"Absolutely."

Gary looked relieved.

"If she isn't here, they'll have to go to wherever they're keeping her, and we can just follow them again. Maybe they'll lead us to her. Maybe they won't. But it's a chance, Gary, and I think we have no choice but to take it."

"And if they do lead us to her… we can call the police?" he asked again.

"Of course."

"Okay, that all sounds good." Gary looked thoughtful. "What if she *is* already on the yacht and Anatoly has his fingerprints all over this?"

"She won't be, I'm sure of it. But for arguments sake, let's just say she is. There's no doubt it will be easy enough for Anatoly to provide proof of life to keep us quiet, so… in a way, we'll be no further forward. But just maybe we might be able to identify where she is from the background of the photograph or some other detail. I don't know. These guys are scary bastards, but they don't seem too bright to me. Something like the background on a photo might not mean that much to them, but it could be all we need to determine whether she's at the hotel or on the yacht or somewhere else. Even if it's not definitive, it might enable us to at least rule some things out. I know it's a long shot, but at least we're calling the tune for a while, and you never know, we could get lucky."

Paul knew it wasn't perfect.

Alisa was back on the phone. She was agitated, and with good cause. The Russian's response had been swift and not exactly what Paul anticipated. He knew that sending the text carried a certain amount of risk; he was now forced to consider the very real possibility that he had just made things a whole lot worse.

"They've replied," she said.

"Okay," said Paul, "what *exactly* does it say?"

"It says they will hunt us down like vermin and kill us both and then our families."

Paul registered the very genuine sense of fear in her voice. The girls knew exactly what Giorgi and Boris were capable of. They had good reason to be fearful.

"Shit! Shit!" Paul's mind raced. "Let me think… Let me think…"

No one spoke. Alisa's sobs were the only distraction. Moments later, Paul was back on the phone.

"Wait…" he said. "Wait, it's a good thing! We've got them scared!"

"Are you sure about that?" Gary looked pale. "I'm shitting myself here."

Paul focused on Alisa.

"No… listen to me. It's fine. Don't let them get to you. They're just trying to frighten you."

There was no doubt it was working.

"It's Boris and Giorgi who are panicking now, and that's a good thing," Paul reassured them all with a steely conviction. "They still believe they're up against just Alisa and Kira. That's a good thing too. We can use that."

He played his last card.

"Alisa," he said, "text them back with this, just this, nothing more…" His instructions were crystal clear.

Alisa typed a translation into Kira's mobile phone: **У вас есть 45 минут.**[3]

And then, as instructed, she typed the single word *Barabus* into the email's subject box and hit *Send*.

If the Russians thought the girls were bluffing before, then giving them the name of Anatoly's yacht might just undermine what remained of their confidence. At the very least it would get them asking questions about who they were up against. How could Kira and Alisa know about Anatoly? How could they possibly know about *Barabus*?

One possibility was that they would think that Alex had survived his beating and was helping them, and that suited Paul just fine. Alex was either dead

---

3. *You have 45 minutes.*

already or safely tucked away with the local gendarmes at his hospital bedside for company. But, if the Russian's thought their fixer was working against them, that would certainly carry more of a threat than the girls working alone.

Paul was certain he'd just significantly raised the stakes.

The battered front doors of the hotel flew open, banging on their hinges. The two huge Russians ran out and dived back into the Mercedes. Moments later, the powerful silver car roared out of the hotel car park towards the main road. Paul slammed the black hire car back into gear and set off after them.

"It looks like you got their attention, mate!" Gary suggested, somewhat superfluously. "This is it!" he said, with a very real sense of optimism.

After a few nerve-jangling kilometres, they approached the turning to the Cap Ferrat. Boris turned a sharp right without indicating, hit the brakes hard and the Mercedes ground to a halt.

"Damn it! What the hell are they doing now?"

Boris had brought the car to an abrupt and unexpected halt well short of the next intersection. Paul couldn't just hammer the brakes and park up behind them. It would give them away immediately. Boris stopped the car in the middle of nowhere. It just sat there idling at the side of the road for no apparent reason and Paul was closing in fast.

He needed to decide: drive on past and lose them, or pull up and give themselves away? He was out of time and out of options. Paul was right behind them now and he knew that any realistic opportunity to stop the car discreetly was gone. The road ahead was completely clear. There was no reason for the Mercedes to be stationary and certainly no reason at all for Paul to stop behind them.

Boris was either on to them or just being ultra-careful. Sending the text messages had forced them to react, and Boris and Giorgi, for once, had reacted intelligently. Paul didn't know if they'd been spotted, but he was certain he'd just squandered their one opportunity to find Maria before Friday. Boris had executed his manoeuvre well; perhaps it was a well-rehearsed piece of tradecraft, quite possibly lifted directly from the pages of some Cold War spying manual.

Even if the Russians thought they were dealing with a couple of young girls, they'd suddenly woken up to the threat. The mention of Anatoly had resulted in an immediate and intimidating reaction; the mention of *Barabus* got them running scared.

The game was up. Paul had a split-second decision to make.

"Just look straight ahead – no eye contact," Paul said.

Gary was on the case. He was an old hand by now and didn't falter. He just stared straight ahead, focusing resolutely on a distant point on an equally distant horizon. Paul drove straight past the Russians and turned into the main road that led all the way back to Katia's villa. He watched in the rear-view mirror as Boris sped away in the direction they'd just come from. Once again, they were no closer to finding Maria.

Increasing the pressure had certainly provoked Giorgi and Boris into action, but it had also made them wary. The Russians had simply raised their game.

*****

Five minutes before the deadline expired, Kira's iPhone lit up. They had their proof of life. Maria was still very much alive; Paul had never doubted that.

You don't buy toiletries and pizza for a dead hostage.

The backdrop to the photo was unambiguous yet impossibly vague. She was sitting on the ground looking up at the camera. Behind her was a large green bush and over her shoulder a small part of the stunning coastline could be seen hazily in the distance. It was an elevated location and would have been beautiful if the circumstances were different. Held in her hands, an iPad displayed a familiar French news channel, the time and date clearly visible. Maria looked tired and vacant with the iPad held close to her chest. The date on the banner at the bottom of the screen was today's, and according to the time barely five minutes had elapsed since the image was taken.

Tomorrow was another day. Tomorrow was Friday.

FRIDAY

Chapter 50

FRIDAY

It was 7 am, Maria had been missing for nearly sixty-eight hours.

For Paul, it was another restless night, yet it was Kira who was the first out of bed and already in the bathroom. He rolled over to see Alisa staring straight back at him from the far side of the bed. Neither of them had slept well. He raised the covers a little and she responded to the invitation, easing herself across the huge bed and melting into his arms. They lay there silently for a while, until the bathroom door opened abruptly and a plume of steam accompanied Kira back into the bedroom.

"Get a room, you two," she joked, as she dropped onto the bed and set about her hair. She regarded Alisa through the mirror thoughtfully.

"*Ne plaisante pas lui autour. Il se soucie vraiment de vous. Vous savez sûrement que!*"[4] she said.

Alisa looked displeased for a moment and then smiled sweetly. While the girls chatted away in French, Paul busied himself checking the phones. His was fully charged, as was Alisa's new Samsung Galaxy that lay, as yet unused, by its side. They skipped breakfast and before too long they were up, dressed, and ready to meet Gary in the hotel lobby.

Paul was pleasantly surprised to see that his colleague had beaten them downstairs and already recovered two sets of car keys from the concierge. The vehicles were parked up line astern on the hotel forecourt.

"Right… I think we're all set."

Paul studied them intently, each in turn.

"You know this could be dangerous."

No one faltered.

"You're sure?" he said, stressing his point.

"We're sure, Paul. Let's just get on with it." Gary spoke for them all.

"Okay!" he acknowledged.

---

4. *"Don't mess him around. He really cares about you. Surely you know that!"*

He proceeded to set out the large-scale road map on the bonnet of the Opel Corsa.

"Let's just go through this one last time…"

The suggestion was met with a chorus of groans, but Paul insisted.

Finally he was satisfied and he folded up the map before handing it to Gary. He turned to Kira.

"Show me the message again."

Kira tapped away on her iPhone and passed it to Paul. Alisa was at his side.

"Is that right?" he asked fretfully as he held up his iPhone alongside Kira's. The same message was displayed in English on one and in Russian on the other. Alisa checked the translation one last time.

"Paul, honestly, the translation is perfect."

"You're sure?"

"Trust me," she said, "I'm certain."

Paul closed his iPhone down and put it in his pocket.

"Right… Let's go."

Gary was the first to leave. He drove the red Opel Corsa off the hotel forecourt as Paul and the girls watched him go. Paul knew it would be a long day for Gary as he set off for the Cap Ferrat and back to Katia Shapiro's stunning villa once again. But this time he would be there completely alone.

Paul fired up the black hire car and the girls climbed in.

As he drove, his mind drifted. First the doubts resurfaced, and then the questions, and each chipped away at his confidence and compelled him to second-guess everything he thought he knew. But there was still so much he didn't know. Why were Boris and Giorgi so determined to snatch this girl? Why Katia Shapiro? What did Norilsk and Anatoly have to do with any of it? And, somewhat more prosaically, why on earth had he allowed himself to become so involved. But perhaps far more importantly, especially as he was now so completely involved, it was the "How" and "Where" that mattered most. And more immediately, what exactly did that red cross on the photograph actually mean for the potentially ill-fated chauffeur?

He drove directly into Casino Square and dropped Kira off outside the Hôtel de Paris. She looked very much the part as she climbed out of the car. She made her way to the driver's side window and held out her hand. Paul passed her Gary's BMW car key, complete with its Ferrari key fob attached, and Kira closed her fingers tightly around them.

"Be careful," he said, fighting the urge to call the whole thing off.

"I will, don't worry. I know I can do this."

Paul smiled nervously. Alisa looked even less certain. It was only the thought of Maria that stopped either of them dragging Kira straight back into the car.

"Don't forget. We need the parking ticket too, if you can manage that," Paul said, his apprehension growing by the second.

Kira still looked every bit as confident as she sounded. Alisa leaned across from the passenger seat and squeezed her friend's hand.

"*будь осторожен, faites attention*, be careful!" she said.

"*я буду, je vais*, I will."

Paul watched her go.

"She'll be fine, Paul… don't worry," Alisa said, smiling nervously.

Paul headed back out of town. There was still plenty of time, but he was impatient to get into position as soon as possible.

Twenty minutes later he was reversing the car away from the main road and out of sight. They came to a gentle stop fifty feet back from the carriageway. It was exactly where he'd previously marked the spot with a red X of his own on the road map he'd handed to Gary earlier. All he needed to do now was wait for Gary to call.

The hours drifted by: ten o'clock, eleven o'clock, twelve o'clock. At least he had Alisa for company, but the others were alone, and the waiting would be so much worse for them.

Kira was on the phone. Paul answered.

"What's happening?"

"Nothing yet, Kira. Just hold on for now. Alisa will let you know the second we hear anything," he reassured her.

But he could tell Kira was nervous. She was isolated and afraid, and the polished veneer of confidence had finally slipped. He could hear her voice break, and then he sensed the tears that had almost certainly started to fall. So much depended on her.

"Kira, it's okay, it's going to be fine…" But he couldn't find the words to help. He hated himself for leaving her alone in such a position. He put the phone on mute and turned to Alisa.

"I need to find another way. She's not going to be able to do this."

Kira's sobs continued unabated.

"Can't we just stop them here, when they come by, and tell the chauffeur not to take Katia into town?"

"We could…" Paul considered for the thousandth time. "But the chauffeur would do the only sensible thing he could and take Katia to ground. He'll get Katia to somewhere safe and it will all be over for Maria. If Katia doesn't show, I dread to think what Boris and Giorgi will do with their hostage… If we want to get Maria back, this is the only way."

"Give me the phone," Alisa demanded.

"Kira," she said, and then she continued in Russian. "*Эти злые гады будут убивать Maria. если мы не будем делать это, то они придут после нас! Там нет другого пути, вы сказали, это самостоятельно. Теперь соберись и получить с него. Я знаю, вы можете сделать это. Павел знает, что вы можете сделать это. Я верю в него, Kira. я ему доверяю больше, чем любой человек, которого я когда-либо встречал. Если он говорит, что вы можете сделать это, я знаю, ты можешь…"*[5]

"Знаю, знаю…"[6] Kira said, sobbing.

"I love you, Kira. Be safe," Alisa said, signing off and reverting to English.

She hung up and threw the phone towards Paul. She was furious with him, but he was no less disgusted with himself for potentially putting Kira in so much danger. He could see Alisa boiling with a mixture of fear and anger, but he needed to know what her exchange with Kira meant for the plan.

"Well?" he asked apprehensively.

"She'll do it. She knows she has to. We don't have a choice… do we?!" Alisa snapped.

The mood had suddenly changed. The optimism of the morning had dissipated in an instant as the reality of the situation set in. Paul was shattered. He sat in silence for a moment, wondering what he was even doing there. There was a real anger in Alisa now, and it was all aimed directly at him. Time dragged on.

It was one-twenty when Gary made his call. Paul put the iPhone on loudspeaker.

"Right," he said, "they've just left the villa. The chauffeur is definitely driving. I can only assume Katia is in the back. They should be with you in about fifteen minutes. I'm right behind them. I'll call you back when we're a bit closer."

"Read out the car registration number please, Gary." Paul wasn't leaving anything to chance.

Gary obliged and Alisa quickly wrote it down. Her mood was no better, but things were starting to happen and, as far as Paul was concerned, that was all that mattered. The plan was simple. Gary would follow immediately behind Katia's car and then hold the traffic back at the last minute to create a gap. Paul intended to slip his car in closely behind them as Katia's chauffeur drove past their location.

Alisa began to climb into the back seat without having to be reminded. She

---

5. *"These evil bastards will kill Maria. If we do not do it, they will come after us! There is no other way, you said it yourself. Now pull yourself together and get on with it. I know you can do it. Paul knows that you can do it. I believe in him, Kira. I trust him more than any man I've ever met. If he says you can do it, I know you can…"*
6. *"I know, I know …"*

knew the plan as well as anybody. Paul had insisted she would be safer in the back of the car when they returned to the city.

Ten more silent minutes passed, then Gary called again.

"Right… they'll be with you any minute now."

Gary was spot on.

Paul fired up the engine as they watched Katia's car pass serenely by. Alisa checked the registration plate as he eased the hire car out into the road behind them. The red Opel Corsa came into view a full fifty yards to their rear. Gary had done exactly what was asked of him, and as they entered deeper into the city, he indicated left and peeled away as planned.

Alisa updated Kira. She was calmer now but Alisa continued to reassure her friend in Russian while glaring angrily at Paul from the back seat. He allowed himself the occasional glance in Alisa's direction through the rear-view mirror, but otherwise he kept his eyes firmly on the car up ahead.

"If anything happens to her, Paul…" she said, fuming.

"I know, I know. It won't, I promise."

He followed Katia's car past the entrance to the Monaco–Monte Carlo railway station as the chauffeur continued to make his way steadily through the busy city traffic. Paul had anticipated their route. It was straightforward enough and made sense. It was the shortest and most logical route and Paul was increasingly comforted to find there was no deviation. After a short while they turned right onto the Avenue Saint-Michel towards the underground car park at Casino Square. The car in front slowed, crawling to a halt, and Paul mirrored its movements precisely.

The rear passenger-side door opened and Katia Shapiro stepped out unattended by the chauffeur, joining the steady flow of pedestrians as she headed for the restaurant. She was as beautiful in life as she was in the portraits in the magazine. She was confident and at ease, elegant and poised, and as unaware and totally vulnerable as Paul feared she would be.

"We have to try and help this girl," Paul said.

He heard Alisa's breath shorten. It was all very real now. He sensed her shrinking away from the car windows, deeper into the sanctuary of the back seat of the hire car.

The chauffeur pulled away from the kerb and headed for the car park entrance. But the mood had changed again. Alisa wasn't angry any more. She looked pale, frightened, and she bit down hard on her lip and wrung her hands in her lap. She didn't speak, but just stared out of the window and watched Katia Shapiro disappear from view.

"It's okay, Alisa, I won't let anything happen to Kira, or Katia. I won't let anything happen to any of you, I promise." And he offered his hand through the gap between the front seats.

She clasped it firmly in her own and took a deep breath as if it were her last. The car began the spiralling descent from the bright autumnal sunshine into the dark, shadowy gloom of the underground car park.

Only a few metres separated the two black 5 Series BMWs, with their limousine-style black windows, as they slowly navigated the car park. Paul held back a short distance as Katia's driver pulled into a "Réservé" parking space on "1er étage", next to the pedestrian exit at the far end of the car park.

It was definitely étage, he allowed himself to consider.

The chauffeur completed his manoeuvre and Paul slid casually by. He found a free slot, just five spaces further on, and quietly rolled the car to a full stop, nosing it in and killing the engine.

A tall athletic man in a white, open-neck shirt and dark tailored jacket climbed out of Katia's car, a pair of expensive shades strategically positioned on a finely groomed head of thick black hair. He locked the car and the lights flashed reassuringly as he made his way to the lift lobby. Paul watched him closely. He dropped the car key into his right-hand jacket pocket and, ignoring the lifts, took the stairs two steps at a time.

Paul slipped out of the car and followed the chauffeur into park Prince Albert. He watched him walk directly to a news stand. He picked up a paper and exchanged a few well-rehearsed pleasantries with the vendor. They shared a joke and parted as if they were old friends. Next, he headed off in the direction of the Häagan Dazs restaurant where Kira was already holding station.

Paul dialled the phone and Kira answered it at the first ring.

"Can you see them?"

"They're all here, just like you said. I can see the three girls and the bodyguard. He's sitting alone at a separate table."

"Okay, Kira, well done. How are you feeling?"

"I'm fine," she said. "I can do this."

"I know you can. Just stay calm. The car key is in his right-hand jacket pocket."

"Okay, right... *droit?*" she asked, checking.

"Yes. That's right. *Droit...* on the right," he confirmed, urgently trying to recall the rudimentary French he did learn at school.

"His right?"

"Yes... his right."

"Okay."

"Don't forget," he said reassuringly, "Gary will be with you shortly, so you're not on your own. Just stay calm."

Paul hung up and headed back to the car.

Chapter 51

FRIDAY

The car park seemed darker, more oppressive than before. It felt soulless, colourless, uncomfortably humid, and for now, completely deserted. Alisa was hidden from view, tucked away behind the blacked-out glass of the BMW. She was out of sight and so much the safer for it.

"Stay here," Paul said. "And keep the doors locked."

Alisa looked so pale in the gloom, a sepia version of herself as the interior light washed over her, briefly illuminating her features in the monochrome world of the Casino Square car park. He closed the car door and the interior light faded back to black.

Paul took out his Swiss army knife and selected the screwdriver attachment. He immediately went to work on the number plates of the hire car. First the front plate; that one would be the easiest and the most discreet. The car was nose in, facing the wall, and therefore away from prying eyes and out of the field of view of either of the CCTV cameras.

Two plastic screws attached the number plate to the bodywork. He removed them both and then set them down very deliberately, strategically, next to the car on the concrete floor. Taking the front plate with him, he headed to the rear of the car.

The second number plate was in full view of anyone who might enter the car park on that level, so staying unobserved would be tricky. He needed to be quick. But the CCTV was a very different proposition. It would be almost impossible not to be recorded in the act, given how they were located.

He checked for any signs of movement but there were none – the area was still deserted. He turned his attention to the cameras. It was only then he noticed that the LED indicators on the CCTV cameras were dead. Could Boris and Giorgi have already worked their magic? The CCTV cameras in the underground car park appeared to be every bit as dead as those at Alex's villa only a few days before. He waited. Perhaps they were an intermittently flashing version, like a smoke detector, flashing every thirty seconds or so. He thought back to Wednesday when he was last down there. The LEDs were definitely flashing then. He checked again – still nothing. He was certain now that the cameras where dead.

Whatever happened next would go unrecorded and unobserved. Paul took some comfort in the anonymity he knew that afforded him, but it only served to reinforce his concern for the chauffeur. Something terrible was going to happen, and the disabling of the CCTV cameras simply lent further weight to what he'd suspected all along.

With the cameras out of action, and no one else around, he went to work on the rear number plate. He set the screws to one side, as before, and then headed down the line of parked cars with the hire car's numbers plates tucked under his jacket.

He stopped at the side of Katia's immaculate black BMW in the VIP parking space and wasted no time. He exchanged both number plates on the second of the black BMWs and then checked again for witnesses. With no one else in sight, he walked back to his own car with Katia's registration plates at his side. Moments later, he'd fixed them into place.

He allowed himself a moment and then froze. If the cameras had been knocked out, at least one of the Russians must already be nearby. The thought was sobering. He needed to know.

Leaving Alisa securely locked away in the back seat of the hire car, he headed deeper into the car park. He checked every level, but there was no sign of Boris, Giorgi or the silver Mercedes. That done, he headed for the surface and the reassurance of a few bars of signal strength on the iPhone. He called Gary and brought him up to speed. Gary was keen to get back into the action.

"Wait there, Gary. Stay where you are and give it a bit longer. They have to come past you to get to the car park. Something is going to happen down there. They've already killed the cameras, so just keep your eyes open and let me know the minute you see either of them. Then get yourself down to the restaurant and don't let Kira out of your sight."

"I know. Don't worry. It's done!" he said. Gary knew the plan well enough too and was going nowhere.

The next move was down to Boris and Giorgi.

As time dragged on, the doubts returned. Where were Boris and Giorgi? Why hadn't anyone seen them yet? Had he got this right? What if he'd missed something, something vital that would bring the entire plan crashing down around them? Paul knew it was only natural to second-guess himself, but he tried to answer and then dismiss each question as it came into his mind. But... what was it? Something still nagged at him – what had he missed?

The phone rang. It was Gary.

"I've just seen the Merc. Boris is driving. There's no sign of Giorgi, he's not in the car"

"How far away is it? How long have I got?"

"Just heading down the ramp to the car park now. You'll see it any minute."

The realisation was instant.

"Shit! That's where I've got it wrong. Shit! Shit!" Paul hung up without explanation and sprinted down the car park steps and into the lift lobby. He was quickly across the car park and on his knees at the rear of the hire car. Alisa was still in the back seat, waiting and now terrified by the unknown, unexplained emergency that had Paul in such a flap.

How could he have got this so wrong? Paul pulled out the Swiss army knife and set about the rear number plate. He was signalling frantically for Alisa to get out of the car.

"What is it?" she shouted from the sanctuary of the black BMW.

"I've got this all wrong. I shouldn't have changed the number plates yet. You have to hide. Get out of the car, out of sight while I sort this out."

Alisa dived out of the car and edged further down the line of parked cars and into the shadows.

Paul fumbled around with screwdriver and the second screw.

Boris and Giorgi already knew the registration number of Katia's car! Of course they did! It was the registration number alone they would rely upon to confirm its location. In changing the number plates too early, Paul had just handed them the hire car with Alisa gift-wrapped inside. How could he have been so stupid?

But there was no time. Boris would, all too soon, be cruising into the car park to locate Katia's BMW for himself. Paul forced himself to calm down. He only needed to exchange the rear plates on each of the cars. They were both nose in in their respective parking spaces. It wasn't perfect but it was the best he could do.

The first number plate was now free so he sprinted over to Katia's car. The second rear plate was off in an instant, but he was still in trouble, and precious time ticked relentlessly by.

Paul saw the Mercedes exiting the ramp and making its way down the first line of parked vehicles. It would only be seconds before Boris was upon him. Paul rammed the first screw home and tightened it hard. It would have to do. There was no time for the second. He forced the number plate square under the tension of the single fixing and dived down the side of the car. As the Mercedes crawled to a stop behind Katia's BMW, he threw himself to the floor and crawled to the front of the car in the next bay. He froze, hardly daring to breathe.

A man climbed out of the Mercedes and paced around the side of the black BMW saloon. He tried the door. It was locked.

"*Da!*" he growled.

It was Boris.

Boris stalked back to the Mercedes and climbed in. It pulled away menacingly slowly. He drove past Paul's hire car; the missing rear registration plate appeared to go unnoticed as far as he could tell. Finally, Boris steered the Mercedes into a parking space at the opposite end of the car park and stopped. Paul watched silently as he killed the engine, climbed out and headed for the pedestrian exit.

His attention turned to Alisa. How could he have put her in such a perilous situation? Swapping the number plates too early was a stupid error to make and had exposed Alisa to real danger. If Boris had found her, the whole plan would have been compromised and he would have left Katia and Maria helplessly exposed and entirely at the Russian's mercy.

Paul took a moment to regather his thoughts.

With Boris gone, he guided Alisa back into the rear seat of the hire car.

"I'm sorry," he said. "It's okay now. You're safe. Just stay there."

Paul still had work to do. He needed to concentrate. He fitted the second screw to the rear registration plate on Katia's car and then reinstated the original rear plate on the hire car. Both would have to come off again later, but at least Boris had confirmed their target vehicle and that was a good result under the circumstances. Both cars would have dual identity for a while. The front plates on each had been exchanged, but they each sported their own original identities on the rear.

Alisa looked terrified once again, but she was safe enough for now. Paul headed back to the sunlight and the reassuring comfort of full signal strength on his iPhone.

There was a missed call from Gary and another from Kira. Paul rang Kira back first and she answered at the first ring.

"Katia and her friends are getting ready to go," she said breathlessly. "And it looks like the chauffeur is going to stay at his table and wait, just like you said. As soon as they go I'll try and get the keys."

"Just be careful, okay. I'll keep my eye on you as best I can, and Gary's on his way down to you too."

"I know. I'm just a bit nervous, that's all."

"I know you are, but I know you can do this, and you know it too. Don't forget, the chauffeur's a decent man on a break from his job. He's not one of the bad guys here."

"I know, I know… and he's hot too…" she said, giggling. It was a nervous giggle but Paul sensed a strength there too. There was a little bit of Silvi about her now.

Kira hung up.

As Katia and her girlfriends made their way to the shops, Paul rang Gary.

"What's happening?" Gary asked impatiently.

"I had to make an adjustment, that's all," he said, with as much reassurance as he could manage. "Just get yourself down to that restaurant and make sure Kira is safe."

"I'm already here, mate. Kira's making her move."

Chapter 52

FRIDAY

The chauffeur was sipping a double shot espresso and thumbing a newspaper he'd already scanned once before. His jacket, recently removed, was draped casually over the back of his chair. The sun was at its hottest but a mild breeze and the positioning of the canvas sails provided good shade. The chauffeur settled in, in the absence of his charge.

As Kira approached, he set the newspaper down on the table and, while continuing to read, rolled up his sleeves in a well-practised fashion. The crisp white cotton, when folded back, revealed a designer watch, strong forearms and an even tan. He stretched and flexed a little, and Kira couldn't help but register the impressive contours of a powerful physique under his tailored shirt.

She coughed quietly, swallowed hard, and fought back the consuming urge to keep on going, to walk straight past him and away to the relative safety of the park beyond.

He folded the newspaper on the table and switched his attention to his smartphone. He began scrolling through it, casually passing the time. Just a few more steps and she would need to make her move. It was now or never. He looked up, spotted her, caught her eye and held her gaze just a little longer than could be ignored.

Kira swallowed again. She tried to moisten her tongue, her lips, her mouth, all rendered dry through the nerves that began to overpower her. She kept on going, Silvi at her shoulder. *You can do this! You can do this!* her inner Silvi urged. She regathered herself and forced a smile.

"Do you mind if I join you?" she purred.

He appeared flustered for a moment and then returned her smile; it was instinctive, innate. It was a look she'd seen so many times before. To her, it was nothing less than a buying signal, a vulnerability she knew only too well how to exploit. It was a sign of weakness, no less revealing than a poker player's tell. Kira tested her read.

"I'm sorry, I hope you don't think me rude…"

"No, not at all. Please do," he spluttered.

She'd gauged it perfectly. It was time to go to work. It was just a matter of pushing the right buttons and reeling him in. Nothing more than a game, and he wouldn't even know he'd been played.

The chauffeur looked her up and down. His eyes flared a little as he took her in. Kira looked stunning: Alisa's short cream skirt, the obligatory tight-fitting t-shirt, her long rose-coloured hair cascading over both shoulders, her makeup impeccable and her tone irresistible.

"Please…" he said, indicating the chair opposite.

"I saw you looking at me earlier," Kira said, scanning his features and assessing the threat. He was clearly very strong, good-looking, confident, mildly confused perhaps, but there wasn't even a flicker of suspicion. "I wondered if you might come over to *me* earlier, since you're here all on your own. I thought you might like to join me."

"I'm sorry. I didn't notice you before… I was—"

She cut him off before he could finish. She intended to keep this brief.

"What is your name?" she purred again.

She stood close to him, too close. She imposed herself within his personal space, and he relinquished it without protest. Kira moved the game on and casually ignored his offer to sit.

Then, against the odds, against her innate understanding of her quarry, he drew back.

"I'm working," he said. "I'm sorry. It is not a good time. Maybe another day. Now is not good for me… but another time." But he was already starting to mellow. "Another time, I would be flattered."

Kira approached him again, very deliberately. There was something about him. She knew he was still under her control but he was showing signs of fighting back. Perhaps not just like all the rest after all. There was something about him that she liked – could he be drawing her in? He was more resistant to her than she first thought, but for now she dismissed it as part of the joust. Her inner Silvi was buzzing with confidence and enjoying the challenge. But she was short on time and went for broke.

"May I borrow your phone?" She was at her irresistible best. He hesitated. Had she overplayed her hand?

"What are you going to do with it?" he asked.

But there was his tell again – a split-second of hesitation. She held out her hand and he weakened, folded. He passed her the phone. His question was nothing more than a token gesture.

"You'll see…" she replied, beaming.

"But—"

He didn't get the chance to finish. She placed a single finger on his lips and sashayed provocatively behind him. She leaned over him, her breasts firmly, purposefully pressed against him for maximum effect. She could feel the heat from his body and smell the heady perfume of his aftershave as she brushed her cheek softly against his.

"Smile," she said, as she dropped one set of car keys into his right-hand jacket pocket and then picked up another. She could feel a credit-card-sized piece of plastic in his pocket and palmed that too. It wasn't the car parking ticket she'd expected, but under the circumstances she took it anyway.

The chauffeur snuggled in for the shot. She'd set the phone in camera mode and now she held it out at arm's length before snapping a couple of shots in quick succession.

"Let me see," the chauffeur said.

He was starting to enjoy the attention, and all the pretence of his professionalism had gone. It was all too easy. She dropped the car keys and plastic card into her handbag and turned to face him. Kira placed a lingering peck on his cheek. Snap. Snap. Snap.

She peeled away behind him mischievously, resisting his efforts to see the shots she'd just taken.

"One more…" she said with a smile, and he was putty in her hands.

This time he struck a pose, and she presented the image to him for his approval. They made a very handsome couple and he beamed inanely at the prospect. He made a grab for the phone but Kira snatched it away playfully.

"Not yet, not yet," she said, teasing him.

She tapped away on his iPhone for a few more moments. It wasn't part of Paul's plan, and it was a risk, but she was sure now, certain he wasn't like all the rest. She handed his phone back to him. Seconds later there was a shrill ring from her handbag. She feigned surprise and made great play of retrieving her own phone. She opened up her iPhone, and with a flourish showed him the duplicate of the picture he still had displayed on his own.

"You have my number now," she said coyly. "Why don't you call me sometime? Perhaps when it *is* a good time for you…"

"Stay…" he said, completely smitten.

She bent down and gave him a lingering kiss on the lips, and then, with a little giggle and an outrageous turn, she took her leave. He was hooked. The chauffeur scrolled through the images on his phone, and then she caught him watching her glide sensuously away.

"My name is Mikael," he called after her.

She raised her hand and waved without looking back, her fingers a steady ripple as she walked. Just as she was about to disappear from view, she glanced back over her shoulder and gave him a well-practised, irresistible smile.

Kira's job was done, her pulse racing and her breath short. She felt the thrill of an electric charge surging through her as she recalled the kiss, the warmth of his touch, the musk of his aftershave drawing her in. Then it was over, her moment of reflection shattered. Gary was at her side.

"Brilliant, you were brilliant… just amazing." Gary was in love too.

She handed him the car keys and the plastic card. Then, as planned, she headed off through the gardens to the Café de Paris, where Gary would pick her up later.

*****

With Kira safe, Gary made his way over to Paul at the entrance to the car park.

"I don't know if this is any good. It was all he had in his jacket pocket apparently."

"I think it will do fine," Paul said, studying the plastic card. "It's a VIP season ticket for the car park, unless I'm very much mistaken. It will do very nicely indeed."

Paul had immediately recognised the name of the car park, and Katia's car registration number, embossed into the plastic. The registration number itself was seared into his memory. He couldn't help wondering if he would ever forget it.

"She was amazing, Paul. Did you see her? Could you see from here?"

"Yes, Gary, I did, but just get her out of here now. Keep your phone free and stay alert."

Paul took the chauffeur's car keys from Gary. "As soon as the chauffeur gets up to leave, call me. I need as long as possible to validate the parking ticket and then get back to the car. There won't be much time."

"Will do, mate, no problem." Gary changed the subject. "His name is Mikael, by the way."

"Who?"

"The chauffeur… his name's Mikael."

"Shit, Gary, I've got to watch that poor bastard get the treatment later. Knowing his bloody name doesn't make that any easier, does IT?" Paul was unreasonably angry. Perhaps it was just guilt kicking in.

"Sorry, wasn't thinking," Gary said. Then he changed the subject again. "Have you seen Boris over there?"

Gary was discreetly pointing in the direction of a large shadowy form some distance away through the park. "He was watching the whole performance. He definitely didn't recognise Kira, I'm sure of that, but he didn't take his eyes off the chauffeur for a second."

"Yes, I've seen him. Don't worry about Boris. Keep your eyes on the chauffeur. Just keep your attention on *Mikael*."

Paul was well aware of Boris's presence and found it strangely reassuring. Knowing Boris's movements was a good thing, essential even, although his proximity to Kira did nothing to settle his nerves.

Even now Boris was still glaring at the chauffer, impatiently waiting for him to make his move.

"Get going," Paul said.

As Gary set off in the opposite direction, Paul returned to the car park. He headed directly to the VIP parking area holding the liberated set of BMW car keys in his hand. He pressed the key fob once, and Katia's black BMW unlocked instantly with a single bleep and a double flash of its lights. Kira had played her part perfectly.

Paul jumped in, started the engine and quickly manoeuvred the car to another empty space adjacent to the car park exit. He took the precaution of reversing it in this time. He knew they would need a quick getaway and, of course, the front number plate had already been changed.

Alisa switched from the back seat of the hire car to the back seat of Katia's relocated BMW. He then moved the hire car into the "Réservé" parking space Katia's BMW had just vacated. This time he nosed the car in, taking great care to park it exactly as the chauffeur had left his only an hour earlier.

Next, he climbed out of the hire car, shut the door and stepped away. He waited. It needed to be unlocked when the chauffeur came back. He knew that was important and it might just buy them a little more time. There was no bleep or flashing of lights and the car remained unlocked. There was just one more job to do. Paul swapped the rear number plates for the second time. Finally, each car fully took on the identity of the other.

There would be another long wait now as Katia Shapiro and her friends spent the afternoon maxing out their respective credit cards, as they chatted and gossiped over some of the world's most expensive cocktails, and as they whiled away a relaxing afternoon on the elegant terrace of the Crystal Bar at the Hotel Hermitage. Only then would Katia call for her chauffeur and for her immaculate black BMW 5 Series, and only then would Paul truly know, if, after all the mistakes, the doubts and misgivings, after all of that... had he actually got it right?

Chapter 53

FRIDAY

Paul sat quietly in the driver's seat of Katia's car. Alisa was in the back seat fumbling uneasily with a small silver canister she'd recovered from the depths of her handbag. He adjusted the rear-view mirror and saw her smiling apprehensively back at him. He knew it would be of little comfort to her, but it occurred to him that she was almost certainly safer now than at any other point during the day. Katia's car was so much more than its pale facsimile in the "Réservé" parking space it had until so recently occupied.

Both were fitted with similar limousine black windows, but on Katia's car they were thicker and a shade darker, reinforced in some way and quite possibly bulletproof. It drove differently too. There was more power and yet more weight. At slow speed, it manoeuvred beautifully under its power-steering, but there was no disguising the additional burden of reinforced body work and the potentially jaw-droppingly expensive set of run-flat tyres. It was a beautifully engineered armoured limousine. Quite possibly the only reason anyone would need to dissuade them from attempting to snatch Katia in the same way they had attacked the little white Audi. Katia's BMW was half armoured vehicle, half luxury saloon, elegantly packaged but anonymous too; the pragmatic choice of a doting father or a chauffeur with close protection uppermost in his mind.

He studied the second BMW for a moment. It was positioned accurately, diligently, very deliberately located and aligned in the VIP parking bay just a few spaces down. Would his misdirection work? There could be no certainty that it would. It was clear that the cars weren't truly identical, not even close. But all the charade needed to accomplish was to confuse the chauffeur just long enough to ensure the deception wasn't exposed before the Russians made their move. What happened next was outside his control, and as time stood still, it would be Katia herself that would fire the starting gun on whatever drama unfolded.

The next move would be Katia's.

*****

Having returned to the top of the car park steps, Paul could see Boris's animated shadow moving menacingly backwards and forwards as the tension continued to build. He noted a reassuring four bars of signal on his iPhone. Alisa was still safely locked away in Katia's black BMW with a small silver canister of pepper spray for company.

Finally, it began.

Boris's shadow became more agitated, and then it disappeared from view altogether for a moment. The iPhone lit up. It was Gary.

"He's on the move. Get going."

Paul was already on his way down the steps. Three bars, two bars and then the phone went dead.

His breath came in short gasps and his legs began shaking uncontrollably as he took the steps two at a time.

The ticket was already in his hand. He'd dismissed the idea of using the VIP season ticket. It was clearly linked to the registration number on Katia's car, but he had no idea how that worked. He couldn't risk getting to the exit barrier only for it to refuse to open for lack of a PIN code or any number of other security considerations.

He slid the ticket into the pay machine at the third time of asking, His hands were trembling, his mouth dry. Stinging beads of perspiration formed at his temples and he could feel a trickle of cold sweat running the length of his spine. It was instant; the adrenaline had kicked in and Paul was starting to flap. He drew a deep breath.

"Twenty-six fucking euros!" Even at a time like this, the car parking tariffs in Monaco made him wince. He jammed the credit card into the machine. It took an age. Paul could only assume that Mikael and Boris wouldn't be far behind him, and he was desperate to be back in the sanctuary of the armoured BMW with Alisa long before either of them got to the ticket machine at the bottom of the steps.

The ticket machine had other ideas. He'd used it several times before, but now, when it mattered most, it seemed to be working conspiratorially slowly.

What language did he want to pay in? *Come on! Really!* He selected English.

What currency did he want to pay in? *Any damn currency. It's a fucking credit card.* Paul selected pound sterling.

"Enter PIN". He punched it in.

"Verifying transaction"! He waited.

"Remove credit card". He did it instantly.

"Printing ticket". *For fuck's sake, come on!*

The ticket was produced at a snail's pace and then with a final flourish the screen read "*Merci, bon voyage*". *So much for language options!*

Paul raced into the car park and over to Katia's BMW in a flash. Alisa leaned over the front seat and released the driver's door as he approached. He pulled the door closed with a reassuring clunk and hit the central locking button. The locks whirred, and with a final definitive click, the doors secured and the interior light slowly faded to black.

Mikael casually entered the car park as he must have done so many times before. He'd donned his jacket and was fumbling in his pocket for his car keys and his plastic VIP parking pass. His stride stalled for a moment as he failed to find either. He looked down as he recovered an unfamiliar Ferrari key fob with a BMW ignition key attached. He checked his other pockets and then patted his trousers. His confusion redoubled when he spotted the strange car parked exactly where he'd parked a similar black BMW 5 Series only a few hours earlier.

He approached the car with a look of disbelief on his face. He checked his pockets again and then stared at a sign displaying "1er étage" on the wall nearby. He was in the right place. As he turned to the car one last time, the huge Russian gangster went to work.

It wasn't subtle, but it was violently effective. It was no straight fight, and the chauffeur was smashed twice with a brutality and physicality that permitted no response. He crashed awkwardly to the floor, hitting the concrete hard before he had time to react. His attacker struck again. Now Boris had something in his hand, a cloth. He rammed it forcefully into the chauffeur's face, covering his nose and mouth. The resistance, such as it was, faded almost instantly and the stricken chauffeur fell limp. It took less than ten seconds. Mikael had been taken out of the game with brutal efficiency. Paul had never seen anything quite like it. He knew Boris was strong and very capable, but witnessing such unrestrained aggression was shocking and unsettling. It was all far too easy. Mikael didn't stand a chance.

Behind him, Alisa had flinched with every blow. She gasped for air and covered her eyes as Boris went to work. She sat back as far as she could in the rear seat, as if trying to disappear into the fabric of the car, covering her eyes and melting into the shadows with the bottle of pepper spray held tightly in her hand.

Boris grabbed the car keys from the unconscious chauffeur's hand. He pointed the remote control at the car. There was no reaction at all. No reassuring bleep. No compliant flash of the lights. He didn't seem to notice. Why would he? He probably assumed the chauffeur had already unlocked the car as he'd approached.

Now Boris fumbled around at the rear of the car and the boot opened at his bidding. The chauffeur's substantial frame was bundled inside with as little ceremony as their previous target only the day before. Next he pulled something out of his trouser pocket. He set to work, leaning into the boot and bearing down on his victim. The unconscious man was being bound using the same plastic cable ties that Paul had so recently tried to release from Alex's wrists and ankles. Mikael was unconscious, bound and helpless. Paul took a deep breath and started the car.

He put the car into gear and recoiled at the sound of a boot lid being slammed down. The violence of it stirred him into action. He didn't wait to see any more. He was already navigating his way out of the car park. Then, as Paul started up the spiralling exit ramp, he caught one last glimpse of Boris rounding the car and heading for the driver's door. Boris disappeared from view as he pulled the hire car's front door open. But in that instant, Paul knew he'd got it right. Boris and Giorgi had intended to use the car in exactly the same way he did. With that option gone, did they have a plan B? What would they do now?

Paul inserted the ticket into the exit barrier and it opened on cue. He was calmer now. He took a moment to adjust the rear-view mirror as the barrier rose. Alisa was ashen-faced in the rear seat, pressed back as far as she could get and now looking as small and vulnerable as he'd ever seen her. She stared blankly back at him.

"Did he kill him?" she said, sobbing.

"No, he's not dead, of course not," Paul reassured her. "Boris wouldn't waste his time tying him up if he'd killed him, would he?" Paul had no idea what he was talking about, but it seemed logical and he needed Alisa to get a grip. As they drove out into the sunlight he could see her wiping tears from her eyes. Paul saw a little of the steel return to them, and he could only hope she was back on board.

"I'm sorry. I'm just being silly," she said, and flashed him the weakest of smiles.

"It's okay. I know it was terrible, but you have to get it together. It's your turn now. You'll have seconds, that's all. It's all about Katia now."

"Yes, I'm fine," she said, the same weak smile trembling across her lips.

It was just a short drive from the car park to the Hotel Hermitage. No more than five minutes if the traffic was flowing, and it was.

As he pulled away, Paul pictured Boris in the gloom of the car park, losing his mind in a car that wouldn't start. He pictured him tapping away on his phone making a call that would never connect. He imagined him smashing the phone against the dashboard in a frustration that had no resolution. He pictured him examining the key, perhaps polishing it and trying it again to no avail. He pictured him losing his cool and tossing the key aside as he worked out what to do next. He imagined him slamming the car door shut with the power and aggression that could shatter the glass, and he pictured him setting off on foot for the Hermitage. The thought of it hit him hard. He redoubled his grip on the steering wheel and focused on the road up ahead. It was all Boris could do now, and if events didn't work out as Paul had planned, that one stark inevitability would almost certainly bring him face-to-face with the vicious Russian himself.

Paul knew he would come. They both would.

It was obvious that would have to be his next move. Boris would head to the Hermitage on foot. He would know that Katia Shapiro would be leaving the Hotel Hermitage in the next few minutes, that she would be expecting to be picked up by a chauffeur that as far as Boris was concerned would never arrive. The Russians' plan had fallen apart, but Katia Shapiro still remained very much their target.

Turning off the main road, Paul cruised quietly into the crescent in front of the magnificent hotel. He immediately spotted Giorgi posing as a tourist. He was admiring the elegant lines of one of several Ferraris currently being fawned over by an animated group of enthusiasts. He seemed oblivious to their approach for now, but how long would that last?

He drew the BMW to a gentle stop and unlocked the car doors. The highly polished hotel lobby doors opened and Katia stepped out into the glorious Mediterranean sunshine. She was smiling, oblivious, and bidding a fond farewell to someone still inside the hotel. She only turned to face the car as a concierge gracefully reached for the door.

It was then that Paul saw Giorgi spark into life. He had his phone pressed to his hideously deformed ear and was gesturing to someone in the distance. Paul could see Boris haring down the street two hundred yards away and making good progress. It was a short drive from the car park to the Hermitage, but it was just as quick a journey on foot through the arcade. Boris was on the far side of the road, across the gardens of the Square Beaumarchais, and closing fast. Giorgi was on the move too, his injured leg doing little to slow him down.

The concierge opened the car door with a flourish and Katia, with her back turned slightly towards the vehicle, slid inside with all the grace and elegance a Swiss finishing school could bestow. It was only then that she realised there was someone else in the back seat of her car. It was only then she noticed Paul at the wheel, the blackened windows having weaved their spell of anonymity in his favour.

Katia immediately panicked. She attempted to climb back out of the car, but the concierge was in the process of closing the door and pressed it firmly against her shoulder. Alisa grabbed her arm to pull her back and spoke to her in Russian. It sounded reassuring, but Katia's sudden realisation rendered all words redundant. She just wasn't listening.

Katia struggled to break free and lunged for the door once more. She found an unfortunate ally in Giorgi. The huge Russian barged the concierge out of the way and grabbed the door handle before the door lock could fully engage. The car door rattled noisily as he tried to pull it open without fully disengaging the lock.

Paul was already accelerating away, a gaggle of tourists hindering his progress and Giorgi keeping pace.

Alisa was doing her best to calm the girl. She looked terrified by the two strangers in her car. "Remember the flowers?" Alisa said. "We sent you the flowers. We're the friends you didn't know you had. We're here to help you. Please stay calm," she pleaded. "Let me explain…"

The door was rattling on its half-latched lock as Giorgi re-secured his grip on the handle. Katia looked confused and terrified. Paul could only imagine what she must have been thinking.

Alisa threw herself across the terrified girl and grabbed the armrest on the door for all she was worth.

Katia was desperate.

"Help me! Help me!" she screamed through the glass as the lock finally slipped.

"No, Katia, he's the one you need to be afraid of!" Alisa screamed back at her. "Don't let him open the door… Help me! Help me!"

It was all going wrong. It wasn't supposed be like this. It was meant to be so simple, reassuring and calm – nothing like this. Another group of tourists were blocking Paul's path as they admired a soft-top Bentley with stunning white leather trim. Paul hit the horn hard. They stepped back stunned, but it was too late. Giorgi had forced the door open and was dragging Alisa out of the car as she clung to the armrest with all her strength.

Suddenly something clicked, and Katia grasped at the door handle, frantically trying to stop the door from opening further. She'd seen the second man racing towards the car and that seemed to tip the scales. He was huge, and a look of pure malice contorted his face already grotesque through exertion, his features smeared with blood. The fear redoubled in her eyes. She was frantic now, but was it already too late?

Katia screamed out as she came to Alisa's assistance. She pulled at the armrest too, but the man with the scar was too strong. As she lost what hold she'd managed to secure, she grabbed at Alisa's wrists in desperation but her grip continued to fail as the door inched open, her grasp sliding down Alisa's arms. It was hopeless. They were both being dragged out of the car.

Paul braked hard and slammed the car into "Park". It rocked violently on its suspension. Giorgi stumbled forward but still maintained a vice-like grip on the door. The sudden stopping of the car, even at such a slow speed, jerked the rear door fully open and the huge Russian fell forward violently. The girls released their grip on the armrest and began scrambling back into the car and as far away from Giorgi as possible.

Paul seized his chance. He grabbed the driver's door handle and smashed the car door open with as much power as he could generate. The full weight of it caught Giorgi fully in the face, crushing his nose. Blood sprayed from his damaged features and he collapsed to the floor, but he still determinedly gripped the car's rear door handle. He was utterly relentless.

And now Boris had reached the car too. He was breathing hard but was equally as committed as his colleague. He grabbed at the rear passenger-side door handle, but Alisa saw him coming. She slammed the lock across as he made a desperate attempt to open it.

With both doors on the driver's side still open, and Giorgi still maintaining his grip on the rear door of the two, Paul slammed the car back into "Drive" and hit the accelerator. The group of startled tourists scattered. Two concierges made a grab for Giorgi, but he was already out of their reach and being dragged along the cobbles, refusing to release his hold on the car.

The front passenger-side door swung open and Boris lunged in. He smashed down on Paul's arm, causing the car to swerve violently to the left, the two open doors on the driver's side flapping widely as Paul pulled away. He corrected the steering as best he could with his right hand and hit out furiously with his left.

Ignoring what blows Paul could manage, Boris tried to climb into the car, his legs dragging on the cobbles as they picked up speed. With one arm he hauled himself across the passenger seat while the other flailed powerfully in Paul's direction. Paul hit out as hard as he could, only connecting weakly with the Russian's nose. But despite the frailty of the punch, he felt a dampness spray across his hand. He looked over to see what he fully expected would be blood dripping from Boris's face, but there wasn't any.

Katia and Alisa had reached through from the back seat of the car. Each girl held a handbag-sized canister of pepper spray in their hands and were furiously discharging the contents of both bottles into Boris's face. The effect was immediate and overwhelming.

His eyes slammed shut involuntarily and his flailing arm went straight to his face. The massive arm levering him into the car did the same. Paul lashed out again and caught him more strongly this time, but it was the pepper spray that did the job. With his legs still dragging helplessly on the cobbles, he slowly slid back out of the car and into the street.

Paul glanced into the rear-view mirror and could see both Russians lying in the road. Both were holding their faces, and blood was pouring from Giorgi's nose. Katia grabbed her door and slammed it shut, hammering the lock into place.

"Sit back, sit back, I'm going to brake hard!" Paul called to the girls.

He waited until they'd braced themselves and then stood firmly on the brake pedal. The car dipped savagely on its suspension and the front passenger-side door swung shut. With all four doors now firmly closed, he hit the central locking button one more time. Now they were safe.

There was a long silence.

Paul steadied the car and joined the light afternoon traffic on the Avenue d'Ostende. He took a moment to regather his thoughts. They'd pulled it off. It hadn't been as he imagined it would be. It was traumatic and dangerous, but they'd done it and now they were on their way out of Monaco and as far away from Boris and Giorgi as possible. But where was all the security? It had seemed so responsive and efficient on Wednesday, but there was no obvious reaction at all. It had all happened in seconds – even the concierge could do nothing to help.

He dismissed it all from his mind. All he needed to do now was clear the city and, somewhat perversely, hope the Russians could do the same.

Katia looked terrified.

Alisa began to explain, but Katia wasn't listening and went for her phone. Alisa needed to stop her. She knew Katia couldn't make that call. The girl was frightened, her face pale and drawn, yet she was, in truth, safe now despite the terror of her ordeal. Alisa grabbed the phone from her and threw it into the passenger-side footwell at the front of the car. There was a furious exchange in Russian but eventually Katia calmed down.

"But you said you were my friends?" Her tone was resigned and desolate. Her English perfect.

"We are, but I need to explain. Give me five minutes to explain, and if you want to make a call once you know everything, I promise you I will give you your phone back." Alisa was composed and reassuring.

As compelling as Alisa sounded, Paul was never going to allow Katia to make that call. They needed to get Maria back first, but the promise seemed to reassure Katia and she settled back in her seat.

Alisa began to explain; first she spoke in Russian, morphing effortlessly into English. Paul could only assume it was for his benefit, but the Russian heiress seemed equally at ease with either.

Katia seemed to gradually regain a measure of composure as Alisa patiently explained. She left little out. She told her who she was and what she did, and the unguarded honesty seemed to take Katia by surprise. Alisa gave a compelling yet sanitised account of how she came to be attacked by Giorgi in room 732 at the Palais de la Méditerranée. The heiress looked genuinely distressed and even sympathetic. She explained about the magazine article, the stolen photographs and what she knew of the Russian gangsters. She told Katia all she could about Paul, and in doing so, he realised just how little they actually knew about each other.

Alisa explained about Alex and the situation with the police. She told her about the man in the dark suit from the Negresco and their concern for her when he made another appearance at the gates of her beautiful villa. Katia was shocked. He was a trusted friend, a family retainer, and she told Alisa his name was Oleg. The thought of his betrayal clearly hurt her deeply and she appeared to genuinely fear for his safety.

Alisa explained about the exchanging of the cars in the underground car park and what happened to the chauffeur, and Katia looked dismayed to hear it.

Then Alisa told her about Maria, and finally Katia understood.

It wasn't until Alisa uttered the name Anatoly that her demeanour changed again. Alisa had merely mentioned his name, but it was enough. Despite all Katia had just gone through, and everything Alisa told her, Paul had never seen anyone look so afraid at the mention of a name. The fear was consuming, debilitating, her face blanched white, the sound of his name overwhelmed her, and she began to shake uncontrollably.

"Who is Anatoly?" Paul asked, as Alisa took Katia in her arms and gave her what little comfort she could.

More softly this time, Paul tried the question once again.

"Who is Anatoly?"

"He is the Devil," she said, and the terror in her eyes redoubled.

Paul saw her distress but pushed for more.

"Does this 'Devil' have a last name?" he asked.

"Malokovic," she answered, and recoiled at the sound of it.

Alisa took a deep breath and shot Paul a look.

"Malokovic," Alisa repeated, as the colour drained completely from her features.

It was four-thirty in the afternoon.

Paul called Kira on the iPhone. She answered at the first ring and he told her to send the text message they'd prepared earlier. Paul was focused and single-minded now. There was no way Boris, Giorgi or Anatoly were ever going to harm Katia Shapiro. But it was all about Maria now. In truth, it always had been.

Chapter 54

They arrived back at the hotel at four-fifty in the afternoon. The hotel forecourt was crowded with Secure Co. delegates, some taking in the air, while still more polluted it with their nicotine of choice.

Paul turned to the two girls in the back of the BMW. Despite the crowded hotel forecourt, they still enjoyed a measure of privacy behind the blackened windows. Katia sat silently gazing out of the car and Paul thought how strange everything must have seemed to her. One minute she was enjoying cocktails with her closest friends, the next she was plunged into a world of violence and danger with her at the very centre of it all.

"Katia, we need your help," Paul said.

She seemed distant and distracted. Paul tried again.

"Katia, I know this must be very frightening for you, but I need you to listen to me."

"Why have you brought me here? Why can't I go home?" She turned to face him. "I want to go home. I want to go home now!" she demanded.

"You will, but not yet. We need your help, but once we get Maria back I will personally make sure you get home. I promise you that."

Katia appeared confused, even angry.

"Am I *your* hostage now? Is that it?"

"Please, Katia, it's not like that at all."

She glared at him from the back seat of the car and his patience broke.

"Look, I know right now this may not mean that much to you, but we did just save you from those two animals back there, so surely that must buy us some credit."

He could almost see her working through his argument. She stared straight back at him.

"You are safe," he reassured her. "You are completely safe, but Maria" – he paused for effect – "she is in very real danger. We need *your* help now. It's no more than a favour really. We just need you to agree to give us a little more time, that's all."

Paul raised the stakes.

"Katia, we know what Boris and Giorgi are capable of. We've seen it for ourselves. They've threatened to kill Maria, and I have no doubt they will do it if they get backed into a corner. I can't take that chance. We just can't afford to risk it."

Katia continued to glare at him, unmoved. He had no means, and certainly no intention, of getting what he needed from her by force, but he did need her cooperation. He raised the stakes again.

"But there's more to it than Boris and Giorgi. There's another man involved… this 'Devil' of yours. He's right at the heart of all of this. He's pulling the strings and seems to terrify everybody that comes into contact with him. This man, Anatoly Malokovic…"

Katia winced and recoiled at the sound of his name. Paul capitalised on her obvious fear of the man.

"If you know anything about this man at all, you must know what Anatoly is capable of. I suspect you know that far better than we do. Saving you from Giorgi and Boris is only half of the story. Anatoly Malokovic is behind all of this. It's not over, not yet. Anatoly is still out there and Maria is still missing. We must get her back, and that means we need you to work with us. It's not about you any more, Katia. This is about Maria now – that's it, nothing else matters."

Her composure began to desert her again. It was that name. The possibility of Anatoly's involvement landed like a hammer blow to Katia. She was intimidated by it, unnerved, shrinking in stature every time his name was mentioned.

"You are not our hostage, Katia. If you insist on getting out of the car right now, neither of us is going to stop you." Paul gambled.

Katia appeared uncertain.

There seemed to be little prospect of her doing anything of the sort – her fear of Anatoly saw to that. Why would she? The car was potentially no less secure than the state-of-the-art safe room Paul imagined was installed back at her villa. In some respects, it was potentially even safer, being mobile, anonymous, all but impregnable and ferociously quick off the mark. Suddenly Katia's appetite to get away from her new "friends" had waned completely. Her mood changed again.

"Yes… I know, the poor girl," she said. "I'll help if I can. But what can *I* do?"

Her voice trailed away and Paul could see she was still in turmoil. He gave her a few moments as she struggled to piece together all that was happening to her. Katia drifted quietly into her own thoughts. She shifted uncomfortably as Alisa tried to reassure her. Gentle Russian words were exchanged between them.

Katia appeared less frightened as the seconds ticked by, perhaps reassured, sheltering inside the familiar sanctuary of her armoured limousine. Suddenly her mood changed again, her body stiffened and her eyes closed tightly shut, as if bracing for an impact that would surely come. Something had suddenly fallen into place. She was piecing it all together, and the picture it completed appeared no less distressing to her than the fear she held for Anatoly himself. She shook her head as if trying to be rid of it, but there was no escaping the images taking shape in her mind.

"No!" she wailed. "Oleg, what have they done to him?"

Paul waited for more.

She slumped back in the seat. Her eyes moistened but she refused to cry. She fought it and instead began to talk, her head down, facing the floor, lest a single tear betray her. She rambled at first, confused and disorientated, but slowly an order began to emerge.

She talked about Oleg, Mikael and her father. But it was Oleg that troubled her most. He was all but a friend to her, an old family retainer, loyal and faithful, a man whom her father trusted without question. But he'd changed, and she knew something was wrong. He hadn't been himself for weeks.

"I thought it was a private matter, nothing to do with me, perhaps a family illness," she said, her voice breaking with emotion. "Oleg said nothing. He just let me believe it. If only I'd known… if only he'd told me."

Katia paused for breath.

"Oleg became withdrawn. He kept unusual hours. Sometimes he just disappeared without explanation," she continued.

Oleg's betrayal troubled her deeply.

"Why would he betray me to a man like Anatoly?"

Katia fell silent.

Paul saw no reason to mention Oleg's one-way trip to the yacht. Now wasn't the time. Katia was distressed enough. But he needed more from her and so, with a degree of trepidation, he changed the subject.

"Tell me more about Anatoly Malokovic, Katia?"

She shook her head slowly.

"He's a terrible man," she whispered. "He's vicious and dangerous. It isn't easy for me to talk about him."

Paul could sense her reluctance but pushed her for more.

"His father was in business with my father… that was before he died. He's Valentine's only son, but he's nothing like his father. I've known him all my life, but he's sick and twisted. He enjoys hurting people."

Paul studied her for a moment.

"Why does he want to hurt you, Katia?" he asked quietly.

She looked up ashen-faced. The terrifying truth of it hit home. The Devil, Anatoly Malokovic, was coming for *her*.

"I don't know. I hardly know him anymore. I haven't seen him for over three years... I can't talk about it... it's too hard."

"Does he own a yacht called *Barabus*?"

"Yes, it was his father's. It was his pride and joy. Why do you ask?"

"Did you know that *Barabus* is in the harbour at Villefranche?"

"No... No... Anatoly's here in France? Why?" Katia was distraught. "Oh my God! Why? Why? You have to help me. Please don't let him find me... please."

Alisa placed her arm around her shoulders and pulled her close. A single tear slipped silently, defiantly down her cheek.

"You're already safe, Katia, trust me. You *are* already safe... But we think the two men that attacked your car are working for Anatoly. We don't know why yet, but that's why we need your cooperation."

"Anything, anything, just don't let him find me..."

Katia's strength failed her and she collapsed into Alisa's shoulder, gripping her hand as if her life depended on it.

Paul pushed on.

"Katia, I was told that Anatoly would never 'set foot on French soil'. Those were the exact words used. Do you know why that might be?"

Katia thought for a moment.

"I don't know. I don't ask. When it comes to him, I just don't want to get involved."

She took another deep breath and then looked up. There was something else; a memory was forming. She tucked her hair behind her ear as she regathered her composure.

"My father told me Anatoly was a marked man in France," she continued more brightly. "I remember that. My father took great comfort from it. He thought it would be safer for me to be in France because of it."

She smiled weakly. It was something perhaps. She looked at him imploringly.

"Surely that is something."

"Yes, it is, definitely," he said.

Paul's lack of conviction did little to comfort her.

"It isn't safe for me, is it? It's never going to be safe for me here, or anywhere." As the prospect took root, a second tear followed the first.

"You do need to stay with us for now, Katia. We can keep you safe and then get you away from here, somewhere safe once we get Maria back."

"I can't stay in France if Anatoly's looking for me," she whimpered. "I just can't."

"We'll work something out. Maybe we could take you to Italy. It's so close we could just nip over the border once things settle down. Would that help?"

"No! Anatoly keeps the yacht in Genoa. He knows a lot of powerful and dangerous men in Italy too. I need to get back to my father. He will know what to do. I need to get back to St Petersburg."

"It's okay. We'll work something out."

There was a loud tap on the window. The concierge was at the side of the car, all smiles and efficiency. Paul let down his window and gestured him away for a few minutes more.

"Of course, *Monsieur* Smith," the concierge replied, with a deference Paul assumed was afforded to any guest that valet parked a fleet of cars at the hotel. He closed the car window and returned to Katia.

"I know this must be frightening right now, but we have a room here at the hotel. No one else knows you're here, and you will be safe as long as you stay with us. Will you do that? Just for a short while?"

She nodded.

"We need you to give us some time. We need the Russians" – Paul was increasingly aware that everyone involved in the drama, other than himself and Gary, were all Russians. He needed to be far more specific – "the two men who attacked the car at the hotel," he clarified. "We need them to genuinely believe that you've been abducted."

She looked terrified as his words took shape in her mind.

"Katia, we can't tell anybody that you're safe right now, not yet. I can't stress to you just how important it is that Anatoly doesn't find out where you are, or who you're with. It's too risky. We don't know who your father can trust either, or how many people Anatoly has working for him. If he can force a man like Oleg to work against you, we can't be sure of anyone right now."

"Mikael… He would never betray me…"

"That's true," Paul conceded, as a fresh wave of guilt broke over his already guilty conscience. "He's stayed loyal to you, there's no doubt about that…"

"What's happening to me…?" she said, sobbing. "Why is this happening?"

She was falling apart in front of him, and what he was about to say next wasn't going to help.

"Katia… Boris and Giorgi need to believe that we are prepared to exchange you for Maria. It's the only way to keep Maria safe."

Katia recoiled in horror at the prospect, and she withdrew her hand sharply from Alisa's. Her eyes flashed with alarm and she looked pleadingly at the girl who had, until now, been a source of much-needed consolation.

"No… no…" she cried.

"It's okay, Katia, we'll never do that… Never…" Alisa reassured her.

Paul spoke gravely and deliberately.

"Katia, I assure you that will never happen. We won't do anything that will put you at risk. I can't emphasise that enough. Nothing is going to happen to you. But we need until tomorrow afternoon before you can contact anybody. I know it's a lot to ask, but Maria is in such terrible danger. I need this. I need some time to get her back?"

"Please…" Alisa applied her own gentle pressure.

Paul waited.

"What about my father? Surely I can tell him I'm safe?"

"I'm sorry, Katia, not even your father at this stage. If this gets out, if Anatoly finds out you're safe, Maria won't survive. I can't let that happen."

Katia fumed quietly for a moment and then sat bolt upright in the back of the car.

"Please," she said firmly, "may I have my phone back?"

The request felt like a test.

"You understand what I'm asking of you?"

"Yes, I understand."

She held out her hand for the phone.

Paul rummaged around in the footwell of the car to recover it. He handed it to her. She tapped away briefly and then handed it back to him.

"When Maria is safe," she said quietly, "will you ring my father and tell him where I am. This is a private number. It is always answered and only my father and Natalie, his secretary, know it."

And with that one simple act of good faith, it was agreed. Paul discreetly set the phone to silent mode and slipped it into his pocket. He knew it would ring incessantly once the news of Katia's abduction broke. That was a distraction he just didn't need.

Gary parked up the Opel Corsa immediately behind the BMW. Paul noticed the concierge becoming increasingly agitated because the two cars had completely blocked the space available at the front of the hotel.

Moments later, there was another tap on the car window. Gary was all smiles with Kira at his side. Paul lowered the window, and the sounds of bustling traffic on the promenades and the thick aroma of cigarettes invaded the cabin.

"Are you ready, mate?" Gary beamed as he looked straight past him. "Hello, luv," he said, with all the familiarity in the world. "Very nice to meet you."

Katia responded graciously with a smile.

"Yes, Gary…" Paul said. "I think we are…"

Chapter 55

The underground car park was dark, brooding and silent. The Mercedes was gone, but the BMW hire car still remained in its parking bay, exactly where he'd left it.

As they approached, Paul paused for a moment at the spot where the assault took place. The memory of it disturbed him. It had been vicious and uncompromising, the images replaying in his mind vivid and raw. There was nothing to betray what happened there – no blood, no damage, barely a scuff mark on the polished concrete floor. But it was cold and unsettling all the same.

He studied the black BMW in the VIP "Réservé" parking space. There was nothing to indicate the presence, or otherwise, of the chauffeur in the boot. Maybe he'd already made his escape, or perhaps some passer-by had let him out. The car *was* still unlocked; anyone could have opened the boot from the outside if the chauffeur had made his presence known.

"Are you going to open it?" Gary asked, and he took an involuntary step backwards.

Paul let out a breath and made his decision. He scanned the car park. They were completely alone. The tell-tale red LEDs on the CCTV cameras remained inert, the cameras still out of service.

He pressed the boot release and slowly let it rise. Before it travelled more than a few inches there was visceral roar from within, an explosion of activity and the boot lid swung forcefully upwards to the full extent of it hinges. It sprang back, hammering down again as Paul stepped away in alarm. There was another roar from the confines of the car boot and the lid sprang up a second time, kicked with enormous force by the man trapped inside. The boot lid slammed against the limit of its hinges again, then smashed down with increased energy. The only impediment to it slamming shut completely was the flailing tethered feet of the chauffeur as he made his bid for freedom.

Paul grabbed the boot lid and pressed his full body weight against it. Mikael was trapped, the cold metal of the car boot biting into his claves.

Paul hadn't known what to expect, but he should have been better prepared. He was certain the chauffeur had been out cold when Boris dumped him in there, but now he was very much awake and desperate to make his escape. Surely Mikael would have worked some of it out for himself. He would know he was in the boot of a car, but of what car and where it was parked would be questions without obvious answers. And the car could have been dumped anywhere while he was unconscious. It could have been driven over the border to Italy, or abandoned at the docks, or left on a remote mountain track, or maybe his imagination, intensified by fear, would have him considering the very worst. Was he, even now, unwittingly awaiting the massive hydraulic jaws of a car crusher that would end his ordeal once and for all. Mikael could have no idea, but this was his chance, and he was making a determined attempt to take it.

It was stalemate. Paul pressed down hard as he considered his options. He couldn't let go of the boot lid and there was no way he could secure the lock; the chauffeur's substantial legs were still in the way. Paul needed to do something. He looked around for inspiration. There was nothing obvious and Gary was keeping his distance. Even the slightest release of pressure resulted in the trapped man kicking out wildly. The stalemate couldn't go on.

"Gary, get over here."

Then, suddenly, the man in the boot fell silent. Perhaps he was regathering his strength for another attempt. But it was a chance, and Paul didn't hesitate.

In a single movement, he released the boot lid and grabbed Mikael's legs. Paul adjusted his grip and then, using Mikael's bound legs as a leaver, he forced the chauffeur back down hard inside the boot. He slammed the lid shut. The chauffeur responded with a serious of muffled expletives in what Paul assumed was a Russian dialect.

Paul fumed at himself for not being better prepared and cursed at Gary for being no bloody use at all. But even now, as he battled to keep Mikael under control, he felt for the chauffeur. Just as there was no way Mikael could know who had attacked him in the first place, he could have no idea who it was that had just opened the boot. It was, perhaps, his only chance to get away, and he'd tried to take it with all of his formidable strength. But he'd failed, and now that the boot lid was securely shut, he was trapped inside once again.

There were more muffled cries from within, but nothing discernible. It wasn't just the boot that made Mikael incomprehensible, and it wasn't the language barrier either. It was obvious, from the muted, indistinct tones that Boris had gagged the chauffeur as well as binding him.

Gary had taken a few more backwards steps.

"What the fuck!" he exploded.

"Get over here!" Paul demanded, his eyes flaring, sweat pouring from his brow.

"But—"

"Gary, just get over here." Paul was short on patience. "Look, he's taken a severe beating. He's bound to be confused and disorientated. He probably thinks we did this to him in the first place."

"So…"

"He's not a threat! Get over here and keep hold of the boot just in case."

"In case of what?"

"Just do it!"

Reluctantly Gary added his weight, securing the boot and giving Paul time to think.

"What the fuck…?" Gary's vocabulary hadn't improved. "I thought you said he was one of the good guys!"

"He is, but look at the state of him. He has no idea what's going on."

"What now?" Gary demanded.

"Shush!"

Paul was suddenly conscious of someone entering the car park at the far end. The man was wearing the branded overalls of a security company and carrying a stepladder and a large metal tool box. The decommissioned CCTV cameras were about to get some attention.

"We can't go on like this," Paul declared, lowering his voice to a whisper. "I've got to get him out of here."

Gary stepped back from the car and just looked lost.

"Right, get back to the girls. I'll deal with the chauffeur," Paul whispered.

Mikael began his assault on the boot lid once again.

"What are you going to do?"

"Right now, I don't know, but I need to get him out of here. We can't just leave him in the boot. It's my hire car. It's my details on the contract."

At the far end of the car park, the CCTV engineer set up his stepladders below one of the disabled cameras. He began rummaging around in his toolbox. The sound of Mikael's struggle was masked only by the noise of the engineer setting about his work.

"We're out of time. That guy's going to hear Mikael's efforts to escape, but even if he doesn't, he could have those cameras up and running any minute. There's no way I'm letting Mikael out down here, not now, not with a witness or CCTV, and certainly not while he's as agitated as this. I don't see any way of calming him down right now either."

Gary looked hesitant.

"Just get out of here, Gary. I won't be long," Paul said. He located the BMW car keys in his pocket. "Just get back to the hotel. I'll deal with this and catch up with you later."

Moments later the BMW purred into life. Paul switched the radio on and wound up the volume. As he approached the exit barrier he spotted a familiar Ferrari key fob and BMW ignition key on the passenger seat. *My lucky day,* he thought, as he pulled up to the barrier and recovered the keys. The VIP car parking ticket worked its magic in an uncomplicated fashion. If only he'd known it would be that simple earlier, but he couldn't have taken that risk with Katia's safety hanging in the balance. He slipped the car out of the car park and into the cool Mediterranean evening sunshine.

As they hit the road, Mikael renewed his bid for freedom, kicking and hammering at the boot with every ounce of his remaining strength. Paul retuned the powerful, and frustratingly complicated, radio to a station playing rock ballads and ramped up the volume still further. The pounding bass and guitar riffs created more discomfort for his passenger, but they also drowned out his all-out assault on the BMW's luggage compartment.

Paul made his way out of city and up into the mountains.

Before too long he was powering along the Grand Corniche and scouring the road ahead for anywhere discrete and secluded to deposit his cargo. He dismissed several improvised viewing points along the way. Each provided parking for a few cars on compacted gravel, but Paul drove on – they were all far too public.

The good news... at least Mikael had survived the encounter with Boris. He felt no small measure of relief about that. But what next? Paul was comfortable enough that Mikael had nothing more to fear from Boris and Giorgi. If they did have further plans for the chauffeur, then they would have taken him with them when they recovered Alex's Mercedes from the underground car park.

He approached a narrow dirt road that headed further up the mountain towards a ridge where a few ancient olive trees lined the route. Paul stopped the car and turned off the radio to consider his options. The trail was steep, rocky and neglected; it would have to do.

He reversed up the track, bearing hard left as it climbed away from the main road and then straight on again for another hundred yards. He stopped and hit the central locking button, more for reassurance than in any expectation. There was a dull aborted whir; the locks were already engaged. From the security of the car, he pressed the boot release and waited. There was an instant flurry of movement and the car rocked on its suspension as the chauffeur seized his opportunity.

As Paul waited, Mikael scrambled out and the car lifted appreciably as his weight spilled out awkwardly onto the dirt. He allowed the car to roll forward fifty yards and then brought it to a stop once more. Reflected in the wing mirrors he could see the chauffeur struggling in the dust where he'd fallen. He looked dazed and in pain. His efforts to stand were futile, and Paul took pity on him.

He unlocked the car door and stepped out. He walked cautiously to the back of the BMW and closed the boot. It shut with a thud. The chauffeur stopped his struggle for a moment and strained to turn in Paul's direction. A rag was still wedged firmly in his mouth. His distress was all too clear. Paul pulled out his Swiss army knife as he approached and Mikael started to struggle ever more frantically as he neared.

"It's okay. I'm not going to hurt you," Paul said, trying to reassure him. But he could see the alarm on his face, the terror in the eyes of a man who had all but accepted, with a compelling certainty, that his time had finally come. His distress only intensified as Paul pulled the blade from the body of the handle.

"It's okay," he said for one last time, and he gently tossed the Swiss army knife in the stricken man's direction. It landed just short of his hands and he scrambled eagerly towards it.

"I'll have that back next time we meet," Paul said. Then he added superfluously, "It was a present." The image of a cosy Christmas spent with Sophie suddenly flashed inappropriately across his mind.

He dashed back to the car before the chauffeur could make any meaningful use of the lifeline Paul had just gifted him. As he looked back through the rear-view mirror, he could see Mikael bringing the blade to bear to some effect.

Not before time, he felt he'd finally shown the man in the photo, the man with the ominous red cross, the victim of a premeditated and vicious attack, some small measure of consideration. Paul knew it was the very least he could do.

Chapter 56

Boris fired up the stolen iPhone and read the message for the thousandth time.

The incoming text read:

У нас есть Катя Шапиро. Мы обменяем ее для безопасного возвращения Марии. Подробная информация опорядке обмена, будет отправлен завтра в 8:00 утра точно и должны строго выполняться. Отправить еще одно доказательство жизни. Должна включать подтверждение даты и времени или нет сделки.[7]

Boris threw Alisa's iPhone onto the table.

"These people have no idea who they're dealing with," he growled.

He stalked the room rubbing his eyes.

"Those bitches have made fools of us," he declared, breaking the short silence and drawing the unavoidable conclusion. The day had been a complete shambles from start to finish.

He turned to Giorgi, who was occupied nursing his nose with a damp cloth and holding a swab of bloody cotton to his injured thigh. Their recent exertions had reopened the original wound yet again. Giorgi said nothing.

"If we live through this…" Boris shook his head as if the odds weren't in their favour. He seemed resigned, almost unwilling to conclude his sentence lest he made the odds worse still. "Know this, Giorgi," he said, pointing a nicotine-stained finger in his colleague's direction, "you will die every bit the fool you have always been. You were born an imbecile and you have learned

---

7. *We have Katia Shapiro. We will exchange her for the safe return of Maria. Details of the exchange will be sent tomorrow at 8 am precisely and must be followed precisely. Send further proof of life. Must include proof of date and time or no deal.*

nothing. This is all your fault, all of it! You've been an idiot all your life. You and that whore… She is the cause of all of this… Will you never learn? Why did you let that girl get away from you? Why didn't you just keep your mouth shut and that file out of sight?"

Giorgi was about to protest but Boris cut him short.

"Too late. It's all too late, Giorgi. You're always wise after the event – why never before? Why do you never think? Why do always react like an animal!"

He held his hand up, forbidding any response.

Boris stood at the window squinting at the view. He still couldn't tolerate the full blinding intensity of daylight. Even as the power of the sun diminished, the early evening light still forced his eyes shut against his most determined efforts to keep them open.

"Look at the state of us!" he said, as he pressed a cool wet cloth to his face.

Still Giorgi held his counsel.

"Well? What have you got to say for yourself?"

Boris didn't pause to let Giorgi speak.

"Anatoly will kill us both for losing Katia Shapiro, and if Alex isn't dead already, he'll be next. Maybe you should have done him a favour and finished him when you had the chance. Anatoly will make an example of all of us…"

Giorgi could stay silent no longer.

"But we can still exchange the girl… the text…"

"That will never happen. It's too late. How long do you think that bastard is going to wait? There's no way we're going to get our hands on that girl in time. What am I supposed to tell Anatoly? He's expecting a call now. He's expecting Katia Shapiro tonight, and all we have is a washed-up old whore instead. We're out of time, Giorgi!"

Boris was pale and drawn, his body language that of a man anticipation the potential cost of their failure.

He caught sight of the sodden cloth in his hand trembling, agitated by the involuntary shaking of his fist. It was fear, a genuine fear. It was alien to him but real enough. He dumped the cloth on the table. Fear was bad for both of them. Fear could make him weak, stop him thinking clearly. He couldn't afford to let his own fear of Anatoly divert him now. There was no time for weakness and distraction – he needed to concentrate. It was Giorgi's mess but Boris knew he would have to do the thinking for both of them. If they were going to get out of this alive, he needed to put all that to one side, and he needed Giorgi to focus and exercise some control over his volcanic temper.

"But the exchange… they want to do it… Why can't we just make the exchange and then…"

Boris knew that Giorgi meant well, but he was missing the bigger picture. No matter what happened next, Anatoly would exact a heavy price for all their mistakes.

Giorgi tried to make his point yet again. It was all so black and white to him. Where shades of grey did exist, they were usually tinged with red, lots of red. Blood and violence were his stock-in-trade. Subtlety and nuance had no place in Giorgi's world.

"We can exchange the woman for Shapiro," Giorgi pleaded.

"Shut up! I need to think."

Boris turned away from the window and rubbed his eyes dry on his shirt sleeve. His eyes were badly swollen and bloodshot, his breathing remained shallow and laboured, and the effects of the double dose of pepper spray continued to take its toll. He slumped down in a chair.

Giorgi found his voice again.

"I should have killed that whore when I had the chance," Giorgi growled from across the room.

Boris exploded.

"You should have screwed the whore when you had the chance and nothing more."

Giorgi was about to protest, but Boris was out of his chair again and at his side.

"You should have drunk your damn beer, screwed the whore and kept your fucking mouth shut. What's the matter with you?" Boris paced menacingly in front of him. "Just keep your mouth shut! Surely you can do that now!"

There was nothing else to be said.

The room resembled a triage suite. Bottles of saline solution, fresh bandages, liniment, antiseptic swabs and a large packet of painkillers lay discarded on the table. Pizza boxes and bloodstained bandages littered the floor. A bottle of Polish vodka sat on the kitchen drainer next to a sink full of dirty pots.

A plastic carrier bag of unused female toiletries sat by the front door undisturbed. Boris had genuinely intended to ease the discomfort of their hostage, but things were so much more complicated now. Cleaning up the hostage was a courtesy now neglected as events continued to spiral out of control.

Boris stalked the kitchen, pausing at the sink to rinse his eyes yet again. He blinked hard and attempted to focus on the view from the window. It was another stunning vista, similar to the one from Alex's villa. He'd found the vacant property only a few hundred yards up the hill from Alex's home. It was far enough away for them to feel secure, yet close enough for them to be surprised at the speed that Giorgi's lack of self-control was discovered by the police. He had assumed it was just bad luck that Alex was found so soon, but after all that had happened since, Boris wasn't quite so sure. As convenient as it was to use Alex's villa, he knew at the time they couldn't stay there for long. At least he'd been right about that.

"Polish shit!" Giorgi exploded, as he took another sip from the vodka bottle on the drainer.

Polish shit or not, it took the edge off and both men set their prejudice aside to feel the warming spirit ease a little of the burden.

"These fuckers are going to die! If we live through tomorrow…" Giorgi said coldly, grabbing Boris's shoulder with a grip that would have crippled a lesser man. "I promise you, if we live through tomorrow, I will kill every last one of these bastards."

Boris took no comfort from his unhelpful and typically ill-considered outburst, but he let it pass unchallenged. *"If we live through tomorrow!"* That was all that occupied his thoughts for now.

Boris took the bottle from Giorgi and drained the last of the vodka from it. He turned to face the view again. His vision had cleared a little, but the pain remained as the sun slowly set, turning the sky blood red over a darkened sea.

"You listen to me now, and listen well," he said. "Tomorrow you do exactly as I say. You may be my brother, but trust me, if you don't, I will let that mad fuck Anatoly kill you for kicks." There was a hint of a smile on his face.

"I will," his brother said meekly. "I will."

Boris lifted the vodka bottle to his lips once more and then cast it aside, a single meagre drip his paltry reward.

"Give her some food, Giorgi… water too, but don't touch her. Don't even go near her. Stay away from her, Giorgi, I warn you. None of this is her fault, and I need her alive and unharmed for tomorrow… I'm going to call Anatoly."

He tossed the stolen iPhone to his brother.

"When she's had something to eat, take her outside and get another photograph. Make sure you can read the time and date on the iPad like last time."

Giorgi reluctantly got to his feet and dragged himself out of the room.

Boris stepped outside and stood alone on the terrace. He focused on the horizon, staring out over the rooftops. He wasn't given to emotion, but even he had to admit it was a beautiful spot, and he allowed himself a few moments to enjoy the view.

He'd left it as long as his nerves would allow. There were seventeen missed calls on his phone, every one of them from the same satellite phone number. It was eight o'clock in the evening. It was more than four hours since they'd lost Katia Shapiro, and he knew he couldn't stay silent any longer. He needed to make the call.

He dialled, the line connected and Anatoly erupted.

"Who got there first, you incompetent bastard? How could they? Are you simple? Do you take *me* for a fool? You're a dead man if you're trying to play games with me. There's no more money for you. You won't live to spend it. Trust me… I'll—"

"I don't know who they are—" Boris interjected, attempting to answer the first of the questions.

"You're finished unless you find that girl. I'll kill you myself!" Anatoly screamed down the phone.

"I have another—"

"Another what?" Anatoly interrupted venomously.

"Another hostage, Anatoly. All is not lost. They want to trade the Shapiro girl for this other woman. We have her here with us. All is not lost. I just need more time to—"

"What are you talking about? Who are these people? What other woman? What the fuck is going on there?" Anatoly was raging.

Boris took a moment to compose himself and allowed Anatoly to burn himself out. Boris explained from the start. Anatoly seethed as he listened.

"Bring this other woman to me," Anatoly commanded without waiting for all the details. "Do it now."

"It's not safe. There was a scene at the hotel. We only just got away before the police arrived. The police will be looking for us. It's not safe to move right now."

There was a pause.

"Why do they want this other woman? What is she to them?"

"I think she's their mother, Anatoly. I can still get the Shapiro girl if we can just—"

"Bring her to me now," he demanded again. "The police wouldn't dare board my yacht. Bring her now." He paused as if considering his options. "I want to meet this mother of whores."

"No, Anatoly, in the morning, at first light. I will do it then. They will give us instructions for the exchange at 8 am. I will get her to you before then."

Refusing Anatoly's demands was dangerous in itself, but Boris needed more time to let events settle down. And what more could Anatoly do to them now that wasn't already on his mind? They had a hostage. They had Maria. She represented greater value to them now than ever before. As long as they held Maria there was still a chance they could get out of this mess with their lives. Boris didn't even care about the money any more.

"Do it!" Anatoly ordered, and the line went dead.

*****

The deck was illuminated by a dozen hurricane lamps, and soft chill-out music drifted out from the saloon. The sea was calm and the huge yacht glowed in the fading light as the sun continued to set. Anatoly didn't care for details. It was only outcomes that mattered to him. He turned to the man at his side, the ambience doing nothing to soften his mood.

"Katia Shapiro has been taken, Christoff," he said coldly. "She may not be my hostage yet, but she is a hostage all the same. This is good. I can wait until tomorrow to meet the lovely Katia, but you make the call to her father tonight as planned. I don't care who has her right now. She is lost to Nikoli, and that is all he needs to know. Make the call. The board meeting goes ahead tomorrow, 6 am Moscow time, exactly as planned."

Christoff turned to leave.

"Wait. Use this number," Anatoly said, unfolding a piece of paper he'd just taken from his trouser pocket. "It's their *secret* number apparently. I have no doubt that ringing Nikoli on this number will guarantee you his full attention."

Christoff studied the numerals intently.

"The handwriting is very poor," Anatoly added dismissively. "Alex told me Oleg was a little nervous about handing it over. I think the betrayal was a little too much for him."

Anatoly allowed himself a smile and Christoff nodded slowly in acknowledgement.

"It's fine," he said. "I'll make the call."

As Christoff retired to the saloon, Anatoly took in a draught of bracing sea air and stared out aimlessly towards the shore. It wasn't perfect, but things were still on track as far he was concerned. He would take care of the bitch Katia Shapiro in the morning, and as for the fools who lost her in the first place... he would take care of them too. One way or another, Anatoly Malokovic always took care of business.

Chapter 57

In room 733, Gary, Alisa, Kira and Katia had made themselves comfortable. The minibar was already showing signs of wear; its contents were sparse indeed. Empty plates and half-eaten bowls of salad were strewn across the desk. The mood was subdued and there was still a deep sense of anxiety as Paul entered the room.

Katia's expression was one of concern. She didn't dare ask, but Paul already knew the question.

"He's going to be fine, Katia. Mikael's got a few cuts and bruises but other than that he's in good shape," Paul reassured her.

"Where is he?"

"I've no doubt he'll be making his way back to your villa as we speak. Honestly, he's fine."

Katia appeared unconvinced. Gary shot Paul a glance as if *he* needed further confirmation, and Paul nodded reassuringly.

"He's going to be fine," he repeated entirely for Katia's benefit.

"Thank you," she said.

Mikael had survived, but Paul knew full well he had all but conspired with the Russians to get the chauffeur out of the way. Any thanks from Katia were misplaced at best.

Alisa got to her feet and walked past him into the lobby.

"I saved you this," she said, taking the final 8 euro bottle of Peroni from the minibar.

She grabbed Paul's hand and dragged him, albeit willing, over to the bed. A space was made and, kicking off his shoes, he shoved the collection of pillows and cushions to one side. He sat with his back against the headboard, his feet on the bed and the bottle of beer in his hand.

The first draught of cooling liquid hit the spot.

"I could use a few more of these right now," he said ruefully. "Any news from Boris?"

"Nothing yet," Alisa confirmed, checking Kira's iPhone.

He was in no doubt that Maria would still be alive. He was certain Boris and Giorgi needed her more than ever. What troubled him most right now was the fate of the would-be kidnappers. Everything depended on them still being at large. It played on his mind. Why the delay? Why hadn't they responded to the text message? If the Russians had failed to get away, if they had been arrested by the police, Maria was in a completely different kind of danger. She might never be found. He needed the proof of life not for its own sake, but because it was the only way he would know if the Russians were still in the game.

With nothing left to do but wait, the events of the previous few days bore down on him. Quite suddenly he felt a consuming, immediate need to be alone. It was 8.30 pm. How long could Maria afford for him to wait?

Paul stepped out onto the balcony and pulled the sliding door shut. He could still hear the others talking inside, but their constant nervous ramblings seemed aimless and distracting; nothing they said added much. Nothing they said seemed to help.

The balcony door slid open again and Alisa stepped out before closing it behind her.

She placed some cutlery, a plate of cold meats and a small green salad on the table and then joined him at the handrail as he stared out across the square.

"Are you all right?" she enquired, placing her left hand softly on his right.

"I'm fine. Just a little tired, that's all."

"Do you want me to tell the others to be quiet?"

"No, it's fine. It's good to see everyone letting off steam. How's Katia holding up?"

"She's okay. She understands, I think. Now she knows us a little better, she seems to be fine." She paused. "She's very concerned for her father. He is an old man, and when he hears she's been kidnapped she is worried about his health. She doesn't know how he'll react if he thinks Anatoly has got his hands on her." She looked directly at him. "Anatoly... from what Katia has told me about him, he sounds like a terrible man. Paul, are you sure there's no other way?"

"I'm not sure of anything right now. I just need to think. What I really need is for Boris or Giorgi to text us back. I need to know they're still out there. If they've been arrested, Alisa, I don't know how we, or anyone else for that matter, will find Maria."

Alisa smiled up at him. She seemed to have a confidence in him he feared was unwarranted. What if he'd got it wrong again? He'd made so many mistakes before and was haunted by the possibility that the next one could be fatal.

"Why don't you eat something? You must be hungry?"

Paul wasn't hungry at all, but he sat down at the table anyway and, with Alisa sitting opposite him, he ate everything on the plate.

"Is that better?" she asked after a long silence.

"Yes," he said, surprising himself. But he knew things were far from better, he shook his head unintentionally and let out a sigh.

"What is it?" she asked quietly.

"I just want to finish this, that's all. The waiting… it's the hardest part."

"I can't believe what you've done for us. No matter what happens from here, Paul, no one could have done more."

Paul wasn't so sure about that. Surely he could have done so much more. "Come on!" he said, and ventured a smile. "Let's go back inside."

"I need to tell you something first," she said, seeming reluctant.

"Okay, what is it?"

"I told you about Chris… when we were in Cannes together. Do you remember?"

"Of course."

"Paul… Chris knew Maria long before he knew me…"

"Okay, you mentioned that."

"I know, but they shared a lot of history."

"You mentioned that too."

"He knew Alex as well. I mean, Chris *really* knew him. Alex worked for him from time to time. They did a lot of business in Marseille together."

"Where's this going, Alisa?"

"His name was Malokovic, Paul. His full name was Christoff Malokovic."

Paul took a deep breath.

"You think he's related to Anatoly?"

"Yes, Paul, I do."

He sat back in the chair and exhaled loudly. "Okay…"

"What do you think it all means, Paul? Do you think Chris is involved in all of this?"

"I don't know. I just don't know, Alisa."

She grabbed hold of both his hands across the table.

"I'm scared, Paul. He scares me. After what happened with Maria, he's capable of anything."

"What did happen between Maria and Chris, or should I say Christoff? What is this history they shared?"

"Maria confided more in Kira. I shared history with Chris too, so she never really opened up to me."

"Okay, but just tell me what you do know."

"She lost a baby. It was terrible, and she was very ill afterwards. I think the baby might have been Chris's. I don't know, maybe it was. I just don't know."

"Okay… What else? … Is there more?"

"Whatever happened, Maria nearly died. It was awful. Alex took her in and looked after her. I think that's when she fell in love with him. She can't have children any more, Paul, that much I do know. I think that's why she's the way she is with us. We're like her family and she loves us… she takes cares of us.

"I do know she couldn't work after what happened, and Alex just took her in. She owes Alex a huge debt for looking after her. He is a good man… I know I keep telling you that, but truly he's been very good to her, and he cares for us too."

Paul considered the latest revelation.

"Okay… I don't know if this Christoff is involved or not, but let's just keep this between us. I don't see any benefit in upsetting Katia or Kira any more than they already are. It's all about Maria for now. Let's not allow things to get more complicated. I want to focus on Maria, and one Malokovic at a time is more than enough for us to deal with. If Christoff shows up, we'll deal with him then. Agreed?"

"Agreed. I'm sorry, Paul. I should never have involved you in all this."

"Shush now. I am involved, so there's no point worrying about any of that. Come on, let's go back inside. I've got a lot to do to get ready for tomorrow, and we could all do with some rest."

As he stood up to leave, she threw her arms around him and squeezed him to her. It felt amazing, but it wasn't helping. It served only to heighten his growing sense of impending loss. Paul eased her gently away and planted a kiss on her cheek.

"You're very special you know," he said unintentionally, and then he stepped back into the bedroom before she could respond.

Alisa watched him go and remained on the balcony for a few moments more. She seemed distracted and deep in thought.

Chapter 58

FRIDAY

Paul called Gary to him.

"No more beer, mate," he said. "We need to talk. It's just you and me tomorrow and we've got some work to do."

"No problem," Gary said resolutely. And in a singular display of intent, Gary placed what remained of a bottle of Peroni on the desk. "Done!" he said. "Let's use my room. It'll be quieter and there'll be fewer distractions."

Paul gave Gary a weighty pat on the back as he headed for the door. He let him go and paused to speak to Kira.

"Promise me something, Kira…"

"Of course," she replied without hesitation.

"Promise me, none of that coke nonsense tonight. Do you understand? I'm relying on you."

"I promise, Paul. I'm sorry… I'm so sorry."

Paul took her in his arms and squeezed her like it was for the last time.

"Look after Katia for me, and call me the instant Boris or Giorgi texts you."

"Do you think they will?" Kira looked doubtful. "Text, I mean?"

"I'm certain of it," Paul said, with as much conviction as he could manage. She smiled weakly.

"One more thing," he said. "Text me the address of Alex's villa and Maria's apartment too. It's really important."

"I'll do it straight away," she said.

*****

Boris read the text message one last time. It was eight forty-five when he finally sent his response. He tapped out his vitriol, attached the photograph Giorgi had taken earlier, and then hit *Send*.

"Those fools have no idea who they are dealing with," he growled, and then he threw Alisa's stolen iPhone back down on the kitchen table in disgust.

*****

Paul and Gary were already halfway down the corridor when Kira's phone buzzed in her hand. It was an incoming text, Alisa's phone number clearly displayed on the screen. A grainy image of Maria was attached and the time reference stamped in the corner confirmed it had been taken just fifteen minutes before it was sent. Alisa read the message again and again.

"Stay here and keep the door locked, Katia. We'll be straight back," she said, dragging Kira out of the room by her arm.

Moments later, Alisa and Kira caught up with Paul and Gary as they crossed the lift lobby on their way to Gary's bedroom.

"What does it say?" Paul demanded, urgently closing the attachment down and focusing on the hieroglyphics in the message. He instantly dismissed the image as inconsequential. Maria was still alive, but he'd never doubted that. The new text message was the proof the Russians were still in play. With that settled, he was desperate to hear what they had to say.

Alisa translated. **Fuck you and your whores.**

Nice opener! Paul thought.

Anatoly will have her by then. You make your bargain with the Devil himself.

Gary's shoulders dropped.

"We're fucked!"

Kira burst into tears.

"Shut up, Gary," Paul snapped. "Tell me again."

Alisa re-read the message as they stood in the middle of the lift lobby.

"Again," he demanded.

The lift doors opened and a couple made their way down the corridor as Alisa studied the phone. They were of no concern to Paul. The text message was all the mattered, and he was convinced the Russians had been indiscreet. But he needed to be certain. Surely it was another error. Despite the brevity of the message itself, it was possible they'd inadvertently given away too much. It was a relief to finally receive their text, but it was so much more than that. If he was hearing it correctly, the Russians had just made another mistake. Paul saw a chance.

"Tell me again, exactly what it says," he demanded, rather more aggressively than he intended.

Alisa repeated the words.

"And you're sure?" he asked again, conscious that this wasn't the time to be adding to the tally of his own mistakes.

"Absolutely!" Alisa confirmed. "I'm absolutely sure."

Gary butted in. "It's a disaster! They think we know Anatoly and how to contact him, from all the proof of life stuff." Gary was utterly deflated. "We're screwed!"

Paul ignored him.

"The bit about 'Anatoly will have her by then' – is that absolutely correct? No ambiguity?"

Alisa could see it was important, so she read it silently to herself, agonising over the words.

"None!" she said. "No ambiguity at all. It's what it says."

"Change of plan, Gary. We're going right now."

Paul turned to Kira.

"Go and fetch the Samsung. It's still on charge by the bed."

Kira sprinted to the bedroom.

"Gary… get the lift and hold the doors."

Gary hit the call button.

"The Galaxy, Alisa, have you used it for anything?" Paul was dreading the answer.

"No, nothing, I haven't had time to do anything with it yet," Alisa replied.

"No phone calls, no text messages, no emails to the new account?"

"No, nothing. I've put a few contacts in, that's all. Is it important?"

Kira was back at Alisa's side.

"Seventh floor, doors opening," the lift interjected.

Gary stepped in, his foot wedged against the door and his finger rammed down hard on the *Hold Open* button.

Paul took the Galaxy from Kira and checked it. There were a few messages from the new network provider that were all in French and, as far as Paul was concerned, completely irrelevant. Other than that, the phone was completely unused, and, just as importantly, it was reassuringly one hundred per cent fully charged.

"Don't forget to send me those addresses, Kira – directly to my phone though. Absolutely nothing to the Galaxy. Nothing at all."

Paul dived into the lift and hit the ground-floor button.

"Doors closing."

"I'll call you later. Just stay in the room and keep the phone free… I love you," he called to Alisa as the lift doors began to close.

Gary shuffled uncomfortably from one foot to the other. He looked confused. There was a "lift car" silence between them more typical of complete strangers inadvertently thrown together for a few awkward moments. They didn't speak, and Gary avoided eye contact as the lift slowly descended.

Finally, Gary broke the silence.

"Er… mate…" he began. "Did you just propose or something?" Gary was a little wide-eyed.

"What? Don't' be ridiculous. She knows what I mean. I just meant… She'll know what I meant. It was nothing."

"It didn't sound like nothing to me."

"Gary, just shut up will you!"

And mercifully he did.

Chapter 59

Paul took the lead, navigating to the underpass before powering away down the Promenade des Anglais in Katia's BMW. Gary followed closely behind in the rather more modest Opel Corsa.

"What's the plan?" Gary asked, his phone wedged between his ear and his shoulder.

"Work in progress, but we need to get to the quayside in Villefranche as soon as possible."

"I don't get it. What's all the rush?"

Paul was still working out the details for himself, but Gary persisted.

"What's going on, Paul?"

"It's simple. It's that text message," Paul explained impatiently. "It said 'Anatoly will have her by then'. It was quite specific."

"So?"

"So? The point is, Gary, he doesn't have her now."

"So?"

"Think about it. If he doesn't have her now, that can only mean one of two things…"

There was a silence from Gary's end of the phone as he mulled the options over.

"What two things?" He'd completed his mulling to little effect.

"It's simple. They either take Maria to Anatoly, or Anatoly has to go to them."

"Okay, that makes sense, but why the rush?"

"We don't know when they're going to make the handover. They could be doing it right now for all we know. We need to get to the quayside so we can see when they make their move."

"And once we do, we call in the cavalry – right?"

"Right."

As far as Paul was concerned, Katia being safe simplified everything. They only had one objective now.

"As soon as we find Maria, Gary, we make the call and the authorities can do the rest."

Gary stayed silent. Paul couldn't help wondering if they'd just lost the phone connection.

"Sounds good," he said after an exaggerated delay.

"I've got a lot of work to do when we get there, so we need to get set up as quickly as possible. I thought I'd have all night to sort things out, but that text message has changed everything."

"What do you need me to do?" Gary asked.

"When we get to Villefranche, I want you to park up at the top of the village, where the road drops down to the harbour. You'll either be the 'early warning' or 'last line of defence'. I don't know which yet, but I'll work all that out later. I'll show you where to park. You just need to stay put and keep your eyes open. Okay?"

"Okay, I can do that."

Fifteen minutes later, Paul performed a U-turn and then pulled over to the edge of the quayside a short distance beyond the restaurants. He had a clear view of the jetty where the small white tender remained securely tethered. It bobbed restlessly on the modest swell and the dark blue pennant fluttered in a gentle sea breeze.

"There's no sign of them down here," Paul reported. "Settle in and keep your eyes open. When they make their move we need to be ready."

"Ready for what precisely?"

Paul didn't have an answer just yet, so he chose to ignore the question altogether.

"Just keep the phone handy. I'm going to check to see if the tender's been used recently."

"How does that help?"

"I need to know… If that tender has been used, there's a distinct possibility that Maria could already be on the yacht, but I don't think they've had enough time to do that yet."

"I don't understand. Why are you so convinced they'll take her to the yacht? How do you know Anatoly hasn't come ashore and they've handed Maria over already?"

"Norilsk, Gary. Because of what happened in Norilsk."

"You can't take that as gospel!"

"Actually, Gary, I think I can."

There was a brief pause and then Gary was on the phone once again.

"Okay, but even if you're right about the Norilsk stuff, they've had since four o'clock this afternoon to get Maria to the yacht. That's over four hours ago!"

"No, they haven't."

Paul was adamant. If Alisa's translation was half as good as he thought it was, there could be no doubt about that. Russian was Alisa's first language after all, and her English was "almost" perfect. There could be no possibility of a mistake.

"Think about it, Gary. Think about the message. 'Anatoly will have her by then. You make your bargain with the Devil himself.'"

Paul quoted the text message word for word. It was no less seared into his memory than the registration number of Katia's car.

"We received it no more than twenty-five minutes before we got down here," Paul explained. "There's no sign of Boris or Giorgi, and the tender is still moored up, right here. They haven't had enough time to get her to the yacht and get the tender back to shore in the twenty-five minutes since we received the message."

Gary stayed silent.

"Are you sure?"

"Certain!" Paul snapped. "Look, Alisa's language skills are top draw. She knows how important this is, and she was certain her translation was spot on. Have some faith, Gary, or better still, go with your intuition… it's your call."

"I'm with you, mate. Let's get on with it."

"Okay," Paul replied, with a disproportionate degree of relief. "I need to check that tender and then find a decent Wi-Fi signal."

"What?"

"Just keep your eyes open, Gary. I'll ring you back."

Paul killed the call.

This was it. They were getting closer to finding Maria, and Paul felt his pulse quicken as he climbed out of the car and headed for the jetty.

It was a cool, pleasant evening. Only the lapping of the water at the quay and the muffled sounds of the restaurants and bars disturbed the peace. It was a lovely spot, all the more so now the marauding hordes had made their way back to their respective cruise ships. There were none of the behemoths at anchor that evening, and the view out to sea was much improved as a result. By day, it was a busy little harbour, but as the evening drew on the activity waned, the pace slowed and a sense of tranquillity replaced the bustle. In the bay, dozens of elegant sailing yachts swayed languidly at rest, and further out, the somewhat more imposing hulk of *Barabus* lay brooding a good distance from the shore.

The vast yacht appeared to be a little further out to sea than Paul recalled; a trick of the light maybe or just an aberration of his errant memory? Why would they move her? What might that mean if they had? He dismissed it for now. He had more pressing matters to attend to.

Without breaking stride, he walked the length of the jetty and stood for a moment as if admiring the view. It was lovely, restful, a delightful spot. The atmosphere at the quayside felt relaxed and completely at ease. He scanned the quay, and a lone dog walker he hadn't noticed earlier slowly rounded the corner, leaving him completely alone.

He stepped gingerly onto the tender and made for the outboard motor. The small boat bucked and weaved underneath him rather more than he anticipated. He struggled to maintain his footing and, falling awkwardly, braced himself against the side of the boat. The pitching and weaving pushed him forward again and he toppled full length onto the tarpaulin in the bow. As he regathered himself, he remembered, with a sense of trepidation, that it was under that very tarpaulin that Boris and Giorgi had stowed Oleg on his trip out to *Barabus*. Paul lifted it anxiously, in dread that their victim might still be under there. To his relief, he wasn't.

The storage area it concealed was far larger than he imagined, but it was completely empty except for a length of blue nylon rope and three large white plastic fenders. A congealed pool of dark liquid marked the deck – perhaps it was Oleg's blood, the inevitable result of someone being battered senseless with the butt of a gun. Several unsettling smears of what appeared to be yet more blood stained the fenders a stomach-churning shade of pink. All of it was dry now, but it was only too evident that the stains were recent.

Paul regained his balance as he allowed the tender to settle back into the natural swell that slapped rhythmically, incessantly at the hull. More cautiously now, he made his way to the stern and placed his hand on the exhaust housing of the engine. It was stone cold. The boat had certainly not been used recently in Paul's estimation, and while it confirmed nothing much in particular, it was very much as he'd hoped.

Back on the quayside, he headed away from the car and towards the gentle buzz emanating from the restaurants. All were busy, but he soon found a suitable table at a café-bar with a "Free Wi-Fi" sticker stuck on the door. The majority of windows along the bar's frontage were concertinaed open, with the tables inside fully occupied. In front, a line of smaller tables, with chairs at either side, faced across the road, past a small seating area at the water's edge and out over the bay. Paul took a seat and waited to be served.

"*Oui, monsieur?*"

"*Une café au lait, s'il vous plaît, et le code pour le Wi-Fi, merci.*" At least he'd tried.

"*Oui, monsieur… une café au lait, et le code est HOTEL2014.*"

"*Merci.*"

Paul recovered Alisa's brand-new Samsung Galaxy from his pocket. He set it down on the table alongside his own iPhone and the iPhone Katia had given him earlier in the day. He knew there would be missed calls and took a moment to scroll through them. What father wouldn't try ringing his lost daughter? He'd set it to silent in expectation of the desperate calls that would surely follow her disappearance and, although it did stay silent, it had, none-theless, received dozens of calls. They were all from one number, a number he now knew to be Katia's father's. Paul couldn't begin to imagine his agony.

He set Katia's phone to one side and opened up Alisa's Samsung Galaxy, checking for emails and text messages just in case. There were several, but none were compromising, just setup and welcome messages from various service providers and of no real concern. He deleted them all. Next, he checked the contacts list for the telephone numbers and email addresses Alisa had loaded into her new phone. He deleted them all one by one, then felt a flutter of excitement for no rational reason as he came across his own name. He deleted that too, with a misplaced sense of reluctance. Finally, he reset the phone to its factory settings, taking care to preserve the email account that had been so helpfully set up by the shop assistant in Cannes.

"Right..." he said to himself, "where the hell do I start?"

He checked his own iPhone before he started doing anything at all. There were two messages. He instantly dismissed the first, a recurring reminder to "Phone Sophie", and immediately opened the second from Kira. Two addresses were displayed on the screen.

He fired up the Galaxy for the second time and typed in the Wi-Fi code. He waited anxiously for it to connect. After a brief delay, it logged on with excellent signal strength. Result! Next, he opened up the browser and went to work.

Paul had attacked Google and Wikipedia with a sense of urgency on Wednesday evening in preparation for what he needed to do next. He'd sourced five agencies in all and amassed no less than fourteen email addresses covering a complex law enforcement infrastructure.

First among them was the Police nationale, or local civil police. Next, he found the Gendarmerie nationale, the military police that operated under the authority of the French Ministry of Interior. The Gendarmerie maritime, or coast guard, were next. Paul located three email addresses for INFRA, the rather snappily titled International Fugitive Round-up and Arrest depart-ment, whose principal purpose was to target international criminals. Finally, a further four email addresses were loaded for the IBMTF, the equally snap-pily named Integrated Border Management Task Force, who concentrated on maintaining an integrated approach to border security.

That done, he needed to write the emails. He began with an account of what happened to Alex at his villa. Paul included the villa's address, kindly supplied by Kira, and a brief description of the cellar with the chair placed ominously at its centre. He listed Alex's most obvious injuries, including a reference to the cable ties and a how the emergency services were called to his aid. It was, as far as it could be, accurate and verifiable. It was intended to be as compelling an account as possible, to ensure the rest of the email would be taken seriously.

Next, he detailed the kidnapping of Maria, an event he was still convinced the authorities would know little, or perhaps even nothing, about. Paul included the address of Maria's apartment, again courtesy of Kira's recent text message.

Paul continued the email describing the incident at the Hotel Hermitage and the attempted abduction of Katia Shapiro by Boris and Giorgi. Despite the lack of any obvious response by the local law enforcement community at the time, he was certain the incident would have been reported and the two Russians would, without doubt, be "Persons of Interest" to the police.

The email went on to detail the part played by Mikael, Katia Shapiro's chauffeur, and the price he paid personally at Boris's hands. Paul confirmed where, and how, Mikael was attacked, and how he was later, on that same day, released on a remote dirt track in the mountains just off the Grand Corniche.

Finally, he detailed the involvement of a mysterious Russian, but left out his name and any reference to the yacht. It was all about Maria now, and he couldn't afford for the authorities to target Anatoly prematurely. He needed to be absolutely sure where Maria was and only then trigger the police response.

The email ended stating that a further message would be sent at some time during the next few hours. It would confirm everything the authorities needed to know to effect a rescue for Maria, and to scoop up any number of Russian targets in the process. It also included a stark warning that the final location could be either at sea or on the mainland, and that the kidnappers would, without doubt, be armed and dangerous. Finally, it urged the authorities to prepare for an immediate response, because when the email landed it would, almost certainly, be a matter of life and death.

The second email was short and to the point. He saved it to the *Drafts* folder for use later in the day, then agonised over when precisely he should send the first. He closed down the phones and finished his coffee. It was stone cold by now, but he barely noticed.

It was eleven o'clock when he made his decision. The Russians still hadn't shown their hand and the quayside was quieter now. The last of the diners were departing to their hotels or boarding their tenders and gently powering back to their respective yachts.

He made his decision. Paul loaded all fourteen addresses into the *To* options in each of his pre-prepared emails, selected the first, took a deep breath and then hit *Send*. That done, he headed back to the car for what he suspected could be a very long night indeed.

SATURDAY

Chapter 60

SATURDAY

At 2.30 am, Maria had been missing for eighty-seven hours.

The calculation helped to keep Paul awake at first, playing on his mind and inviting unwanted images of a woman he barely knew. Each image felt darker than the one that preceded it. Maria tied to a chair, tears streaming down her blood-smeared features, beaten, lying on a featureless floor in an anonymous room. The images began to flash in sequence: Maria, then Alex, Maria again. Now the floor was smeared with blood, Alex's blood, as he lay bound with the cables ties that had become Boris and Giorgi's signature. The darkness and isolation of the quayside taunted him. He felt a chill. He felt Maria's loneliness and sensed her fear. Outside the car every sound carried a threat, every shadow was filled with uncertainty.

A noise startled him, nothing more than a cat calling out in defence of its territory, but the picture in his mind was of Maria calling out in pain and desperation. Paul let down the window, fresh cold sea air filled the car and his body shook with a chilling apprehension. When would they come? Surely, they would come…

As a distraction, he re-read the email he'd sent earlier. He considered all the details he could have added to make it even more compelling than it already was. He closed the window as something close by fell to the ground, or was it kicked, a clattering sound that echoed in the stillness? The cat perhaps, or was there someone else out there in the dark, watching him? He scanned the road ahead and then each mirror in turn as he sat alone in the car – nothing, there was nothing at all. But they were out there somewhere. Giorgi and Boris were both out there, planning their next move. He watched the shadowy form of a street cat mount the sea wall and drop down out of sight. Silence retuned and the darkness closed in around him, a little blacker than before.

*****

Above the harbour, Gary shuffled uncomfortably in the driver's seat of the red Opel Corsa. He too was quite alone, but streetlights kept the darkness at bay and the incessant buzz of air-conditioning units disturbed the night. Gary turned the radio on for company and hummed along to the familiar tunes and tapped the steering wheel in time with the beat. He didn't have much of a view, but Paul had been very precise. The car faced up the hill and away from the harbour. It made sense. If Gary was to be Paul's early warning system, he was now facing the only direction that Boris and Giorgi could approach the quayside from; it was the only route down to the harbour from the main road, and Gary was bound to see them. If he was to be the last line of defence, he was facing the only direction that Anatoly could be travelling, in the unlikely event that he did actually come ashore.

Paul called him every thirty minutes. It was a boost to each other's morale, but there was little to report. Paul kept the calls short.

*****

By three-thirty the village was quiet and the quayside utterly deserted. Simply staying awake was becoming a challenge. Paul was determined to stay alert, but in all honesty he couldn't be certain that he hadn't drifted off from time to time. It was dark and cold, and there was nothing to be done but wait, to kill the minutes that dragged into hours as he fretted endlessly about what would happen next. He had only his recurring doubts and mounting trepidation for company, and sleep beckoned constantly.

At four-fifteen Paul stretched his legs. Leaving the sanctuary of the car, he wandered up and down the quay a few hundred yards in either direction. He felt better for the exercise and determined to recommend it to Gary next time they spoke.

It was a crisp, clear night and the moon reflected brightly off the water as it lapped endlessly against the antique stone. He stood a while, taking in the fresh salt air and feeling his tired limbs steadily coming back to life. All was quiet, *Barabus* lay silently brooding far out in the bay, and the tender remained tethered to the jetty close at hand and undisturbed.

Paul was chilled to the bone, but despite the temptation, he resisted starting the car and enjoying the warmth its powerful heater would no doubt readily provide. It was still very early and the quayside remained completely deserted. It occurred to him just how reckless it would be for Boris and Giorgi to fire up a noisy outboard motor. With so little activity and nothing to mask the sound, the roar of a powerful engine would cut through the peace, inviting attention, perhaps even a degree of scrutiny from the locals.

Paul was now convinced, more than ever, that the most sensible course of action for the kidnappers was to wait until the morning – just a few short hours – when the ebb and flow of everyday routine would legitimise even their activities.

The iPhone lit up. It was Kira's phone, but it was Alisa on the line.

"I couldn't sleep. How are you?"

"Fine, nothing's happened yet. I think they'll wait till morning now anyway. It's just too quiet here."

"You will be careful, won't you?" she whispered.

It was almost rhetorical. Careful is what he'd been from the start.

"You know I will," he said. It was almost an apology. "Where are you?"

"On the balcony. The others are still trying to get some sleep, but I can't."

"It's good to hear your voice," he said wearily.

"And yours," she whispered.

"How's Katia?"

"She's okay, tired and scared, worried about her father."

"I'll call him when I can. It must be terrible for him not knowing. Perhaps even thinking Anatoly has her."

There was a brief silence.

"Paul?"

"Yes… what is it?"

Another brief silence before she spoke again.

"Nothing really." She hesitated. Whatever she'd planned to say, she had clearly changed her mind. "It's okay," she said quietly. "Just be careful, that's all. I want you to come back safely. We all do."

"Don't worry about me," he said. "I'd better hang up. I want to save the battery just in case. I'll phone you when I can. I need to give Gary a call and make sure he's still awake."

Alisa laughed, and Paul could almost feel the warmth of her smile.

"Okay, be careful," she whispered once again.

*****

Before Paul could summon the will to dial, his phone lit up and Gary was on the line.

"Wakey, wakey, you old bastard!" Gary exploded down the phone.

"Not so much of the old," Paul countered, stretching his arms and legs in turn, forcing a little vitality back into each.

"I hope they come soon. I'm not sure my arse can take too much more of this." Gary sounded wide awake.

"They'll come, don't worry about that."

"Are you sure? We've been here for hours."

"I know they will. Just stay with it for now – it won't be long."

Paul heard Gary yawn and followed suit involuntarily.

"They'll come, Gary, they have to. If I'm right, they don't have a choice."

"Whatever you say, mate. You're the boss."

Paul killed the call and scanned the road ahead. It was getting light.

As five o'clock came and went, a few people started to appear. A couple of the working boats set out to sea and the sounds of the bars and cafes opening up for another day's business drifted in on the breeze.

Time passed.

The tiny bell on the Chappelle Saint-Pierre in Villefranche-sur-Mer quarter-chimed three distinct strikes. It was a quarter to six on a beautiful Saturday morning and things were starting to happen.

Paul ended the call, put his phone down on the passenger seat and picked up Katia's iPhone. There were dozens of new missed calls from various numbers, mostly from her father. Paul scrolled through them, thirty, forty, maybe more. Sitting in Katia's BMW, he had so much time to think, he could only imagine the agony of a father fearing for the safety of his only daughter.

Chapter 61

Just fifteen minutes later, as the tiny bell on the Chappelle Saint-Pierre in Villefranche-sur-Mer chimed six times, the antique Empire clock struck seven in St Petersburg. The boardroom was silent.

Thirteen men sat apprehensively at the table, each lost in their own thoughts, with Nikoli at the head. Following Yuri Barkov's untimely death, Vasily Grankin, the company's newly appointed lead counsel, sat immediately to his right. Two more men held station to one side, each guarding bundles of legal papers set out on a credenza. Natalie fussed around at the other end of the credenza arranging coffees and pastries.

"This is ridiculous, Nikoli. We have better things to do on a Saturday morning than indulge this madman. We do have families, you know!" Grankin was impetuous and outspoken, yet blessed with a legal mind as sharp and incisive as his much-revered predecessor.

Nikoli let his unwelcome contribution pass without comment.

Most of them had family – brothers, sisters, wives, children. Many had grandchildren too, and Nikoli was only too aware of it. He had family himself – one daughter – and although he'd shared his fears with no one else, it was the desperate concern he felt for Katia that had convinced him to call his colleagues together at such an hour, and at such short notice. There had been two phone calls the previous night. The first was from Anatoly's fixer, Christoff, and the second from Mikael, his daughter's chauffeur and bodyguard.

"Why are we here?" Pavel Vasin called from the far end of the huge table. "What is the meaning of all this?"

There was a murmur of support from others. Only one spoke up for Nikoli.

"I'm sure there's a very good reason for all this, so let's just get on with it," Timor Dimitriev said calmly. Then he shot Nikoli a meaningful look.

Nikoli eased himself to his feet.

"There is just one item on the agenda this morning, and I am at the mercy of these two gentlemen as to what that matter might be."

He nodded in acknowledgement of Anatoly's lawyers, who stood solemnly at the side of the credenza.

"I am sure we shall know their purpose in due course. All I can do in the meantime is ask you all for a little forbearance."

Time ticked by, and the room became restless once more. One rose to leave, but it was half-hearted and symbolic. He knew as well as anyone that they were going nowhere until Nikoli closed the meeting.

"We don't have to indulge Anatoly any more. Why are we still here?" Yulian Ivchenko demanded. He targeted his question at the two lawyers, who, despite their own obvious discomfort, remained stubbornly silent.

Nikoli stood up to address them again, his manner formal, his delivery grave.

"Gentlemen, you know as much as I do, I'm afraid. But, when Anatoly says it is a matter of life and death, I for one take that seriously. We are not indulging this man, I assure you. We are exercising caution where we all know extreme caution is merited. Please, gentlemen, have some more coffee."

Only one man rose to take up the offer. He brushed past the unwelcome visitors on his way to the credenza. He poured himself a cup of black coffee and started back to his seat, pausing momentarily to scan the top page of the documents the lawyers had so meticulously set out. He was immediately ushered away by the first lawyer, who insisted, without recourse to any legitimate authority, that the senior accountant go back to his seat at the furthest end of the boardroom table. Maxim Petrov dismissed him with a mild expletive before taking his place, planting his coffee cup down noisily on the exquisitely polished walnut table.

A mobile phone rang, and the senior of Anatoly's lawyers recovered a smartphone from his inside jacket pocket and took the call. The conversation was one-sided and brief. The mood in the room changed as he approached the table.

"I am authorised to issue the documents, gentlemen. You will have one hour to read them, and then sign them in the order dictated by Appendix One. There can be no deviation from the order. Once the document is signed, I will confirm the same to our client, and he will then honour his part of the bargain."

The room was in uproar.

"Who do these people think they are?" Yulian's indignation was widely shared.

Bogdan Noskov stood in protest. "What is the meaning of this?"

Each voiced their objections, but the instructions were clear. They had one hour to read the documentation and Nikoli bid them do it.

The junior of the two lawyers proceeded to hand out the bundles as they had been instructed. Neither knew the substance of the resolution they delivered, as neither had played any part in its drafting. Once the documents were distributed, they were both to leave the room.

"One hour, gentlemen. I'm afraid that is all you have," the senior lawyer reiterated, as they retired to the anteroom, closing the boardroom doors quietly behind him.

Nikoli read the first few lines, only to have his worst fears confirmed. The first sheet contained only threats and consequences. It was plainly written and chilling in its simplicity. The rest of the pack was legal in nature and to be complied with exactly.

On reading the words, Nikoli's world stopped dead. Nothing mattered now. It was his gravest fear made devastatingly real. Mikael's call had been everything he feared it would be. It was shattering, his worst nightmare, but now the full horror of it hit him hard. He felt his heart break. The despair was overwhelming.

Mikael had made the second call. But it was Anatoly's noxious sidekick Christoff that had made the first. Christoff had called him directly on a telephone number he should never have known – a private, secret number, a number known only to Katia and Natalie. It had been a brief and bitter exchange. Christoff's message was singular and unambiguous, an extraordinary meeting of the board was to be convened. In that one brief shattering phone call, Anatoly Malokovic had set out his demand and Christoff Malokovic had delivered it.

In the second phone call of the two, Mikael had delivered his own terrible news. Katia was missing. Nikoli's beloved daughter was gone.

The call from Christoff Malokovic had haunted Nikoli. But, until now, there had been room for optimism; maybe the two events were unrelated. Nikoli had dared to hope they were. But as he scanned the page again, there was no doubt left. All hope was gone, cruelly banished by the words printed on the document in front of him. With all hope gone, his strength failed him.

He choked back the urge to vomit as tears welled in eyes, and each despairing heartbeat pounded in his chest. He was disorientated. He steadied himself on the desk with one hand, wiping away tears that even now evaded his most resolute attempts to contain them. He was proud, too proud to let the weakness show, but too old and weak to keep such emotions in check for long.

She was gone. His beautiful daughter was gone. Lost to the very worst of men. Lost to Anatoly Malokovic.

A fist slammed down hard on the boardroom table, breaking his malaise. The gasps grew louder as each man came to the same inevitable conclusion. It was clear to all that if Katia was to be returned, if Katia was to live, the resolution needed to be signed in accordance with the instructions set out. Nikoli knew that would never happen. How could he expect them to agree to this? It was just too much to ask.

In return for his daughter's life, the board would hand control of the company back to Anatoly. It would be the end of the company, and an end, in itself, for each of them. He knew the board would never give in to such a demand; it was too high a price. This was blackmail, pure and simple, and no board worthy of the name would give in to it. But this was Anatoly, held in contempt by all, but feared too.

Each member of the board would have to search his own conscience. Not all, but most, would have to consider the safety of their own loved ones. They each knew with an unsettling certainty that there were few limits to Anatoly's depraved machinations. Today, it was Katia and Nikoli who were the victims of his insane attentions. How readily, almost inevitably, those same attentions could be visited upon any one of them.

There were a few members of the board who only had themselves to consider. These men had never known the joy of a family, or the debilitating weakness that such joy translates into at times such as these. Others had never been married, wedded only to their desks, and one, Maxim Petrov, had lost his wife recently and lived only for his work. So many of them had given their lives to the company; how could they be expected to give in to such demands? But, and Nikoli's heart broke with the certainty of it, to refuse Anatoly now would mean the end for Katia, a death sentence Anatoly would relish executing. The new constitution made no difference. All that his great friend Valentine had arranged was about to be torn apart. Nikoli was in agony. His beautiful daughter! His only beautiful daughter. His strength failed him completely and he slumped onto the table. It was all too much to bear.

"Water, get him some water," Timor called out.

Water arrived but he waved it away. The tough old man's eyes welled up as the colour drained from his face.

"My God!" he cried. "My God!"

"This can't be legal. It's coercion. We can fight this," Pavel bellowed.

His was a forlorn voice raised in anger from the far end of the room. He threw his bundle of documents to the table in disgust.

It was coercion, of that there was no doubt. It would certainly fail at the first hurdle if a legal challenge was mounted. There was undoubtedly a case to be answered. But who among them would mount it? Who would stand up for the company and watch their family pay the price? Anatoly was a madman, and legal probity had nothing to do with it.

Through it all, Nikoli held his counsel. Nothing mattered to him now. Not the company, not his wealth, nor the power that went with it. There was nothing left of consequence. All that mattered was his daughter. Anatoly had made this all about Katia, and now Nikoli would have his say.

"Gentlemen," he finally interjected, "I will vote with my heart and ask no favour of you in this matter. Each man must look to his conscience, and I for one will judge none that votes this day. This is a matter for each of you, and I pray we can all live with our decisions."

The board descended into chaos, every man speaking at once. Nikoli turned his attention to the document. He was to sign first but he knew it would count for little. Valentine's new constitution saw to that. It required a majority of the board, in addition to his own vote, to carry a resolution of such gravity. He would sign, and it would mean nothing. It would be decided by the others and that is how it was arranged.

The boardroom door opened, and the two lawyers returned uninvited and unannounced. The hour was up, and the voting had to commence.

A single document was set down in front of Nikoli. The young lawyer leaned over and turned to the back page. It listed thirteen names and, next to them, two columns. The first was headed "For" and the second "Against".

Nikoli picked up the pen, his agony no less than Valentine's three years earlier. His pen hovered over the paper but he couldn't bring himself to sign. Either way he would lose his daughter. Anatoly would take it all and would still never release Katia. Nikoli knew Anatoly, and though he taunted him with a forlorn hope that she might be spared, he feared he would never see his beloved daughter again no matter how the board voted.

"There is little time, sir," the lawyer reminded him, with no comprehension of the gravity of the task at hand.

"This is outrageous." Timor came to Nikoli's aid. "This is cruel. You leave him till last. We will sign your damn paper, and may you rot in hell for what you ask of us today."

"But there can be no deviation. Those are my instructions," the lawyer protested. Procedure was all that mattered to him. His instructions were specific.

"Do you want your damned document signed or not? Do you want to be the one that goes back to that monster and tells him that you've failed? Do you have children of your own? A wife? A son maybe? Do you? Do you have any idea what you are asking this man to do?"

Clearly he did not.

Timor was seated to Nikoli's left-hand side, and he snatched the paper from his faltering grasp.

"You have no idea what kind of animal you're working for. God help you if you ever find out," he snarled.

Both lawyers took a step back.

Timor turned to Nikoli. "Allow me, my friend."

Timor signed the document without delay and passed the paper to the next man. He too signed, as did the next, and the next. Nikoli fell forward. The first signatory took to his feet to console him.

"This is outrageous!" he boomed, and offered the old man the water he still wouldn't accept.

Yulian Ivchenko was next, and he took no longer to make his mark than the first. He passed the paper on. The next man was the sixth, and Pavel displayed no hesitation. He passed it on again.

The old accountant looked at the page before him and studied it analytically. He was the seventh man to sign, and as he scanned the page it was clear to him that he alone had the power to decide. All before him had signed in the same column. The next signature in that same column would carry the day. Making his mark in the opposing column would pass the full weight of responsibility to the next man, and then the next, until finally it would be back to Nikoli himself, merely a hostage to the decisions already taken.

Maxim had no one to consider but himself, but he felt the full burden of responsibility as he raised the pen. He felt Nikoli's eyes burning into his soul as he made his decision. It wasn't meant to be like this. The constitution specifically ensured that no one man would hold the balance, and yet in this, he did. If he signed in the same column as the six men before him, he would be choosing for them all, or forcing that same decision onto the next man. He had the casting vote should he choose to wield it. The future of the company and the life of an innocent young woman lay mortally exposed to the sweep of his pen.

He signed it and passed it on.

Bogdan signed and passed the document to Vasily Grankin. He paused for no more than a few seconds before making his mark. Finally, the paper returned to Nikoli.

Suddenly, the boardroom door flew open and Natalie ran to Nikoli's side with a mobile phone in her hand.

"You have to take this," she cried. "An Englishman says he needs to speak to you. He's calling from Katia's mobile phone."

Natalia handed the phone to Nikoli.

"Mr Shapiro?" the voice said.

"Yes, I am Nikoli Shapiro."

"I have your daughter, and she *is* safe, but I have to ask something of you, and you will need to trust me."

"Who are you?" The old man was calm and measured, a note of scepticism in his voice. "Where is my daughter?"

"Mr Shapiro, we have her, and that's all I can say for now, but I promise you she is completely safe. She wanted me to let you know as soon as I could. She's concerned that you might think she's with Anatoly Malokovic."

"She is not with Malokovic? She is not with Anatoly?"

"I have to be clear with you here, Mr Shapiro. Your daughter is safe. Katia is not with Anatoly. I give you my word."

Nikoli couldn't speak for a moment. He looked around the room, seeing only expectant faces. "Katia... it's about Katia..."

The room erupted.

"Mr Shapiro?" It was the voice again.

"What is it you need me to do?"

"Are you alone?"

"No, my friend, I am not alone."

"No one can know Katia is safe... No one!" There was anguish in the caller's voice. "You have to do this one thing for me, then I will get Katia to ring you herself. No one else can know she's safe. Another innocent woman will die if this gets out... if Anatoly finds out. I beg you not to make me regret giving you this news. The other woman is as innocent as Katia is in all this, but she has no one to look out for her. Mr Shapiro, I'm all she has right now. You must help me keep her safe, as I have kept your daughter safe from Anatoly. I only need a few hours."

There was a moment of silence. Nikoli felt stronger now, composed and more commanding.

"How long do you need?"

"Three hours, maybe less. I'll call you when Maria is safe."

"You have your three hours, my friend. No one will leave this room. No one else will know of this."

"Thank you. I'll get Katia to call you as soon as I can."

"Thank you, my friend, thank you. Tell me, what is your name?"

"That's not important right now... Three hours... right?"

"Yes, my friend. That I can do."

The phone went dead.

"Seal the office, no one is to leave," Nikoli bellowed. "I'm sorry, gentlemen, but I have given my word. We all stay here for now. News of this has to stay in this room."

Two security guards arrived at Natalie's instruction.

"Take their phones," Nikoli barked. "Sit down over there. You two are going nowhere."

The two lawyers did as they were ordered without protest.

There was no dissent in the boardroom. No one complained and each man embraced Nikoli in turn and shook him by the hand.

The old accountant, Maxim Petrov, was the last to congratulate Nikoli on the good news. He shook his hand formally and then hugged him with a strength that belied his years. He stepped back and looked the old man in the eye.

"Here..." he said, handing him the document with twelve signatures already in place. Just one space remained incomplete.

"You should see this, my friend." He smiled warmly and left the old man to his thoughts.

All twelve signatures were in the same column. They had each, without exception, chosen Katia over the company. The old man slumped back in his chair. He was completely overwhelmed.

Chapter 62

SATURDAY

Paul had no choice but to trust the old man now. He hadn't expected there to be a room full of people, but it was done, and Katia's father had given him his word. Paul stuffed the phone into his pocket. He could only hope he'd done the right thing.

Paul lit up the Galaxy and stared at Anatoly's name typed into the subject bar of the second email. The email itself still languished in the *Drafts* folder awaiting dispatch. Paul shuddered at the sight of it, with no real appreciation of why. Anatoly Malokovic. There was something about that man, about that name; the very sound of it induced fear. He read the email aloud and then retyped the words "VILLEFRANCHE" and "YACHT BARABUS" in block capitals for emphasis. It was going to be one or the other. Paul would just delete as appropriate when the time came. But time was his enemy now, creating doubt and repeatedly posing questions – questions he just couldn't answer.

How would all it play out? How quickly could the authorities respond? Paul knew he needed to call them into action the very instant he could confirm Maria's location. He would have to give them as much time as possible, but no matter what happened, they wouldn't have long. Paul was suddenly fighting an urgent, compelling need to do something to slow Boris and Giorgi down. It had worked once before; why wouldn't it work again? Why hadn't he thought about it earlier?

He rang Gary.

"I'm going to disable the tender," he said.

"What? Now?" Gary was incredulous. "How? What the hell do you know about boats?"

"Nothing, but I'm sure I can break one."

"Why didn't you do it earlier?"

"Maybe I should have," he said irritably. "I told you this was a work in progress."

*****

Less than a mile away, a silver Mercedes turned right off the main road, cruised past a red Opel Corsa, and headed down the hill towards to the quayside.

*****

Paul climbed out of the car, opened the boot, and located the stout metal bar that made up part of the BMW's wheel jack assembly. On the occasions it might be called into service, it could, quite possibly, save the day. But Paul was confident it was equally well suited to use as an instrument of destruction and mayhem.

He was more careful this time as he boarded the tender. The boat bobbed and weaved but his footing was steady. There were a few people going about their business on the quayside, but that didn't worry him. He was suddenly alive, wide awake and energised by a new sense of purpose. Time was running short and other people were the least of his concerns.

What did concern him, however, was the unmistakable sight of a silver Mercedes approaching the jetty from the direction of the customs house. Paul knew Gary was keeping watch; he couldn't have missed it. He must have seen the car and decided it wasn't the kidnappers, otherwise, surely, he would have called him.

He went for his phone to check for missed calls. He pulled out *a* phone, the Galaxy, and he checked his other pockets. He located Katia's iPhone but nothing more. Paul froze like the proverbial rabbit, caught in the very real headlights of the approaching car. He was struck by a temporary paralysis as he realised he'd left his iPhone on the passenger seat of the BMW.

"Shit!"

Paul needed to move and he needed to move fast. It was them. It was Boris and Giorgi. It was Alex's silver Mercedes, and there was no time to disable the tender. There was no time at all. He couldn't get back to the car and he couldn't get back to the jetty. The Mercedes eased to a stop at the quayside. He needed to get out of sight. His choice was simple. He could bail over the side, before the Russians saw him, or he could get under the tarpaulin and hide.

Neither option was good, but hiding felt like the right thing to do and, somewhat perversely, the bravest. If he bailed, the Galaxy would be finished, no second email, no police and no help for Maria. Getting under the tarpaulin meant he could try to send the email and, once that was done, he would just have to take his chances with Boris and Giorgi.

Paul forced his way as far back into the prow of the boat as he could, drawing the tarpaulin over himself. He tried to keep a line of sight through the mass of stiff material but it proved almost impossible. He still had no idea if Maria was with them, but he assumed she must be; it was the only reason for them to be in Villefranche. Nothing else made any sense.

Paul grabbed the redundant fenders that were still lying stored under the tarpaulin and placed them in front of him. He then eased himself even further into the prow, with the fenders strategically placed as best he could. They couldn't hide him completely if the heavy canvas cover was fully drawn back, but they would act as a barrier if they forced Maria under the tarpaulin as they had previously with Oleg. There was just a slim chance he could stay concealed, but that seemed all but impossible. Paul had made his decision on instinct alone and was now resigned to the prospect of being discovered. Only one thing mattered. He needed to send the second email, but with the approaching Russian voices ringing ever more loudly in his ears, would he even have time for that?

Paul eased the Galaxy out of his pocket. The tender rocked violently as one of the huge Russians boarded. The phone lit up and sparked into life. Paul needed to get the message away now, before it was too late. He tried to shield the illuminated screen with his hand, but even that didn't matter. He just needed to navigate his way to the pre-prepared email and hit *Send*. There was one solitary bar of signal. Paul hadn't even considered that earlier, but one bar would have to be enough.

"VILLEFRANCHE" and "YACHT BARABUS" blazed out from the screen. Both could be right, but he was out of time. He needed to decide. He didn't hesitate. *Barabus* was their most likely destination. He quickly deleted VILLEFRANCHE and hit *Send*. Once, twice, three times he hammered the screen and then lay there silently watching the activity bar as it made its way across the screen. The rate of progress was heart-stoppingly lethargic. It was so painfully slow, but it was steady. The email was on its way and, with just a few more seconds, there would be nothing Boris or Giorgi could do about it.

Suddenly, it was done.

Paul checked the phone was still set to silent and then closed it down. The tarpaulin was pulled halfway back, and a woman he'd never met before was eased to the deck rather more gently than he would have expected. Incredibly he remained undetected. Neither the woman or either of the Russians saw him as the tarpaulin was rearranged back into place.

Paul remained silent, completely immobile, not daring to breathe. The woman was lying only a few inches in front of him but she had no idea he was there. Discovery still seemed inevitable; it was just a matter of time. He was reconciled to that. Paul found an unexpected calm in the knowledge that there was nothing more he could do. He'd finally found Maria, and she was still very much alive. With a bit of luck, half of the French Navy and the Côte d'Azur gendarmerie were en route to their aid… and if they weren't? What more could he do now? The plan, such as it was, had always been something of a work in progress…

Chapter 63

SATURDAY

The tender settled restlessly in the water as the second of the giant Russians took his seat. The engine fired into life at the first time of asking. The powerful outboard motor roared as it became fully engaged, and the tender steadily pulled away from the jetty.

The pace was slow at first, but the whine of the motor, the churning water astern, and the melodic slap of the swell against the tiny hull served Paul well, masking the sound of his erratic breathing as he frantically fought to control it.

Maria shuffled uneasily, instinctively forcing herself further back against the fenders and closer yet to Paul. He was certain she would become aware of his presence at any moment; they were only a few inches apart. She was so close to him he could feel her distress. He wanted to reach out to her, to comfort her in some way, perhaps to reassure her and ease a little of her suffering. But what could he do? What could he say?

He felt his body cramp with the effort to stay immobile. He mustn't move. Any reaction from Maria at all could betray his presence to Boris and Giorgi, and there was nothing to be gained from that. If he was discovered now, it would squander any tiny advantage he might still have. Paul's heart went out to the terrified girl lying in front of him, but he remained completely still and utterly silent.

The engine note changed and the tender picked up speed. He could only speculate that they were out into open water and free of the restrictions of the tiny harbour.

He renewed his grip on the sturdy steel bar in his hands, the wheel brace seamlessly morphing from wrecking tool to weapon, and he felt emboldened by its cold utility. His mind drifted back to the violence he had witnessed in the car park, Boris launching his brutal assault on the chauffeur. The violence was extreme, yet controlled, and completely uninhibited. It was Boris's cold-blooded disregard for any consequence, that made the attack so totally overpowering. Paul determined then that he would suspend all caution, any regard for outcomes, if he got the chance. He would take any opportunity that came his way, and he would take his lead from Boris.

Still they headed out to sea, and suddenly a sense of dread washed over him. What if they weren't going out to *Barabus* after all? What if the Russians were just taking Maria out to deep water? No witnesses! No loose ends! His mind raced and his pulse quickened still further. He'd lost all track of time. Any effort to calculate distance travelled was lost in the rhythmic momentum of the tender and the numbing necessity to remain silent and undetected.

Finally, the engine pitch changed again and their progress slowed. The tiny craft rocked disconcertingly as one of the huge Russians got to his feet and made his way to the front of the boat. Beads of stinging sweat formed at Paul's brow and ran irritatingly into his eyes. He fought the compulsion to wipe it away and blinked furiously as he anticipated the flood of sunlight that would ultimately betray his presence.

He felt a gentle collision as the tender reached its destination. The relief was overwhelming in its own way, yet he was almost instantly consumed by a fear of what would happen next. He felt the craft lift slightly in the water. A substantial element of its burden had alighted to the chorus of vitriol that passed for conversation between Boris and Giorgi.

Paul's pulse rate soared. He could feel his heart beating as if trying to break free from his chest, and he felt the sound of it alone could give him away. He renewed his grip on the steel bar once again and braced himself for the inevitable. He was ready…

The sound of more Russian voices, unfamiliar to him but close at hand, was all it took to modify his ambition yet again. The voices were strong and powerful and laced with aggression. There was a dangerous edginess to their encounter, with each man sounding warily alert to the other. Paul heard Boris address the two new arrivals coldly – Viktor and Dimitri – but it was clear from what he could hear of the exchange, that it was Viktor that was giving the orders.

There were at least four Russians now: one still on the tender and three on the yacht's hydraulic mooring platform. There was no possibility he could take them all on with any realistic chance of success. His attack would be as futile as the chauffeur's efforts to escape the confines of the BMW. He remained completely still, barely allowing himself to breathe lest it betray his presence under the tarpaulin.

"Out!" someone bellowed. Paul recognised the voice immediately. It was Giorgi, the animal that had started all this in the first place. Sweat was pouring from him now. It was hot under the tarpaulin, stifling and rancid.

"Out! Get out!" Giorgi repeated.

Maria started to slide out from under the tarpaulin. For the first time, Paul caught a proper glimpse of her, but only from behind. She was smaller than he imagined. She was slim yet shapely, with delicate shoulders and long dark hair that hung limp and lifeless down her back in matted braids. She was unclean and unwashed from days of privation. Her blouse, once white, was filthy and torn, and her dark skirt was ripped and soiled. She had suffered trauma and degradation at the hands of her captors and now seemed submissive and broken. Her hands and feet were free, but Paul could see her ankles and wrists bore the signs of shackles probably only recently removed. She moved painfully slowly.

"Out!" Giorgi demanded one last time.

Paul could see the Russian's thigh, and a large bulge in the denim betrayed the presence of a bandage still applied to his injury. He noted it as a potential weakness, maybe a target if nothing else presented.

Giorgi grabbed Maria as she struggled to get to her feet. She was battling the rolling of the boat and her own fatigue. He lifted her bodily from the tender and deposited her on the jetty. Paul watched through the folds of the tarpaulin and saw Giorgi reach behind his back and draw his gun. He meekly handed the weapon to the owner of one of the voices that, until only a few moments earlier, had been barking demands of his own. Paul noted the lack of goodwill between them. It was evident that only Anatoly's most trusted men carried weapons on his yacht.

Then Paul's world went dark once again as the tarpaulin fell back into place. A wave of relief washed over him, and he silently released a breath he hadn't realised he'd been holding in the first place.

The voices drifted away. He was completely alone.

Chapter 64

SATURDAY

Paul recovered the Galaxy from his pocket and sparked it into life. The screen lit up brightly, exaggerated by the unremitting darkness under the tarpaulin. Self-consciously he shielded the screen with his hand as he navigated his way to *Sent Items*.

The email had been sent successfully as far as he could tell, and his spirits lifted a little. It was listed, reassuringly, immediately below the only other email the phone had ever been required to send. He deleted them both.

There were two messages in the inbox, and he opened them quickly one after the other. They were both in French, but he recognised them immediately for what they were: two identical automated replies, both from the Police nationale. He took comfort from the confirmation that at least two copies of the email had got through but none at the prospect that, even now, they might not have been read. It was more than eight hours since he'd sent the first email and a good thirty minutes since the second. He'd played the only cards he had.

Suddenly, a raised voice shattered the peace. It was a good way off, above him and to his right. Paul tuned in as best he could. Viktor's baritone boomed out from onboard. He shut down the smartphone and the comforting blanket of darkness returned once again.

He could see nothing but sensed something bad was going down. Things were escalating on board the yacht. He'd detected a palpable air of tension between Maria's abductors and Anatoly's welcoming committee, but this was something more.

He eased the tarpaulin to one side. He was alone in the tiny vessel, still moored securely alongside the yacht. *Barabus* was truly vast. It took on an even greater scale at such proximity. Paul took in the scene. He could still make out Villefranche, the customs house and the broad sweep of the busy quayside. It looked idyllic but remote. *Barabus* had been moved further out into the bay as he suspected, and as a consequence the sanctuary of dry land seemed impossibly distant.

He surveyed the length of the yacht. It was extraordinary, more than eighty metres long in his estimation, with the tender moored towards the stern. A huge door in the side of the vast vessel had been hydraulically lowered to form the mooring platform at which the tender was now expertly tethered. A pop-up handrail protected all but one side of the platform, with the elegant teak and cork decking suspended just a few inches above the swell.

Inside the storage bay Paul could see two smartly liveried tenders; they were larger in size and sophistication than the one used by Giorgi and Boris. Both were still set resolutely on their mountings, with a pair of powerful jet skis parked to one side. A collection of wetsuits and diving apparatus hung along the back bulkhead, and a selection of fishing and, perhaps, even hunting paraphernalia was stowed alongside them. An open-fronted storage rack displayed a range of lethal-looking diving knives.

The two huge chrome hydraulic rams that lowered the mooring platform into place, gleamed in the morning sunshine, and despite the obvious utility of the storage bay, it all seemed obsessively orderly and sanitised. Everything about the yacht was huge and magnificent, the sheer scale of it uncompromising and intimidating. It was an unapologetic display of unimaginable wealth, but still the ship had a sinister aura and a deep sense of foreboding. A craft designed solely for pleasure and display, it felt joyless and ill at ease.

Paul moved warily towards the side of the tiny boat as it rolled gently on the swell. On the far side of the yacht's storage bay he could see an open door in the bulkhead where sunlight streamed into a narrow stairwell. To his right, and perhaps twenty feet above his head, was the quarterdeck – the source of all the shouting.

Two further decks towered above him. They were staggered away from the stern so each enjoyed a measure of exposure to the Mediterranean sunshine. But all the action was on the lower of the three.

Paul could see Giorgi standing at the rail, facing the shore with Anatoly's men at either side. Giorgi was silent, but the most vocal man from the welcoming committee was, once again, in full flow. Viktor was tearing into him.

If Giorgi looked in Paul's direction now he would spot him instantly, but there was something about his demeanour that indicated he had far more compelling issues to contend with. Viktor was to Giorgi's left and furthest away from Paul, and he was becoming increasingly animated. He held something in his hand and now he had it jammed hard against Giorgi's head. It glistened in the brilliant early morning sunlight as Viktor twisted it threateningly at Giorgi's left temple. There was a moment of silence, but still Giorgi didn't move; he didn't even attempt to speak – the huge Russian was totally compliant. Just as suddenly as it started, the silence was over and Viktor began to pour his vitriol into Giorgi's ear once again, spitting out his words like venom.

Paul recognised the mystery object as a large handgun, but it had a strange overly long barrel, much extended and fatter than seemed familiar to him, albeit from his somewhat limited experience of guns, all of which was derived solely from Hollywood movies. Giorgi was in big trouble. If Viktor was only intending to intimidate Giorgi, then the gun alone would achieve his aim; the presence of the silencer implied a more sinister, graver intent.

Suddenly the relocating of the yacht further out to sea had a purpose. The increased remoteness from the shore added further significance to the deadly implications of the scene that was unfolding on the yacht.

Paul stepped off the small boat and crept silently across the mooring platform and through the huge storage area. He could hear voices through a second door on the left-hand side of the tender bay, a door that had previously been hidden from his view by the yacht's liveried tenders themselves. The voices were female and sounded frantic. He froze and held his breath. He saw a young girl in a blue monogrammed polo shirt and a light brown skirt scurry past the open door without giving him a second glance. Whatever was happening on the main deck was causing a stir throughout the vessel, and the air of panic was unmistakable.

Paul waited at the bottom of the stairs, the sun blinding him as he redoubled his resolve and raised the wheel brace pre-emptively in his right hand.

There were more voices now, all raised and with an even greater sense of urgency. The panic in the first girl's voice seemed to have gripped yet more of the crew, and a general sense of alarm seemed to spread throughout the ship.

Paul waited no longer. He passed quietly through the bulkhead door, turned right and headed up the flight of steps into the sunlight. He stopped at the top of the stairs and took a discreet peek through the main salon window before crouching back down out of sight. He could hear the voices more clearly now. Not crew this time, but the same visceral tones as before. Viktor was still in Giorgi's ear.

There was one last corner before Paul would get a view of what was happening on the quarterdeck, but he was suddenly aware of increasing activity in the main salon. He slowly rose to take a second look, the wheel brace lowered by his side.

The glass was tinted against the vagaries of the sun, but he could still make out the disposition of the sumptuous sofas, the indulgent armchairs and a huge, highly polished dining table at the far end.

Directly opposite Paul, and across the salon, was a pair of sliding doors. They were fully opened, revealing a stunning view out to sea and the horizon beyond. In the mid-distance, he could make out the silhouette of a large ship heading on a direct bearing towards *Barabus*. To each side of the approaching vessel was what appeared to be a pair of small black dots on the sea's surface, flanking the main ship but powering on ahead.

Surely this was the help he was hoping for? The emails had worked and the French Navy was reacting magnificently to his plea for help. But would they get there in time?

The growing sense of panic from below decks was now ship wide. Inside the salon the crew were dashing in all directions. Paul could see another set of sliding doors at the rear of the salon and they opened up onto the main rear deck itself.

Paul got his first sight of what was unfolding.

Boris was standing in the middle of the quarterdeck. His features were contorted with rage, his eyes fixed exclusively on a man ten years his junior who appeared utterly unfazed. Maria was on her knees, her head bowed and her arms listlessly by her side. Boris stood over her, a towering and intimidating figure.

The object of Boris's displeasure stood behind the starboard bulkhead, as if hiding from the seaward side of the yacht and the approaching ship. He wore white trousers, a tight-fitting black V-neck t-shirt and a disconcerting air of authority. He had a handgun stuffed casually into the waistband of his trousers. He was dismissive of Boris and was barking orders down a deck phone fixed to the bulkhead. He wore dark glasses and exuded a poisonous aura that emanated in all directions, gripping all but Boris, who alone seemed to have his measure.

A man in the all-white uniform of a senior maritime officer appeared at the far end of the salon. He strode purposefully along its full length as Paul watched silently through the window. He confronted the man in the V-neck t-shirt, who was still on the phone screaming orders when the officer arrived. He snapped to attention as etiquette might demand of a captain addressing the ship's owner, and Paul was certain it must be him. The man in the V-neck t-shirt had to be Anatoly Malokovic, but that was where all such proprieties ended. It was the captain's turn to have his say, and he delivered a salvo of his own.

Whatever was being demanded of the captain was clearly being questioned, perhaps even refused, given the furious nature of the exchange.

The reward for the captain's impertinence was a vicious punch to the stomach, which left him reeling, then his legs gave way and he slumped to the floor. The man in the V-neck t-shirt kicked the officer in the groin as he lay defenceless on the plushest of carpets. The man barked one last order into the phone before smashing his foot down hard on the officer's face.

The reaction was instant.

The yacht's engines spooled up with a deafening roar, coming to full power in a matter of seconds. The vessel hammered forward, the prow of the yacht rising precipitously out of the water, setting her at a pitch that left all but Anatoly scrambling to keep their feet.

Across the salon, the sliding doors now framed the approaching French naval ship as it made good speed, and the two black dots slowly took on a more distinctive form. Paul imagined them to be exactly the sort of powerful, low-profile craft a special forces unit might use for such occasions. The lightweight, high-speed black boats forged ahead, bristling with antenna, a plume of white water raging behind them. He could make out the individual forms of men dressed head to toe in black. He imagined them armed to the teeth, expertly trained, focused and motivated to complete the task. The rigid insertion craft were so close now that they would disappear from view in a matter of seconds on the seaward side of the yacht.

Paul's sense of relief was almost overwhelming but short-lived, as the yacht powered away. It was obvious that Anatoly wasn't going to give up readily. The pursuing ship changed course aggressively to parallel the fleeing *Barabus*, increasing power massively and throwing up a huge wave of white water behind it.

Paul ducked down once again. He made his way to the final corner at the far end of the salon. Once rounded, he would have a clear view of Giorgi, with Viktor to his far side and Dimitri closest to Paul on Giorgi's right. He took a moment and drew a deep breath. It was time to make his move.

Chapter 65

Barabus picked up speed and Villefranche disappeared into the distance and behind the headland of the Cap Ferrat. Paul could no longer see Anatoly, Maria or Boris – it was just Giorgi flanked by Viktor and Dimitri who held his attention for now.

Time seemed to have stood still.

And then, suddenly, everything happened at once.

Giorgi made his move and Paul broke cover.

As Giorgi launched his attack on Viktor, Paul was spotted by Dimitri.

Dimitri turned to face him and went for his weapon. Giorgi hammered his fist into Viktor's ribs, who, even now, even as the blow struck home, maintained the silenced gun at Giorgi's head. Both of Anatoly's men were engaged simultaneously. It was Giorgi against Viktor and, for his part, Paul now had Dimitri's full attention.

The situation was desperate and immediate. Paul didn't have time to raise the steel bar, but his instincts finally cut in. In that one adrenaline-fuelled instant he recalled the single-minded brutality of Boris's attack in the car park, and he struck.

He smashed the wheel brace upward, through and beyond his target, directly into the softest and most exposed tissue of his adversary. The wheel brace tore into Dimitri's throat before he could fully recover the gun from his waistband and he fell limp and ragged to the floor with a speed and finality that sickened Paul. Dimitri might not be dead, but he'd gone down hard. It was as brutal and conclusive as Paul feared it would be, and the horror of the attack churned at his stomach. In the blinking of an eye, the first man was down and now there was Viktor.

Giorgi's punch had connected powerfully with his target, but Viktor's gun had gone off as he struck. The huge Russian tottered at the side of the railings before falling lifeless to the floor. Any hint of life that had been Giorgi was gone before he even hit the deck. Blood flooded from the wound and surged backwards as the deck pitched and weaved under the awesome power of the engines.

Paul didn't hesitate. Appalled as he was at the sight of the dead Russian, it energised him and vindicated the horror of his first strike on Dimitri. Viktor was his target now. Paul slammed the steel bar down hard, letting out a roar of anger as it landed. Viktor screamed out in pain and Paul heard and felt the bone shatter from the massive impact. The gun flew from Viktor's grasp and slid across the deck to where Maria was slumped at Boris's feet. Viktor hit the deck in agony.

Boris was motionless. He just stood there staring at his fallen colleague. Maria reacted first, grabbing the gun, but she barely possessed the strength to lift it. Her instincts were good, and although it was Boris and Giorgi who had taken her hostage, she clearly knew it was Anatoly who called the shots and only he could make it all stop. It was Anatoly she targeted as the French naval ship continued to close in.

Then, suddenly, *Barabus* lurched to starboard in a bid to deter the approaching ship. Paul heard the special forces craft slamming into the side of the huge yacht as the sudden, unanticipated change of course left them floundering, requiring an immediate recalculation of their final assault.

Back on board, the first man Paul had hit remained prostrate, unconscious on the deck, face down, his weapon drawn at his side, and Viktor was still on his knees reeling under the crippling weight of the second blow. But he wasn't finished yet. He was as tough as any of them and struggled to his feet. Paul could see the intent in his eyes even with his arm hanging limply at his side. Viktor stopped suddenly at the sight of Maria struggling to take the weight of the silenced gun. She was still slumped at Boris's feet but was now galvanised into action.

They all stopped. Time stopped.

The French ship was upon them. Paul could see the snipers on her deck targeting the *Barabus* with their powerful weapons. A loudhailer engaged them, demanding restraint, but no one was listening; all eyes were on Maria.

Paul crouched down and backed up behind the bulkhead, out of sight of the ship bearing down on them. He could hear the shouting from the French special forces as their assault began from the seaward side of the ship. He could hear them calling to each other over the massive roar of the engines and the churning, battering ferocity of the enormous tide that spewed out behind the yacht as it powered forward.

The booming tannoy demanded the crew stop the ship and submit to boarding. But the yacht roared on. With the captain absent from the bridge, lying unconscious in a crumpled heap on the floor of the grand salon, perhaps their fear of Anatoly was far greater than anything the French Navy could threaten them with. *Barabus* powered on regardless.

Italian coastal waters could only be a few nautical miles away. *He knows a lot of powerful and dangerous men in Italy*, Paul recalled Katia confiding in him earlier.

Paul could hear the powerful special forces boats again as they hammered against the hull, keeping pace, the sound of yet more men climbing the side of the ship and making their assault. He could see the marksmen more clearly, their sights stabilizing, finding their range as red laser dots hit the white guard rail that ran the length of the main deck. They acquired and then lost their targets.

It was obvious that Maria was a target too. She alone held a weapon. She alone presented a threat to life. Paul could barely look as she tried, with all her remaining strength, to level the gun at Anatoly, who cowered pathetically behind the bulkhead, unseen by the ship-borne snipers.

Paul prayed she wouldn't find the strength. It would be the last thing she would ever do, and everything would have been for nothing.

Boris caught Paul's eye as he crouched at the side of the bulkhead. There was something in his look now, unspoken and ambiguous. Boris had witnessed Paul taking down his colleague's killer and one more man besides. There was a growing sense of comprehension in Boris's eyes, and in that instant, he seemed to remember.

The only previous occasion he'd seen Paul was a brief and painful experience. They'd grappled in the front seat of the black BMW as Katia and Alisa had emptied their pepper spray into his eyes. The flicker of recognition was clear now, as was the malevolence in a tortured smile that caused his lips to curl and his eyes to flare.

Paul's heart stopped. Where were the French special forces? What was taking them so long? Instinctively, he lunged forward and grabbed Dimitri's abandoned gun. He took it in his right hand, transferring the wheel brace to his left. Now he too was armed, and a potential target if the snipers could find their mark. Paul backed up, taking cover and taking aim.

But what Boris did next took him completely by surprise. He plunged his hand into his pocket, leaned down to Maria and passed her an envelope and a mobile phone. She took them and held them to her chest like they were the most precious things in the world. But Boris held something else in his hand. He turned to Paul and then slid the item across the deck in his direction. It was a plastic bag containing a stained piece of monogramed white cloth. Paul leaned forward and picked it up. As he did, he held his target firmly in his sights. Boris looked unconcerned.

Then, the giant Russian reached down to Maria one last time, her eyes full of tears as the burden of the gun trembled in her hands. Her strength had failed her, the barrel pointed at a shallow angle downwards, towards the deck and posing a threat to no one. Red dots flashed across the guard rail again. One took up station on Viktor who had remained frozen to the spot. Other dots lurched across their targets, struggling to hold them in the swell.

The huge Russian spoke briefly to Maria. She turned to face him with a sorrow and resignation in her eyes that tore at Paul's emotions. Is this how it's going to end? Was Boris about to take the gun after all this and finish Maria even now? He couldn't allow that to happen.

Paul took up the tension on the trigger...

Maria released what little grip she still maintained on the massive weapon as Boris closed his enormous fist around its handle. Paul looked on as Boris fixed his finger on the trigger.

"Shoot him now!" Paul screamed in frustration as the red dots danced frantically around the deck. "Shoot!" But his cries were lost as the engines roared and the massive concussive plume of water churned and boiled behind them. It would have to be him. He would have to take the shot himself. Paul felt the trigger of Dimitri's gun firm against his finger... just the slightest squeeze would discharge the weapon. Paul waited.

But now Boris held the gun in his left hand. With his right he pulled Maria to one side and behind him. It was as if he was protecting her. Why would he? Something had definitely changed. Boris raised the gun and, in a single action, aimed and fired.

As he fired, there was a second shot, and then a third.

It might have been Boris's intention to empty the entire magazine into his target, but he only got the first shot away before the snipers finally did their work, ultimately saving Paul the task. It was devastating. The first high-velocity round hit Boris in the temple. The impact flung him to his left, then, as his huge frame started to fall, the second hit him in his neck, almost severing his head from his massive shoulders. That same impact propelled his contorted body across the deck and rendered it lifeless and disfigured at the feet of his dead colleague.

Paul selected another target.

Anatoly lay crumpled in a heap at the side of the sliding doors to the salon. But he wasn't finished yet. Anatoly held a gun of his own and it was levelled at Maria. Paul hesitated no longer. He fired once, twice, both shots found their target and Anatoly's body convulsed with the impacts. Anatoly had taken three bullets, one from Boris and now two from Paul. His twisted frame lay propped against the bulkhead, suddenly drained of menace. Yet, incredibly, life still held a tenuous grip, despite the pool of blood forming at his side.

Viktor raised his one good arm in surrender as a red dot danced across his face. A second laser played at his chest and then a third.

The huge yacht forged ahead.

Still out of sight of the snipers, Paul crouched a few moments more behind the bulkhead. Only now could he see her properly. Other than in the grainy images on an iPhone, it was the first time Paul had seen Maria's face. Tears flowed down her cheeks, and her eyes were swollen and reddened from her trauma. Her features were pale and drawn. She looked haunted and desolate, but he could see she had been beautiful once. There remained something extraordinary about her, and he could sense her inner strength, which seemed far greater than the physical that had deserted her in the end.

She turned to face him and her natural spirit appeared to surge through her fleetingly. "*Merci, monsieur,*" she mouthed silently, and then she turned away and sobbed uncontrollably at the side of the dead Russian.

Two members of the crew were quickly at her side, and that was where he left her. Finally, Maria was safe, and Paul took his leave.

Chapter 66

Paul threw Dimitri's gun overboard and slipped back down the passageway to the top of the stairs. He started down, taking two steps at time and sliding his free hand down the stainless steel handrail for balance. Below him, another of Anatoly's loyal lieutenants blocked his path. Surely he would let him pass? With the naval ship bearing down on them, the marksmen finding their targets and the French special forces swarming the forward sections of the yacht, surely he would just step aside? But he held his ground.

Paul threw the wheel brace at the man's head in an act of pure desperation. It was parried but still struck him hard on his exposed forearm, drawing blood and eliciting an involuntary roar. Paul launched himself down the stairs, leaping from the fourth step and leading with his knee. He piled into the man, who was ill-prepared and stunned by the speed of his reaction to his presence. He drove his knee hard into the man's face and he crumpled to the deck at the foot of the stairs. He felt the bone in his adversary's cheek fracture, deforming under the weight of the impact, and then, without a second thought, he attacked. There was no hesitation, no restraint at all, Paul's fists clenched as he tore into him, his face, his throat, both unprotected and open. He was defenceless now, pinned down helplessly by the full weight of the assault. Paul felt a sickening sensation as the flesh on his own knuckles tore and peeled back as he struck. But he couldn't stop now; he wouldn't stop. Again and again he hammered his punches home, his victim was barely conscious, but still he continued. It was instinctive, brutal and completely overpowering.

Paul screamed insanely as he vented the full depth of his fury. Previously controlled and repressed, he found release in yet one more series of crushing blows.

And then it was done. Paul stood over his victim, a man he'd never seen before, and the extent of the wounds he'd inflicted suddenly sickened him and a deep churning clawed away at the pit of his stomach; bile caught in his throat as he retched.

And then the sound of approaching special forces flooded back into his consciousness; he needed to focus. If he was going to get away from all this, he needed to move. He crossed the tender bay leaving the stricken man to his fate. Then he stood at the edge of the opening in the side of the ship as the yacht careered onward. The lowered mooring platform was still in place, battered by the formidable bow wave as the yacht's massive propellers forced the ship dead ahead at full speed. The tiny tender bounced frantically in the raging swell and the yacht sliced relentlessly through the water. The roar of the churning sea was deafening, echoing alarmingly in the cavern created by the open-sided hull.

Paul needed to make a choice. He could either stay and face whatever censure was coming his way, or he could get off the ship and leave the whole terrible episode behind. As Maria was safe, his instincts were for the latter.

He grabbed a diving knife from the selection in the rack on the bulkhead. If he was going to get away before the special forces team swept through the ship, it needed to be now. Dismissing his fear and harnessing the remnants of adrenaline that still coursed through him, he made his bid to escape. He ran the length of the tender bay, out onto the platform, and with a single burst of well-timed aggression he leapt unflinchingly into the flailing tender.

The tiny boat fell away from him as he braced himself for the impact and then surged back up forcefully to meet him on the swell. It slammed into him hard, throwing him to the side and nearly bucking him overboard in the direction of the yacht and the raging waters. Paul clawed frantically at the sides, the seats, the canvas – anything that he could use to secure himself inside the tender. It was all but hopeless, and it was all he could do to hang on as the ship's mighty props, rotating at a massive rate, churned and chopped at the water beneath the huge yacht, drawing in countless gallons of water beneath it before forcing them out again with devastating power. He was thrown ragdoll-like to the back of the boat and had to grapple his way forward with the vicious-looking knife in one hand. He needed to cut the tender free.

Finally, he saw his chance. He worked feverishly on the rope that tethered the tender to *Barabus*. The knife made light work of it, and it was only as the last few strands finally gave way that he fully appreciated the sheer scale of the wash behind him. He was in the mountainous, surging water in an instant, then plunging down deep into the swell, several metres below the waterline, before surging up to the surface at a heart-stopping rate. He hung on as the boat leapt out of the water and bounced and spun in the wake. As it settled, he ventured a look over the side, barely raising his head. Now free, the liberated tender bobbed endlessly in the diminishing swell.

The yacht powered on for a few minutes more and the naval ship mirrored her course and matched her for speed. The two black special forces craft were nowhere to be seen, but the men they'd delivered were storming *Barabus* in force. They boarded towards the bow and were even now in the process of clearing her to the stern, securing each part of the yacht as they went. There were still a few of Anatoly's men on board, but they appeared to be offering little resistance and were being taken down without a further shot being fired. Once more, brute force and targeted aggression had won the day and finally, inevitably, brought the mighty *Barabus* to heel.

Paul could still see the two young crew members tending to Maria. As he watched, they were forced to the deck and secured in the same ruthless manner as everybody else. The two crew members were forced flat on their faces and had their wrists and legs secured at the point of a gun. Maria was treated with more empathy. At least she among them was treated like the victim she truly was. A special forces' medic set purposefully to work.

Chapter 67

Maria briefly resisted attempts to help her. She clung to Boris, sobbing uncontrollably at his side. The medic spoke to her in reassuring tones, but she didn't hear his words. She was broken, exhausted and tormented by her experience. And now there was this. She stared at the shattered body of her captor, transfixed.

Boris was dead, and the brutality of his passing sickened her. His flesh torn, ripped from the bone, which in turn lay shattered and hideously dislocated from his lifeless body. It was true that Boris had taken her and held her against her will. It had been Boris who had deprived her of her freedom and threatened the girls she had come to love as if they were her own daughters, the only family she would ever know. But it was Giorgi who had caused it all, and Anatoly who'd forced their hand.

She alone heard the arguments and recriminations as Boris exerted control over his volatile and dangerous brother. It was Boris who had stayed his hand when for all-the-world it seemed he would beat the life from her in the hallway of her own apartment block on Monday morning.

It was Boris who arranged for her to be given water, what little food she was allowed, and had shown her the small measure of compassion he afforded her. He'd saved her from Giorgi's hate-fuelled rantings and had given her what little dignity her captivity allowed. It had been Boris who'd protected her from the violent excesses of his own brother.

And it had been Boris alone who'd prevented Giorgi from beating Alex to death in the basement of his own home. She'd been bound and blindfolded at the time, but his agonies were made only more acute as she imagined the violence that elicited such cries. Defiant at first, Alex had goaded Giorgi, but as the blows had rained down, the manic howls of the aggressor drowned out the snarling curses of the victim. She'd pleaded with Giorgi to leave him alone, and despaired for Alex when he wouldn't. She'd screamed for help and struggled against her own bindings, begging for him to stop, but Giorgi had been deaf to it all in his rage. Alex's resistance held, until finally the fight had been beaten out of him. His desperate, involuntary whimpers had been replaced by the sound of what remained of his breath being expressed forcibly from his failing lungs, all sounds finally giving way to a bitter silence as consuming as death itself. Alex's fight for consciousness had already been lost, his fight for life desperate, marginal. Only then, when she had already lost all hope for him, and as the brutality of Giorgi's frenzy became even more feverish and demented, did she hear Boris's footsteps hammering down the kitchen stairs.

And now with his final act, he had shot the man who caused it all – Anatoly, a man known to her for all the evil that he did. Anatoly Malokovic was the man who had controlled and intimidated Alex for as long as she had known and loved him. He alone had turned Alex into a dangerous yet reluctant gangster, manipulating him to his own ends through threats and fear.

She hated the very sound of it: Malokovic. That name ran like a weeping sore through her life. If it wasn't Anatoly, it was his twisted cousin Christoff who taunted her, enduring only misery and heartbreak in that name. There was so much pain at Christoff's hands, and death too – an innocent life, her child, taken from her and her life broken beyond repair. So much pain, perhaps enough to destroy her and challenge what remained of her own humanity. It had been Alex who saved her then. If it hadn't been for him... She owed Alex her life. She owed him everything.

But now her tormentor, Boris, had avenged his brother and saved her from herself. Had she the strength she would have pulled the trigger willingly, dispatching Anatoly without a second thought. Although her part in it would be diminished by circumstance, she would still have murder on her conscience if she had survived. But she knew that would never happen, even as she strained to level the gun at her target, her survival was never a possibility either. She knew it just as certainly as Boris did when he took the gun from her. She would have faced the sniper's fire as inevitably as Boris did, and suffered the same fate for shooting the monster that was Anatoly. She sensed Boris knew the snipers had their targets, and still he took the gun and did for them both what she was unable to do for herself.

So she clung to Boris as the medic comforted her and gently released her grip on his jacket one finger at a time. It didn't make sense that she mourned his passing, but to her, his death was an end in itself. She knew she was safe for now, but was it over? Could it finally be over?

Chapter 68

SATURDAY

From the tender, Paul watched as the yacht suddenly started to slow, the huge boiling plume behind her dissipated, yet *Barabus* continued to edge further away under her own momentum for a while. She began to settle, drifting restlessly on the tide as she rounded a headland and all but out of view. The naval escort powered back and bobbed furiously on the wake before coming to an unnaturally abrupt full stop.

Suddenly, the sound of an approaching helicopter split the air. As if from nowhere, it was powering towards him. He scrambled for cover, diving under the tarpaulin and grabbing handfuls of the heavy cloth to prevent it being ripped away in the downdraft as the aircraft hovered overhead.

Where the hell did that come from? he asked himself. *Why didn't I see it before?* But none of that mattered. *Is it too late? Have I already been spotted?*

As suddenly as the helicopter appeared, it flared, hovered for a moment more and then powered away again, forcing the boat to spin in the unnatural storm-force gale created by the rotors. It headed off in the direction of the subdued *Barabus*.

Moments later he was alone in the tiny tender. Paul looked back in the direction of Villefranche, to where he knew Gary would be awaiting news, but instead he found himself contemplating the unmistakable landscape of Monaco, and even that seemed an eternity away.

Barabus had set a course heading full speed for Italian waters, but Paul wondered what good it would have done her. Surely the French would never have stopped despite the strictures of archaic maritime law; surely the Italians would have given their approval for the assault to continue or diligently turned a blind eye. None of that mattered now. The magnificent French Navy and her incredible special forces had arrived almost on cue, Maria was safe, and Anatoly... As far as he could tell, Anatoly was just one more victim in a terrible episode. He doubted there would be many that would mourn his loss.

Paul suddenly felt isolated in the silence, but he was glad of it for a while. The gentle rocking motion of the sea was calming at first, but then he became consumed by a nausea so sudden and overpowering it rendered him helpless. He threw himself to the side of the boat and his body convulsed. He hung there, staring down into the vastness of the water, hoping the feeling would pass. It didn't.

Later, with the tender drifting on the tide, Paul started up the outboard motor. It wasn't unpleasant for a time, just guiding her back into harbour once the nausea had finally eased. He lay low in the boat, enjoying the cool sea air and the gentle rocking motion as he made his way back to land.

He pulled the Galaxy from his pocket and sparked it back into life for one last time. There were no less than twenty-four emails in the inbox. He scrolled through them all without opening a single one. He didn't even turn the phone off; what would be the point? He quietly, deliberately let it slip through his fingers over the side and into the cool crystal-blue Mediterranean water.

It was one hour and forty-five minutes since Paul had last spoken to Nikoli Shapiro. As the first bar of connectivity registered on the screen, Paul made the call. It was answered at the first ring. Paul told him the news and released him from his promise. From the solitude of the tiny boat, he heard the room erupt with emotion for a second time, and he knew the message had been enthusiastically relayed. Nikoli was as good as his word, but now, overjoyed and energised, he wanted to know all that had happened. Paul couldn't face talking to anyone much right now. He made his excuses and politely hung up, leaving Nikoli to enjoy the extraordinary moment in the company of friends.

Paul regretted not having his own phone with him. It would have been good to let the others know too, but he would tell them all the news soon enough. He'd left the car unlocked, with the keys in the ignition and the phone on the front seat... None of that had been part of the plan either.

The quayside was a busy place once again. Paul wondered just how much of what transpired out at sea, if any of it, had been witnessed from the shore. Paul could see several police cars, an ambulance and two dark blue tactical response vehicles parked by the customs house at one end of the quay, the BMW was still parked, somewhat reassuringly, at the other.

He took a circuitous route back to the jetty, sticking close to the shore and meandering through the yachts at anchor. He could see Gary waiting at the quayside looking relaxed, and then becoming reassuringly terrier-like the instant he recognised it was Paul at the helm. He threw Gary the rope, who then made a predictably ham-fisted attempt of tying her off.

"Where's Maria? Is she all right… Are you all right?" he said, buzzing with energy.

"Maria's going to be fine," Paul said calmly.

"What happened? It all kicked off down here after you disappeared, there were police everywhere! Someone got picked up for sure, I thought it was you. What happened to you, I was trying to call you—"

"I'll tell you later, but right now I have to make a call of my own…"

Gary didn't argue.

"I'll get you a beer, mate… I'll get you a beer."

"Mineral water," Paul called after him. He was still feeling a little queasy.

Paul dialled Kira's iPhone and Alisa answered it at the first ring. He told the girls that Maria was safe and was greeted with screams and tears for his pains. He asked to speak to Katia as the girls fussed and hugged and cried. He told her to phone her father, that he was holding up well under the circumstances, and was desperate to hear from her. Next, he spoke to Kira. He told her she could return one of the many missed calls she'd received from a certain chauffeur. Paul knew, more than anybody else, that he owed Mikael an explanation.

Finally he spoke to Alisa, and once her tears of relief had subsided, he told her he was desperate to see her again, and that his feelings for her would never change, especially now that all the excitement was finally over. He was desperate for her to know that his feelings for her hadn't changed at all.

Chapter 69

Gary and Paul arrived back at the hotel to a jubilant welcoming committee.

Alisa, Kira and Katia were beaming wildly. A tall, dark, athletic man, who Paul instantly recognised as Mikael the chauffeur, was standing at Kira's side. A small crowd had gathered under the porte-cochère and, completely oblivious to the reason for all the fuss, watched on in growing numbers.

There was a good-natured scrum as the girls enthusiastically hugged and kissed Paul and Gary in turn. As things settled, Paul threw a set of car keys to the waiting concierge and then walked over to Mikael, who was now standing quietly to one side.

He held out a second set of car keys and the VIP parking pass for Mikael to take.

"These are yours I believe," he said.

The chauffeur stood stock still. Paul wasn't sure which way this was going to go. Mikael put his hand inside his jacket pocket and recovered a small, but familiar, Swiss army knife.

"And this is yours, my friend," he replied in broken English with a heavy Russian accent.

The two men exchanged items and then Mikael tossed the second set of car keys to the waiting concierge. The chauffeur held his hand out and Paul took it. Moments later the powerful Russian held him in a bear hug.

"Thank you, my friend. Thank you. What you did for Katia…"

Paul allowed the bear hug to run its course. Once released, Paul took a step back and tugged at his jacket sleeves. He regarded Mikael for a moment.

"How's your throat?" he asked.

He could see the redness that still betrayed the impact of the first of three venomous blows. Paul winced slightly for him.

"This?" Mikael said dismissively. "This is nothing."

It wasn't nothing! It was the result of a truly debilitating blow. Boris had delivered it deliberately and accurately and it had rendered Mikael

414

disorientated and left him reeling in the gloom of the underground car park in Casino Square. It had been the first strike of three, and it had taken him out of the game instantly. He was completely neutralised even before the second impact could land.

Boris hammered that home too, a massive, destructive forearm to the jaw before Mikael had any chance to recover. It was delivered with the full weight of Boris's body forcefully behind it. Paul raised his hand to his own jaw.

"This…" Mikael boomed. "It is nothing, my friend." The Russian's bravado was impressive, but the huge weal on the side of his face told a different story.

"And…" Paul's eyes dropped a little.

The Russian flinched.

"This…" the huge Russian said, cupping his own groin for emphasis. "This, my friend? This is not nothing." And he shuffled awkwardly on the spot but somehow still managed a grin.

Paul was uncomfortable with the ambiguity for a moment.

The coup de grâce had been delivered with a full strike of Boris's boot, aimed directly to the stricken chauffeur's groin. It had resulted in the already unconscious Mikael adopting the tightest of foetal positions on the concrete floor. It removed completely even the slightest possibility that he might yet threaten some measure of resistance.

Paul offered his hand once again and smiled. Mikael took it, and with an approving grimace he registered the damage to Paul's knuckles, the ingrained blood that stained his fists, his shirt, and even the few stray spots of blood on his neck, the evidence of Paul's own brutal encounters with Anatoly's men.

"I'm sorry, Mikael," Paul said finally. "I couldn't think of any other way."

"What you did, my friend… you did a good thing."

Kira came bouncing over, her charming enthusiastic self. She wrapped her arm around the chauffeur's, her hand reaching up and almost involuntarily squeezing his impressively over-developed bicep.

"Come on, we're going to the bar," she said, rubbing the Russian's arm with genuine affection.

"No hard feelings then?" Paul asked rhetorically.

Mikael's grin broadened. There was no doubt Kira had liked the look of the chauffeur from the start, and for his part, he'd been hooked from the first moment he saw her. It just took him a little time to realise it.

The bar was busy, but Gary had already managed to get a couple of bottles of champagne on order. He'd spotted Doug and called him over to join the party. He'd already started to fill in the blanks and Doug just sat there open-mouthed. Much to Paul's embarrassment, Gary was enthusiastically saving

Paul the job of explaining his own consistently erratic behaviour throughout the entire conference.

As the champagne arrived, Gary distributed the glasses and then went around topping them up. He was less than impressed with the obvious closeness of Kira and her chauffeur, and Mikael suffered a short measure for his pains. Gary was about to target Katia with his not inconsiderable charms, perhaps in consolation, when Paul stepped in.

"Your father, how is he?" Paul asked, putting Gary off the scent for a few more minutes.

"In your debt. He wants to meet you."

"I just wanted to thank you for helping us, Katia," he said. "We couldn't have done it without your cooperation. Maria is safe because of you and your father. You both did the right thing when she needed it most, and for that we're all in your debt. I think we can call that even."

"I'm not sure my father will see it that way. I owe you everything. Anatoly would have killed me... You do know that, don't you?"

Paul had never doubted it for a moment.

"Champagne, you two?" Gary said, interrupting them. He made a gracious host and now everyone had a glass.

"We need a toast. Come on, Paul," he demanded excitedly – the terrier within was back once again. "Toast, toast, toast..." He started a chant that generated a life of its own and they all joined in.

Paul was under pressure. He couldn't think of anything appropriate.

"Toast, toast, toast..."

He looked from Kira to Katia, and finally his attention settled on Alisa. She was more beautiful than ever.

"To Maria!" he offered, his embarrassment obvious, but his eyes never moved from Alisa's as she beamed her approval.

"Fuck that, mate!" Gary bellowed. "To you, mate. You're a fucking legend."

The toast was to Paul, and he'd never felt more uncomfortable in his life.

*****

Later, Alisa was at his side. She was all smiles and had borrowed a spray of Kira's heady perfume that he'd first encountered in the early hours of Tuesday morning. He allowed himself a self-conscious smile.

"They're all going back to Katia's villa later, but I thought we could stay here and have some dinner, just the two of us, and maybe I could stay tonight. What do you think?"

Alisa already knew the answer.

*****

As Gary distributed the last of the champagne, Mikael borrowed Paul's Swiss army knife one last time and headed off in the direction of the hotel car park. The ever-genial concierge turned a blind eye while Mikael performed the honours with the registration plates, reuniting each car with their own. A few minutes later, and back at the wheel of Katia's powerful black saloon car, Mikael made his way to the hotel entrance, where Paul, Gary, Doug and the girls awaited his arrival.

Moments later, Paul and Alisa were left standing arm in arm at the side of the promenade, watching the magnificent 5 Series BMW disappear out of view.

"Now," she said, "where would you like to eat? It's my treat."

"Anywhere, I don't really care," Paul said casually.

They dined at one of the seafront restaurants. They both chose fish, a dessert to share and an espresso to finish. Alisa paid, despite his protests, and then they walked hand in hand down the promenade for a while. It was a warm autumnal evening, and Paul found himself wishing it would never end. For him, Alisa was the most beautiful girl in the world, and in a few short yet traumatic days, he felt she had changed his life forever and in ways he could never have imagined.

Later, they returned to room 733. They made love, and afterwards Alisa fell asleep in his arms.

SUNDAY

Chapter 70

SUNDAY

Paul awoke slowly.

The room was untypically gloomy. The curtains twitched and billowed wildly, caught by strong gusts of wind that whistled through the open bedroom window. The balcony furniture slid across the tiles, scraping in protest as the patio doors rattled in their frames. Heavy rain lashed against the glass as the monumental storm that was forecast to break arrived on cue.

The morning already felt very different.

He could still smell the scent of Alisa's perfume on the pillow. He took a deep breath, savouring it before turning over in the bed, fully expecting to see her lying there. He might watch her sleep for a while, or lean over and give her a kiss, maybe just hold her until she awoke. But something imperceptible already told him that the bed was empty. Paul sat up and called her name.

"Alisa."

There was no response.

"Alisa?" he called again.

Still nothing.

He rose quickly and walked naked to the bathroom, but it was all too obvious – she was gone.

As he returned from the lobby he could see there was a note; with Alisa it seemed there was always a note. Paul sat on Alisa's side of the bed, picked it up from her bedside table, and began to read.

Thank you for everything you have done for me. I will always love you for it. You will forever be my Nice man.
  Love always, Anna

And there was an *X* for a kiss.

He turned the page over. It was Alisa's handwriting once again, and from just a few short days earlier. It read:

Call Sophie.

And again there was an *X* for a kiss. There was always a kiss.

*****

The rained hammered down on the pavement as Alisa stepped out from the revolving door. The concierge smiled, produced a large branded hotel umbrella and opened it with the push of a button. Alisa took it gratefully and headed for town.

Despite the umbrella, her jeans were soon soaked through, the rain bouncing off the ground and splashing up from the waterlogged pavement as she ran. The wind gusted through the empty streets, whipping in off the sea, stinging and bitter, laced with salt. Unabated, the deluge continued.

A sudden blast turned the umbrella inside out, and she was drenched in seconds. Alisa struggled to right it, then discarded it and ran for cover. She avoided the puddles where she could but the rain was invasive, her sodden clothes sticking to her body and her hair flattened against her head. She pushed on but her sadness began to overwhelm her. Her progress slowed. It was all too much. She felt her heart breaking with every step and the tears began to flow. She stopped in a doorway and slumped to the ground. Her sense of isolation tore at her emotions; the loss she felt crushed her; she ached inside.

Alisa didn't feel the rain anymore; she didn't even hear the wind. As she forced herself to continue on her way to the flower market, she heard nothing other than Paul's final words to her as she had drifted sleepily in his arms.

"I love you, Alisa," he'd whispered, as the night closed in around them.

But the girl he loved was never real. There were moments, a few intense moments, that felt genuine enough, but it couldn't last. It never did. The girl Paul loved was an illusion, nothing more than a fantasy. It would all change now that the fiction was over. There was no future for Alisa. She was nothing more than a veneer, and now Anna's tears fell in torrents – authentic, raw, unrestrained and very, very real.

Even as she took a seat in the familiar café the tears continued to fall. Even as the waiter placed the hot coffee on the table and offered her a towel she'd never asked for, still they came. As Kira approached her past the tables, her arms already outstretched to embrace her, they flowed down her cheeks and mingled with the pooling water that dripped ceaselessly from her hair. The truth was, Alisa was gone forever, and Anna had never felt so completely alone.

*****

Paul showered, dressed and packed. Before he left the room for the last time, he sat down on Alisa's side of the bed once more. He looked around the room. So much had happened since he'd first arrived. But it was all over now, and it was time to move on. There was just one thing he needed to do, He knew it was wrong, but he felt compelled all the same. He tapped 5555 into the iPad and started a new search.

The result was immediate but initially unsuccessful. There was no Anna. angel???.nice@msn.fr, although there was a depressingly long list of alternatives displayed. Halfway down the page he saw it, and his heart sank. Alisa. angel656.nice@msn.fr.

He could barely bring himself to click on the link in dread that it would truly be her, but the compulsion was too strong. Moments later he discarded the iPad onto the bed and stepped out onto the balcony. It was all too obvious. Alisa had never been real. The girl he came to love didn't exist. That was the truth of it. That was the end of the excitement Alisa had told him about. She had been right after all. It could never be the same; he understood that now. He had never truly known her at all.

Wearily, Paul collected his bags, removed his credit card from the energy saver and closed the bedroom door behind him. He would delete his cookies and history files when he got home. It would be nothing more than a symbolic act of contrition and good housekeeping, but it would be an end to it all. He couldn't do it straight away. He just couldn't bear to delete Alisa from his life like that; at least not yet.

Chapter 71

The automatic doors slid open and Paul walked out into the arrivals hall at East Midlands Airport. There was a small group of taxi drivers holding up cards with passenger's names on them and a less ordered scrum of people waiting excitedly for the arrival of their loved ones. Among them was Sophie. She looked genuinely delighted to see him, and her enthusiasm clawed at his conscience.

"How are you? … How was the conference? … Did you have a good time? … You'll have to tell me all about it," she gushed. "I've got the car. I thought you might like a lift." Her smile cut right through him.

She kissed him on the cheek and gave him a hug he knew he didn't deserve. She drove him back to *her* apartment, where "dinner for two" was well under way. She put the first load of his washing in while he sat lost in introspection on the sofa they had so recently chosen together. She made him a cup of tea and fussed around him, talking excitedly about how well her work was going and the new miniseries starting on TV later that evening.

"I thought you could stay over tonight," she said. "I picked up a few things from your place this morning. Then, tomorrow, I thought I could drive you over to pick your car up from the service centre." She seemed certain that Paul would see getting a lift to the BMW garage was a nice gesture, particularly after the petty sourness the night before he'd left for the conference. "It'll save you getting a taxi…" she continued, not that any further explanation was even remotely necessary.

Later, she gave him his set of *her* house keys back. Her sister wasn't coming after all, and Sophie seemed genuinely angry with her for not being able to make up her mind.

"Why the radio silence?" she asked eventually. "I thought you'd fallen out with me or met another woman while you were out there…" She laughed. "I'm sorry I didn't call you. I couldn't. Work's organising me a new mobile and it's been a bit of a pain to get sorted."

424

Paul was numb.

"Sorry about that," he said blankly. "It was all a bit hectic."

Sophie just smiled. He was home now, and she appeared to have made plans of her own.

"You must be tired," she said. "Shall I run you a bath? Take a shower if you like…" There was a little mischief in her smile. "I really have missed you, you know…" she purred.

He couldn't help it… his mind drifted back to Silvi and room 733. Inappropriate images formed in his mind. He was lost for words, but now he knew more than ever that they needed to talk. He already knew it was more than that. He was resigned to it. It would need to be "the talk". Only this time, for the first time, it would be him doing the talking.

THREE WEEKS LATER

Chapter 72

SUNDAY

The new mail notification appeared in the bottom left-hand corner of the screen. It displayed the first few lines of the message for a few seconds then melted away before he could hit the reveal option.

He closed down the quote he was working on and clicked the email inbox. There was the usual flurry of spam and a few that would need dealing with, some urgent, others not so much. The sheer volume of rubbish people incessantly inflicted on each other through the medium of email never ceased to amaze Paul. He deleted the spam as it appeared – delete, delete, delete – and then he stopped.

The last email to appear was from a Silvi.angel787.nice@msn.fr.

It had been three weeks since he'd arrived back home from Nice, and not a single day had gone by without him thinking about Alisa and her friends. He clicked on it and then copied and pasted the entire message into his old friend Google Translate.

It was instant.

Hi Paul

I hope you are well.

I thought you might like to know that Maria has made a full recovery and is with us at the apartment for now.

Alex has told us not to worry about the 5000 euros, in case you were still thinking about that. He was happy for us to have it, but he is still furious about being charged 200 euros by the hotel for the missing towels from room 732. He can be so funny sometimes.

Katia is a good friend to me and has introduced me to some of her friends too. They are kind to me and so rich. They find all my stories interesting. They think my life has been very exciting and very glamorous? I do know that I am a bit of a novelty for them, so they will probably get bored with me soon, but I think Katia will stay friends. She is a lovely person. I still can't bear to think about what those men would have done to her.

The doctors say that Alex will need to use a stick for a while, maybe a year, but he could still make a full recovery too, given enough time. He will be out of hospital soon and Maria is going to live with him to look after him. She's always been a little bit in love with him ever since she lost the baby. He was so kind to her then and it will be good for her to have someone she loves to look after. I think she feels it is a way that she can repay him for all the kindness he has shown her in the past. She is looking forward to having him around.

Things are so much better for me here now. I am sure you will be pleased to know that I don't work any more and I am still with Mikael. I think he is a special man. He is my "Nice" man, Paul, and I think it might work out for us.

Anna finally got to read her mother's letter too. Maria gave it to her. It was the first thing she did when we went to see her in the hospital. She even got her phone back.

I keep telling Anna to write to you, but she knows she hurt you very badly and regrets it now, but things are still very complicated for her. She has been hurt so much before. I know she did care for you. She just won't let anyone get close to her any more. She won't admit it, Paul, but I know that you did.

She doesn't work any more either and has started studying again. That seems to help her. She is doing very well and is even planning to take her exams again. She has given up on getting any of her certificates from England. I think she will go back home when she passes her qualifications. She misses her family and seems so lonely and sad these days. Perhaps it is since you left. Nothing seems to be the same any more and maybe she misses you more than she will admit. You were her "Nice" man after all. I don't know what it is, but I do worry about her and I know I will lose her if she goes home. I will never go back to Russia, never.

Alex is looking after everything for us and he won't even take our rent money any more. I know Anna told you he was a good man. He has been truly wonderful since it all happened. He knows you saved his life too, and he knows about everything you did for all of us. He said he would like to meet you one day, but I don't suppose that will ever happen. It is a shame. He is not the man you think he is. He's a good man in his own way, but life is complicated.

We never had the chance to say goodbye to you, so I wanted to write and thank you for everything you have done for us, for me, Anna, Katia and Maria. They all send their love. Maria knows she owes you everything.

We miss you.

Thank you with all our hearts.

Love always

Kira

The email was finished with an *X* for a kiss.

Paul read the email one more time, drafted an appropriate response and then deleted it. That chapter of his life needed to be over now; he simply had to move on.

Chapter 73

It was inevitable. The French police were bound to contact him eventually; too much had taken place for his part in it to be overlooked.

The two French detectives were accompanied by an English liaison officer, but the meeting seemed somewhat perfunctory, at least at first. They demanded some form of ID, merely routine, they assured him. As they waited patiently in the lounge, he retrieved his passport from the safe in the office. The senior of the two French detectives gave the document little more than a cursory inspection. He handed it back and took a seat.

"We already know most of it from other witnesses, Monsieur Smith," he said calmly. "We just require some assistance from you on a couple of points." He paused and consulted his notes, then looked Paul up and down. "Won't you take a seat, monsieur?" he suggested with a firmness cultivated from a lifetime in authority.

"I'll stand. What assistance? How can I help you?"

"First of all, please appreciate this is a sensitive matter. We need a degree of discretion on your account. Do you understand what I'm saying to you?"

"No. No, I don't. What is this all about?"

"We need your discretion, monsieur. To be absolutely clear with you, once we are done here, we need your silence. In return for that, I can confirm that there will be no charges against you and no investigation. Is that plain enough for you?"

Paul didn't respond. The words were certainly plain enough but the stakes were high, so he played for time before giving any reaction at all. The French officers exchanged glances. The first effected a cough and indicated that the English liaison should leave the room. He stepped out into the hall and closed the door.

"I can confirm, monsieur, that there is already no official record of your visit to France in September. It is safer for you that way."

"Safer? What do you mean?" Paul was incredulous. "How can you do that? Why would you do that?"

"The *why* is not important for you to understand." The officer glared at him, as if an explanation should not be necessary. Then he relented. "The incident is, shall we say, the tip of a very dangerous iceberg, and, as a consideration to you, we are offering you the opportunity to distance yourself from it. You would be wise to accept."

Paul glared back. The officer continued.

"Monsieur Smith, what you do need to understand is that the list of potential charges against you is substantial." He shook his head slowly as if considering the sheer enormity of Paul's jeopardy. "The list of your offences is impressive indeed."

Paul held his nerve. It seemed to amuse the French officers to list them one by one, pausing for effect as they took turns to read them out.

"Interfering with a crime scene."

"Conspiracy to pervert the course of justice."

"Theft of a motor vehicle."

"Kidnapping."

"False imprisonment."

"Blackmail."

"Several counts of common assault."

"Actual bodily harm."

"Grievous bodily harm."

They paused.

"Monsieur Smith, do you see this could be very serious for you?"

Paul didn't respond. It was evident they hadn't finished with the list just yet.

"Breaking and entering."

"Burglary."

"Possession of class A drugs in your hotel bedroom."

"Leaving the scene of an accident."

"Illegal use of a firearm."

The first officer couldn't resist the temptation to embellish the charge. "That offence carries a long custodial sentence on its own, Monsieur Smith."

Paul lost his patience.

"Where the hell is this all leading?"

The senior officer raised his hand.

"Several breaches of international maritime law, monsieur, and the non-payment of a parking fine in Monaco." The officer smiled. "That last one we can't do much about. It's not our jurisdiction. It will need paying, I'm afraid. You can do that online if that's not too much trouble."

Paul waited impatiently as the officer rummaged around in his pockets.

"Voila," he said, handing him the paperwork with the principality's impressive crest embossed on the top.

Paul took it without comment.

"Of course, we already know it was you on that yacht too, monsieur. Naturally, we can produce the evidence to prove that, should it be necessary."

Paul said nothing. He avoided eye contact with either officer and took the seat he had previously declined.

"The steel bar, the hire cars..." he continued. "We know all about room 732, and your face is all over the CCTV footage covering the incidents in Monaco." He turned to study Paul's reaction. "There's nothing in the car park, of course, but I suspect you know that yourself. But the restaurant, Casino Square and the Hotel Hermitage... it's all there..."

"We're not looking for a confession, Monsieur Smith," the second officer interjected. "We merely wish to conclude our enquiries and close the matter."

"Ideally," the first continued, "we would like to conclude this matter quietly and discreetly. There are some matters of a sensitive nature at stake here. Matters of international and political sensitivity."

Paul had heard enough.

"Why are you actually here? What do you need from me?" he demanded. He felt emboldened. If they were going to arrest him, he was convinced they would already have done it. "What precisely do you want from me?"

"It's just procedure, sir. But... there is one pressing issue we do need to discuss with you... It involves a UK national, so, as I am sure you will appreciate, we do need to handle this matter with sensitively too."

Paul shuffled uneasily in his chair.

"Three men died that day, Monsieur Smith, and another is still unaccounted for."

He felt himself tense uncontrollably as the officer spoke.

"Oleg Gusev is still missing,"

"I'm sorry to hear that, but I still don't see how I can help you."

The officer held up his hand for a second time.

"Two of the men that died were brothers, Boris and Giorgi Berezin..." he read from his notebook.

"They were brothers?"

"Yes. They were twin brothers, Monsieur Smith."

Paul said nothing but registered the news without surprise. It explained Boris's reaction to the loss of his colleague; everything had changed in that instant. When Giorgi was killed, everything about Boris had changed.

"The third man was a…" He consulted his notes. "A Christoff Malokovic," he said without emotion.

He flicked the notebook shut and studied Paul for his reaction.

The name reverberated around his head for a few seconds. He was confused, how could he have heard that right? *Christoff Malokovic? Not Anatoly?* Paul tried to process the information. It was unexpected. He was certain he already knew the identity of the third man that died. Surely it had to be Anatoly. After everything that had happened, he needed it to be Anatoly.

"Monsieur Smith… are you all right?" the officer asked.

"I'm fine," he said, still playing for time.

The officer consulted his notes again, as if checking *he* hadn't made a mistake. It was a ploy and Paul recognised it for what it was. It was merely an excuse to repeat the unexpected news once again, and a second chance to read Paul's reaction to it.

"Christoff Malokovic," he repeated, drawing out the name for emphasis and watching Paul with a forensic intensity.

Paul's heart rate surged wildly and his breathing shortened. How could Anatoly have survived? Paul recalled it all. He remembered the blood. He saw Anatoly taken down. He watched him fall, first to a single shot from Boris, and then the Russian's body convulsed twice more as the shots he fired found their mark. Surely no one could have survived that?

"How did this Christoff die?" Paul asked, as the police officers maintained a professional silence he felt compelled to break.

They looked at each other before responding. Their ploy had worked. The senior officer effected a second cough and reviewed his notes once again.

Paul dreaded the answer. An image formed in his mind. He'd fought against that same image night after night, dismissing it, only for it to return again and again, each time more bloody and grotesque than before. But he couldn't dismiss it any more. He could see his victim all too clearly, almost hear the man's cries, even feel the power of his blows as he recalled them hammering into his face and neck. He could still feel it, the sickening sensation of his victim's throat collapsing, surrendering to the weight of his all-out assault. Could that man have been Christoff Malokovic? Could he have been Alisa's Chris? The man who broke her heart and, before that, Maria's abuser? The man he left unconscious at the foot of the stairs – could that have been Christoff Malokovic?

Paul forced himself to re-engage.

"How did he die?" he asked again. The question felt reassuringly measured, non-committal. Paul felt it gave nothing away.

The second officer consulted his own notes. It was a tick they both shared, a well-practised tactic, as was the exchange of glances that followed it. It was obvious, all too obvious, the notes were nothing more than a prop. They already knew everything they needed to. Paul was sure of it.

"Let me see…" he said, as he consulted them again. "Yes… a special forces team found Christoff Malokovic beaten to death at the foot of the stairs. His body was found next to the tender bay…"

He paused for effect and then closed his notebook with an air of finality.

"So, our question for you is a simple one. What can you tell us about his death, monsieur?"

The French police officer fixed him with a stare as he spoke. He shook his head slowly and very deliberately as he delivered the question.

Paul hesitated.

"The problem, Monsieur Smith, and it is a delicate one, is that this Christoff Malokovic leaves a widow and two children. And more than that, she is an English widow and they are her two very English children. You English can be a little tiresome when it comes to these matters, monsieur. As a result, we are required to exhaust all lines of enquiry in our investigation… in order to satisfy your very British sense of fair play and thoroughness. I'm sure you understand our predicament, monsieur." He waved his hand dismissively.

The other officer gave a Gallic shrug and tutted loudly.

"As I say, tiresome indeed."

Paul focused on the man doing the talking. He was still shaking his head and now raised a finger as if forbidding him to speak.

"You are simply one more line of enquiry we need to exhaust, sir," he continued.

Paul resisted the temptation to fill the void as the officer continued to shake his head. The message was clear enough.

"So, Monsieur Smith," the second officer continued, "we'll take your silence as your answer. We are both very comfortable with that as an outcome. If you are unable to help us further, that will be the end of our investigation. It is probably for the best, monsieur, I'm sure you agree."

Paul agreed completely, but remained stubbornly silent.

"It is of no concern to us now. I strongly suggest you do not trouble yourself further on the matter."

The officers appeared to have made their point. They had asked their questions and seemingly exhausted their enquiries. Paul was only too happy to agree. But he was under no illusion. He was certain they knew it was him. They knew exactly what had happened on board *Barabus*, and he was equally certain they knew every detail of his part in it. But it was also abundantly clear there was no interest in pursuing it further. Paul was unaware of the sensitivities involved but was only too happy to take their lead. The question had been asked, and now it was evident that its posing was the limit of the French police officers' interest in Christoff Malokovic's demise.

Paul held his nerve. He couldn't help speculating which part of the massively complex French law enforcement community the two officers represented in the first place. They were definitely not run-of-the-mill gendarmes. He was sure of that.

"Christoff Malokovic was a nasty piece of work," the second officer continued casually. "A dozen international arrest warrants were settled that day. Perhaps we will just never know what happened to him."

Paul tried to narrow it down. He suspected they were spooks of some sort.

"It's funny," the second officer said, "Christoff, Maria and Alex were all known to us. We were surprised to see them mixed up in this together after everything that happened to that poor girl."

Maybe organised crime, Paul speculated as they stood to leave. He waited for the officer to continue but they just headed for the door.

"What did happen to her?" Paul asked quietly.

"It was nasty, monsieur," he said. "She was left for dead in the boot of a hire car after a botched backstreet abortion. It was a miracle she survived at all."

Paul could feel a renewed sadness beginning to bear down on him.

"The hire car was rented by your friend, Alex."

"He's no friend of mine," Paul objected, but despite the strength of his reaction, he already knew they had got it wrong. Alex might have hired the car, but Paul was sure he would have played no part in Maria's ordeal.

"They found the girl severely dehydrated and suffering from a massive loss of blood. She was completely helpless, yet he still left her in the boot of the car, bound with plastic cable ties and gagged. It was all very sad. When they removed the gag she just kept calling out for someone called Christoff."

Paul let the officer talk.

"We found him eventually. He was just another Russian villain. He tried to reinvent himself as a respectable businessman." Both officers shrugged dismissively. "He set himself up in London... even married an English girl. He had a couple of kids with that poor woman, both boys as I recall. Of course, she's a widow now," the officer continued. "It's all very sad."

"But in reality, Christoff was no better than his cousin." The second policeman took up the theme.

"His cousin?" Paul asked. It was the obvious question.

"Yes, Christoff Malokovic... He was Anatoly's cousin."

Paul feigned his surprise. "Small world," he said without emotion. "What about Anatoly? What happened to him?"

The officer shrugged his shoulders.

"Anatoly is not your concern, monsieur. He is no longer in France and that is all that any of us need to know."

With that, the police officers thanked Paul for his time and took their leave. They would contact him again if they needed any further information, but, as things turned out, they never did.

Once they had left, Paul went to his office and tapped his new default passcode, 7777, into the discreetly hidden wall safe behind his desk.

The lock whirred and the bolts drew back.

He pushed the plastic bag with the bloodstained, monogrammed piece of white cloth further back into the tiny space and placed his passport securely and safely inside. He knew that piece of cloth was important, but in truth, he hoped he would never actually find out why.

Chapter 74

WEDNESDAY

Two days later Paul received a voicemail from his bank. Apparently, a substantial deposit had been made into his personal account and his investment manager was keen to speak to him at his earliest convenience. Paul dismissed it as nonsense. He hadn't made a substantial deposit into any of his accounts, and he didn't recall ever having an investment manager. He certainly had no need for one.

Later that same day his curiosity got the better of him and he logged into his bank account. A single transaction stood out from the rest. There was a credit of £1,187,400 sitting in his current account. From the detail that accompanied the entry, he could see it was the British pounds equivalent of a cool US$2,000,000. It had been transferred into his private bank account only two days earlier.

His jaw dropped.

He thought there must be some mistake, but there was no mistake. The single line entry carried a reference: "*Ot Vashego blagodarnogo drugu, Nikoli.*"

Paul copied and pasted it into Google Translate. The result was, as it so often had been, instant and reassuringly unambiguous: "*From your grateful friend, Nikoli.*"

TWELVE MONTHS LATER

Chapter 75

"… and that, gentleman, is only a fraction of the story," Gary finished with a self-conscious flourish as Paul approached from the bar with another round of drinks.

Gary effected a nervous cough and folded away the piece of paper he was reading from.

"What's going on, Gary."

Paul set the tray down on the table and started to distribute the contents. A pint of bitter for Gary, a Peroni each for the three newbies, and a double malt for Doug. They were all staring at him in silence.

"What is it? What's going on?"

"Nothing, mate, I was just telling the new guys about last year."

Gary looked sheepish. Doug looked embarrassed.

"You're doing what? I thought we'd discussed that!" Paul snapped.

"It's all right, Paul," Doug interjected calmly. "He's only telling them the stuff that's already in the public domain."

"What are you talking about?"

"Show him, Gary."

He rummaged around in his pocket for a disproportionately long period of time. Then, reluctantly, he recovered the piece of paper he'd been reading from and held it out for Paul to take.

"A member of the crew on *Barabus* has done a kiss and tell, mate," Gary said.

"What?"

Paul snatched the piece of paper from his outstretched hand and everyone else remained silent. He unfolded the crumpled sheet of A4, and as he did, a newspaper clipping fell onto the floor. Paul picked it up and scanned the text. It was several weeks old and printed in French.

"There's a translation, mate," Gary said.

"I can see that," Paul growled, and he began to read.

The first paragraph was enough to make him gasp.

"It's been published, mate, so I didn't see the harm," Gary said.

"It's a wind-up, right?" one of the newbies blurted. He picked up his fresh Peroni, offered a genuine salute of thanks to Paul and then looked him up and down, assessing his new colleague with a critical disdain. The newbie looked unconvinced and turned his attention to Gary. "And you're telling us that Paul's this unnamed mystery man – is that right? The man who 'allegedly' took out all those bad guys singlehanded! You're talking bollocks, mate! You're just taking the piss."

Paul was appalled, furious even, but knew he needed to contain things.

"He does the same thing every year, lads. Take no notice," Paul replied.

He managed to grin back at them through tightly clenched teeth. "Talking bollocks is when Gary's at his most fluent," he added, giving Gary a gentle punch on the arm. "Same thing every year... Just don't fall for it."

Doug laughed self-consciously, but he clearly recognised the change in mood. Paul's grin was still locked resolutely in place, but now he was staring directly at Gary and fighting the impulse to kick him to the floor.

"You're full of shit, Gary," one of the newbies slurred with all the eloquence of a relapsing alcoholic.

Paul ignored the outburst and guided Gary to one side. It looked casual enough, yet Paul maintained a firm grip on Gary's arm as they walked. His grip tightened even more when Gary opened his mouth to protest. As far as the newbies were concerned the matter was over – just an insignificant bit of banter at their expense. But it was more than that...

"Sorry, Paul, I didn't see the harm," Gary said.

"That's the harm, Gary!" Paul hissed. "Making that link between me and *Barabus* – that's the harm!"

"It a great story, lads," a newbie shouted over to them before draining his glass. "Is there a punchline?"

Gary turned his back on the table and lowered his voice to a whisper.

"You never told us what happened on *Barabus*. I was just having a bit of fun," Gary said in an attempt to defuse the situation. "Is that shit real? Is that what happened out there?"

"Look, Gary, just go back and tell them it's a wind-up and leave it at that. I'll explain another time, but not here and not now. Understood?"

"Yes, mate, understood, but—"

"Just tell them, Gary. Get some more beer down their necks. They need to believe that all that is just some 'fresher' bullshit and nothing more."

444

"Okay, leave it with me, but we need to talk about this sooner rather than later, mate. It's important."

"Fine, but sort *them* out first. I want to read the rest of this." He waved the sheet of A4 in Gary's face. "I'll meet you at the bar in five minutes."

Paul headed to a quiet corner and read on.

It was all there, a full account of what happened, and his role was at the very centre of everything. The translation was typed in a clear font, yet it was still very difficult for him to read. It brought it all flooding back. Memories he'd determinedly locked away over the months came pouring back as vividly as if it was the day itself.

He read the words and tried to detach himself from the events. The unnamed man had taken out Dimitri with a steel bar, a single crushing blow to his throat. It was hard to stay detached. He could feel the weight of the blow as it landed, reheard the sound of his victim's flesh tear and the gasping of a man close to death. After all this time, it was still so real. Then Giorgi's desperate attempt to overpower Viktor, only to be shot at point-blank range as Viktor, himself, fought for breath.

Paul swallowed hard and forced a breath of his own.

Next, the unidentified man struck again, landing another crippling blow that brought Viktor to his knees.

The image replayed in his mind as he forced himself to read on.

He skipped some text, his eye drawn inexorably down the page to a description of Boris's death in the next paragraph. It detailed how Boris took the gun from Maria and shot Anatoly, only to be brutally killed himself by the ship-borne snipers.

There was no escaping the images now. Each one a graphic, haunting, portrait of violence and death. He could hear it, feel it, even smell it. The bucking of the deck, the blood, the roar of the engines, the chilling echoes of men dying and the ear-splitting sound of gunfire.

He felt every muscle stiffen. He was rooted to the spot, unable to move. So much detail… even the small package being slipped across the deck from Boris to the unnamed man was there. Then the speculation. The article contained the sort of speculation that could get a man killed. It was highlighted and underlined. Why the focus on that one detail? What was so important about that piece of cloth in a plastic bag?

Paul exhaled loudly and steadied his nerve.

The article was insightful, well-reasoned and compelling. If the speculation was as accurate as the account itself, that piece of cloth linked Anatoly to Oleg Gusev and a crime Paul had always suspected had been committed in the first place. According to the translation, the package linked Anatoly to

Oleg's disappearance and perhaps even to his murder. It was like a grenade bursting inside his head. That package was a ticking time bomb, and now its existence was out in the open, in the public domain, the fuse had been lit and, even now, it burned inexorably away, contained only by the feeble security of his office wall safe.

But there was more. The unnamed man was credited with unleashing two further rounds, both hitting home, slamming into Anatoly's body. Then he discarded the gun and quietly slipped away, unnoticed by the special forces operators storming the yacht.

There were no names printed in the article or in the translation. There were no clues as to victims and certainly nothing to give away the author. But the translation was good. The English was almost perfect, and at the bottom of the page there was a single name and an X for a kiss. With Anna, there was always an X for a kiss.

Paul carefully tucked the newspaper clipping inside the A4 sheet that translated it, folded it, and stuffed them both into his jacket pocket. He headed for the bar.

A glance was all it took to see that Gary was doing his best to kill the conversation. He was paying a heavy price and was clearly the butt of an unending torrent of good-natured abuse. As he watched, all three doubters turned to look in his direction. Paul propped himself up at the bar and ordered a whisky. It was Doug's latest recommendation.

"Make it a double... Put it on room 733 please?" Paul requested absent-mindedly.

"I'm sorry, sir, we don't a have a room 733. Can I take your name?"

"Smith, Paul Smith," he said.

Gary was at his side. He started humming the James Bond theme tune.

"Very James Bond, Mr Smith," he said, a massive grin on his face. "You expect me to talk... No, Mr Smith, I expect you to die!" He was high on life as usual.

"Not funny, Gary."

Despite Paul's assertion to the contrary, Gary was highly amused, but he got the message.

"It's done, mate. They all think I'm a jackass, but they've moved on to other stuff and Doug's promised them a whisky tasting later."

"Thanks," Paul said with a sense of relief.

"So..." Gary said, "not over *her* yet then, mate?"

"What?"

"The old 733 room number thing?"

Gary had been at his side longer than Paul realised.

"I guess not…"

"I don't blame you, mate. She was a looker."

"Gary, it's not all about that…" Paul started, but then he lost the will to continue his protest. "I take it you stayed in touch with the girls then."

"Just the odd email here and there," he said, grinning. "Someone had to… and then she sent that clipping and the translation. I was going to show you later. I didn't mean to piss you off."

Paul shrugged.

"Forget it. It's not important now, but just don't link me to all that shit again. I mean it, Gary. What happened on that yacht was bad, but it's in the past and it has to stay that way."

Gary seemed distracted. He had something in his hand and placed it on the bar.

"Your phone was ringing so I brought it over. You left it on the table."

Paul took it unenthusiastically, but at least it was a distraction. He'd mastered resolution number two after all. He'd completely broken his habit, in contrast to Gary, who was as bad as ever. Even now, in the early hours of the morning, he was consulting his iPhone yet again. There could be no possible rationale for it, but he looked uncharacteristically downbeat when there was, as so often happened, nothing of any significance to be seen.

And resolution number one? That was, without doubt, still a work in progress. He'd actually got around to changing his passcode, but he'd only done it the once since getting back from Nice. He still used the same code for everything, and its security value was no greater than the one he'd been so determined to upgrade in the first place.

Paul's mind wandered. As for resolution number three – being honest with Sophie – Paul shrugged as the thought occurred to him… so much had changed since he'd made it. He hoped she would be happy now, but there had never been any real prospect of things working out between them. He told her the news on his first night back from Nice. He was finally honest with himself but spared her the details. They'd lost touch since, but he recalled she'd taken the news rather better than he would have expected. The thought saddened him now, or was that just a little alcohol-induced self-pity? He couldn't be sure.

Gary turned on his heels and bounded back to Doug and the newbies of the Secure Co. International Sales Conference 2015 on the far side of the bar.

Same old shit, just a different location, Paul thought. At least it was easier to get to this year. A quick drive down the M1 and no stuffing DJs into a suitcase. Everything transported on hangers in the back of the brand-new black BMW 5 Series he'd recently treated himself to.

"Not over her yet then mate?" Gary had asked... *Probably not...* he had to concede.

There was a missed call. He didn't recognise the number but tapped the screen to return it anyway. He wouldn't usually have bothered at this time of night – who the hell would be ringing at one-thirty in the morning? But returning a call to an unknown number was still a marginally more palatable option than re-joining his newly initiated, yet sceptical, fan club.

He recognised the voice immediately. The caller hadn't waited for Paul to speak.

"Hi, are you in London?" the caller asked, in a tone that implied they already knew the answer.

Paul was stunned.

"Yes..."

"Are you at the conference?"

"Yes, I am but—"

"Where?"

"I'm in the bar... why?"

The phone went dead.

Paul was about to press redial when he saw her.

Standing in the entrance to the bar was Anna. She was wearing a light green top, a short cream skirt cut well above the knee, and a pair of trainers that, with what little knowledge he did have of the fashion industry, appeared to be "so last year".

She was as beautiful as he remembered, and her presence immediately created a stir, as it had once before at a pizza restaurant on the Promenade des Anglais. Paul remained frozen to the spot. She started to walk towards him as the buzz intensified around the bar. The last few paces she ran and then threw herself into his arms, kissing him deeply and wrapping her arms around him.

The bar went wild.

A cacophonous roar went up interspersed with raucous cheering and an impressive series of wolf whistles. The mob was led by none other than Gary, and even Doug was on his feet.

Paul didn't notice any of it. He returned Anna's embrace and held her tightly. She pulled her lips away from his and looked into his eyes for a moment, and then she kissed him passionately once again. This time he heard the cheers and a fresh volley of wolf whistles that rang out over an unexpected round of applause.

Paul self-consciously raised his hand for calm. He took her by the arm and led her to a quiet corner. All eyes were on them, but that would pass. There was so much he wanted to ask her, so much he needed to say.

As they passed Gary and the newbies, he heard Doug's voice boom out.

"About fucking time!" he said, as he drained the contents of his whisky glass and held it up in salute.

Paul had never once heard Doug swear before.

Gary had both thumbs in the air and a huge smile on his face. If he were any more excited, he would surely combust.

"Did you know about this?" Paul mouthed as he led Anna away from the crowd.

"Mate, we both did." His grin was wider still.

As they sat down, Anna brushed her hand sensuously down the short length of the cream skirt he'd once bought for her. She held his gaze with a smile that lit up his world.

"I told you I loved it," she said, and kissed him again by way of a convincer.

EPILOGUE

Epilogue

It was only then he saw them.

Two men were standing at the entrance to the bar. The first was Viktor, his arm hanging awkwardly at his side. Immediately behind him was Dimitri, he had stepped around his partner into the light and Paul recognized him immediately. A huge man, his throat cruelly scared where Paul had left his mark during their close encounter on Barabus's quarterdeck. That was twelve months ago, almost to the day.

Both men scanned the room with intent, seeking a mark of their own.

"Anna, we need to get out of here," Paul said calmly. "That newspaper article has changed everything."

Without another word he led her quietly away. With the entrance to the bar blocked by Viktor and Dimitri he had no choice. The only other exit was marked "Staff Only". He didn't hesitate.

For Paul, the conference was already over…